Kirov Saga:

Doppelganger

By

John Schettler

KIROV SERIES:

The Kirov Saga: *Season One*

Kirov - Kirov Series - Volume 1
Cauldron Of Fire - Kirov Series - Volume 2
Pacific Storm - Kirov Series - Volume 3
Men Of War - Kirov Series - Volume 4
Nine Days Falling - Kirov Series - Volume 5
Fallen Angels - Kirov Series - Volume 6
Devil's Garden - Kirov Series - Volume 7
Armageddon – Kirov Series – Volume 8

The Kirov Saga: *Season Two*

Altered States– Kirov Series – Volume 9
Darkest Hour– Kirov Series – Volume 10
Hinge Of Fate– Kirov Series – Volume 11
Three Kings – Kirov Series – Volume 12
Grand Alliance – Kirov Series – Volume 13
Hammer Of God – Kirov Series – Volume 14
Crescendo Of Doom – Kirov Series – Volume 15
Paradox Hour – Kirov Series – Volume 16

The Kirov Saga: *Season Three*

Doppelganger – Kirov Series – Volume 17

More to come...

Kirov Saga:

Doppelganger

By

John Schettler

"We are past the end of things now, but I don't want to leave."

—**Richard Ford:** *The Sportswriter, 1986*

"The vision recurs; the eastern sun has a second rise; history repeats her tale unconsciously, and goes off into a mystic rhyme; ages are prototypes of other ages, and the winding course of time brings us round to the same spot again."

— **The Christian Remembrancer,** 1845

Kirov Saga:
Doppelganger

By
John Schettler

Author's Note:

Dear readers, this is the opening volume of the third "season" of the Kirov Saga, *Doppelganger*, and a proper continuation of the events presented in *Paradox Hour*. The challenge facing the ship on 28 July, 1941, only just began to manifest in the previous novel, and will reach a full resolution here. In writing this, I thought long and hard about the Paradox facing the ship as it approached that date from both the future and the past. That collision in time promised to be as harrowing as the strange incident with the cruiser *Tone* at the end of *Pacific Storm*. Then again, it might be nothing at all.

The mystery inherent in time travel has long been at the heart of this series. You sat with me, patiently watching Fedorov and Volsky slowly peel that onion, discovering what was moving the ship in time in Rod-25. *Men of War,* introduced yet another major element of that mystery when Fedorov inadvertently discovers the natural time rift aligned with the back stairway at Ilanskiy. The connection of this event to 1908, concurrent with the Tunguska Event, took the mystery of time displacement to another level, particularly when Inspector Kapustin discovers that elements used in the making of Rod-25 were mined near the epicenter of that event. The importance of Tunguska in what is now happening is far from over, and more of this segment of the mystery will be revealed in upcoming books.

You have also watched the slow evolution of Director Kamenski's character, from a whimsical old man discussing battleships with his grandson, to something quite more. I have used this character to be a mouthpiece for some of this mystery of time travel, a sounding board for Fedorov as he struggled to understand what the ship and crew might be facing soon, and the consequences of his own actions in the past.

Kamenski's revelations concerning the Russian nuclear test program were another peek behind the curtain and, in *Paradox Hour*, he spends some time trying to explain the nature of time to Fedorov, and also reveals one other startling fact—like Elena Fairchild, he has been the keeper of a strange artifact from the future.

The "Keyholders Saga" was first introduced as the final scene in my five volume Meridian Time travel series, which was reprised in an edited version in *Paradox Hour* to help explicate events that are now unfolding in the Kirov Series. Another enigmatic figure, Sir Roger Ames, the Duke of Elvington, also served to slowly plant the seed of the tree that is now growing when he took us on that strange retreat to the castle of Lindisfarne, yet another hidden natural rift in time, secured, and opened, by a key from the future.

The mystery and purpose of these keys soon became an imperative in the naval chase that saw *Kirov* sail with Admiral Tovey's HMS *Invincible*, first in the hunt for the *Hindenburg*, and then in the desperate effort to save the battleship *Rodney*, and the secret cargo it was transporting to Boston. Readers should know that this mission by *Rodney* was not a device arising from my own imagination. It was entirely historical. I merely inserted the key in the base of the Selene Horse in my Meridian Series. When *Rodney* sets sail to rendezvous with *Kirov*, those two story worlds also begin to join in *Paradox Hour* with the introduction of Lieutenant Commander Wellings—another historical figure whose identity was filched by an enterprising Physics Professor, Paul Dorland.

Readers of the Meridian Series will know this man well, along with the other team members from the Meridian Project. Some of you have even written to me asking whether the Meridian team was going to discover what *Kirov* was doing on its chaotic sorties through WWII. Now you have your answer. As the Kirov Series progresses, you will occasionally meet the Meridian team members operating from their Arch facility in the Lawrence Berkeley labs. Considering what has happened to Director Kamenski at the end of *Paradox Hour*, Professor Paul Dorland now steps in to help explain the Paradox, and further unravel this Gordian knot of time travel.

Through the mind of Professor Dorland, you will now gain an understanding of just what is happening to the time continuum. In this regard, I have included the lexicon of his time travel terminology as developed in the Dorland theory here at the end of this volume as an easy reference. (Just be sure you don't peek at the ending if you navigate there!) If you listen carefully to the Meridian team leader here, you will soon come to understand why *Kirov* experienced all those strange effects, Lenkov's fate, and by extension the fate of the entire ship and crew. You will also learn just what Elena Fairchild fears, even though she does not quite understand it, when she speaks about a "Grand Finality."

Beyond that, there is a great deal more to come as *Kirov* finally faces the effects of *Paradox Hour.* An intriguing story line develops that will further explore this mystery inherent in time travel, and explain how the Keyholders relate to it all, while also taking us towards the year 1942. Yes, though these two volumes are heavy on the time travel angles in the story, the alternative history of WWII will also continue in season three.

There's a lot of military action yet to come. Operation Barbarossa gathers momentum, as well as Volkov's war with Sergei Kirov on the Volga front. In that regard, the fate of Captain Karpov will take an interesting turn here, for he must also stand before Time's court, and answer for the many misdeeds he has committed. In this book you get the verdict.

The Japanese will soon be entering the war, and the Americans right on their heels. Meanwhile, the shock of *Kirov's* missile technology, and the appearance of Brigadier Kinlan's unstoppable 7th Armored Brigade, will prompt Germany to launch crash programs to develop new heavy tanks, jet engines, and rockets. The WWII looming ahead will be profoundly influenced by these developments, and Kinlan's troops will be in the thick of that action.

To faithful crew members, my readers who have been with me from the first book, this volume will finally take us *through* the fateful date of 7/28/41 and lead to the progression of the war in 1942. Thank you all so much for staying with this story. I promise you another exciting ride here in season three. So without further preface, let us begin! *- John Schettler*

Part I

Fire & Steel

"The hardest steel is tempered by the hottest fire."

— **Proverb**

Chapter 1

Tovey stood on the bridge of HMS *Invincible*, struggling to resist the urge to pace. Somewhere within him, he ladled up the cool waters of that reserve of calm he could call on—when his temper wasn't hot and fired. He was fire and steel, the cold strength of well tempered metal, the heat and energy of the flames, all in one.

My god, he thought, as he noted the tall seething column on the horizon, rising like a thunderhead, up and up. He had seen this before... *somewhere...* He could not recall when and where it was, but the sight of that awful grey mushroom chilled him to the bone. What was happening here?

The plaintive reports from *Rodney* harried him as well, and though *Invincible* was running all out at her best speed of 32 knots, it would never be enough. The old battleship he hoped to keep from harm was already stricken, hit by an enemy torpedo, and the gaping wound was battered open again by the hard steel of shells from the *Tirpitz*. He did not know that his charge had already slipped from his grasp, falling inexorably into the depths of the murky sea, the light of the glittering bars of gold bullion slowly fading as they fell.

"Message from Captain Tennant sir." It was the Flag Lieutenant, Commander James Villers, a dark haired, blue-eyed man, tall and aristocratic in bearing, with a stiff posture and equally stiff manner, particularly with subordinates. He had been the tutor of Tovey's young protégé, now Captain Christopher Wells, and he eyed the message with some concern.

"Emergency to Admiralty and C-in-C, Home Fleet. From BC2 – Sighted battleship and battlecruiser, bearing 220, distance 21 miles. My position, course, and speed to follow. Requesting permission to engage."

Tovey looked up, squinting at his Flag Lieutenant, his eyes narrow with thought. Villers walked slowly to the Admiral's side, handing him the signal. "That's twelve more 15-inchers on the field," he said.

"Yes," said Tovey, still thinking. "Yet with bloody thin skin."

"They've laid on a bit more deck armor for *Renown* after that bomb damage she took."

"Quite so," said Tovey, "but nothing that will stop the steel being flung about by that German battleship. Any more word from *Rodney*?"

"She's in bad shape, Admiral, foundering with a hard list to port. Captain Hamilton is of a mind that we may lose her, yet he's still in the fight."

"Then order Captain Tennant to engage at once. Tell them we're coming with all the speed we can muster."

"Very good, sir." Villers started away, looking to collar a signalman, but Tovey spoke again.

"What about the German carrier?"

"Apparently the Russians put the fire to them, sir. Hamilton reports he can see a considerable column of smoke to his northwest. Good of them to get one in like that, but where in bloody hell are they now?"

"I wish I knew, Mister Villers. And between you and I, that ship has maneuvered to make good its attack. I want no talk on the ship of magic tricks, miracles, and disappearing acts. I'll want to see every member of the morning watch in my cabin after this is over."

"As you wish, sir."

Tovey wanted to keep a lid on what had happened to the Russian ship. *Kirov* had been there, right in the vanguard of his small formation, not half a mile on. Then, when he turned his head to look again, there was little more than a cold wisp of fog that quickly dissipated on the light morning breeze.

The Admiral knew at that moment, with a sinking feeling, that something had happened. The ship had a habit of bouncing about. Something deep within him grasped that, an inner recollection that he knew was his, yet one he also realized he had never lived in this world. It was as if he was now being haunted by some unseen duplicate of himself, a strange Doppelganger who had made the acquaintance of this Russian ship and crew long before Tovey ever set eyes on it in this world. Then again... the old memory returned to him, from his days with the China Squadron as a young Lieutenant. He *had* seen this ship before, and he was certain of that now. In fact, his first order upon taking command of *King Albert* when its Captain had been felled on the weather bridge, had been to turn every gun he had on the demon, rushing in, just as he was now, to the fire and shock of a battle at sea.

The shouting voices still echoed in his mind from that distant memory...

"Port thirty, and signal all ships to follow!"

"Port Thirty, aye sir!"

"Come round to two-seven-zero and set your range!"

"Sir, coming to two-seven-zero," the helmsman echoed back.

"Range 9,000 yards, aye sir, and all guns ready."

"Steady... Steady... Commence firing! All ships to fire in turn!"

He could still feel the vibration on the deck beneath his feet when his own ship trembled again with the impact of yet another enemy shell, this time at the base of the conning tower where it rattled the heavy armor. Yes, he remembered it all now, they had a fire amidships, one funnel sheared off and bleeding smoke, one of his stacked casement guns on the starboard side blasted away, the weather deck gone and the Captain with it, but still he did the one thing that instinct and honor demanded, and drove relentlessly on.

It was the grandest battle he had ever seen at sea, with all of forty ships or more dashing forward in a wild surge of steel and violence. It was Armageddon and he was right in the middle of it all, thrust into battle with a nemesis that would haunt him the remainder of his long life. One day he would see this ship again, and the strange, unnerving feeling would settle in his gut as he reached for the faded memory of that hour. He would wait, through long decades, unknowing and unaware that this demon before him would return again and again. Once it had been a dire threat, and then the face of his enemy had returned, yet the demon had become a guardian angel.

The unseen enemies he had fought decades ago had become friends, but just as they vanished from the swirling fire of that battle so long ago, the ship was missing yet again. Where have they gone this time, he wondered? On what grey sea do they find themselves now, and will they ever return?

He had come to know the Russian Admiral, and the intrepid young Captain Fedorov, so very well. They were not the demons he had first made them out to be, but men of honor, reason, and strong moral fiber. And the coming of their ship had been a godsend this time. If not for their intervention the previous year, *Hood* may not have survived its first encounter with Admiral Lütjens. And it was equally clear to him that *Kirov* had been an unflinching bulwark of strength in the Mediterranean as well, bludgeoning the Italians, French, and Germans alike.

Men from the future, he thought, still shaking his head inwardly. Boxes full of files, photos and reports from the future as well, detailing his intimate involvement with this strange interloper on the high seas. Yet now the ship had vanished again, right in the midst of the engagement that was before him—another battle, another mad rush at sea, and the hard fire and steel of war.

God go with you…

It was a silent wish and prayer for his lost comrades, and the sight of that awful mushroom cloud shook him from his reverie, and he returned to the moment at hand.

"What is the situation with Captains Patterson and Leach?" he said to Villers when his Flag Lieutenant had returned.

"We had them about 120 nautical miles out, sir. I have the position in the Flag Plot Room."

"And what about Holland?"

"Another hundred miles behind," said Villers with a shrug. But the two carriers are coming up fast, and we should get some air support in due course."

Tovey was plotting it all out in his mind. Patterson had *King George V*, with Leach commanding *Prince of Wales*. Holland was on the *Hood*, and he had a strong right arm with the newest battleship to enter the fleet, the *Duke of York*. The two carriers were *Ark Royal* and *Illustrious*, racing to the scene behind the forward advance of Patterson's group. In the long run, he had sufficient power here to prevail, he knew, but in the short run…

"Things will be dicey at the outset, Mister Villers," he said. "It will be the two battlecruisers and *Invincible*, and we must expect to be facing everything the Germans have. If *Rodney* still has some fight left in her, all the better, but we must plan on going it alone for some hours until the rest of the fleet can come on the scene."

"And what about that fleet air defense cruiser?" said Villers.

"The *Argos?*" Tovey squinted again, noting the rising swell in the sea, still shadowed by the overweening presence of that distant mushroom cloud. "They're out there to the east, and may have to fight it out with the others until we can get there."

"With those naval rockets, sir?"

Tovey gave Villers a look. "I suppose we shall have to see… Very good, Mister Villers. That will be all."

He looked at the sea, noting a sudden wave come sweeping in, seeing it break heavily over the forward bow, feeling it lift the entire ship. It was the fading swell of that thing out there, he knew. Even here, maybe sixty miles out, we feel it lift the ship with its anger, a weapon so powerful that it can move the sea itself.

He remembered Admiral Volsky speaking of this power, yet he could scarcely imagine how it had been achieved. Fire and steel, he thought. What will war become in the decades ahead? Is it any wonder that these ships and men flee to us here?

And now the memory of his own voice, the young Lieutenant shouting all those many years ago, sounded hollow. *Port thirty and signal all ships to follow…* But there was no one in his wake now, and HMS *Invincible* was alone.

* * *

Gordon MacRae was considering what to do now, standing behind the Captain's station, as he often did, wanting his feet on the deck in any good fight, and not his ass in the chair. Mack Morgan had returned with Miss Fairchild's consent, indeed her order, to stand the men up, and he had just put the crew to their battle stations. *Rodney* was finally on their horizon to the north, and the smoke there was certainly cause for alarm. He could see the distant flash, and hear the dull roar of the guns, like far off thunder. Somewhere over that horizon to the northwest, the German battleships also had *Rodney* on their horizon. The white geysers of shellfall seemed tiny in comparison to the awful wrack that now fisted up into the morning sky.

"What happened to that Russian sub?" Mack Morgan had an 'I told you so' look on his face. "And who the bloody hell is flinging nukes about?"

The tall column from the massive explosion to the north had been most alarming. The Russian sub was out there somewhere, supposedly on point. MacRae figured they had nukes aboard, but it never occurred to him that they would resort to their use. It was completely unexpected, a level of anger and violence that might have been par for the course in the world they came from, where he knew the hunter killer subs of his day had those shark's teeth in them, and little hesitation to use them. But not here, not now, the ugly mushroom cloud blighting the sea for the first time in the history of this world.

"Lord almighty… That's done it," he said to Morgan. "Someone has one heavy hand out there."

"Has to be 15 to 20 kilotons," said Morgan. He was still watching the horizon, transfixed. Like MacRae, he had expected to see nuclear weapons in easy use in the war that was brewing back home, but not here. "It either came off that Russian boat," he said, "or that bloody *Astute* Class we were warned about must have fired the damn thing."

They had received one hurried radio message on the secure system, stating a British *Astute* class submarine was now on the scene, and that is when the whole scenario began to spin off like a wild Irish jig. Acting on pure reflex, MacRae had sent out an all channels message to try and stand the submarine down. Minutes later the crackle of static came over the airwaves and the horizon had erupted with the broiling mass of a good sized warhead.

Yet now they had no sign or word from either sub. It was as if they had also disappeared, just as the Russian battlecruiser had vanished some hours earlier. Were they down there, backs broken, and slowly sinking into the murky depths? He had no idea what was going on, but the sight of *Rodney* now was enough to rattle his reflex for battle again, and he knew he had to act.

The Germans were obviously closing in for the kill, and MacRae did not have to guess where the enemy ships were as the British might. His Sampson radar had their exact positions pegged, and he knew it was now time for *Argos Fire* to join the action. After seeing that mushroom cloud, anything he fired might seem a feeble thing by comparison, but he knew he could still influence the outcome of this battle if *Argos Fire* engaged.

He leaned in toward Morgan, lowering his voice. "Did her Ladyship say anything about our missile quota this time around?"

"Not a peep, Gordie. She seems particularly invested in the health of that ship out there."

"Aye…" MacRae considered his situation. They had used seven of their precious GB-7 missiles in the Med, and only ten remained. He had already engaged the enemy planes swooping in to attack *Rodney*, his Aster-15s wreaking havoc with the German formation. Now the battleships were in range, and he needed to weigh in.

"The ship will ready for missile fire," he said with as much calm as he could muster. "Ship-to-ship. Spin up three GB-7s, and be quick about it."

The warning claxon sounded. The target was noted and assigned. "Let's get after that number two ship in the enemy formation out there. I make it to be their flag. Engage!"

The missiles were up to greet the morning sun, their hot tails of fire pushing steel. The GB-7 was fast at Mach 3, and it would barely have the time to accelerate to its full speed before it had the target in its radar cross section, swooping down and then boring in at sea level to make the final run.

MacRae smiled. The bar fight was on, and he was just about to break a beer bottle or two over someone's head out there. They've gone and picked a fight with the wrong man, he thought, folding his arms. Now let's see about it.

Chapter 2

Kurt Hoffman had been on the weather deck off the bridge of *Scharnhorst*, clenching his fist with those last hits on *Rodney*, and knowing they were finally going to get their pound of flesh against the Royal Navy. Then he was stunned to see the massive explosion on the sea, driven by the expanding gas bubble of Gromyko's heavy nuclear torpedo. It erupted in a crest of dark surface water followed by the expanding ring of white "crack," and then the huge spray dome, rising upwards into a column of seawater and steam.

The plume would rise some 5000 feet, nearly a mile high in the sky, and out from its base a tsunami of water surged out in every direction, creating a circle around the blast that was over three miles wide. As it careened down into the sea, a series of smaller waves were generated, the first about 100 feet in height. Then a haze of mist expanded, some 1,800 feet high and forming the enormous dome, like some demonic behemoth that had emerged from the sea, its head suddenly crowned with the serrated bloom of the topmost edge of the detonation chimney.

God was in his heaven, thought Hoffmann, but what was in the sea? It looked as though hell itself had risen from the depths in a massive volcanic eruption from an unseen seamount. That was all he could think of as any possible reason for the calamity on the horizon, for it never entered his head that such power could have been the result of anything made by the hand of man. Then he felt the heavy swell as the shock wave finally reached his ship, feeling *Scharnhorst* rising up as though lifted by some mighty giant.

The wrath of Neptune was heavy on the sea, and the guns on every side were stilled, all eyes riveted at the scene on the horizon. The detonation had occurred some twenty miles off, far enough to spare the ships any real damage, but was spectacular in its sudden appearance, imposing a stunned hush on the scene. Then, if the madness of that moment were not enough, Hoffmann saw the sky clawed by three thin streaks, his heart leaping with the realization of what was now happening.

The missiles came like spirits fleeing from the awful scene on the horizon, just as crews on each side had finally recovered, and the shouts of officers urged them to resume their own little war on the sea.

The Germans returned to the heat of their action against *Rodney*, when *Tirpitz* fired again, and now Hoffman looked to see the British battleship was in serious trouble. He could clearly see the fires foreword, and heavy smoke, but the list caused by the damage it had sustained was more pronounced, as the ship had been rolled heavily by the shock wave of that terrible eruption, though it continued to fight on. Then the high watch above shouted out the alarm—*Rockets!*

Hoffmann was already watching them, tense and guarded when he saw the telltale contrails coming at them. They had not been fired from *Rodney*, he knew, and he first thought they might be something hurled into the sky by the detonation. Yet soon he could see order within the chaos of their approach, and knew the worst. There's something else out there, he thought, just beyond the horizon— another ship. They must be getting signals from the battleship to guide those rockets.

Up they went, then they fell to the sea, and he knew what was coming next. There was no way the gunners could stop them. They moved too damn fast!

In they came, until the bright fire at their tales could be seen as a hot glow on the sea. For a moment it seemed he would suffer the nightmare yet again, endure the fate of *Gneisenau*, already bludgeoned and fallen off the battle line. Then, to his astonishment, he saw the rockets execute a precision turn, angling right off his starboard beam and vectoring in on the *Tirpitz!* It was as if they had eyes, as if they were piloted. He found himself casting a quick upward glance at the skies, thinking he might see some aircraft being used to radio control these demons, but all was clear. Then came the roar and thunder of the rockets as they struck home, and he leaned over the gunwale, looking back to see the bright fire and explosions enveloping the forward segment of the *Tirpitz*.

Topp's flagship had been hit hard, once on Anton turret, once at a point on the hull just below this, and the third hit behind Bruno at the base of the tall conning tower. He was transfixed for a moment, seeing the hot rolling smoke and fire. Then the watch shouted again and he looked to see two more ships had suddenly appeared on the horizon. He knew them at once. These were the British battlecruisers.

Hoffman had seen one close enough to duel with in the Norwegian Campaign the previous year off Lofoten Islands. Gunther Lütjens had been in command at the time, and they had come upon the battlecruiser *Renown* escorted by a pack of other smaller ships, which Lütjens took to be cruisers and destroyers. A brief action resulted, with both *Gneisenau* and *Renown* sustaining hits until Lütjens believed the British destroyers rushing in were much larger vessels, and broke off the engagement.

Always the reluctant Admiral, that one, thought Hoffmann. Only later did we learn that those were merely destroyers, and all that frenetic gunfire reported was well out of range. We could have stayed in that fight, but instead Lütjens ran off into the Arctic Sea. And where is he now?

In one brief moment, the situation had taken a major turn. *Rodney* had finally ceased firing, but now those two battlecruisers would bring another twelve 15-inch guns to the battle. How bad was the damage on *Tirpitz*? If those forward guns were compromised by that rocket attack... And what had caused that terrible eruption in the sea?

He soon learned that the damage looked far worse than it was. Anton turret had been temporarily put out of action, though its heavy armor had protected it from serious harm, in spite of numerous casualties there from the sheer shock of the attack. New crews were rushing to get it operational again, and fight the deck fire that resulted. The conning tower armor had also weathered the hit. The missile that struck beneath the forward guns had hit a segment of the hull above the main belt, where the armor was thinner at about 145mm. There was serious blast damage there, and yet another fire, yet none of these hits were fatal. The smaller 200kg warheads on the GB-7s did not have the punch to defeat heavy armor like this, and their effect was mainly one of heavy shock and fire.

Yet those punches had been enough to prompt Topp to turn to port. It would allow him to get his rear turrets in action, and also serve to put him on a better heading to disengage if that became necessary. Hoffmann saw the maneuver, and though he could see no signal flags on the battleship, he shouted orders to keep station and turned ten points to port. He could already see the flash of distant guns on those battlecruisers, and now he made the decision to shift fire to engage that new threat.

How long before those rockets find my ship, he thought, the memory of *Graz Zeppelin* still burning in his mind. My god, will we lose our whole squadron? What is that out there? He could not take his eyes from the still rising column on the horizon, mayhem and madness from another time, where two unseen warriors battled beneath the sea.

* * *

Aboard the *Hindenburg*, Admiral Lütjens was staring through his field glasses at what he first took to be a rapidly rising thunderhead. It had to be thirty or forty miles off, and how it could have appeared in the clear morning dawn mystified him. Yet there it was, billowing up in the distance, dwarfing the smaller columns of black smoke where he knew *Graf Zeppelin* must have died, and other ships must surely be burning with the fire of war.

Adler came to his side, both men on the weather deck, staring at the scene in silence. "Perhaps that is good news, Admiral," he suggested. "That British battleship may have blown up!"

"That has to be over a mile high," said Lütjens, gazing, beset with a deep inner feeling of misgiving. That was no storm, not on a day like this. That was death and destruction, but what on earth could have caused it?

"Send to Topp at once. Can he see that? What has happened?"

Then he felt the upwelling of the sea, just as all the others, which did little to still the feeling of disaster that was rising with that cloud on the horizon. It was not long before he saw what he had feared. The scoring of rocket trails in the sky, lancing up and speeding away towards the distant battle he now hastened to join.

They are here, he thought with some alarm. Yet we believed the *Invincible* was well to the southeast. Could those spotting reports we had be in error? He needed to know, and immediately ordered an Arado seaplane launched to overfly the battle ahead and report positions of anything in the vicinity. He knew that was risky. Those rockets could strike down aircraft as easily as they pummeled ships. He stiffened with a sudden chill, though the morning was not all that cold. The moment Adler returned he put his squadron on air alert, not for planes that might soon come, but for those rockets that would surely seek his own ships if they persisted on this course.

"Rockets," said Adler. "Topp reports three hits—all from those rockets, but the damage is controllable. He does not know what has happened with that eruption, nor do I. What could it be, Admiral?"

Lütjens gave the scene another narrow eyed look, his face grim. "Three trails in the sky, and three hits. Such accuracy! If we could do that with our guns we would destroy anything we encounter. And here we get yet another report of these rockets striking with unfailing accuracy. Whatever means they have discovered for guiding these rockets, it is the greatest breakthrough of the war. Now it comes down to what we discussed earlier, Adler. Just how many rockets do they have out there? And how many hits can we absorb before we get into gun range? The ship will come to battle stations. Now we see what that new armor may do for us. Tell the Chief of Engineers that he may deploy his hydraulics. And as for you, Captain, in another half hour you get your battle."

* * *

Elena Fairchild was now on the bridge, her eyes also pulled to the rising column of steam and vapor on the horizon. MacRae explained it in frank starkness.

"It's one hell of a donnybrook out there, and who knows where it might have come from. Mack thinks the Russians got spooked and made a bad call. In any case, they believed they were in jeopardy, and they lit one off."

"Lit one off?"

"That has to be fifteen to twenty kilotons out there," said MacRae. "Probably fired it on one of their Type-65s. Believe it or not, that would be standard operating procedure against a major threat in our day. It's the one warhead that would be almost certain to take out the target, even if they missed. This is what Morgan thinks."

"They got that spooked? From a U-boat contact? I thought this Russian sub was the best they had."

"That's the odd thing," said MacRae. "They sent us a flash radio message saying they thought they had an *Astute* Class sub on their tail. I know it sounds crazy, but our man Haley says he thinks he heard torpedoes in the water—*Spearfish*. Those are British weapons, but from our time, so this message is starting to have a nice ripe smell."

That took Elena by surprise. "A modern British submarine? Here? How did it get here?"

"I was thinking to ask you that myself," said MacRae. "They wouldn't happen to have another box and key like the one you've fished out of Delphi, now would they?"

Elena had a strange feeling now. She found herself staring at the sea outside, the tall lowering cloud in the distance chilling as it overshadowed the scene. It was as if the power and dreadful terror of the next war made all they were doing here in this one seem ludicrous and insignificant."

"Any word from our X-3?" She wanted to know what had happened to the Russian battlecruiser.

"They've been up an hour," said MacRae. "All the British ships are just where they were, but the Russians are gone, and now there's something else out there. Sampson radar has it too. We've got a string of seven more surface vessels about 20 kilometers out off our port side. X-3 says they look for all the world like *Point*-Class sealift ships—four of them, and a few other auxiliaries, including the *Ulysses*."

Elena knew the ship, a transport ferry of Irish registry. "*Ulysses?*"

"And fancy this…" MacRae forged on, thinking to dump the whole unseemly lot out at one time. "We picked up a message on a secure channel—coded channel used in Royal Navy operations in our time. Well, we've got the equipment here to decode it, seeing as though we're wearing the uniforms ourselves. Morgan says he thinks it came from that sub the Russians were squawking about. They were sending to the *Diligence*—fleet Auxiliary and repair ship—and asking about the Destroyer *Duncan*. That's a Type 45 destroyer, which would make it our long lost cousin, would it not?"

"There's another British destroyer out there too?"

"Not that we know of. We have nothing on radar, and we'd damn well know it if another Sampson system was operating here. No, I think this is starting to add up some other way, crazy as it might sound. Morgan thinks there was a Type-45 out there, riding shotgun for those seven merchant marine ships… In our day that would make perfect sense. He did some digging and found out that there was a fleet order to get RoRo ships down to Mersa Matruh. They were going to pull the 7th Armored Brigade out of Egypt and move them to France."

Elena's eyes narrowed, and all she could think of now was the discussion she had with the Russian Captain concerning how he thought Kinlan's troops had suddenly appeared here. Someone lit one off to go after them as well, and apparently it blew a hole right through the time continuum, sending Kinlan's entire brigade here, to the same place that box in her cabin had sent the *Argos Fire*. That convoy would have made another nice target, and if the Russians used a nuke...

My god, she thought. It's coming apart at the seams! Eighty years on the Russians are enemies, and yet here we must embrace them as allies. Yet both are throwing nukes around like there was no tomorrow... That thought gave her considerable pause, for it was exactly what she had warned them about, sheer calamity, a stony silence from the future that spoke of real doom. Now the Russians were suddenly gone, but in their place they had a whole string of uninvited guests. What to do about this?

"What about *Rodney*?" The urgency of the moment returned, pushing all these other incongruities aside. "We've fired missiles?"

"Aye, I sent three along to see if we could dissuade the Germans, though I'm not sure how much good we did. Thing is this, Elena. We've na' but seven more missiles under the deck, and without the Russians they won't be enough to decide this little disagreement. The battlecruiser is gone, and now we've no word from their submarine either. This situation is going from bad to worse. Now then. What would you like me to do here, mum?"

Chapter 3

The Germans were going to answer that question for MacRae, and in a most uncomfortable manner. The battle continued, this time with *Tirpitz* and *Scharnhorst* slugging it out with *Renown* and *Repulse*. With only seven anti-ship missiles remaining, MacRae decided that was a very thin margin for the defense of the ship.

"I think we'd have to salvo fire at least five missiles to seriously discourage one of these battleships," he said. "That will leave very little under the deck, but we can also weigh in with the deck gun"

"Well will it hurt them?" Elena folded her arms.

"It's a 155mm naval gun, a six incher that can outrange anything they have. I could even engage over the horizon. It may not penetrate their side armor to do serious harm, but it will be damn annoying if we hit their superstructure."

"Do it. A stiff jab is better than nothing. I knew we should have considered a heavier missile, but who could foresee this? Are the Russian missiles that much better than ours? They seemed to have no problem with these ships."

"Some have warheads more than twice what we have on the GB-7, and they weigh three times more. That's a lot of excess fuel to burn."

"Very well, use your best judgment, Gordon. I'm going to huddle with Mack to see if we can sort out this mess with those other ships, and find out what's happening with *Rodney*."

MacRae gave the order to deploy the forward gun, the deck panels sliding open and the hydraulics lifting the turret into view. It was a modified BAE Mark 8 naval gun in an angled stealth turret, using a new barrel and breech designed for the AS-90 self-propelled gun in the British Army. Fairchild had purchased one on a special order, and implemented a BAE plan to up-gun the older Mark 8 turret with this newer 155mm third generation maritime fire support system.

The Captain wasn't bragging when he talked about over the horizon engagements. The gun could hurl 6-inch rounds out over 100 kilometers, 62 miles, and hit with a circular error of no more than 50 meters at that range. At ten rounds per minute, the rate of fire could deliver a punch similar to a battery of six 155mm howitzers, which would indeed be damn annoying to any ship forced to endure that pounding.

MacRae decided to concentrate on the two contacts arriving from the east, leaving the British battlecruisers to their duel with *Tirpitz*. This second German squadron was led by the *Hindenburg*, he knew, though it was not yet on his horizon.

This will be a nice little surprise, he thought.

* * *

Aboard *Hindenburg* Lütjens was quite startled when the sea suddenly began to sprout up with the splash of shellfall. "Watchman," he shouted. "Where is that fire coming from? Adler?"

"We don't know, sir. There's nothing on our horizon!"

"What? Don't be a fool. Those are small caliber rounds—a secondary battery or guns off a light cruiser or destroyer. Does the radar have anything?"

"Nothing sir!" The edge of frustration in Adler's voice was obvious.

"Damn incompetence," said Lütjens, raising his own field glasses and scanning the horizon. He knew the mainmast above would have a much better view, and they should easily see any cruiser or destroyer in range to fire those shells, but the sea was empty. His next thought was that a submarine might have surfaced and was using its deck gun, but he dismissed that as sheer madness. No U-boat Captain would be so brash as to challenge a pair of battleships like this, and besides, the rate of fire here was well beyond what any deck gun on a sub could achieve. He watched, astonished, as three rounds plowed into the sea just ahead of *Bismarck* in the van, the third welling up right on her starboard side. That had to be a salvo from a triple barrel naval turret, but where was the damn ship? This was madness!

It was not long before the first rounds struck home, one landing amidships on *Bismarck*, a second striking *Hindenburg* right on the forward deck and exploding with a hail of shrapnel—damn annoying. Then a line of three shells came plummeting down to rake right across the ship, one striking his heavy Bruno turret with a loud explosion. Lütjens felt the whizz of shrapnel go right past his cheek, and realized he was in grave danger here. He rushed for the safety of the armored conning tower, still amazed by what he was seeing.

"Aircraft?" he said with an exasperated tone.

"Nothing sir, the sky is clear, except for that storm on the horizon."

"Clear? Then this cannot be happening, Adler. Who is firing at us? We have no ships sighted on any horizon, and surely this is not a U-boat? What is going on?"

Chief Engineer Eisenberg had been ready to raise his newly fitted armor plates as a defense against rockets, but the plunging fire of the rounds prompted him to delay. It was this extra measure of defense on many of the outer decks in the superstructure that greatly aided *Hindenburg* now. Yet Lütjens could see several small fires on the *Bismarck*.

This is insane, he thought. These rockets find our ships unerringly, and now we take gunfire that must be coming from well over the horizon—a range exceeding even that of our main batteries—and clearly from a small caliber weapon. This cannot be happening! No cruiser I know of could fire at such a range, and hit with such accuracy. Could they have a submarine correcting their fire, or an unseen seaplane? Yet how could they achieve such range from what must be a five or six inch gun?

Now he began to have a deep feeling that something was very wrong here. The British had stunned and amazed them with the sudden shock of their naval rocketry—now this! How could they be seeing us? Could it be some highly advanced form of new radar?

The hard crack and explosion of yet another round on the lower deck shook the ship again. This time they lost a secondary battery to a direct hit. His mind went on and on... Rommel... The man had reported the British had a massive new heavy tank in the desert. He had dismissed it at first, but now he began to re-think the rumors and talk he had heard about it—twice the size of the old Matildas, and with armor that was impervious to a direct hit from an AT gun, even from the vaunted 88. How could they be so far ahead of us? Why... it's as if these weapons have come from another time, a generation or more ahead of anything Germany had developed. Yet, at the same time, the British still flew off those old *Swordfish* biplanes from their carriers, still fought in their lumbering Matildas. It made no sense.

These new weapons have appeared only in very select places. Goering sent wave after wave of our bombers to smash London. One would think that a prime target for the British to defend with the very best weapons they have. Yet there was not a single instance of any of these rocket weapons that have proved to be so lethal to our planes. That *Stuka* attack put in by the last planes off *Graf Zeppelin* was shot to pieces in five minutes! Those anti-aircraft rockets are so deadly that I had to order the *Goeben* to stand down and break off to the west. No use throwing those last three *Stukas* away. I see this, astonished, and yet the British let us pound London without firing a single rocket. Something is not what it seems here. Something is very wrong. In the meantime, how much more of this must we endure? Thankfully we should be coming in range of the *Tirpitz* in due course.

MacRae's deck gun had been more than annoying that morning. There was damage on both *Bismarck* and *Hindenburg*, small fires that were controllable, but the casualties had mounted up. On the *Hindenburg*, they lost a secondary battery, a gun director, had lifeboats blown to pieces, and an Arado seaplane exploding amidships with a direct hit.

The action between *Tirpitz* and the British battlecruisers had shifted well away from the foundering *Rodney*. There the *Scharnhorst* had taken one hit forward near the Anton turret, And *Tirpitz* suffered a hit on her heavy side armor, shrugging off the blow. *Renown* had not been so lucky. Topp's gunners had straddled that ship on their fourth salvo, and the next one put a 15-insh shell right through the forward deck, with *Scharnhorst* hitting the ship amidships for good measure.

"Adler!" Lutjens shouted. "It's now or never. Drive off those battlecruisers!"

Captain Adler was only too happy to comply, the frustration of taking all these secondary battery hits had been mounting for the last fifteen minutes, and now the enemy would hear the roar of the *Hindenburg*, like a great elephant wielding its mighty trunk and trumpeting in anger. At long last, he had something to shoot at.

The British battlecruisers saw the arrival of *Hindenburg* and *Bismarck*, and knew their time for battle had run out. They began to angle off to starboard, still firing, yet edging away and opening the range to prevent the new German ships from engaging.

All the while the plumes of small caliber rounds were still falling around Lütjens squadron, and the Admiral had a very keen eye. He was watching the enemy battlecruisers very closely with his field glasses, and could clearly see their main batteries firing, and mark the fall of those heavier 15-inch rounds.

Yet they aren't even using their secondary batteries, he thought. And there is no way these shells could be fired by the *Rodney*. Our Arado reported that ship to be listing over and sinking. So that narrows down the list of suspects. The British had destroyers with the *Rodney*, yet they were reported to have broken off with that fat troop ship liner. They would be well east by now. There was also a cruiser said to be approaching *Rodney*, most likely to render aid and pick up survivors. Could that be the ship firing at us? I could turn hard to starboard now and swing east to find *Rodney* again…

At that moment, his lookouts shouted—ship off the port beam. A battleship! The Admiral rushed back out onto the weather deck, heedless of the danger now. There he could clearly see the tall mainmast and conning tower appearing on the horizon, and that could be only one ship. His Arado seaplane soon reported it as well—battleship with three triple turrets, his nemesis, a match for the *Hindenburg* itself. It could be no other British ship but HMS *Invincible.*

There you are at last, he said. You've come a long way in my shadow, and now we finally meet. Was this the ship that had been announcing it coming with those troubling small caliber rounds, like hail at the edge of as thunder storm? He looked again at the massive clouds on the horizon, the only weather in sight, yet it seemed an unearthly spectacle, out of place, and deeply disturbing.

"Adler! Come about to port! We will engage this newcomer. Leave the battlecruisers to *Tirpitz*. Now It will be your nine 16-inch guns against theirs, and god go with us."

The time for this insult of small caliber rounds was finally over. Now it was time for the heavy artillery to decide the issue, and Lütjens was determined that it would be settled here, one way or another. If this was the ship flinging those damn rockets about, he would settle the matter, once and for all.

* * *

Argos Fire was finally up on the scene of *Rodney*'s travail. The battleship was in a heavy list, down at the bow, where the weight of those three massive turrets seemed to be pressing the ship into the sea. The list was too bad for any further gunfire, but thankfully the battlecruisers had arrived and the action had shifted away from *Rodney*, off to the west and over the horizon.

MacRae could already see life boats in the water, and he quickly gave orders that they should launch every boat they had. He had kept up a withering gunfire against the second German squadron, and was certain he caused them much misery. But he knew he wasn't going to sink a German battleship here with his deck gun.

Now look at us, he thought. There's men in the water, perhaps seven or eight hundred souls on that stricken battleship. That's

45,000 tons of steel about to roll over and go under out there, and all the King's business will soon go with it. He looked at Elena, back at his side again with a look of despair in her eyes.

"We're too damn late," she breathed.

"Aye," said MacRae. "We've had them on the radio. They took a couple hits low near their forward torpedoes, and the whole magazine went off there. Word is that cargo hold was completely flooded. There was no way in hell we were ever going to get in there. All we can do now is get as many men out of the water as possible."

"That could be a problem. Too many eyes, Gordon."

"We can't bloody well leave them out there? I've gone and launched all out boats to lend a hand."

"Yes, do what you can to pull them onto the boats, but there's a big troop ship off east. Let's see if we can quarter the survivors there."

"That'll take time, Elena. What if that battle out there comes our way while we're at it?"

"How many missiles left?"

"Seven."

Elena folded her arms, determined. "If anything so much as sticks its nose over that horizon again, you damn well hit it with everything we have."

Gordon nodded, one eyebrow raised. "Well enough," he said. "Aye, we can hold the field here a while if we have to, but what's the plan now, Elena? What about those other ships out there?"

"I've got Mack on it," she said. "He's talking with the Captain of the squadron now—a chap named Dowding. He's on that auxiliary you mentioned, the *Diligence*. There are four fleet transports, an oiler, and then the *Ulysses*."

"Quite a flock," said MacRae. "Useful ships."

"Yes, and with *Rodney* going down, I'm afraid they're all our watch now. If we can finish up here, I plan to head to Madalena or Ponta Delgada in the Azores."

"Makes sense," said Gordon. "We can't very well sail into Portsmouth with that lot, can we?"

"Not bloody likely," said Elena. "Any further word on the Russians?"

"Quiet as mice," said MacRae. "I've been thinking what may have happened. Do you suppose they were on the wrong end of that mushroom out there in the garden?"

"That ship was reported missing long before that, wasn't it?"

"Aye," MacRae nodded, "and then the whole plan went bonkers on us. That other British Admiral must be having fits out there."

"Tovey? Probably so. Let's get a message off to him and let him know *Rodney*'s status. How long do you figure we have?"

"She's listing at well over ten degrees from the look of it," said MacRae. "And that is likely after they've already counter-flooded to try and correct it. She'll most likely go down within the hour."

Elena nodded, her eyes vacant, searching. "Get as many men on those boats as you can," she said. "I don't care if we have to use every raft on the ship—even the helicopters if necessary. Two of the destroyers with *Britannic* are on the way as well. At the moment, I'm going to have to arrange a meeting with this Captain on *Diligence*."

"He's going to have one hell of a story for breakfast," said MacRae with a knowing smile.

"Elena shrugged. "I'll be in my cabin," she said, her hand touching his elbow for the barest moment, their eyes meeting, with much said there without words.

Part II

The Final Shift

"The strangeness of Time. Not in its passing, which can seem infinite, like a tunnel whose end you can't see, whose beginning you've forgotten, but in the sudden realization that something finite, has passed, and is irretrievable."

— Joyce Carol Oates

Chapter 4

Fedorov was also facing down the cruel whims of time that night. The dilemma they now found themselves in was confounding, and he could not determine what was happening to the ship and crew. Were these strange effects the result of impending Paradox? The fate of Lenkov, the threatening sounds reported, and now the disappearance of key members of the crew, all convinced him that this was so. Yet what was really happening?

Have we so altered the course of history with our actions here that it has had fatal effects on the life lines of the missing men? We searched the ship's records, both digital and analog, and found no evidence that these men had ever existed. There would have been hundreds of data points to prove the existence of a man like Orlov on this ship, he thought. He would have signed off on all the section chief crew assignments, but we find nothing, not a single trace that he was ever here. Orlov exists only in our memories now, and that can only be said of a select group on the ship.

He remembered Orlov clearly enough, and all the other missing men as well. Yet the Admiral and other senior officers seemed foggy when he first asserted Tasarov was missing. Indeed, he realized that he had also been oblivious of Tasarov until Nikolin came to him and insisted his friend had gone missing. Once the looking glass of his memory was dusted off, however, he could suddenly recall everything. And he had been able to jog the memory of Admiral Volsky and the other senior officers on the bridge at that critical moment. Now they were among the knowing few on the ship, but as he made his rounds, he soon discovered that most other crewmen knew nothing of Orlov, while others remembered him clearly enough.

Sergeant Troyak was a perfect example. He clearly recalled Orlov being assigned to his Marine detail after he was busted, and the details of his mission to Ilanskiy on the *Narva* were also clear in his mind. In fact, most of the Marines remembered him with no problem, but other crewmen, even those who might have had daily interaction with the Chief, seemed oblivious.

His first thought was that this was an effect that resulted from their sudden shift. Every other time displacement they had made, left the ship and crew remarkably intact, but not this one. The more he thought about this, the more he came to believe his worst fears were now slowly being realized.

Paradox… It wasn't just a seeming contradiction, or a thorny puzzle to challenge the logic of one's thinking. No. It was a real force, and one capable of reordering the physical reality of the universe, changing and altering everything. It was the force of annihilation, the cruel imperative in any equation that demanded a zero sum—and it was killing them. The missing men, the missing data, were all evidence of the deadly hand of Paradox.

Now that the ship had phased, shifted again in time, he still had no real idea what their position was on the continuum. Was it still May of 1941, or had they moved to some other time? Did they shift forward, or slip deeper into the past? If the disappearance of these men was the result of Paradox, then he was inclined to think the ship might have moved forward again, to a point in time where they were now suffering the consequences of their many interventions. They had changed the course of events to a point where the life lines of Tasarov and the others were fatally compromised. This was all he could deduce at that moment.

The only thing he was relatively certain of was that Paradox was somehow involved. As the ship had sailed closer and closer to a moment in time where it already existed, these effects became more pronounced. The hand of fate was on them now, and he could see no way they could avoid it. His fear now was that the process was still underway, and other things could change—go missing, just like Kamenski and the others.

Yet just a moment, he thought. The ship doesn't simply exist in time. It also occupies space, and the combination of its spatial position and its temporal position would define it as an event in *spacetime...* Then something struck him with thunderclap surprise. Two discrete objects could easily exist at the same time, but they could not exist in the same space. Therefore they could also not exist together in the same spacetime, which was a unified expression of both space and time.

Physicists and theoreticians were always trying to nail things down on a chart, just as he plotted the position of the ship for navigation. He was often asked to set an intercept course that depended on many variables, and this was always a chancy prediction. He could know an enemy ship's last reported position, course, and speed, and then compare that with similar information on his own ship. This enabled him to set a course and speed that would potentially bring the two ships together in the same future moment of spacetime. And when this was happening with two opposing warships, battle would result, with one ship ruling the moment and prevailing, and the other either driven off or destroyed.

Just like two chess pieces trying to occupy the same space on a board, one or the other had to prevail. But we are not on an intercept course in *spacetime*, only in time. Our last reported position was just a few hundred nautical miles west of Lisbon, but that other ship, the one we arrived on, will appear in the Norwegian Sea. Two discrete objects can easily co-exist in the same time, but not the same spacetime. If this were so, then it suddenly occurred to him that it was not simply a collision in time that he should fear, but a collision in *spacetime.*

Was this the source of my confusion? I believed we were on an intercept course with that other ship, with our own selves as we appeared on July 28th of 1941. They are approaching that event in spacetime from the future, while we are approaching it from the past. I have been obsessed with the timing of the event, and I was ignoring the spatial element. We'll reach July 28th, 1941 if we continue to move forward here, *but that will be a separate event, from that defined by the other ship.* We won't be in the same spatial location, and therefore we won't be in the same spacetime as the ship arriving from the future!

Now he remembered that terrifying moment when *Kirov* was in the Pacific. The ship had begun to pulse, its position in spacetime wavering and undefined. They had used Rod-25 to try and remove themselves from danger, then there came that strange event, where the cruiser *Tone* had appeared and seemed to plow right through the ship. He could still see it in his mind's eye, and feel the terror of that experience. It was as if a ship of ghosts had sailed right through them on a collision course, spectral phantoms from another reality.

At that moment we were fortunately not in the same spacetime as the *Tone*. Otherwise the two ships would have had a fatal collision. He had been thinking about this all wrong, believing he had to be in a different temporal location when *Kirov* was slated to arrive from the future. Yet could they avoid the Paradox he feared by simply being at a different spatial location? That could be easily arranged. Was the solution to this dilemma that simple?

Then one troubling note sounded an objection in his mind— Alan Turing's watch. Why did it vanish, only to be found later in that file box that must surely have also come from a future time? Why did time find it necessary to move that watch? What complication was it trying to avoid? Was something else happening with that watch, something unrelated to the possibility of Paradox?

Two ships… one arriving from the future, another arriving from the past, and both wanting domain over a single moment in time, but not in the same location in space…

Now he found his thinking falling through to yet another level. Were there really two ships? Wasn't *this* the ship that arrived from the future? It's already here… and if we haven't moved elsewhere, it will still be here come July 28, 1941. It isn't arriving at that moment from the future this time. Now it is arriving from the past.

All these thoughts swirled through his mind, like a great spiraling whirlpool of possibility, and he felt like a swimmer adrift in that maelstrom, and desperately struggling to keep his head above water. Quite literally, only time would tell which of these conflicting theories would hold true. There were only three possible outcomes. The first was that the ship he was now standing on would vanish, as it seemingly had, and its place in 1941 would be claimed by the ship arriving from the future. This was the chilling reality he feared they were now facing. They had vanished, and pieces of the puzzle that had once been *Kirov* in 1941 were now obviously missing.

The second possibility was that the other ship would be prevented from arriving from the future, and for a number of reasons. The most obvious was that the long chain of causality could never replicate itself to produce the circumstances that sent *Kirov* back through time.

Now his thinking about that stack of plates and teacups returned. All the events from 1941 to 2021 extended out like a stack of fragile china, eighty years high. Wouldn't these changes they were making to the history cause catastrophic changes in the future? This was what the butterfly effect argued. It held that something as simple and insignificant as the flapping of a butterfly's wings could cause just enough of a perturbation in the air to prevent the formation of a hurricane in the future. Small things now have big effects much later, and the changes they had caused in the history were not small things—they were huge.

In their first displacement they had altered the entry date of the US in the war, and by so doing, changed the entire course of the war in the Pacific. There was no way he could see the design and building of *Kirov* after what they had done, let alone the assignment of all the exact same crew members, and the same exact decisions and events being taken to eventually result in the ship being displaced in time as it happened. How could that future moment repeat? How could it arise now from this terribly convoluted past?

That was logic enough, he thought, and there is one more reason the future *Kirov* cannot arrive here—*because the ship was already here.* If this were so, there was no real threat, even though they were now suffering all these ill effects. Something else could have caused the oddities that were occurring—our instability in time—the pulsing

I have observed many times before. Perhaps Orlov and the others *were* still here with them, but strangely out of phase? Yet if that were so, why did so many seem oblivious to the fact they ever existed? Why was there no physical evidence they were ever here, their possessions, ship's records?

So in these first two options, the chess game example holds true—only one piece can occupy a given square, and it would be left up to fate and time to decide which would prevail.

Then there was yet one more possible outcome—*both* ships could arrive on July 28, 1941, one from the future and also the one he was on now, arriving from an earlier moment in time, arriving from the past. He had first thought this co-location would be impossible, and become the root of the Paradox, but if his thinking about spacetime was correct, then this was now a real possibility. They could *both* be in the same time, as long as they did not occupy the same space, and he knew that could never happen.

For this to be so, it would mean that the ships were *different*, not the same at all—that they had originated in different worlds. Is this the way it worked? He knew the ship slated to arrive from the future could not be coming as a result of the history extending forward from this moment. It had to be coming from some other time line—some other meridian in the continuum. In fact, it had to be coming from the same exact world they left when they first raised anchor at Severomorsk. No other time line, assuming multiple lines were possible, could result in the unique set of circumstances that sent the ship back through time. And here is the riveting truth—I'm standing on that ship. This is the *Kirov* that came from that meridian in time. So if another ship does arrive here from the future, then it must be coming from some other meridian, *not the world we left at Severomorsk.*

That thought shook him, for it depended on there being many alternate universes, which was something he could never prove or know for certain. Could such an alternate world produce the same exact event that first sent the ship back in time—the live fire exercises, the accident aboard Orel, Rod-25, all of it? The odds on that seemed impossibly small, but assuming it did so, would the ship come here, to this alternate time line? Why? Is there really a world for every possible circumstance and replaying of these events?

He shook his head. Trapped in the loop of his own thinking. Yet he realized that one of those three outcomes must happen. *Kirov* will either be prevented from arriving here because of the changes we have made to the history, or, if it does arrive here, then it comes from some other world, and not the world in which we now sail. Assuming that, it will either replace us and rule unchallenged in these waters, or else *both* ships will survive.

Kamenski had tried to tell him something else about this... *Kirov* was not a thing, not an object, but a process, an activity, a verb. *"Yes, my friend, everything in the universe is like that. Everything is a verb. There are no nouns, if you really think about it. That is just a pleasant and useful convention. Everything is a process."*

We are just an activity—we are just something the universe is doing, thought Fedorov, and now he remembered Kamenski's incredible discourse on that topic.

"Time is not what you think it is... There are no 'moments,' only a constant expression of motion.... Old Zeno tried to prove motion was an illusion, that life was like a series of frames in a movie—or a series of positions in a chess game, but he actually had it backwards. This notion of fixed moments in time—that is the illusion, a mere convention of thought... 1941? 2021? These are not places, Fedorov, they are activities, movement in a dance. To go to one or the other you simply have to change your behavior—step lively, and learn the dance of infinity. You see, anything can be expressed in that dance..."

Anything... If Kamenski is correct, then I am just a maelstrom of particles, in this very peculiar shape called Fedorov. I'm just something the universe is doing, just as a whirlpool is something the river is doing, an activity, a temporary arrangement of particles that seem to persist, though we know it is impermanent. And none of those particles can ever be said to be in any particular place. This was what quantum theory asserted, Heisenberg's Uncertainty Principle. The particles were always in motion, never in any one "place" and always retaining the possibility of being somewhere else. It was just as Kamenski had argued… *"To put it simply, things don't stay put… there is only constant change and motion—constant uncertainty. And if they are never here, then they are never anywhere else either."*

If another ship does arrive, it will be another arrangement of particles, will it not? The two ships will not be the same. In fact, it would be impossible for them to ever be the same, to have every unique particle of their being doing the exact same thing on both ships, acting out the exact same steps in the dance Kamenski had talked about.

Damn… this ship had combat damage, missiles expended from our magazines, men missing, and all the souls here forever changed by what we have experienced, what we have endured. But *that* ship would be fresh from the docks at Severomorsk, its magazine full, undamaged in any way, and with a full crew of innocent souls who had no idea of what they were about to face.

They aren't the same…. It may appear so, but on a quantum level the two ships would be distinctly different, two whirlpools in the stream, two expressions the world might simply call *Kirov*, but they would be completely different, like identical twins—doppelgangers. And considering they would not even be occupying the same spacetime event, being in two completely different locations… Was it possible that both could exist at the same time? And if this is true…

There is no Paradox!

That thought struck like the bell of hope ringing in his weary mind, yet one question still remained unanswered. If this were true, then what was happening to us now? Something told him his hope might be standing on shaky ground, and in this instance, his deep unconscious objection to his tortured logic was quite correct. For all of his assumptions and suppositions were simply wrong…

Chapter 5

The time for speculation and pondering the physics was over. The grey fog that still surrounded the ship persisted like a funeral shroud, and Fedorov knew they had to do something.

"I have never seen sea conditions like this," said Volsky. "The ocean is still and calm, and this sea fog is impenetrable."

"For the cloud deck to extend up so high is most unusual," Fedorov agreed. "Every compass on the ship is spinning like a top, which is probably an effect from that uncontrolled shift. But the weather?"

"How long before it will break?"

"Hard to say, Admiral. Advection fog like this usually forms when a warmer air mass migrates above the colder sea surface air. Yet for this to extend up so high that the KA-40 could not find clear air is unheard of. It's usually confined to the boundary layer of the warmer air mass, and just manifests as surface fog."

"And we have no wind," said Volsky. "So here we sit, stuck in the doldrums."

"True sir, but I am beginning to suspect that this is not advection fog. It seems… almost unnatural."

"What do you mean?"

"Well it's clear we shifted, as we've lost all contact with the British and Gromyko. So something happened to disturb the ship's position in time. Who knows why? The ship was beginning to exhibit signs of instability, just like that time in the Pacific after the last air strike we faced. Remember? We turned north, well ahead of the cruiser *Tone*, but then it just appeared because I think we were pulsing, phasing, moving in and out of the time we were in. That allowed *Tone* to close the distance, because it was moving in space when we phased."

"Then no time passed for us when that happened?"

"The evidence seems to support that. *Tone* should not have been able to catch up with us that quickly, so when we phased, we must have been in a kind of suspended time. And yet, I never lost the sensation that we were in the sea the whole time. We don't know where we go when this happens, but we are clearly somewhere, because the ship remains stable and afloat on the sea, just as it is now."

"You mean you believe we are in one of these phasing states now?"

"I can think of no other explanation for this heavy fog. It simply cannot manifest all of a sudden like it did, nor could it expend up beyond the ceiling of the KA-40. You are correct Admiral, these sea conditions are nigh on to impossible. It is unnatural."

That gave Volsky a chill as he looked about them, the grey fog so close on the ship that the bow was barely visible through the forward view screens.

"So we are somewhere," he said. "Elsewhere, a kind of purgatory where we sit in judgment at time's court. Is that what has happened?"

"That is a colorful way of thinking about it sir, but you may be correct. Then again, all these effects we've been experiencing may simply be the result of our approach to Paradox. To be equally colorful, it looms like a vast hidden ice berg out there in that fog somewhere, and there we were, sailing blindly along as the days ticked off and we came ever closer. Something was bound to happen sooner or later, and it did."

"Sooner," said Volsky. "It was only May when we disappeared this time. Why is that, Fedorov?"

"I don't really know, but it happened. Perhaps the event we were facing was so critical, that it created effects that undulate out through time. We arrived here from the future, like a stone falling in a still pool, and we clearly disturbed the waters here, sending ripples out in all directions. We know those ripples affect the future from the point we entered here in July of 1941. Might they also affect the past? If this is so, then the effects we've been experiencing, Lenkov, men missing, the physical changes to the ship itself, might all be the result of these waves in time we created ourselves with that first arrival."

In this Fedorov was quite correct, and Volsky nodded as if he could sense this. "I understand," he said. "At least I follow your metaphor. Then we may be riding one of these waves now. But what about Admiral Tovey and his ship? Is he lost in a grey fog as well?"

"Who can say, sir, but I would think not. *Invincible* was native to the time we were in. it belonged there, even though it was the result of profound changes we caused to the time line. There were no odd reports coming from Tovey; no men went missing there."

"I see… Then we are affected more because we do *not* belong here. Yes?"

"This is what I am thinking."

"These waves, Fedorov, will they get worse?"

"The effects do seem to be progressively worsening, sir. It started with Tasarov and Dobrynin reporting that strange sound. Then we lost Lenkov. After that…"

"Men started to go missing," said Volsky grimly. "And I cannot believe I stood here on this bridge and could not remember Tasarov."

"Nor I, sir, until Nikolin jogged my memory. And now we have hit a wave that has had a broad physical effect on the entire ship and crew. We have phased completely, moved again, though we do not know where we are, or even *when* we are."

"Will we ride this wave, Fedorov? Will we re-appear in May of 1941 again until the next wave hits us?"

"I'm not certain. We might, but if these effects continue to worsen, the next wave…"

Volsky took a deep breath. "Well I do not think we can sail about like this for weeks waiting for a look at the stars. We may never see them unless we do re-emerge in that time we were in. Who knows, we might have been swept out into the seas of oblivion for good this time. We might never return to the place and time we were. That is good luck for the Germans, and bad luck for Admiral Tovey. From his perspective we must have simply vanished, and we've left him there alone to face the *Hindenburg* and all the rest. I was going to destroy the entire German surface fleet, Fedorov. We had the missile power left to do so. And then there was Gromyko. Whatever we failed to sink would remain easy pickings for him. The Kriegsmarine was on its last fatal sortie, or so I saw it when I decided to engage. It was not an easy decision—never easy to kill, particularly other sailors. Yes, we made them our enemies, but we are kinsman of sorts with them. The ocean we sail on, the depths below, are all our graves in waiting. Every sailor who ever set sail knows that, fears it. The sea holds them up, sustains them, yet it also waits for them, as the sharks wait, to devour their souls."

"Time is that way, sir. We're all sailing on the seas of time, from the cradle to the grave."

"Yes? Well we have started to founder, Fedorov. It is now clear to me that we are taking on water from that sea, and this ship is sinking. So what would we do if that were the case in the ocean? We counter flood to correct a list. Damage control, yes Fedorov?"

"What are you thinking, sir?"

"We must do something. We cannot just wallow here until that next wave hits. We have the power to act, and we must do something. Is that second control rod ready?"

"Aye sir. The engineers have it mounted."

"I can tell by that face that you hesitate to use it, Mister Fedorov."

"There is always some risk, Admiral. Look what happened to us last time—we shifted in spacetime, not simply time. It was as if we were held in suspension while the earth rotated, and then dropped into the Atlantic. If that had gone on a little longer, we might have plopped down in Canada! Then there is one other problem—we could sustain additional structural damage. The ship has had difficulty phasing. When we displace in time, we must manifest somewhere else, and re-sync with that timeframe. We've seen clear evidence that the ship is not manifesting in a stable manner on these later shifts. We've been discussing all that just now, but it is only speculation. Running from the problem before we know what really happened is somewhat daunting."

"What other choice do we have now, Fedorov? We either run this procedure and take our chances, or we sit here for days on end, wondering where we are, waiting for the next impossible thing to happen."

Fedorov thought of his hand, his boots, and the Admiral did not have to persuade him further. "Agreed sir," he said. "There's no use speculating any more about this. What you say is obvious. We are foundering, sinking in time, and if we don't take some action the sharks will have the final say. Shall I send the order down to engineering?"

"Make it so."

Fedorov complied, using the overhead handset for the ship's intercom. "All hands, all hands, this is the Captain. We are going to make an attempt to move the ship from our present location in time. Stand ready. Engineering—initiate rod maintenance procedure and keep the bridge informed. That is all."

Fedorov looked down at his boots, glancing at the Admiral. "I hope I will not need another pair soon," he said glibly.

"Yes," said Volsky. "And let us also hope we do not have another incident like Lenkov."

He swallowed, and for a moment Fedorov thought he saw his eyes glaze over with emotion. The Admiral looked at him, the light of appreciation warmly in his eyes as he extended his hand, placing it on his Captain's shoulder.

"Mister Fedorov," he said quietly. "I want to thank you for all you have done since I first had the wisdom to make you my *Starpom*. You have lived up to my expectations, and exceeded them, and without you I do not think we could have survived all that has happened to us. To put it plainly, you are simply the finest young officer I have ever served with, and you are to be congratulated."

Fedorov felt the emotion come, and unable to speak, he simply nodded. All about them there was a silence on the bridge, and it held within it an understanding that a moment of great significance was now upon them all.

"I second that," said Rodenko, smiling and shaking Fedorov's hand." And every man there, though they were glued to their stations, extended that same handshake in thought. They were all there, every hand one on top of another, a solidarity of minds, hearts, and lives that had come so very far together.

The Admiral eyed the intercom, thinking, a strange, lonesome look on his face. He took a deep breath, then stepped over and took the handset, giving Fedorov a wan smile as he did so.

"All hands… This is Admiral Volsky…" He paused, thinking, an expression on his face akin to sadness, as though he were about to say goodbye to a dear friend, and take a very long journey fraught with peril. Then he spoke, his voice clear and steady.

"We have come a very long way together, through fire and steel, embracing the impossible, and yet enduring as one ship and crew. We have seen battle, lost friends, good men all. And we have stood by one another in every circumstance, brave to a man… We do not know now where we may end up. Yet that is so for every day we live, is it not? We are the same brave ship and crew that first sailed from our homeland so long ago, and yet now we are something more. Who knows, perhaps we'll make it home one day, to our own time again, and a world where life is still possible. I cannot yet offer you that to a certainty, but we can try, and so we will. Yet there is one thing I know, and without any doubt. You must know it as well. I see it in your eyes, your strong backs and arms as you bend to complete the work of the ship. I have seen it each and every day as we sailed and fought together. We stand now aboard the finest ship on this earth, and you are the finest crew to ever stand a watch at sea, as god is my witness. And so I thank you—for your courage… for your perseverance… for your steadfast loyalty… for *Kirov*…"

He reached slowly, replacing the handset, and as he did so, the sound of men cheering resounded through the ship, echoing in every hall and passage, vibrating the bulkheads and hatches, and quavering in the dull fog enfolded all about them. Then the cheers became a song, and every officer on the bridge smiled.

* * *

The smoke-white fog seemed to deepen at first, and then glowed as though illuminated by the cold light of an unseen moon. They heard a strange sound, vibrating throughout the ship, a fearful dirge that filled them with dread. Soon the light around them glimmered and glowed, the fog suddenly thinning, the sea gleaming with a witch oil of phosphor green.

Then the sound deepened, falling... falling.... Until it finally resolved in what sounded like a great kettle drum resounding from the depths of the sea, a heavy rumble, low an ominous. A sudden chill took them all, frosty cold and bone deep, and Admiral Volsky found himself clutching the arm of the Captain's chair, his tooth, the tooth that always bothered him when bad weather came, a sudden throb of pain. He closed his eyes, whispering one word to himself, a silent invocation... *Remember...*

There came a shudder throughout the ship, and when Fedorov looked out the fog was gone, and he could see the stars seeming to move in a wild, wheeling dance, as if the heavens, and all eternity, were spinning about the ship as it fell into some unfathomable void. God go with us, he breathed inwardly. Then something passed over him, threw him, a wave of energy unlike anything he had ever felt before, tingling in every fiber of his being. He had the distinct feeling that it was reaching for him, a yawning hunger, greedy and cruel.

He felt a sudden heat at his side, his hand reflexively moving to his pocket, and finding there the hard metal of the strange key he had found in Kamenski's quarters. It was warm to the touch, and now he found himself surrounded by a strange cobalt glow, that intensified until he could see nothing else around him. The feeling of dread and doom passed, and he felt as though he lay in the palm of God's own hand, protected from the ravages of time and eternity, safe and sound. His hand closed about the key and he felt it slowly cooling with each second.

The light around him dissipated, and for a moment he thought he caught a glimpse of blue light from within his jacket pocket. He looked down at his feet, wondering, fearful, hoping that wherever they were, he would all be there in one piece. A sensation of solidity returned to him, feet firmly on the deck, and boots all intact. Then he heard a voice, his eyes widening with shock and surprise.

"What in god's name was that? Certainly not thunder…"

There came a blinding white light, and Fedorov instinctively flinched, shielding his eyes. The searing light flashed and vanished, leaving the air alive with what looked like a hundred thousand fireflies all around the ship, strange luminescent particles that spun on the cold airs, whirling and dancing as they slowly faded to milky green. When it passed, he instinctively looked out of the forward viewing panes, surprised to see that the ocean itself seemed to light up for miles in every direction with an eerie phosphorescent color. Then the sea erupted in the distance, boiling up in a wild convulsion of sound and motion. The ship shuddered with the impact of a strong blast wave, rolling heavily.

Fedorov spun about, looking to find Volsky in the Captain's chair, but soon realized his greatest fear. The admiral wasn't there! Was he gone? Vanished? Had he fallen out of sync with the shift? Everyone on the bridge braced for further impact. Fedorov extended his hand to the nearest bulkhead, not so much to keep from falling, but to assure himself that the ship and crew around him were real and substantial things. What was happening?

He saw one man thrown from his seat near the helm, his eyes wide with fear and astonishment, as if he could also sense that something terrible had fallen upon the ship. The strident welter of sound subsided, resolving to a sharp cellophane crackle that hung in the air like a wave of heavy static electricity. Then there came another low descending vroom, the sound falling through three octaves as if it had been sucked into a black hole and devoured.

Stunned and amazed, every member of the bridge crew seemed frozen, their faces twisted into expressions of numbed, painful shock.

Then a high, sharp voice broke the silence, barking out an order.

"Action stations! We are under attack!"

In spite of the alarm, he suddenly felt a giddy lightheadedness, swaying briefly on unsteady legs.

And then he fell.

Chapter 6

When he awoke, opening his eyes with bleary awareness, he could see another face looking down at him, warm and smiling. The dark rimmed glasses and white hair were unmistakable, and the man's white medical blazer immediately told him he was now in sick bay. He tried to sit up, but felt a gentle nudge, easing him back.

"Easy now, Mister Fedorov. No need to be alarmed. You are all in one piece, and with little more than a small bruise on your head from that fall you took. Has the dizziness passed?"

Fedorov blinked, still processing what he was hearing. "Fall?" he said, his voice thin and weak.

"So they tell me," said Doctor Zolkin. "Looks like you lost your sea legs up there for a time and keeled right over. Don't feel ashamed. There's been a line at my door twenty men long for the last hour—mostly for bumps and bruises like that knock on the head you took. I trust the room has settled down now and your stomach has quieted?"

Fedorov swallowed, feeling just a little sensation of nausea. He turned his head, somewhat queasy, but there was no dizziness.

"How many fingers?" said Zolkin extending his hand.

"Two."

"Very good. And now if you would kindly just watch the tip of my finger for a moment." The Doctor moved his finger left and right across the plane of Fedorov's face, noting his eyes as they tracked, and seeing that all was well.

"Also good," he said with a satisfied tone. "I've given you something to help with the nausea, which should be very temporary. I think I can have you back on your feet in another hour, so take advantage of the time to get a little rest."

"But Doctor…" Fedorov began. "The ship… Admiral Volsky… Were we under attack?"

"Attack? I don't think so. The sea and sky are somewhat strange, but the ship has secured from battle stations. Admiral Volsky has the matter well in hand on the bridge."

A feeling of great relief swept over Fedorov when he heard that. "Then he's alive? He shifted intact? Do you have any idea where we are now?"

"Shifted? The ship rolled quite heavily there for a moment, but you were the only casualty they brought down from the bridge. Of course he's alive. As for where we are, that's not my job, Fedorov. Yes, you are the navigator, though you seemed to have someone else's coat on when they brought you in here. You can determine our course soon enough when you return to the bridge. For now, rest easy. Things are under control."

"I need to get up there."

"Not just yet, Mister Fedorov. That anti-nausea drug needs just a little time to kick in. I think it best you stay right where you are. Don't worry. I'm sure Mister Pavlov can handle things for a while."

"Pavlov?" The man was a junior bridge officer for third shift at navigation, thought Fedorov. What would he have to do with anything? Then he realized Zolkin must be referring to the navigation issue. Well, he thought, at least I had no trouble remembering that crewman's name, so my memory might still be intact. And the ship appears sound, the walls and bulkheads around them here all looked solid and unbowed. He decided to ask Zolkin about that.

"Has any further damage been reported, Doctor?"

"Damage? To the ship? Not that I know of. Just those bumps and bruises with the crew, though a few seemed a little suspicious. I wonder if our surly Chief has been up to his old ways of late."

That confused Fedorov a bit, for it seemed to him that Zolkin was referring to Orlov. Again, he was inwardly glad the man's name and face came so easily to his mind now. He passed a moment, running faces and names through his head, and inwardly hoping that no more eggs were broken, and the crew was all still there. They would most likely have to run a complete roll call again, and re-check all the ship's records. Fedorov had made a point of keeping a database running, and reinforced with battery backup power after their last head count. He had thought that the magnetic field surrounding the ship's electronics might have served to exert some kind of stabilizing effect when the ship shifted. Perhaps, he thought, that data will remain unaltered.

"The shift," he said. "Did we have any other problems?"

"It's only four bells, Mister Fedorov, 14:00. Shift change comes at eight bells when the new watch comes on duty, which gives you two hours for rest, and perhaps a little food would do you some good as well."

Now Fedorov remembered how the others on the bridge had forgotten names, forgotten that men had ever served with them. It had taken some time before their memory was jogged loose, and he remembered Admiral Volsky saying something about rattling the Vodka cabinet down here with Doctor Zolkin. Yes, it was about Chief Dobrynin. The Admiral said they used to take a nip or two here with Zolkin.

"Doctor," he said, deciding to see if Zolkin remembered the man. "Was there any problem reported with the reactors?"

"Who knows? At least Dobrynin hasn't been in here complaining. You would have to ask him, Mister Fedorov."

"Dobrynin? Then you remember?" Fedorov struggled to sit up now, watched closely by the doctor.

"Remember what?" Zolkin was giving Fedorov a studied glance, as if he were still assessing his overall condition and state of mind.

"Chief Dobrynin. You remember him from engineering?"

"Of course," said Zolkin. "Who else can keep the ship running, and all while listening to Tchaikovsky."

"That's a relief," said Fedorov, though something in the way the Doctor said that seemed slightly off tune. "You speak of him in the present tense," he said. "I suppose it is still hard… considering what happened to him and the others, particularly Lenkov. I'm not sure which was the crueler fate."

Zolkin cocked his head to one side. "Now you are speaking in riddles, Fedorov. What do you suppose has happened to Dobrynin? I would certainly be one of the first to know if he reported sick, and I haven't seen him this morning."

"Didn't you hear the news about him, and the others... Orlov, Tasarov, Kamenski? Haven't you been briefed yet?"

"Briefed? Nobody bothers with that these days, but believe it or not, I hear far more about what is happening on this ship than you may realize. Every rumor and whisper eventually finds its way here to sick bay, much of it hogwash. But I get a good feel for what is going on in spite of that. Yet concerning Orlov and the others, I've heard nothing unusual. That last fellow you mention does not ring a bell. What was the name?"

"Kamenski," said Fedorov, giving Zolkin the same appraising look that he was getting from the Doctor. "Director Kamenski, our guest up in the spare officer's cabin."

Zolkin merely shrugged. "If he isn't ever sick, I probably don't know the man."

"But you examined him yourself," said Fedorov, "right here when we were discussing the discovery of Karpov in Siberia with the Admiral." He gave Zolkin an expectant look, hoping that would be enough to jog his memory, and fearing that he was also suffering the effects of the shift, forgetting things, faces, men, lives.

"It's enough just to put names to all the faces I see here each day," said Zolkin, "and I know a good many—probably know this crew better than any man on the ship, except the Chief. I do have a better bedside manner than Orlov, or so I've been told."

Fedorov smiled. At least he remembered Orlov. "It was hard to lose him," he said.

"Lose who?" Zolkin folded his arms now.

"Orlov," said Fedorov sullenly. "I've been trying to sort it all through, and I was thinking it may have had something to do with the time he spent with that object he found in Siberia. Dobrynin was with it for some time as well, and I had something strange happen to my hand, though I never came here about it."

"Your hand looks fine to me, Fedorov. But what is this talk about an object from Siberia?"

Fedorov took a deep breath. "I mentioned that the last time I was down here, before the shift. Remember? Well, I suppose there's been too much going on around here, but at least you still recall Dobrynin and Orlov, which is encouraging. Hopefully everyone else made it through safely this time, and we have no more business for you with the engineers. Lenkov was more than enough."

"Lenkov... That's twice you mention him now. Well he hasn't been in either. Last I heard of him he was down in the galley complaining again. That man rattles his pots and pans like a woman. Do you know, the crew tells me he has a little scheme going on down there—something about trading cigarettes for extra portions in the mess hall. I'll have to speak with him. Someone should tell him cigarettes are bad for his health. Then again, some of the men say his soup is bad for your health too, so perhaps he's making an even trade." Zolkin smiled, pleased with his quip, but the look on Fedorov's face now gave him pause.

"Something wrong again, Mister Fedorov? Has the dizziness and nausea returned?"

"No... I'm quite fine, but Doctor... I realize that affair with Lenkov was very difficult, but you and I both know Lenkov isn't smoking cigarettes any longer."

"Oh? Then perhaps he has wised up. Or maybe Orlov knocked some sense into him, which is more than likely."

"Doctor Zolkin..." Fedorov was caught off guard, suddenly thinking Zolkin's memory must have been affected after all.

Now Zolkin's eyes narrowed. "Why do I get the feeling that you are sitting there examining *me*, Mister Fedorov? I'm the Doctor here, and you're starting to sound just a little confused. Are you certain there is no further dizziness?"

Fedorov blinked, a strange unsettling feeling sweeping over him that was not nausea or dizziness. Something was wrong here. He could feel it. Zolkin seems to have forgotten all about Lenkov! I can see how he might wish to get that out of his mind, but still... He clearly remembers Dobrynin and Orlov. And yet... The way he's been speaking of them… It was as if he thought they were still aboard—Lenkov too. Could that be so.?Was it just a phasing issue?

"Lenkov," he said. "Don't you remember him? And Orlov… When was the last time you saw him?"

"He checks in every morning to see the shift assignments are in order, Fedorov. You know the Chief's work as well as I do. His nose is everywhere."

"Are you saying he checked in here this morning?"

"As usual. What of it?"

"Did he say anything? Did he report any odd effects?"

"No, he seemed his old surly self. That man always seems to have a headache that no medicine can cure, and of course he takes it out on everyone else."

So Orlov was here before he went to the bridge. Now Fedorov remembered the compass that Orlov had given him, and he reached into his pocket to find it had finally settled down, its fitful spinning stilled, which gave him heart. The ship may have settled with it, and the crew as well. Perhaps the shift they initiated had helped them to sync properly this time, but where were they now?

Looking at that compass, he realized they should have done something to acknowledge the loss of the man, as they did with Lenkov. Yes, there was no body they could wrap in a flag and commit to the sea, but perhaps a ceremony of some kind would be appropriate.

"We might want to do something for Orlov and Dobrynin," he said glumly. As difficult as Orlov was, he had a great deal to do with the running of this ship. The men may not ever have warmed to him, but they respected him. I think another ceremony might be in order."

"Ceremony? What, Fedorov? Don't tell me it's Orlov's birthday. What are you talking about?"

Fedorov gave the doctor a long look, his hopes sinking for a moment. What was going on here? Zolkin clearly seems to be suffering the memory lapse. He remembers some things, forgets others. My god, he thought. This could be happening all over the ship! It could be affecting every man aboard, myself included. I have no way of really knowing if I've forgotten anyone else. It took Nikolin to help me even remember Tasarov, a man I served with on the bridge every day. So yes, the Doctor would not be immune to any of these effects either. I had better find out if anyone else is suffering memory loss. It could be getting progressively worse. If you can get to someone early on after the shift, and jog their memory, things might be saved. But as time passes, the memories might fade away into that grey fog that was all around us.

The irony of that was not lost on him, and he strained to look out the Doctor's port hole window, wondering what the sea conditions were.

Zolkin sighed. "I can see that you will not sit still, Fedorov. Are you so eager to get back to your post? Look here, settle down now and let that medication kick in. Then you may satisfy yourself and go back to the bridge. But for now, you stay right where you are— Doctor's orders."

Part III

Gladiators

"Anyone can train to be a gladiator. What marks you out is having the mindset of a champion."

— Manu Bennett

Chapter 7

As gladiators went when it came to battle on the sea, HMS *Invincible* was one of the best and most powerful ships in the world. Designed after the First World War, the ship was initially conceived more as an answer to naval building programs in the United States and Japan, than to oppose anything the Germans were doing. At that time, Raeder's Plan Z ships were still dreams on the drafting tables, but *Invincible* would soon take shape and form in hard steel.

At nearly 54,000 long tons displacement, it was Britain's heavyweight, outweighing the *King George V* class by a full 12,000 tons, the weight of another decent sized cruiser. Oddly, the ship was conceived as a battlecruiser, meant to be paired with another metal behemoth, the 18-inch gun N3 battleship that had never seen a keel laid down. As such, her nine 16-inch guns were still bigger than anything in the fleet, save *Rodney* and *Nelson*. In some minds, *Invincible* was an upgrade to the former pride of the fleet, HMS *Hood*, correcting all the deficiencies that had been uncovered in that design. It was fast at 32 knots, up-gunned over *Hood's* eight 15-inchers, and much better armored, a fast battleship in every respect.

Invincible was the seventh ship in the Royal Navy to bear that name, taking it after the earlier battlecruiser that had been built in 1907 and destroyed at Jutland. Now she would face down the Germans again, in the long running naval duel that was collectively the biggest engagement since Admiral Beatty had clashed with the German High Seas Fleet in the last war.

The ship was one of a kind, unmistakable on the sea with her unorthodox silhouette. Two of her three triple-gun turrets were mounted forward of the conning tower, and the third directly behind it, amidships. This meant her engineering sections and twin funnels were pushed aft to the latter third of the ship.

Here I am again, thought Tovey, coming late to the scene, and with old *Rodney* up to her knees in seawater. Better late than never. Blucher did well by Wellington at Waterloo, and now it's my time.

The situation looked grim. *Renown* and *Repulse* had been the first to *Rodney*'s aid, two fast battlecruisers that had engaged and compelled the German fleet to turn in order to bring all their guns to bear in the fight. Fortunately for *Rodney*, that turn had taken the fight west, away from the foundering battleship, and over the horizon. The Germans might have detached one of their ships to put *Rodney* down, thought Tovey, but they wisely stayed together. Now they'll outgun Tennant's battlecruisers 17 to 12, and they have much better armor for that fight.

Yet here I come, running full out, guns ready and right in the thick of things. It looks like Lütjens was just about to pile it on and give Tennant much more than he could handle. Now let's see him take on someone his own size.

"Second ship sighted!" came the call from the mainmast watch.

"That will be *Hindenburg* and *Bismarck*," said Tovey to Captain Bennett.

"Aye sir," said the Captain, "and they'll have us outgunned here as well."

"Then we must see that we open the engagement well," said Tovey. "Cool heads but quick action, gentlemen. Give me ten points to starboard and we can get all three turrets into the action. You may indulge yourself. Target the lead ship."

"Aye sir. Mister Connors!"

The warning bell sounded, and the ship shook with the fires of their opening salvo. Two guns on each of the forward triple gun turrets to test the range. The next salvo would be a three plus two, with the last guns on A and B turret joining with all three guns on X turret behind the conning tower. This unique gun arrangement gave the ship tremendous firepower at angles to either side of the bow, where all nine guns could get into action. By comparison, the twin two-gun turrets on the forward segment of the German battleships saw those ships with their firepower cut in half if they turned to close on the enemy, and Tovey was going to make sure the action started with both sides coming nose to nose, for this very reason.

Tovey knew his ship well, and was maneuvering to use every advantage her unique design could give him. He remembered that very first engagement he fought aboard *King Alfred* in the Pacific. That ship had her two biggest guns in a forward turret, and so he had espoused a quick dash in like this as the preferred approach in battle.

Now that moment when the ship's Captain Baker had come up behind him in the officer's mess aboard the old armored cruiser *King Alfred* was clear in his mind again. A few of the men had been discussing tactics, and the general consensus was that a good broadside at range was the best possible play in a sudden one-on-one engagement. Armored cruisers were often used in scouting roles, and would often find themselves in small groups, or even alone when they might happen on an enemy ship.

"*What? A broadside with six inch guns?*" Tovey put in. "*Well we'd have to be damn close to hit anything,*" he had asserted. "*Those casement guns can theoretically range out over 15,000 yards with a heavy charge, but good luck hitting anything that far out. No gentlemen, I'm an advocate of speed at the outset. I'd show the enemy my bow and put on a full head of steam to squeeze every knot out of those boilers I possibly could. Harass them with all our forward facing guns as we come in, then swing round and give them the old broadside well inside 10,000 yards. 8,000 yards would even be better—ideal I should think.*" It was a strategy he would put to use in the future, though the ranges involved would change as gun size increased. Tovey would one day end up leading more than one good fight at sea.

"*Concentration of firepower is always best, at any range,*" came a voice behind him. Tovey had his arms folded and did not know who made the remark, but he batted it aside with the sharp intelligence he would become known for at sea.

"*At any range? On my watch I would use my cannon at the best range suited to them. If that means a little reliance on speed and armor to achieve a better firing solution, so be it.*" The complete silence after his remark prompted him to turn his head, and there was Captain Baker, lips pursed with disapproval. He had come into the mess hall in the heat of the discussion and threw out the remark to test his young officers.

Later that evening he had summoned Tovey to the bridge and took him aside in the plotting room for a private chat. *"See here, Mister Tovey. Concerning your remarks in the officer's mess this evening... If you chance to contradict another officer ever again, you had bloody well better turn your head first and look the man in the eye so you will know who you're speaking to."*

"Yes sir. Of course, sir. I'm terribly sorry. I meant no offense."

"No offense taken, Tovey. This is simply a matter of decorum."

"Yes sir."

"Very good then. That will be all."

"Sir!" Tovey saluted and went to leave, but the Captain scratched his ear, adding one last word.

"You were correct in one thing," he said quietly.

"Sir?"

"That bit about reliance on speed and armor. I gave it some thought and find it sound advice, depending on the circumstances of course. But just remember that King Alfred is the flagship of this squadron, young man. In that role she will be at the head of her formation and expected to lead the battle line in. So in nine cases out of ten we will not be talking about a single ship broadside, but that of the entire squadron. This is concentration of firepower, Mister Tovey. Don't forget that."

Invincible is the fleet flagship now, thought Tovey, and I should be leading in the full power of the Royal Navy, and using that concentration of firepower. Circumstances simply prevent that at the moment.

In that first wild engagement, Tovey had *Kent, Bedford, Monmouth,* and then the light cruisers *Astraea* and *Flora* with him to form that battle line, a long tail of iron on the sea. Now the Admiral of the Fleet was rushing in alone, but he would stick to the tactics he had so ably argued all those years ago, because his ship had all the power of a broadside no matter which way it was facing. Yes, Captain

Baker was correct. Concentration of firepower is always best, at any range, and *Invincible* can give me that every time we fire.

We'll actually have them nine guns to eight at the outset, he realized. With any luck we can get in our licks before they turn, but no matter what happens, I'm coming at them straight as an arrow. When they do turn their silhouettes will present much bigger targets for Mister Connors.

The ship's second salvo fired, the noise even louder now as the three guns behind the conning tower boomed out their challenge. Listen to them now, Mister Baker, he thought with a smile. But dear god, give us the hits.

The almighty, and perhaps even Captain Baker, were listening, and smiling back at him that day. The forward watch soon shouted out the news.

"Straddle! Range is good."

"Black Five!" said Tovey firmly, ordering a flag sent up that was supposed to act as a signal to other ships in this squadron to fire for effect. The flagman looked at him, as there were no other ships in the squadron, and Captain Bennett gave the man a wink and waved him off, knowing his gunnery officer Connors would know what to do. Soon the ship had all nine guns ready, and Tovey knew what was coming, quietly raising two fingers to his ears. Even through that muffled silence imposed by his fingertips, the roar of nine 16-inch guns came thundering through.

* * *

So now the gloves are coming off at last, thought Lütjens, slowly lowering his field glasses. That was very close. His decks were still awash with sea spray from a row of heavy shells that had raked across his bow. Thankfully, none hit the ship directly, but the rattle of shrapnel clattered on the armor there, and he knew his enemy had found the range.

"Ahead two thirds!" he shouted, and Captain Adler looked at

him, hesitating briefly, but wise enough to first relay the order to the helmsman before he questioned it.

"You're slowing to 20 knots?"

"You saw what just happened, Captain. They'll be trimming a little range off their last sighting, and if we slow the ship down, and turn slightly, their next salvo should be well short. Use your head!"

Adler took the sting, nodding grimly, and quickly ordering the ship to turn ten points. He finally had his battle, but he realized the Admiral had been correct. He had been so set on getting Axel Faust into action on the main gun turrets, that he was forgetting to maneuver the ship properly. He resolved not to disappoint the Admiral again.

"Oberleutnant Eisenberg!" said Adler tersely. "I trust you have a firing solution. Answer that salvo!"

"Aye sir."

It was *Hindenburg's* turn to get her main guns into action, and the insult of those small caliber rounds had finally abated. Now it would be steel on steel, the massive weight and shock of shells weighing over a thousand pounds each, flung into the sky by a massive, controlled explosion, and sent careening over the sea to find a target that was over fifteen miles away. As insane as that seemed, this carefully controlled chaos could be managed so well that the battle was almost certain to see hits obtained on either side. It was nowhere near the precision of the smaller rounds fired by *Argos Fire*, but any hit scored would be much more lethal.

"We must close the range, Adler, and make the best use of our armor. The gunners will do their best work inside 20,000 meters."

The armor scheme on *Hindenburg* had been conceived by designers who assumed the ship would most often fight in the misty cold waters of the North Atlantic, where visibility was low and range for gunnery duels was often very short. As such, the layout and angle of the armor was designed to repel flat trajectory attacks, as opposed to plunging fire attacks that might be delivered from shells fired at a greater range.

"Sir, I recommend that *Bismarck* move off our wake and run on a parallel course to our ship as we close. That way they can get a clear line of fire."

"Good, Adler. Now you are thinking like a fleet commander again. Yes, signal *Bismarck* to take station to port, and fire when clear. But mind your signals flags if we have to maneuver."

Down in Anton turret, Axel Faust was peering through his range finder, the man who had smashed the *Queen Elizabeth* senseless in the Med, with a withering blow forward that broke her jaw. His well muscled arms made him look every bit the heavyweight he seemed, and he was already working up a glistening sweat as they sighted for their second salvo.

"Move smartly, boys," he shouted, urging his men on. "They already sent us to the showers with that first salvo, and we were lucky it wasn't a rain of steel. Let's give them hell!"

The guns were primed and re-elevated, the hum of the hydraulics loud in the confined space. The breach was cleared, lights signaling 'gun ready.' Faust waited on Fuchs in the forward gun director, his eyes lost behind the cups of his own optical sighting. They heard the soaring whoosh and fall of more heavy rounds, and knew the enemy's second salvo was looking for them. Faust could feel the ship's engines rev down as they completed the loading action, and he hoped the brass on the bridge knew what they were doing. He was not disappointed. He could clearly see the rounds falling short by at least 500 meters. The speed change ordered by Lütjens had worked as planned.

But those bastards would have put those rounds much closer if we had kept on at full battle speed. They're damn good, and so we'll have to be better.

Anybody could train for this job, but he was not just anybody. He was Axel Faust, the devil's adjutant, and the best naval gunner in the fleet. Seconds later the order came down to fire, though he was not quite satisfied with the elevation on his guns. He was going to nudge them up another degree, but he heard the booming report of

Bruno turret firing, and knew that Hans Hartmann had beaten them to the punch.

No matter, he thought. "Up elevation! One degree. Quickly! Now Fire!" Anton threw the right cross over Hartmann's left hook, and they waited eagerly to spot the fall of their shot. Thirty seconds later he saw the target erupt with fire, but he knew it was too soon to be a hit from their own shells. The British had just given them a full salvo, something rarely done, as the big ships were more prone to fire half salvos given the jarring concussion of the massive guns.

Squinting through his optics, he soon saw two clear shellfalls short of the target, and slightly wide. Hartmann's hook had found nothing but seawater, and a few seconds later his own rounds fell slightly long, but one was very close. He saw the tall plume of water just off the starboard side of the enemy ship, and then noted how they responded by making a slight turn away from the round. He's jogging left, and then right again—a zig-zag approach. And yet he can still fire all three turrets as he comes. Each time he turns he opens the fire arc of that third turret behind the conning tower. This one knows how to fight his ship. In the meantime, none of our rear turrets can get into action, but that will change soon, if we can close the range without serious damage.

The seconds ticked off, agonizingly slow, and the men rushed through their loading evolutions. Then he saw them, evil white geysers dolloping up from the sea, and walking slowly towards the ship. And they were going to be very close...

Chapter 8

Down from the heavens came the demons set loose by the work of Elswick, Vickers, Beardmore and the Royal Gun Factory. They had been blasted into the sky by a 108 ton gun that was over 60 feet long, using 50 pounds of TNT and another propellant charge of 495 pounds. These exploded inside it to create a working pressure of over 21 tons per square inch, and fire a shell weighing 929kg, or 2,048 pounds. It would blast out of the muzzle at a speed of roughly 2600 feet per second, taking all of 40 seconds before it surged down at the targets, which were some 25,000 yards distant.

The rounds of A-turret, or 'Old Elswick' on the *Invincible* would fall in a line off the starboard side of *Hindenburg*, but those of B-turret would be much closer, with the center gun, sometimes called Vickers Delight by the crew, scoring the first hit of the engagement. At that range, the massive shell might have penetrated 10.3 inches of side armor, not enough to defeat the 14 inches protecting *Hindenburg*. Yet that was academic, because the shell was going to strike the forward deck, right beneath the elevated gun of Anton turret. It was coming in at an angle of 24.6 degrees, and could penetrate 3.9 inches of deck armor at that range, and if it blasted through, the magazines that fed the ardor of Axel Faust and his crew were right beneath.

But *Hindenburg* had a very tough shell. The upper deck on the ship was 3.1 inches of Wotan Hart steel, and this was penetrated, decapping the shell, only to find the main armored decks waiting beneath, with another 4.7 inches of steel. The bow of the ship was very strong, based on German experience at Jutland when the *Lutzow* went down when her bow was riddled with hits. It was ironic that *Lutzow* had engaged and sunk the older British battlecruiser *Invincible*, forerunner of the ship now dueling with *Hindenburg*, and her subsequent demise would lead German designers to give the ship the strong chin it now had. So a kind of rematch was now underway as both navies upgraded their ships to the heavyweight division.

Vicker's Delight would not get through this time, which was why the Germans were closing to this range. If this same gun had achieved a hit at a much longer range, the steepness of its angle of fall and kinetic shock would have been much greater. At 30,000 yards it might have penetrated 5.1 inches of deck armor, and 6.5 inches at 35,000 yards. Yet those were ranges that almost never saw the guns accurate enough to score hits, so for all intents and purposes, *Hindenburg's* deck armor was going to shrug off most everything it received inside 25,000 yards in well protected areas over magazines and machinery. In places the decks were even more heavily reinforced by the special new two inch armor plating on hydraulics that Chief Engineer Koenig had rigged, which were now still laying flat, not deployed in their intended position to try and thwart missile attacks. That did not mean the ship could not be harmed, as Axel Faust was soon to learn.

Faust was lucky that hit could not get through to the magazine, but the explosion it caused on the forward deck was so violent that he and his crew were badly shaken up, and the right barrel on Anton Turret was jarred upward so severely, that its training and elevation mechanism gears were badly damaged. Shrapnel flayed the heavy gun turret, but mostly struck the face, which was 15.2 inches thick, and completely impenetrable to anything but a shell fired at near point blank range inside 12,000 yards.

Faust had managed to stay on his feet, but his ears were ringing from the concussion, and several men were down. He took one look at his number two gun and knew it would not fire again in this engagement, but he still had number one, and enough able bodied men to keep it firing. Yet nothing was coming down from the rangefinder's station, and Fuchs was silent.

He gritted his teeth, and was at his optics making his own calculations while the crew staggered back to life, driven on by his deep voice. "Come on! Get up and get your back into it. We still have the number one gun. Let's move!"

He waited, yet no data came from the gun director, and now he was going to have to call the shot himself. They were now inside

22,000 meters by his best judgment, with the range falling closer to 18,000. He knew the Captain would make a turn any minute to get those rear turrets into action, so he wanted to fire before he had to also re-train the gun after that turn. His crew did not disappoint, and they had a ready light in just under 50 seconds. Faust waited, squinting at his enemy through his rangefinder, and then decided.

"Make elevation thirteen degrees! Ready… Fire!"

The boom of the German 16-inch gun shook the turret again, and his vengeance was on its way, guided by the devil's adjutant himself, and followed soon after by another two round salvo from Hartmann in Bruno. Then, just as he expected, he began to feel the *Hindenburg* turn, and he shouted out the new tracking orders.

"Right ten degrees at the double quick. Move!"

* * *

HMS *Invincible* was coming on, and right into the thick of that last German salvo. Axel Faust beamed when he saw a single round strike the ship, and he knew it must be his.

"Got the bastard!" he beamed. "We're counterpunching off the ropes! Let's give them another."

His own 16-inch shell was the biggest on any ship in the German Navy, from the 40.6cm SK C/34 gun, screaming out of Axel's turret at over 2600 feet per second. The shell was heavier than the British round, at 1,030 kg. If the turret had not found its way to the *Hindenburg*, it would have ended up as "Battery Lindemann" on the French coast, in honor of the Captain of the *Bismarck* who was supposed to lose his life this month. Yet that history was now on the scales of time and fate, and Lindemann was still very much alive, and more than happy to cede the turret to Axel Faust.

Invincible was equally well armored, with all of 8 inches on key deck areas, 14 inches at the belt, and 17.5 inches shielding her massive turrets. But Faust was going to hit the much smaller 4.7 inch AA gun mounted right to the starboard side of the conning tower, and it would be completely demolished, and all its ready ammo also fed the explosion, sending off a series of jolting reports, like fitful firecrackers. The shrapnel took a heavy toll on the deck crews near the second 4.7 inch twin gun mount, but when the smoke of the initial blast cleared, the fire there was not serious.

So right at the outset, both sides had landed good punches, and now Tovey saw the German ships begin to angle into a turn. He might have one, or possibly two more salvos where he actually outgunned both enemy ships combined, but they would soon double their firepower.

"Now or never, Mister Connors," he said, and the boom of the guns answered with the ship's fourth salvo, this time four barrels, quickly followed by the remaining five. Of those nine shells, Connors' luck would hold long enough to see one of them strike the *Hindenburg*, and it would be a very telling blow.

Yet even while those shells were in flight, *Bismarck* had put in a good shot with its third salvo, and Tovey felt the hard thunk and explosion of a side armor hit.

"No worry there, gentlemen," he said calmly. "That was on the main belt, and our hide is as thick as they come." The *King George V* class actually had slightly heavier belt armor, but what it added there in protection, it had lost in much needed speed.

"Range?" asked Tovey.

"I make it a tad under 22,000 yards sir," said Connors.

"Let's make good use of it," the Admiral replied. "We'll be inside 20,000 in little time ."

* * *

Lütjens had seen the hit on *Invincible*, and wanted a better look. He was outside on the weather deck off the Admiral's bridge when it happened, the luck of Mister Connors, and the single shell of the nine he had fired that struck a fatal blow—not for the ship, but for the man standing on that weather bridge, the Admiral himself. Lütjens had just raised his field glasses to have his curiosity satisfied.

Let's see what we've done here, he thought, and that was the last thing to run through his mind before the shrapnel came. When Connors' round struck the heavily armored conning tower, protected by 14 inches of Krup Cemented Steel, and with a roof nearly 8 inches thick, the cruel metal splinters suddenly swept the field glasses from the Admiral's hand, and smashed into his right temple, killing him instantly.

For a brief moment, the Admiral's legs still held strength, then his body slumped to the deck, his life's blood bleeding from a catastrophic head wound. In those dark, dangerous seconds, Johann Gunther Lütjens stopped being something the universe was doing, and the process that had begun on the 25th of May, 1889, now ceased, just a few weeks shy of his 52nd birthday. Every experience of his life, and memories recorded in his long distinguished naval career, came to a sudden and absolute end. He would never know what happened to him, how he would die, or have even a single moment to contemplate his fate. One moment he was there, in the fullness of his prime, calmly assessing the damage his guns might have inflicted on the distant enemy. The next moment he was simply gone, the flame of his consciousness blown out, and never to shine again.

At that instant, the overall command of the battle had quickly passed from the calm and calculating mind of Lütjens, to that of his eager, yet less experienced Kapitan Adler. Fate had tapped the shoulder of one key player that had been slated to go into the void of death that very month, though there was an entire ship's crew aboard *Bismarck* that was once destined to die as well. Whether that would happen this day remained to be decided by this terrible contest of guns versus armor.

The blast and shock of the hit shattered glass in the wind screen of the conning tower, ripped away shutters on a nearby signals platform, and shook loose a voice tube on the bridge, sending it gyrating back and forth in a noisome clatter against a nearby bulkhead. Three men were also shaken off their feet, and Adler took a white knuckled grip on the binnacle.

By the time he realized what had happened, and the bridge crew got sorted out, he had allowed the range to continue to close until it was now inside 18,000 meters. The turn he had made was aimed at exposing the rear firing arcs of his ships to bring another eight guns into the deadly calculus of this battle. Yet in the heat of the action he had foolishly forgotten Lütjens last remonstration. *Bismarck* still ran on a fast parallel course, and was now interposed between the *Hindenburg* and the oncoming British ship, still charging boldly into the fray, all guns firing.

The sudden news in the discovery of Lütjens death had also served as a distraction, and no flag signals had been sent to order *Bismarck* to take station behind. Fortunately, Kapitan Lindemann saw what was happening and cut speed to fall off on *Hindenburg's* wake, but not before *Invincible* was able to put another full 9-round salvo right into the formation. This time it was *Bismarck* suffering the hit, and at this range the 16-inch shells striking the belt could penetrate just over 13 inches of armor, which was just enough to do the job. The penetration was not serious, but jets of fiery steel shot through the minor breach to lacerate the inner hull.

"Range at 17,300 meters," shouted Eisenberg. "We'll do better at 20,000, Kapitan."

Adler folded his arms, almost protectively, and still somewhat shocked by the suddenness of the Admiral's demise. His ship had already been riddled by at least fifteen smaller caliber rounds from the harassing attack put in by *Argos Fire*. Now he could finally see his enemy, still bemused to think this ship could have put those lighter hits on them while still over the horizon. Yet *Hindenburg* had also received two hits from heavy guns off the *Invincible*, and Lütjens was dead.

What was Eisenberg trying to tell him? *Open the range!* They were letting the British run in too close. Inside 15,000 meters these monstrous guns could blast right through his belt armor, penetrating 14.4 inches of steel. Both ships had nearly that, and yet both would now be vulnerable. He did not know that to a certainty, not with the cold measurements of a ruler, but he could sense the rising danger as the enemy ship loomed ever larger, and the warning was evident in Eisenberg's statement.

"Helm! Come left fifteen and ahead full battle speed! Signal *Bismarck* to follow." This time he remembered his signals flags, though he knew that if the British ship persisted in its daring approach, it would now be very difficult to really open the range. He finally had his battle, yet the smell of blood was on the wind, tainting the dark rolling soot and smoke with a tinge of added danger.

* * *

"A hit sir!" Connors exclaimed. "Well up on the conning tower. That had to shake them up."

"Nothing like putting one right on the noggin," said Tovey. "Good show, Mister Connors. Look, they're all in a jumble with that turn. And that lead ship has a broken finger. Give them all nine guns!"

Connors was only too happy to comply, as he could now see the aft segments of both ships light up with gunfire, and knew *Invincible* was going to be outgunned fifteen to nine. That was a considerable margin, and if they had to turn and attempt to break away, the very same gun configuration that made *Invincible* so deadly as it charged, would now work against them. There were eight 6-inch guns, all mounted aft behind the funnels, but it would be much more difficult to open up firing arcs for the bigger turrets. X-turret would be completely blind dead aft, unlike a similar rear mounted turret in a more classically configured ship design. To get it into action, the ship would again have to withdraw in a zig-zag, allowing the X-turret to fire at an angle of at least 15 degrees. The two forward turrets would need at least twice that to look over their shoulder and stay engaged. The ship was never meant to run from a fight.

These were all things running through Tovey's mind as

Invincible kept on with its charge. If I turn, he thought, they'll have all their guns available to sight on our full silhouette. For those minutes, the ship will be much more vulnerable, and when we run we can't hit them as hard on those rear firing arcs. What I miss now is a good pack of hunting dogs! Fighting here without a destroyer escort was a clear liability, but there was no way they could trail along through the Med. I counted heavily on the Russian ship standing with me, and now our entire battle squadron has been scattered.

If I turn here, what will Lütjens do? Will he follow and give chase, or merely take his shots and come round to finish *Rodney?* Why should I give him any choice at all? No. All our teeth are right up front, and thinking of the destroyers, I've another little surprise, a legacy of the era that saw this ship built, so let it roll.

"Mister Bennett," he said to the Captain. "Steady on, and make ready on all torpedo tubes."

The Captain raised an eyebrow, yet he knew what Tovey intended now. They were going in, hell bent, and the Admiral aimed to make this a fight to the death. The *Invincible* had a pair of submerged torpedo tubes forward of the A-turret, and carried eight massive 24-inch lances that were driven by oxygen enriched air. They had two speed settings and were already in range of the enemy ships. At 35 knots they could run out 15,000 yards, and at 30 knots that extended to 20,000 yards, the interval that now separated the two sides.

Other ships had them from that era, including *Rodney,* which saw them become the liability that rent her hull open when the *Tirpitz* struck the torpedo magazine. Other ships would normally fire from the broadside, but *Invincible* had a rotating torpedo mount below decks, and could alter the angle of the tubes by up to 15 degrees. This gave him a little flexibility, and the innovation would allow him to fire as he continued to close the range, which was exactly what he intended to do.

Tovey had no intention of turning full broadside. He was running all out, his forward silhouette still presenting a much more difficult target for the enemy as his bow was aimed right at them. All he had to do was make five or ten point zigzags to allow X-turret to fire, and with his slight speed advantage he was inexorably closing on his enemy. He was making a battleship sized torpedo run, as any destroyer might, only he had nine 16-inch guns to use on the way in.

"Set torpedoes to mode one. Speed 35."

That was an obvious choice, as *Invincible* would literally outrun her own torpedoes at the longer range setting. Yet to use mode one, Tovey knew he needed to get well inside that 15,000 yard range marker to give the torpedoes any chance. So it was all or nothing now, and the Admiral was pushing all his chips out onto the table.

The Germans were trying to cross his T, but at the last minute, he would swing hard to starboard to aim his nose at a point well ahead of the enemy formation, and then send four lances out at 35 knots, each one tipped with nearly 750 pounds of TNT. Then he would come hard to port and add four more torpedoes to widen his spread. Unless the German formation turned radically off their present heading, he knew they would face the prospect of taking a deadly hit. Captain Adler had insisted on coming to the ball, and soon, in that wild minute when the watchmen shouted out the torpedo warning, he and his ship would have to learn to dance.

Chapter 9

On came Tovey, standing like a carved statue on the Admiral's bridge of *Invincible,* his face and eyes set. The long bow of the ship was carving through the sea, the wash of grey-green water high over the wet iron anchor chains stretched along the deck. Behind them the massive steel fingers of the guns reached for the enemy as the ship roared out its anger. Connors had shifted to a 6-3 pattern on his salvos, with both forward turrets firing together, while the X turret waited for the ship to turn and open its forward angle as *Invincible* jogged left and right.

The battlecruiser remained a difficult target, even as the range closed inside 15,000 meters, about nine miles from the German formation. The death of Lütjens, and the damage slowly accumulating on the *Hindenburg,* had dampened Adler's ardor for battle somewhat, yet he still believed the day must surely be his. When he saw *Bismarck* score a hit amidships forward of the twin funnels on *Invincible,* he took heart. Yet the damage was not as severe as it might have been on a ship with a more conventional design. The entire area was swept clean to give X-turret clear angles of fire. There was no superstructure built there, and so the 15-inch shell found only the hard steel of the 8-inch deck, and its shallow angle could not penetrate. Shrapnel flailed the turret, causing no harm, and scored the forward funnel, causing it to stream smoke in odd places, but otherwise the ship was not hurt.

Hindenburg also scored a second hit, this time on the belt of the ship. While the flatter trajectory of the shell gave it much more penetrating power in a side armor hit, the angle of the blow was very small given the fact that the target's bow was very nearly pointed directly into the line of fire. This caused a glancing blow instead of a more damaging direct hit had the round come in perpendicular. Again, it was the unorthodox design of the ship, and the way Tovey had boldly chosen to fight with it, that made these hits far less serious than they might have been.

The British gunners had also put additional damage on both German ships. The two forward turrets in Connors' 6-3 salvos had concentrated on *Hindenburg*, and scored yet another hit amidships that smashed a secondary battery and started a bad fire. X-turret also managed to strike *Bismarck* forward on her bow, and very low, with the shell penetrating near the water line in that less protected area, and causing flooding from the wash of the forward bow. A second shell plunged into the water very near this point, struck the ship, but did not detonate, a bit of luck that saved *Bismarck* from serious harm.

The running battle had seen his formation steaming almost due east at about 90 degrees, with *Invincible* coming up from the southwest, steering a jogging course that varied from 30 to 50 degrees. At times the Germans were at 28 knots, and sometimes surged at their top speed of 30 knots, and the angle of convergence was gobbling up the range quickly. Tovey was inside the 12,000 meter range mark in minutes, dangerously close, and he could see the Germans were about to turn to cross his T, which is just what he expected. Now he began to maneuver the ship to prepare for his torpedo launch.

He made his sharp turn to starboard, with the intention of coming quickly around to expose the port side torpedo tubes and fire a spread of four lances at a point well out in front of the enemy ships. It was then that Adler made his first real mistake. He saw the sudden turn, just after that inconsequential hit amidships, but his mind saw much more in the maneuver than Tovey intended.

"Got him amidships!" he shouted. "Good shooting Eisenberg! Look now, he's coming around in a hard turn. He's thinking twice about trying to get any closer. We've crossed his T and he's trying to come around and run with us at the broadside. He's making a bad mistake!"

Eisenberg beamed down from his perch above with the main gun director, and the next three seconds would decide the battle. Adler snapped out an order, thinking he would easily frustrate the British maneuver by turning to starboard himself, using the slight lead he still maintained, and persisting in crossing the enemy's T. It had never occurred to him that *Invincible* was about to fire torpedoes, and if he knew this was happening, he should have turned hard to port instead of starboard, for now he was maneuvering right into the path of the torpedo spread, and actually closing the range even more.

Adler's eyes were lost behind his field glasses, intently watching the other ship and seeing his own shellfall straddle the British behemoth yet again. The torpedoes streaked from beneath the waterline on *Invincible*, and then, to Adler's surprise, he saw the British ship execute yet another sharp turn, this time hard to port.

"What is that fool doing?" he said aloud, looking over his shoulder and pointing. Then he answered his own question. "Ah, he does not want to come to starboard after seeing us turn, because if he comes all the way around he will have to turn his back side to us and all his guns are forward." In his mind the British now looked like they wanted to steer due north as his own formation came round to the south, so the two sides could run parallel to one another in opposite directions instead of running together. He knows he can run with us and exchange broadsides, thought Adler. It never occurred to him that the enemy ship had turned only to present its starboard side and fire yet another spread of deadly 24-inch torpedoes.

If Lütjens had been alive, he might have seen what the British were really doing. His first command had been aboard torpedo boat T-68 in the 6th Torpedo Boat Demi-Flotilla. He served in these squadrons throughout the First War, and dueled with other British torpedo boats off Dunkirk, as well as French destroyers in his first combat actions at sea. Between the wars he had trained on the pre-dreadnought battleship *Schlesien,* again for torpedo firing exercises. In 1936, Lütjens had been appointed *Führer der Torpedoboote* (Chief of Torpedo Boats), planting his flag aboard the German Destroyer Z1, *Leberecht Maass.* It wasn't until the outbreak of the war that he eventually transferred to the bigger ships, commanding the covering force for the Norwegian campaign with *Scharnhorst* and *Gneisenau.*

So the old torpedo man at heart might have seen much more in

Tovey's unorthodox maneuvers than Adler, and in that critical moment, he may have certainly turned to port instead of starboard. But Lütjens was dead, and all of that seasoned experience was gone with him.

"Now we will have him badly outgunned," said Adler, a jubilant edge to his voice. "He cannot trade broadsides with us and hope to survive. Get him, Eisenberg!"

Tovey knew the Germans were not going to be able to come round on 180 for very long. It was only a matter of a few minutes before they would discover their peril, and soon the high mainmast watch on *Hindenburg* shouted out the warning.

"Torpedoes!"

The word shocked Adler, for it was the last thing he expected. In fact, he had no idea that the British ship even carried such weapons, and there had not been a single instance of a battleship using torpedoes since the first world war. The *Hindenburg* had initially included six similar submerged torpedo tubes in her design, but they had been removed in the final construction, thought to be an anachronism. That torpedoes would be used here, in the heat of this intense gun duel, never entered his mind.

Yet now he had to quickly find the danger and maneuver the ship. To do so he rushed outside to the weather deck, where Lütjens body still lay in his unceremonious death, crews only just arriving with a stretcher. Adler had heard the Admiral had fallen, but it was only now that he would see him in his death pose, one arm plaintively extended on the cold metal deck, as if he were desperately trying to point out the impending danger in those oncoming torpedoes.

It was a grizzly sight that shook the Kapitan in spite of the urgency of this moment, for he had to stand on the deck still wet with the Admiral's blood. He looked frantically to the sea, trying to find the wakes of the enemy torpedoes and finally saw that he had steered directly into their approach. Apparently Lindemann on the *Bismarck* had already seen them, and he took it upon himself to turn hard to port. Adler tried to do the same, shouting the orders at the top of his voice, and watching the heavy bow of the *Hindenburg* cutting the sea with the sudden turn.

It would not be enough. The two salvos off *Invincible* had set loose a spread of eight torpedoes, and two were going to strike *Hindenburg* amidships, a third passing behind the ship and narrowly missing *Bismarck*. The combined weight of the blows sent 1500 pounds of TNT against the underwater bulkhead, which was a tremendous shock.

German ships were sturdy vessels, and they had been built with ingenious armor schemes with one single minded aim—survivability at sea. "Steadfastness" was the primary aim of German ship designers, a combination of strength, durability and survivability. To achieve this they combined an excellent system of armor, both above and below the water line, clever watertight subdivisions all along the hull, and the best trained damage control teams at sea. *Hindenburg* had been struck a hard blow, but it would not be fatal to the ship.

The interval between the outer skin of the ship's hull and the main torpedo bulkhead was over 5 meters, a design feature that aimed to absorb the explosive shock of the torpedo. The Germans had tested out their design theory by using the old battleships *Kaiser Wilhelm II* and *Hannover* as torpedo targets. Their work would be so skilled that, in another telling of these events, *Scharnhorst* and *Gneisenau* would easily shrug off numerous hits by 500 pound bombs, and the *Bismarck* would still be floating after being pummeled for hours by heavy guns of British battleships, and struck by no less than nine torpedoes. It would take a bomb weighing over 12,000 pounds, and two of them, to finally sink the *Tirpitz*.

So the mighty *Hindenburg* was not fatally damaged, but the dint to Adler's psyche was more pronounced. He now found his ship had sustained three 16-inch shell hits, fifteen hits from 6-inch guns and now these two torpedoes. The crews were rushing to contain the flooding, and he did not yet know that the damage would be controllable. The battle he had so ardently sought had not turned out to his liking, and now his thoughts soured.

The desperate turn made by the German ships to port now sent them both off on a heading of about 80 degrees east. Meanwhile, Tovey's last turn to fire his starboard side torpedoes had taken him around to 270 degrees west. The two sides were now running away from one another at a combined speed of over 60 knots, which increased the range by 1850 meters per minute, taking the interval from about 12,000 meters to just over 17,000 meters in three minutes.

Invincible then turned hard to starboard again, as Tovey needed to get his main guns into action. The ship swung around in a wide turn until he was heading nearly due north, but the *Hindenburg* ran on to the east still opening the range.

This entire action was still well to the southwest of the position where *Rodney* was foundering, and slowly capsizing into the sea. For another ten minutes, the two sides exchanged fire, with no further hits being scored. During that interval, the range opened another 8600 meters, before the thick smoke of the long running gun duel shrouded the entire scene with heavy haze. The gun directors and spotters could no longer get an accurate sighting, and the last salvo fired by *Invincible*, her 48th, ended the action.

Aboard that ship, a runner came with messages from Captain Patterson. Flag Lieutenant Villers took it and went to Tovey, his expression hopeful. "*King George V* and *Prince of Wales* report they are now thirty miles to our northwest. And better yet, sir, they say they were just overflown by planes off our carriers. Apparently Powers and Tuck are getting close enough to matter."

He was referring to Captain Gerald Tuck on *Illustrious* and Captain Arthur John Powers on *Ark Royal*. Both these carriers had been following in the wake of the oncoming battleships, and were only now coming in range to get their planes off.

"It's starting to feel like I'm actually commanding a fleet again," said Tovey, inwardly relieved that he had come through the mad rush and fire of the battle with relatively little damage. He had been outgunned, yet he fought his ship to take advantage of every innovation in her design, and battled two strong German ships to what must now be considered a draw here. But what to do?

"Radar has the Germans coming around towards 180 sir," said Villers.

"South?" Tovey seemed surprised. Either the Germans were unaware of what was happening further east with *Rodney*, or Lütjens had some other reason for making this turn. He did not know that Lütjens had nothing to do with the decision, and that Adler had decided to look for the *Tirpitz*.

That ship, along with *Scharnhorst*, had fought another inconclusive running duel with the two British battlecruisers that took them well away from *Hindenburg's* action, eventually forcing them to break off. Topp had then turned, thinking he might again eventually find the *Rodney*, but soon seeing that his squadron was now well south of her last reported position. He sent a message to the *Hindenburg* advising him of his status, and Adler had a good long while to think things over. He decided to rendezvous with Topp, call in *Prinz Eugen* and the destroyer *Thor* from their rescue mission near the sinking *Graff Zeppelin*, and then proceed to the Bay of Biscay. The loss of most of his air cover, and the report that British planes had been spotted by the few fighters he had aloft from the *Goeben*, both weighed heavily in his decision.

Adler was now looking to get closer to land based air power, and the safety of ports on the French coast. In doing so, he would also be keeping well east of the remaining British battleships, for after his engagement, he did not now relish the thought of four more British heavyweights coming on the scene if he lingered here.

Tovey waited, thinking to shadow his enemy now until the remaining battleships under Patterson and Holland could join him. He soon received a message from the *Argos Fire* that gave him the exact positions of all the German ships, and he was able to quickly see what they were now doing.

"By Jove, I think we've beaten them, Villers," he said with a smile as he leaned over the plotting table. "From the look of these course tracks, I would say they are running for France now."

"Apparently so sir," said Villers. "Will we give chase?"

Tovey thought for a minute. The gladiators had met, and fought the good fight in the center of the ring. Both would survive to fight another day, though both had wounds to heal.

"Patterson and Holland have been at sea a good long while." He said. "A pity those ships don't have longer legs. They'll be needing fuel soon, and chasing the Germans into the Bay of Biscay would also neutralize our current advantage with air cover. No. I think if we can get in a few licks with the carriers, all the better, but otherwise the fleet will be needing fuel to continue operations. We'd do better to consolidate and head for our base in the Azores. Then we stand our watch again, and see if Lütjens wants any further argument with the Royal Navy.

"Oh… There's one more thing sir," said Villers. "That cruiser we detached reports *Rodney* is sinking. A good number of the crew will be rescued, as *Britannic* is standing by."

"Any word on the Russians?"

"Nothing sir. It's as if they just vanished."

"They may have done exactly that," said Tovey, though he did not elaborate. "Very well. We'll maneuver north to cover *Britannic* now. *Renown* took a couple hard knocks in that fight and will have to be sent home, but *Repulse* is still fit for escort duty."

"That will leave the Germans a clean route to France down here sir," said Villers.

"It can't be helped," said Tovey. "We held our own here, but we can't take on the entire German battlegroup alone. Even with the two battlecruisers we would be outgunned 33 to 21, and we both know they haven't the armor to stand with the German battleships. Any report from *Argos Fire*?"

"They're standing with *Rodney*," said Villers.

"Good enough. My regards to Mister Connors and the lads at the guns. Well fought. I'm off to the radio room."

Part IV

Interlopers

"The soul is no traveler; the wise man stays at home, and when his necessities, his duties, on any occasion call him from his house, or into foreign lands... he visits men like a sovereign and not like an interloper or a valet."

— Ralph Waldo Emerson

Chapter 10

Invincible turned north, and an hour later they came on the scene of the first engagement of that fateful day. *Rodney* was down deeply at the bow, ready to go under any moment. *Britannic* was standing by, watched closely by the *Argos Fire*, and the sea all around them was littered with small boats, and anything else that would float to provide the crew of *Rodney* a momentary safe haven. Around it all, the faithful destroyers that had been escorting *Britannic* circled like fitful hounds, their sonars active for some time until Captain MacRae radioed the squadron commander and asked him to cease their active search, telling them his own sonar was more than capable of providing any warning of an imminent threat from U-Boats.

Thankfully, nothing was found. U-556 had been harassed by the destroyers, who failed to locate the boat, and Wohlfarth had slinked away, already on his way back to the safety of a French harbor. He was looking forward to collecting his laurels, the man who put his torpedo into *Rodney,* and one who could rightfully claim he had sealed the fate of that ship in doing so. It was not the last time a German U-boat Kapitan would skew the lines of history. Between himself, Werner Czygan and Rosenbaum, the three men, and their torpedoes and mines, had had a profound effect on the course of events.

As to the Russian submarine *Kazan,* and the strange appearance of the *Astute* Class submarine it had reported, nothing more was seen or heard. Neither boat could be raised on radio, and it seemed that they had also sailed into the same grey ether that had enveloped the Russian battlecruiser. They were gone.

Aboard *Argos Fire,* Captain MacRae was still somewhat edgy. Radar clearly marked the positions of the German squadrons, and he could see that they had effected a rendezvous some 50 miles west of their position, and were now steaming south, away from the scene.

"I reckon we put enough hurt on them to dissuade them from any further action here," he said to Mack Morgan as they conferred with Miss Fairchild in her stateroom. "That 6-inch we have up front must have been damn annoying. We probably didn't hurt them all that badly, but a good stiff jab is a handy thing in a fist fight."

"We've picked up their signals traffic," said Morgan. "They're breaking off, and heading for France. How long before the other British battleships get here?"

"Three hours," said MacRae. "Their carriers have planes up harassing the Germans, but they still appear to be making a good 24 knots. Predictive plot shows that unless their speed can be cut to 15 knots or less, the British capital ships won't catch up, and even if they did, it would be too close to German land based air power out of France."

"Then this is over," said Elena.

"At least the fighting is over for now," said MacRae, "until the Germans decide to get up a good head of steam and look for convoy traffic again. Will that be our watch?"

Fairchild shook her head. "I don't know what to think now. This whole affair went haywire the minute we dispersed our formation. If we had all stayed together…"

"No use chewing on that bone," said MacRae.

"Well we've failed our mission," said Elena, clearly troubled. "I had come to think that whole run out to Delphi was for me to get here and find this other key, and now it's sitting out there, about to roll into the sea and be lost forever. The Russians have vanished into thin air, and the man who conceived this whole mission, Admiral Tovey, swears he knows nothing whatsoever about it. It's madness."

"No argument there," said MacRae. "I don't see what more we can do about it. In fact, I never quite understood this whole business with the keys in the first place. Very well, I gather they all open a door somewhere, and possibly to places like we found back in Delphi, but what is your charge in all of this, Elena? You've never really come clean with that."

"Sorry, Gordon, but I've told you all I know. We were told the keys were important. I got these orders through the red phone, and that means they came from the Watch, the group Tovey founded, at least in the history we know. Yes, the keys open doors, we've seen that much, and they lead to some rather alarming places. As Watchstander G1, I assumed I was being ordered to secure this key the minute I realized just where and when it first went missing. As for what we might do with it—where it may lead—your guess will be as good as mine."

"Well," said Morgan. "Someone else seems a bit nosy about all this. They fished an American out of the drink. He's been asking to see the Captain."

"Whatever for?" asked Elena, still bothered.

"Something about the cargo being stored aboard *Rodney*, which did give me a bit of a tickle when I heard about it. He's down on B deck if you'd care to have a listen. The chap seemed very insistent—kept looking at his watch like he was about to miss his plane, and insisting he see either MacRae or the British Admiral at once."

"Typical," said Elena. "Cheeky lot, these Americans. They're not even in this war yet and still think they're running the show. Well, see what he has to say, Mack. I've no time to sort his business out."

There came a hard knock, enough to turn heads and raise eyebrows, and the sound of loud voices outside the stateroom. Elena nodded at Mack and he went to the door, one hand drifting slowly to the sidearm he always wore when he heard the shouting. Some kind of ruckus was underway and he was suddenly curious, opening the door cautiously, yet ready for anything.

"Stand where you are I say, or I'll shoot!" Morgan recognized the voice of one of the Argonauts, a Sergeant from the security detail, and he could hear heavy footfalls. There, standing in the corridor, his hands in the air, stood a bedraggled man in a dress white naval blazer and trousers.

"Easy does it," Morgan raised an arm at the three Argonauts now coming rapidly up the corridor.

"I need to see the Captain at once," said the man. "It's an emergency! There's very little time left now!"

"Sorry sir," said the Sergeant. "He slipped off B deck and was half way here before anyone took notice. I'll see to this." The Sergeant reached for the man, but Morgan waved him off.

"Hold on, hold on," he said, stepping up to the man and folding his arms. "Now what's this all about?"

"As I've said. I have urgent information for the Captain, and he must hear it at once. There's no time for delay now."

"Urgent business is it? Well who in bloody hell are you?"

"Wellings—Lieutenant Commander, United States Navy. I was aboard *Rodney* with Captain Hamilton."

"That much I gather, but what's your business here?"

"It concerns the cargo she was carrying—the *Rodney*—the Elgin Marbles. They have to be saved!"

"Too late for that," said Morgan. "But what's your business with any of this?"

"The marbles—"

"Mack," came Elena's voice. "Show the Lieutenant Commander in please."

Morgan pursed his lips, not liking the idea of this character getting right past three of the Argonauts and into the executive suite like this. He stepped up to the American, frisked him quickly and then led him in, casting a disapproving glance over his shoulder at the Sergeant that spoke volumes.

"We'll see to this now, Sergeant. But do keep a handle on anyone else down below. Understood?"

"Sir!" the man saluted stiffly.

"Dismissed."

Back inside the stateroom, Morgan secured the door, keeping a wary eye on the interloper, and noting that MacRae had also interposed himself between the man and Elena.

"Just what is this all about, Mister Wellings?" said Elena, stepping around the Captain.

The man's reply riveted her attention at once, three words. "The Selene Horse," said Wellings.

She stood in silence for a moment, then the questions came. "What about it?" she probed.

"It has to be saved."

"That isn't bloody likely," said Mack again from behind the man.

"I tried to get to it," said Wellings. "That was the only reason I came aboard, but the whole compartment was flooded. Look—you have divers, perhaps a submersible. Yes?"

"Aye," said MacRae, "but nothing that could dive deep enough to fetch that cargo when *Rodney* goes down, and that appears imminent."

"Well, if we can get something into the water at once, perhaps there might be a way—"

"Look here, Mister Wellings," said Elena sharply. "Suppose you tell me just why you have an interest in any of this. I hardly think you're an art collector."

"No," said Wellings. "As terrible a loss as this may end up being, it may be far more significant than the loss of the marbles, or even the gold bullion. That's the least of it."

"Aye," said MacRae. "And that's the King's business, though I still haven't heard why you make it yours."

"Because one of the marbles contained something—an artifact— and it was very valuable. If there is any way it can be saved…"

Elena gave the man a hard look, as though she were trying to see right through the thin disguise he was wearing.

"How would you know this?"

"That's a very long story, and there's no time to explain it all. Look, if there is anything you can do, we need to act now. Then I have a hundred questions, the least of which is what in god's name you are doing here with this ship!"

"We're standing to in the service of the King," said MacRae. "Just like all the rest out here."

"In a Type-45 destroyer? Oh, it's a nice white paint you put over it, and her lines are smoothed out a bit, but this is a fighting ship, and that's a Sampson radar dome up there on your mainmast. It's unmistakable. And who in hell is using tactical nukes? Are you people crazy?"

Wellings gave them a no nonsense look, with just a flash of anger, and MacRae eyed Morgan now, wondering just who this man really was. That statement had clearly changed the entire tenor of the conversation, for only a man from their own day would have been able to finger the *Argos Fire's* heritage as a *Daring* Class destroyer, or know anything about nuclear weapons.

"It wasn't us," said Elena. "Yes, this whole situation is insane, but we've more sense than that. But let's stay focused here... This artifact," a note of suspicion was creeping into her tone now. "Just what might it be?"

"A key," said the American. "A very unusual key, embedded in the base of the Selene Horse."

Only another member of the Watch would know that, thought Elena, and here this man was said to be asking about Admiral Tovey... What was going on? Who was this man?

"How is it you recognize this ship as a Type-45. Not one man alive on this earth outside this ship could have known that. And how is it you know about this artifact, this key?"

"The key?" Wellings said bluntly. "Because I was the first man to discover it, and it will probably not be seen by any man alive on this earth again if we don't take speedy action to salvage it."

"You can forget that," said Morgan. "*Rodney* is finished. There's no way we could risk getting divers aboard now. She'll be heading for Davy Jones locker inside ten minutes."

The American officer shrugged, realizing this was likely true, and yet still animated with a frustrated energy. "Damn," he said, summing up what they all seemed to feel at the moment.

"You were the man to first discover it?" Fairchild gave him an incredulous look. "It's been sitting in the British Museum ever since the 7th Earl of Elgin persuaded the government to purchase the marbles in 1816."

"Yes, yes," said Wellings, "I know all the history. That 35,000 pounds bought the British government much more than they ever realized."

"Oh?" Elena inclined her head, studying the man closely, noting how he glanced nervously at his watch. "This key you speak of," she said. "Might it look anything like this?"

The man's eyes widened as she drew out the key where it had been hanging on a thin gold chain around her neck. "Then you've already found it?" he said quickly, a look of great relief on his face. "How did you manage to get to it with all that ruckus going on out there?"

"I think we'd better sit down, Mister Wellings. You have a hundred questions in mind, and so do I. Suppose we have a little drink and get to the bottom of this. Yet before we discuss this key, and where it came from, I'd like to know who you really are. Clearly you're not who you seem to be, and if you haven't noticed, there's a war on. People take a very dim view of men who put on uniforms without earning the right to do so, and it is clear to me, and most likely to these gentlemen here as well, that you are not a Lieutenant Commander in the American Navy."

"Quite right," said Wellings, deciding to drop the guise and identity he had assumed and do a little digging here himself. "Forgive the uniform, but it was necessary, as was the subterfuge. To answer your question, Madame, my name is Dorland—Professor Paul Dorland, of the Lawrence Berkeley Labs in the United States. And since you seem to be well out of place in this milieu, you may not be all that surprised to hear what I say next. I have come here from the year 2021, and to retrieve that very key," he pointed. "How you managed to come by it is a mystery to me, as was my own discovery of that artifact, embedded in the base of the Selene Horse, right there aboard the battleship *Rodney*, on May 21st, 1941."

Morgan gave the man a frown now. "21st of May you say? Well the last time I checked, and that was this morning, it was the 8th of May, Mister Wellings. Or is it Professor now?"

"Correct," said Dorland. "On this meridian. When I found the key things were... different. You see, this was not the first time I've used this uniform to get aboard that ship out there. I had other business, which there's no time to discuss, and I found that key by pure happenstance."

"You found it?" said Elena. "Aboard *Rodney*?"

"Where else?" said Dorland. "Look, we both know the marbles were being shipped to Boston aboard *Rodney*. Well, you may be gratified to know that they actually got there once. This time things appear to have turned out quite different, but at least you've recovered it. How did you manage it?"

"We didn't manage a thing," said Elena. "In fact this whole operation has been a train wreck as far as I'm concerned. This isn't the key you may be looking for, Professor Dorland, or whoever you are. Now... I want to know how you got here, what you intended to do, and how you even know of this matter in the first place. And I want it straight and narrow—right now."

She folded her arms, waiting.

Chapter 11

"**How** did I get here? That is another long story," said Dorland, "and I suppose it will be as difficult and convoluted as the one you will tell me to explain how a 21st century warship is found here sailing about in the middle of the Second World War! Yet here we are. Let's leave it at that for the moment, as my time is running thin. The real concern now is that key. Believe it or not, I was aboard *Rodney* once before, in another telling of these events, and I believed they had reached a successful conclusion, that is until the final alert came in, and that key went missing."

"Missing?" Elena had a firm grasp on her key now, as though she were suddenly afraid it might go the way of Russian battlecruisers and submarines.

"After I discovered it aboard *Rodney*," said Dorland, "I took it with me, back to my own time—to *our* time, if I may venture a guess. You are also from that future?"

"There was a mishap," said Elena. "Yes, and it was in 2021, right at the outbreak of the war. We were returning from the Black Sea, a business venture involving oil. Yet I have other business as well, and I received certain instructions. Yes, you are correct. It will be a long story, but suffice it to say that it eventually led me, and my ship, here. This key had a very great deal to do with that, and so you can therefore understand my interest in the one aboard *Rodney*. You say you took it with you. Explain."

"The one aboard *Rodney*?" Dorland stumbled a bit. "Are you intimating that is not the same key? There are more than one?"

"Yes. The key aboard *Rodney* vanished, just as you say it did, on the 21st of May, 1941. And yes, that was in another history of these events. We've both seen that the story presently underway is just a little deviant."

"That is an understatement," said Dorland. "We had alerts all over the band, red lines everywhere. At first we traced it all to an incident on the 28th of July, 1941, and then we realized the significance of that date."

Elena held up a hand. "I don't understand what you're talking about. Alerts? Red lines?"

Dorland looked at his watch again, his eyes darkening. "We are a research team established in the Lawrence Berkeley Labs. On the surface the operation appears to be nothing more than a physics lab, yet its real purpose was to investigate something else—the possibility of moving through time." The professor let that sink in a moment before he pressed on.

"You don't seem impressed," he said. "I suppose your presence here is enough of an explanation for that. So let us get round the elephant and grant that both of us know time travel is a very real phenomenon."

"Go on," said Elena, waiting patiently.

"Well we tested our little theory, my theory actually, and discovered a good deal more than we expected. Once the cork was out of the bottle, everybody seemed to be pouring the champagne! You're just the latest wrinkle in this business. How you managed it is astounding. In any case, what we found was somewhat disturbing. If we pulled off the trick, then it was an easy jump to say that others in the future would do so as well."

"You mean they were traveling in time?"

"Exactly, and the sad thing is that there seemed to be a disagreement underway. Oh, let's be plain about it—it was war—time war, and it was getting most uncomfortable. Since we believed our own project pre-dated their operations, we decided to do something about it."

"Aye?" said MacRae. "What was that?"

"Put a stop to it." Dorland took a deep breath, realizing he had too much to convey here, and too little time to do it. "Something happened, and it was somewhat catastrophic. We tried to reverse that outcome, and thankfully, we were successful."

"Catastrophic? What are you speaking of."

"Never mind that now. We prevented it, so there's no use

discussing that. Then we found certain individuals in the future were not pleased with what we had done. This event was a deliberate act, which is the only reason we were able to reverse it. Then we found out there was a great deal more to that operation, and we had to get more directly involved."

"Involved in what?"

"In the war," Dorland hurried on. "We figured out a way to keep an eye on things—the history. When things went awry, when we learned of aberrations and deviations from the history we knew, then we set our minds to correcting them. Believe me, this was no small task, but in the course of events we were quite successful—even in persuading these individuals to cease their little time war, and to stop meddling with things. We *forced* them to negotiate a peace."

"These individuals you speak of," said Elena. "They were not from our day, 2021?"

"No, they were from a future time, though we never really determined how far off that was."

"Then the war was not fatal. It wasn't the cause of the calamity."

"What are you speaking of?" Dorland leaned in intently.

"Grand Finality," said Elena. "It's a term I was given, though I can't really say what it means."

"Yes, I'm very familiar with it," said Dorland. "I was the man who first coined the phrase."

"You?"

"Quite so," said Dorland. "We were the first, you see—the first to open the continuum. At least this was what we once thought. Then I discovered that key, on a mission I was undertaking to set right a little aberration in the history. For an artifact of that nature to be found embedded in the Selene Horse was most alarming. I examined that key very closely, and found it had... properties that could not have been engineered in the past. So what was it doing there in that ancient Greek sculpture?"

"You say you took it with you? After finding it aboard *Rodney*?"

"Correct."

"Took it back to the United States?"

"Yes, to the year 2021… July of 2021, to be a little more precise. Just a few weeks before the final alert came in on the 28th of that month."

"So you've just been flying about like a banshee?" said MacRae. "Traveling through time?" He rolled his eyes, incredulous.

"Yes, we can move in time. That's what our project tested and achieved. My presence here should be argument enough. How *you* pulled it off is the real question I have. You say it had something to do with that key? Well this is what I came to suspect as well. Then a very strange thing happened—on the 28th of July, 2021. I had that key in my possession for some weeks before that, and then it vanished."

"It was stolen?" asked Elena, finally realizing how the key had disappeared in May of 1941. This man claimed he was right there, aboard *Rodney*, and most likely in this very same costume. He claimed he discovered the key in the Selene Horse, and then took it with him. No wonder it was never found again in all the years between that date and 2021.

"Not stolen," said Dorland. "It literally vanished. I kept it on a chain, just as you have that one there, but it vanished. Naturally I wanted to know why, so I came back here to look for it at a time and place I was reasonably certain to find it—the place where I first discovered it."

"I see…" Elena thought deeply now, taking all of this in, somewhat amazed. "Well, Professor Dorland, I do not wish to disappoint you, but as you have determined, this is not the key you discovered aboard *Rodney*."

Dorland smiled. "There are more than one," he said, realization evident on his face, his dark eyes alight.

"Apparently," said Elena.

"How did you come by this one?"

"It was entrusted to me, and that is another very long story."

Now Dorland put two and two together, his eyes narrowing.

"Then you came here to look for it too. You were here to find the key in the Selene Horse?"

"In point of fact, we were, but things slipped a bit, and we weren't quick enough. I'm afraid it's lost now, and I wish I knew what the consequences of that will be. Yes, Professor, there are more than one of these keys about, and they all seem to be associated with movement in time. We came to believe they were engineered in the future, and used to secure, or grant access to fissures in time."

"Fissures?"

"Physical rifts in time, at certain locations. Our mission was to secure every one we could find, but it seems this one has given us both the slip. We'll never recover it now—not unless we get back to our own time and that war settles down enough for us to mount a deep sea salvage operation on the wreck of the *Rodney*."

Now Dorland's eyes brightened. "Salvage operation... Yes... Nordhausen could run that down for me..."

"I don't understand. Nordhausen?"

"Another of our research team members. Professor Nordhausen is our chief historical researcher. Well... You are quite correct that this key will be very difficult to recover in 2021. It might be much easier to look for it elsewhere...." Now Dorland had a strange expression on his face, as though he were experiencing some discomfort.

"Are you alright, Laddie?" said MacRae. "You might fetch the man that drink you promised, Elena. He's white as a sheet!"

"I'm afraid my time is up," said Dorland quickly. Then his eyes widened. "My pattern signature is wearing thin, and they're pulling me out. But I'll be back! The Azores... Look for me on the first of August, 1941. I'll meet you there..."

He smiled, and then, to their utter amazement, it seemed as though he simply dissolved, his image quavering like a hologram going in and out of focus. There came a sudden chill, icy cold, and the sharp tinge of ozone in the air, with a crackle of static electricity. Then this man, like the key he had come looking for, like the Russian ship and submarine, simply vanished.

Mack Morgan stood there, dumfounded. Then he realized that this very ship, and the entire crew, had pulled this same magic trick in 2021, and here they were.

"Well I'll be..." He ran his hand through the air where Dorland had been standing, feeling the palpable cold. "Looks like he was telling the truth!"

Even though Elena had done the very same thing, she still found the evidence of her eyes difficult to believe. Was this man ever really here? It looked as though he was just a digital image! What was that he said about his pattern signature? Clearly there was more to all of this than she had come to learn.

"Everybody started pouring the champagne," she said softly. "The Russians, then we got in on the act, and now this fellow here— to say nothing of those individuals in the future he mentioned. Time war? My god, weren't two world wars enough?"

"Three," said MacRae. "We were just shooting missiles at the Russian Black Sea Fleet before we found ourselves here in this mess."

"What did he mean when he said we might look for that key elsewhere?"

"Your guess is as good as mine."

Elena nodded. "Mack, get busy. Check the ship's computers and see if you can dig anything up on our recently departed Professor Dorland."

"Right," said Morgan. "If his story checks out, I'll find evidence of that in the database."

"Good... Gordon, get hold of Admiral Tovey and see what he's planning."

"I've already done that," said MacRae. "It's just as this fellow had it." He thumbed the place where Dorland had been standing. "He's consolidating the fleet at the new British base in the Azores. These battleships are thirsty buggers, and the fleet has tankers and fuel depots there."

"Alright, then we'll join them. We wouldn't want to miss our next appointment with the good professor."

"You mean to say you think he's going to just re-appear there?"

"That's what he seemed to imply. Let's get there and see whether he turns up. In the meantime, Mack, you can also do a little digging on the Elgin Marbles. Find out when they were first recovered from the Parthenon and taken to England. It will be in the early 1800s. That little remark he made about looking elsewhere may be the cat's tail here, and we'll need to get hold of it."

"Alright," said MacRae, "so we make for the Azores. But suppose this fellow never shows up again?"

"Oh I think we'll see Professor Dorland again, just as he says. Did you follow that business about keeping watch on the history? In a way, that is exactly what I was doing, only my watch was on that damn Russian ship. And did you hear what he said about July 28th? That was the day *Kirov* went missing in that accident in the Norwegian Sea."

"Aye," said MacRae. "The day he claims he was alerted to something. The day he says he lost his key. What's this all about, Elena?"

"That's exactly what I intend to discover. Damn… We need to find out what happened to the Russians. That young Captain of theirs was worried about this. July 28th was the day they were scheduled to arrive here."

"What?" said MacRae. "Another Russian ship? Just like the first? Is that even possible?"

"Who knows," said Elena. "Perhaps this professor can shed some light on that. He seems to claim he invented this whole time travel business, though I was listening very closely to what he said. Did you hear it? He made the claim that they were the first to open the continuum."

"At least that was what they first thought," said Mack Morgan, remembering what the American had said.

"Exactly. You caught that too. Do you realize what he was implying? If they weren't the first… If these keys were engineered in the future as both he and I seem to believe, then the history we were living in was not inviolate."

"What do you mean?" said Morgan, scratching his head. "You're talking about *our* history—all the books I had to read in school—all the data in the computer I'm off to sift through?"

"That's exactly what I'm talking about," said Elena with a smile. "Gentlemen, someone's had their hand on Mother Time's leg for a good long while, and I'm bloody well going to find out who it is."

Chapter 12

Rodney fought for every last minute, even though her crew had been ordered to abandon ship. The close proximity of the *Britannic*, a big steamship liner serving as a troop ship, was a godsend. Tovey's battle with the *Hindenburg* group had taken place about 35 nautical miles southwest of the sinking battleship. He saw that the second German group, badly mauled by the Russians, had eventually turned south as well, and the latest reports had all the German ships forming a new task force, wounded, yet still very dangerous.

The reports coming in from *Argos Fire* assured him the German's were breaking off, and so Tovey took stock of his situation, considering what to do, and what to make of this request for a meeting here aboard *Invincible*. It seemed that Miss Fairchild had something more to disclose.

When *Rodney* finally tipped bow first into the sea, there was a long moment of silence aboard every ship present. Then there came the slow, sedate strains of a small band playing "Nearer My God To Thee," and Tovey turned his head, hearing it coming from *Britannic*. It had been the last song for an old sister ship in the line, the ill fated *Titanic*. The doleful song hung over the sea, until Tovey turned and gave a quiet order to his Flag Lieutenant. Minutes later, the ship's band had assembled on the broad deck amidships, beneath the long steel barrels of X-turret, still warm with the heat of battle. Another song burst forth, resounding over the waves, and it carried quite a different emotion—Rule Britannia!

Tovey looked at Villers, and Captain Bennett turned in his chair, nodding his obvious approval. When the song ended he gave an order to a watchstander to ring eight bells for *Rodney*, the tones that would sound out the last watch of the day at sea.

"That leaves *Nelson* as one of a kind," the Captain said to Tovey. He was referring to the only other battleship remaining in the class, HMS *Nelson*.

"As we are," said Tovey, for there were no other G3 Class ships in the navy. "And looking to our health, gentlemen, please have a full accounting of damage and casualties sent to me in the Admiral's stateroom. I'll be receiving guests shortly."

As he made ready to leave the bridge, he took one final look at the last vestige of the great cloud that had appeared with angry red fire to the northeast. The wind had sheared off its top, and it was only now dissipating. As he looked at it, that ghostly feeling returned, and he knew he had seen something like this before, a clawing memory that gave him a chill.

An hour later, Miss Fairchild came aboard with Captain MacRae and Mack Morgan. They wanted to confer with Tovey, firm up his intentions, and determine what to do with the other ships that had come on the scene, all strange interlopers on this wild day at sea.

"Seven more ships?" asked Tovey. "And all from your time?"

"Apparently," said Elena.

"Well how did they get here?"

"We aren't certain. Perhaps that mushroom cloud on the horizon had something to do with it."

"Just what exactly happened out there?" Tovey frowned. "It's given me the willies since I first set eyes on it."

"Gordon?"

MacRae nodded, then explained. "Tha' was not a natural event, sir." His Scottish brogue seeming right in place. "In fact, it was a weapon of war. We weren't sure if the Russians had them or not, but it seems they do. We believe it was either used by the Russian battlecruiser, or that submarine."

"Yes," said Tovey. "Admiral Volsky discussed these weapons with me at one point, but he was rather vague about it. What kind of a weapon would wrench the sky and sea like that?"

"An atomic weapon, sir. Your government knows about the bomb—that's what we call it in our day. In fact, they most likely have a working program to develop one now. In our day, the history we know, no one had a working prototype here until 1945."

"Then that is where this damn war is taking us?"

"I'm afraid so," said Elena. "And the next one we fight will be quite unpleasant. Knowledge of that weaponry becomes widespread after this war. In our day, at least ten nations possessed them, the newest member of the club being the Islamic Republic of Iran."

"Iran? How would they manage something like that? This is most startling."

"In a word—oil," said Elena. "Your main interest in Iran today is the business of British Petroleum. In fact, that was also the business of Fairchild Incorporated, my company. Oil becomes the witches brew of the modern world, Admiral, and a point of contention and crisis for decades to come. The wells British Petroleum and other concerns sink into the sands of Iran, Iraq, and Arabia, all gush to life in the next few years, but in our day, some eighty years from now, those very same wells will be running dry. The modern world runs almost exclusively on that oil, and speaking of that, I'm told one of the seven dwarves that have arrived here today is an oiler. They'll have fuel for us there. Another is a repair ship and fleet tender. They could be very handy in helping out with your battle damage."

"I see…" Tovey was quiet for a moment, thinking. "These other ships. I think they had best come along with us. It won't do to let them just sail about on their own."

"I quite agree," said Elena. "It was my understanding that you were planning to refuel your battleships in the Azores. Perhaps it would be wise if we lead this little flotilla there. I have spoken with the flotilla leader aboard *Diligence*—the fleet Auxiliary and repair ship I just mentioned. We have just found out that in our time they were en route to Mersa Matruh."

"North Africa?"

"Yes, they were dispatched to move Brigadier Kinlan's troops back to the continent, so you see this is a rather strange twist."

"Indeed," said Tovey, taking that in and wondering at the mystery behind it. "Might their appearance here be somehow mixed up with Kinlan's chaps?"

"It does seem rather odd," said Elena. "In any case, there is another matter concerning the Azores we need to discuss."

She took a deep breath, then tried to explain the appearance, and subsequent disappearance of the American officer, the man named Wellings who later turned out to be something quite more than he seemed.

"Astounding," said Tovey. "Just what in bloody hell is happening here? Are you all going to just pop in from the future and sign on with the Royal Navy? Ships and men have been shuffling in and out of the bar, and nobody seems to know the cause. Well I'll say one thing. I had a number of chats with that young Russian Captain, Fedorov. A good man that one. A pity he's not here to help us sort things through. So you say this American fellow wants a meeting in the Azores?" Tovey raised an eyebrow. "Well I certainly have no objection. In fact, I believe I'll send for someone I would like to include on the guest list. You know that Churchill will have to be informed."

"Churchill?" said Elena. "You're going to ask him to attend?"

"No my good woman. That would be just a tad too risky given the present situation. I was thinking of another man, a chap from Bletchley Park with a good head on his shoulders. I'll want his take on all of this, and I can use him as a liaison to Churchill. In that regard, there is something I would like to ask of you. I hesitated to press the matter with the Russians, and I know it may be a rather delicate request, but I'll ask it nonetheless, since we're all in the family here. You people have been mucking about for some time now, for good or for ill. Needless to say, it has had quite an effect on the course of this war, and it will likely continue to do so. Well then... In for a penny, in for a pound. As to the course of this war. I'd like to know what we can expect in the years ahead."

He waited, watching them closely. MacRae looked at Miss Fairchild, obviously deferring to her judgment on a question of this magnitude. "Perhaps I can have Mack here put together some information for you, Admiral. Mack?"

"Certainly, Mum. Any particulars you might be thinking about?"

"My beat," said Tovey. "A general sense of things would be most helpful. I understand that knowledge is a dangerous thing, and I assure you that anything you may divulge will be kept under my hat, and not revealed to anyone who is not already privy to this… situation we find ourselves in."

"I understand, sir. Yet from what I've been able to determine, things are just a wee bit skewed here. The Germans have already attacked Soviet Russia, and that wasn't supposed to happen until late June. As for the broad strokes, this war is only just beginning. The Americans and Japanese will be in it soon enough, and at each other's throats. I'll fill you in sir."

"Good enough," said Tovey. "Now then, as to this American fellow. You say he's come from your time, and willfully? His presence here was not an accident?"

"Apparently not," said Elena. "He deliberately infiltrated *Rodney* in the guise of that American officer, and he was looking for that key we've been keen to get our own hands on."

"Yes," said Tovey… "The key. Everyone is looking for that bloody key! Strange to think that I have something to do with this, but I can't imagine what it may be at the moment. Well, I think we better hear this man out. If he can come and go as he pleases, that alone is something we'll want to hear about. The Russians seemed to believe their arrival here was an accident, until they gained some means of control over their movements. Yet I find it hard to believe they would slip out the back door like this without so much as a by your leave, or a goodbye."

"Then you believe their disappearance was an accident?"

"It may have been unintentional," said Tovey. "That is fair to conclude. Yet we also have no word from their submarine. That could mean any number of things, though I can't say any of them bode well. I think we must assume that this submarine may have either been lost in action, or else it suffered the same fate that befell *Kirov*. You say there was another interloper out there—another submarine?"

"*Astute* Class," said MacRae. "Aye, we got the call on that from the Russian sub. This class is a modern day Royal Navy boat, state-of-the-art, and one of the very best in the world. Miss Fairchild here has explained how this Brigadier Kinlan managed to slip through to this time. That was another of those atomic weapons, Admiral fired in our day. It seems it blew Kinlan's boys all the way here, and now we're coming round on a heading to think the same thing may have happened with these ships, and that *Astute* Class sub of ours. They would have made a very ripe target in our day. If something similar happened, it might explain how that sub of ours got here. The Russian sub Captain claimed they fired on him, and they wanted us to call in our dogs, but we couldn't get through to stop what was happening. Once those bloody torpedoes go into the water, you have very little time. In our day, they're quick as lightning."

"We figure the Russian sub Captain acted on pure reflex," said Morgan. "It's nice that we've tipped hats here and had our handshakes, but that reflex runs deep."

"As to that *Astute* Class sub," said MacRae, "whether it's still out there or not is anyone's guess. The Russians lit one off on them, which doesn't surprise me, now that I look at it in this light. If our boat survived, that will be a damn good reason for the Russian sub to be running silent. Remember, in our day the Royal Navy is not so cozy with the Russians. That song we heard your ship's band playin' still holds true for the North Atlantic. Britannia still rules the waves on that watch—only it will be the Russians we'll be lookin' out for, and not the Germans. In fact, Germany is our ally in the future. It's the Russians and Chinese we worry about in the next war."

"Indeed," said Tovey. "The whole thing gets turned on its head! Well I think Admiral Volsky and Captain Fedorov were dead set on changing that. I know in fact that they were working here to try and prevent that war you speak of in your time. Whether their intervention here may do some good, I suppose we may never know. The arrival of Brigadier Kinlan's troops, welcome as they are, and now these other ships… Well that all leads me to think things don't turn out as well in the future as Admiral Volsky might have hoped.

Perhaps this American fellow can clue us in. This may make for a very interesting conversation. Just how is he set to return here?"

"We aren't certain. We were told they have some… technology."

"Very well. Then we head for the Azores to keep that appointment he made with us. I think the Germans have seen enough of the Royal Navy for the moment, and with Holland and Patterson coming on the scene, I don't think they'll want to cause any further mischief out here. Unfortunately, we've lost a good ship today, two actually, if we count the disappearance of *Kirov*. But Jerry has taken his lumps as well. The Russians put the fire to that aircraft carrier of theirs, and word is they also lost *Gneisenau*—torpedo damage—so that Russian sub may have weighed in on that one. They did their part, but who knows when or if we will sail with them again. Unfortunately the war won't wait for a happy reunion. Now we must do the lifting ourselves, and I'm grateful you are still with me."

He sighed, catching his breath as his thoughts ran on. "First things first. I'll have a good number of thirsty battleships on my hands soon, so I intend to make for the Azores at once. I think it best that we move the newcomers to the rear of our convoy, and I'll post *Repulse* in their wake. We've another destroyer flotilla in the Azores, and I'll have them form a welcoming committee straight away."

He turned to Miss Fairchild now. "Terribly sorry we've let the King's business go into the sea like that. His majesty will be none too happy with the report I'll have to write this evening, and I daresay Mister Churchill will get up a good head of steam about it as well, not to mention the First Sea Lord. I have a great deal to explain here, and I'll have to be very discrete about it. I don't have to tell you that hat bands can change rather easily in this war, and it wouldn't be wise if Admiral Pound got nosey about all this. I'll have to make an accounting of this action to the Admiralty, and I don't think I can hide the existence of these seven other ships indefinitely. Any objection to my informing the Prime Minister as to what has happened here?"

"My understanding is that he's in the club," said Elena.

"Right," said Tovey. "And he's very keen to know what we might be facing soon, which is one reason I pressed you for... information. Any bone I can throw Mister Churchill may keep the wolves at bay, at least insofar as my fate is concerned, I think it would keep me in the loop, and that will be all for the best. I have just one more question before we retire to more civil matters and sit down to dinner. Do tell me you have no plans to vanish any time soon."

"None that we know of, sir," said Elena with a smile.

"Good," said Tovey. "I do also understand how difficult all this must be for your crew. If there is anything I can do for you, please let me know. In the meantime, let us go and have a bit to eat, and consider what this American fellow might want our ear for on the first of August."

"Don't be surprised, Admiral," said Elena. "But I think it may have something to do with that key. The man claimed he once had it in his possession, until it pulled the same trick the Russians seem to play about with, and just vanished. Then *he* disappeared for good measure, and right before my own eyes. I haven't any idea what he's really up to, but yes, I think this appointment in the Azores will prove to be very interesting."

Part V

Nothing Is Written

"Nothing Is Written, and Everything is Permitted."

- Ismaili Saying

Chapter 13

He emerged in a white mist, effused with glimmering light, with only the reassuring strength of the hard concrete floor beneath him as any point of physical reference. Weak from the sudden return to another time, Paul stooped to his knees, one hand on the concrete floor to steady himself, beset with a queasy sensation of lightness, his mind still a whirl.

The last time he had done this, he was returning from this very same mission, his clandestine infiltration on the battleship *Rodney* in the assumed identity of Lieutenant Commander Wellings. He had gone to see to the sinking of the *Bismarck*, feeding crucial information to the Captain of the battleship *Rodney* to assure he could get that ship into the hunt, for it was *Rodney* that drew first blood against the German warship, scoring a serious hit on her third salvo. The action then had seen him thrown from the ship into the sea, tossed in the wild waves in the heat of the battle, and only just barely extracted from the scene in time. He had returned out of phase, eventually manifesting, wet and bedraggled, yet with a strange souvenir in his pocket, something he had found in the cargo hold when he went below decks to aid a wounded man.

His return shift had been very difficult, as he had emerged in the Berkeley Arch complex, yet strangely out of synch, there but not there, the barest fraction of a second ahead of them in time, and therefore completely invisible to the others until his own clock slowed enough for him to find harmony with them.

They had come to call it "Attenuation," a property of an incomplete time shift, where the traveler manifests across a range of several milliseconds, slightly out of sync or phase with his correct target point in time. He was simply out of tune with everything else, and the effects had also been reported by others who moved in time, the walkers from the future who had been striving with one another in the long, deadly time war.

Now Paul was relieved to hear someone calling his name, though the voice seemed strained and distant. The sound slowly resolved, and the sensation of dizziness faded with the mist around him. There, standing a few feet from the thick painted yellow line that marked the event horizon of the Arch, stood his good friend and fellow team member, Robert Nordhausen.

"Ah," said Nordhausen. "Back in one piece this time. Did you find it?"

"Paul was still a bit dazed from the shift, and for a moment he seemed to have no idea what Nordhausen was talking about. "Find it?" he said haltingly. Then his memory solidified and he remembered why he had taken this risk again, exposing his very being to the strange effects of a time shift—the key.

"I couldn't get to it," he said bitterly. "But my god, Robert, you'll be amazed at what's going on there now. There's a goddamned British destroyer there—a Type 45!"

"What's that?" Nordhausen knew the history inside out—ancient history being his forte, but when it came to military matters he seemed at a loss, particularly concerning anything newer than the 20th Century."

"A modern warship—from *our* time!"

"What? In the middle of World War Two?"

"I was aboard the damn thing, and even spoke to their crew. Look, we need to get busy. It was a ship called the *Argos Fire*. I picked up the name when they pulled me out of the sea."

"You got thrown into the ocean again? I told you to stay away from the gunwales."

"Yes? Well I had plenty of company this time. The *Rodney* was sunk, or at least it was sinking when I left the scene just now. Everyone went into the drink with me."

"Damn," said Nordhausen. "*Bismarck* remains a tough old bastard."

"That's an understatement. Look, Robert, that history is

completely skewed now. The red lines on the Golem module make perfect sense, and I think it all started with that Russian battlecruiser that went missing in the Norwegian Sea."

"That's where we get our first point of deviation," said Nordhausen.

"Deviation? That's not half a word for what I discovered there. The whole history of the war has been turned on its head. There are ships at sea that were never supposed to have been built, and I learned that things have happened in the war that never occurred. The Germans took Gibraltar, and that's just one example. The entire political landscape has shifted as well. It seems Russia never finished its civil war, and the Bolsheviks never united the country."

"I know," said Nordhausen. "The Golems have been slowly returning information, but there's a great deal of haze. I don't understand why I can't get clear data."

"Because this whole thing is in play," said Paul. "There's a Grand Nexus open, and it has something to do with that Russian battlecruiser. As to that key, I just learned that there are others, and I think I have a handle on what their purpose was."

The two men were walking back towards the heavy shielded door now, and into the elevator, ready to take the ride up to the main complex control room where Kelly Ramer sat at the consoles to monitor Paul's shift pattern on the return. He was the math and computer genius in the group, responsible for crunching the numbers to navigate through time by using the enormous power of an Arion module supercomputer.

"Maeve is going to go ballistic," said Paul, referring to the last of the four founding team members. Head of Outcomes and Consequences, Maeve Lindford was as fiery as her red hair, and had been a stalwart defender of the established lines of history. On the night before their first planned mission, a simple jaunt back to see the original showing of *The Tempest* by Shakespeare, she had committed the entire play to memory. In the event they inadvertently did something to affect the history, she wanted to know immediately if a single word had been changed in Shakespeare's drama, and she would stand ready to grill the offender and defend every last punctuation mark of the play if need be. Through the desperate missions the team had conducted, it was hers to sort through the myriad of possible outcomes of their interventions in time, and find the one course that promised to maintain the integrity of the history they knew, all safely preserved in an enormous database, and kept constantly running in a low grade Nexus Point to prevent it from being altered. They called it their Touchstone Database, the "RAM bank" as Kelly Ramer described it.

The four founders had been standing their watch on the history for some months, the Physicist, Historian, Math Wizard and Maeve Lindford's hard hand on the tiller of it all. Just as they thought they had concluded their operations, a final alert had come in on the warning system Kelly rigged to keep watch on the history, and this time the damage was far more severe than anyone expected.

"Are the Assassins behind this?" asked Robert. "Do we have to hold their feet to the fire again?

"No," said Paul definitively. "No, it has to do with the disappearance of that ship. That's where the Golems first led us, to July 28th, 2021, and the direct link to a point of divergence on that same date in 1941. By God, Robert—I think the damn ship moved in time! Who knows how or why, but that is what accounts for these odd Golem fetches that have produced evidence of modern weaponry being used in the war. Those were not fluke prototypes, and I think all those reports you were getting were actually happening—at one point."

"You mean the evidence I uncovered on the use of nuclear weapons?"

"Correct. I think they were real events, not simply something fetched from the Golem stream—not simply possible outcomes as we first believed. They actually happened, but from what I was able to gather, that Russian ship has been bouncing all over the history! I think that information you uncovered concerning the engagements off Sakhalin Island in 1945 were also real events, and that strange bit about a renegade Russian battleship trying to re-fight the battle of Tushima in 1908."

"That was real?"

"I think it was this same Russian battlecruiser—*Kirov*. No, this time it isn't our warring friends from the future—not the Assassins or the operatives of the Order. This time it was the Russians!"

"What in god's name are they doing?"

"Hard to say. I think it was an accident, just as it was first reported on the 28th in our news here. But if I'm correct, and that ship did actually move in time, then it's been ripping the history open from one end to another. Maeve will have a fit."

"And the British destroyer? What has it got to do with all of this?"

"*Argos Fire*... Look that one up the minute we get to the operations room."

The elevator door opened and they started the long walk up the gradually inclined corridor, eventually passing through the heavy titanium door that stood like the entrance to a great bank vault—a bank that held the fate of time and history itself within its hidden chambers. Once through, Paul watched the great door slowly swing shut and seal itself, the heavy metal locking mechanism clinking into place.

"Well, Admiral Dorland? Did you find it?" It was Maeve, hands on her hips, staring them both down with the light of battle in her eyes.

"Oh, he made it there and back again alright," said Nordhausen. "But wait until you hear this!"

* * *

Maeve Lindford was truly shocked by all she had heard. A Russian ship at large in the history of WWII, and wreaking havoc with every missile it fired. The consequences that could result from this were overwhelming, and the thought that it was her job to sort that through was maddening.

Outcomes and consequences—that was her mission in life these days. The dangers inherent in the enterprise of time travel, once only speculation about contamination and fateful effects, had suddenly been made painfully obvious to her. She had an odd feeling that there was something amiss in this whole equation—something she could not quite work out in her probability algorithms, and it irked her like a shirt that needed ironing. It sat like unwashed dishes on her kitchen countertops, and waited like an unpaid bill on her desk—things that she would never allow in the carefully managed space of her own personal life, for Maeve Lindford was a most meticulous woman.

She kept everything in quiet order, and the structure of her world was wholly predictable at any given moment. The steady certainty of her life had been something in which she took great solace—something of her own making. It was an extension of her considerable will power, and the determined competence she thrust against any problem the world would dare to concoct for her. Up until now she had been quite content in her world, with outcomes that were wholly satisfactory—until this latest incident threatened to turn the entire project on its head, and the world right along with it.

Time travel, it seemed, could be quite untidy.

Something was happening now that none of them had a handle on. That uncertainty had become a real feeling for her at that moment—not just a nagging, misplaced cipher in her math. It settled into her with a pulsing beat of anxiety, and it never quite went away, like a thrumming of adrenaline in her chest. The world was not the way she always fancied it to be. Now, nothing was certain; nothing fixed and determined—not even the past.

For someone who had always labored to define clear and well established borders, this defiant 'quantum uncertainty' in time travel was a daunting and frightening prospect. Heisenberg, damn him, was right. He predicted that physical quantities and properties fluctuate randomly, and therefore can never be accurately known. While the effect of this uncertainty was most evident on the sub-atomic level, where things like the speed, spin, and charge of particles could be highly unpredictable, the fact remained that this basic uncertainty was at the core of all reality—if that term could be applied in any meaningful way. Put simply: nothing was written. She realized now that she hated the whole notion inherent in that statement.

Nothing was written; nothing forbidden, and everything was permitted. That was the chaos that now sat hunched in the center of her mind like an old, unwelcome hobgoblin to plague her thinking. She wanted it out, wanted it gone, wanted things wrapped in nice neat boxes again, and stacked up just so. But the world would never be that way for her again. All of her careful habits, all the meticulous checks and balances that governed her life, were futile efforts at imposing order on chaos. It was very unsettling, to say the least.

Perhaps there was something in the human heart that reached for a truth that *was* unalterable. A man's reach should exceed his grasp, wrote Keats, or what's a heaven for? Knowing, or believing that there was something out there that was fixed and permanent, had long been a comfort to the human soul. Now the Arch had proved that anything was possible, and any semblance of truth, as she once knew it, was gone from her life. She had firm ground under her feet when she walked into the Lab that night, but now all was quicksand. Nothing was certain, not even the comfort of finished, printed text in the books that she so loved all her life.

She remembered how they had started that first night with an argument about Shakespeare. They were going to test their theory by simply going to see the original showing of Shakespeare's *The Tempest,* and she was worried that Nordhausen's wayward curiosity might contaminate the time line. The man wanted to go nosing about Shakespeare's office, and she resolved, then and there, that he would not set one foot out of her sight if the Arch actually worked. It wasn't merely Nordhausen's eccentric temperament that she was determined to set a watch on—it was Shakespeare! The thought that the professor might do something to alter a single word of that man's verse was the most compelling argument anyone could make against the time project that night. If Paul's theory was correct, then a carelessly spoken word to a stranger in the past, a heedless stumble in the dark, a mislaid object, could wreak havoc on future time. It would be as if Shakespeare 'never writ.' The most maddening thing was that they might not even know what they had done to alter the record of time. Things would simply change—just like Lawrence's narrative in *The Seven Pillars*. She would reach for *The Tempest* on her library shelf one night and find it missing, gone, annihilated. Worse yet, she might never know the damage was done.

The thought that every book in her library was now subject to sudden revision had become a seed of a deep discomfort, and it was growing in her with each day that passed. She could lose any one of them: Bronte, Whitman, Keats, all blown away with the slightest breath of time. That volume of poetry she had been reading last night—would it be the same tonight? It was more than unnerving to her now, it was frightening. It wasn't merely words and books that could change on a whim, it was everything. Heisenberg's uncertainty principle had finally come home to roost.

She remembered how she had confronted her greatest fear at the end of their first mission. Robert and Paul were still flushed and dizzy with the elation of their return. The Arch was a scintillating montage of light, and the generators were whining as they strained to provide the power required for the retraction jump. She recalled the excitement she had first felt with Robert's return. Then Paul came through and everyone was safe at last. She had the barest moment of relief before that odd rumble shuddered through the Arch, like a ghostly train passing in the night. A howling sound droned in its wake, and she felt the fear gather strength within her.

Things were different.

Something had changed, and she could feel it like a shift in the weather, a faint, yet palpable variation in the certainty of her life. Something had changed. Heisenberg was running wild, and everything was different now.

Time travel was dangerous. Meddling could easily twist the continuum into a confounding loop of Paradox, and when that happened, something lashed out at anything that did not belong on the changed Meridian. Paul tried to explain it to them once. He said that the notion of Paradox was so insulting to time that she would find a way to punish the offenders for their mischief. Paradox was not a mind-puzzle, but a real effect. It was a cleansing and healing force of time that promised nothing less than annihilation for all those who would dare to meddle, engulfing them in the quantum foam of uncertainty, and sucking them away to oblivion.

As much as she tried to put the strange notions in her head aside, that gnawing uncertainty persisted. Now they had discovered that even their own time line had been an altered meridian! Everything she had taken for granted all her life, the history she had fought so stubbornly to defend, was actually just the result of someone's capricious meddling in time. But who was the real culprit? This time it looked to be the Russians, but this business Paul had turned up concerning these keys added another very unexpected twist. Keys, each associated with rifts in time, and found as artifacts embedded in something as old as the Selene Horse of the Parthenon! Who put it there, and why?

Someone was in her kitchen, rattling the plates and dishes of all the events in her cherished china cabinet of history. Cups and plates were shattered on the floor, and that awful feeling returned—she could never be certain of anything again.

Heisenberg be damned!

Chapter 14

"**What** can we do about all this?" said Maeve, the frustration evident in her voice. "You're telling me that all these snippets we've been getting in the Golem data stream were actually real events? Those ships are still back there? Modern warships are setting off nuclear weapons in 1941? My *god*, isn't the war revving up outside enough for them? They had to go back and do this?"

"Calm down," said Kelly, trying to tamp down her emotion.

Maeve flashed him a dark glance, and then bored in on Paul again. "What's going on with these keys, Paul? They've got something to do with all of this. That's why you felt so compelled to go back and try to fetch this one, and to see those damn battleships again. What's going on?"

"Yes," said Paul, thinking. "The keys…. From what I've been able to learn, the one I found was not the only one. This Fairchild woman had another key in her possession, and she claimed it was somehow responsible for the movement of her ship in time."

"The key?" Maeve shook her head. "How would it accomplish that? It took us years of research, all this investment of time and technology and equipment to get a functioning arch complex here and actually prove your theory could work. How does this woman simply upstage this whole project with a goddamned skeleton key?"

"I don't know, but I think this is physical—not a technology based effect."

"Physical?"

"Yes, she claimed they had discovered physical rifts in time, fissures, and that they were secured by these keys."

Maeve's eyes narrowed. "Rifts in time? You mean like that Oklo well you fell into in the Jordanian desert, the one that sent you right back to the time of the Crusades?"

"Perhaps," said Paul. "We had no time to discuss the details, because I knew my shift allocation was running out and Kelly was about to pull me out. The Oklo reaction was something the Assassins set up, as a way of operating off the time grid, as it were. No. I think this lady was referring to something more, something unplanned by the Assassins or anyone else in the future—some natural event that had caused time to fracture."

"The Russians!" said Nordhausen excitedly. "Remember that research I turned up concerning their nuclear testing program. I told you it looked suspicious."

"Yes," said Paul, "that may be part of it. Those effects could be considered physical, like the EMP effect they also discovered associated with nuclear detonations. Yet I think this lady was intimating there was something else in play here, not caused by the Assassins, or the Order, or anyone else deliberately moving in time. I'm thinking there was some natural event that fractured time. That Russian research you turned up may have been a good clue, Robert. Think… Suppose large detonations have the side effect of fracturing time. They don't just disturb space, they disturb the whole thing—spacetime. That's where we live, correct? We don't just live in space, we live in time as well—spacetime. Suppose highly energetic natural events like that have an effect on spacetime? Hell, we already know gravity can warp and bend space. Why not time? And what you can bend, you can also break."

"Fissures…" Maeve folded her arms. "And you say these keys are associated with time distortion?"

"That's what I was coming round to. This Fairchild lady said that there were others—other keys—and that she believed they were engineered in the future, which is exactly what I concluded about that key I found."

"If these rifts in time exist," said Maeve, "then why haven't we discovered them? There's nothing in the Golem data fetches about any of this."

"Yes?" said Nordhausen. "And there was nothing known about King Tut's tomb for centuries either, until it was finally discovered."

"Right," said Paul. "These rifts exist, but we haven't discovered them yet. At least if they are known to anyone in our time, that information remains unknown to us—a secret. Lord knows there is a whole encyclopedia of things that fall into that category."

"Well how does this Fairchild woman know about any of this? What is she doing with that key?"

"She said it was entrusted to her—that she had received instructions. I got the distinct impression that their presence there was not an accident, and she alluded that it had something to do with that key, though I never got the details. There's one thing I do know—she was looking for the key aboard *Rodney*."

"Aboard *Rodney?*"

"Yes, she said they just weren't quick enough. They couldn't get to the ship in time, and *Rodney* was sinking. I think she was on a mission of some kind, to recover that key."

"You say she got instructions? From who?" Maeve was digging now, wanting to get to the bottom of this trench.

"I never found that out, but I'm going back."

"What?"

"Well I have to go back, Maeve. This whole thing is still up in the air. This Nexus Point is wide open. I told them to look for me in the Azores on the first of August. That will be an easy shift to target. I can go back again, and with adequate time to talk to them and answer these questions."

"Why that date?"

"It was a decent interval ahead, and beyond the interference that might be setting up with Paradox time. You know that's risky. There's trouble brewing there around July 28th, the moment that ship first arrived in the past. The Golems were all over that date. It was the first big variation flag discovered by Golem 7. So I wanted to get beyond it. If there is Paradox in the offing, the effects should have already passed by August first."

"You were lucky that you phased correctly this time. Are you sure about this? Another shift, and that close to Paradox Time?"

"Yes. I know the risks, but this is urgent now—imperative. Don't you understand? If this is true, if these fissures or rifts this woman talked about are real, and they were caused by a natural event, then we could be looking at something very serious here—fatally serious. These natural rifts in time could be progressing, developing even as we speak. We could be looking at an ongoing event—the fragmentation of the entire continuum!"

That lit a fire under them all, and Nordhausen was quick to the research station, a hundred questions needing answers. "Alright, let's start with this new ship—*Argos Fire*," he said. "It was a corporate security vessel, a *Daring* class destroyer purchased from the British government by a company called Fairchild Enterprises. I not only found the data on that in the history module, the damn ship was on the news this morning."

"This morning?"

"CNN. They say it was reported missing off the coast of Greece, leaving two oil tankers stranded there without escort. There was speculation it might have been sunk by the Russians."

"The Russians again," said Maeve. "Could this whole thing be planned? Deliberate?"

"You mean the disappearance of *Kirov* in the Norwegian Sea? That's possible," said Paul, "but I think that was probably an accident. It was determined the submarine *Orel* blew up, and they thought it took *Kirov* with it."

"Yes, until the damn ship re-appeared in the Pacific," said Nordhausen, running his hand over his well balded head. "There was quite a mystery surrounding that. NATO couldn't believe they could have failed to track that ship all the way to the Pacific."

"Right," said Paul, "I recall that now. It was discovered by the American Submarine *Key West*, and then it returned to Vladivostok. After that, things began to deteriorate when the Chinese started quarreling with the Japanese over oil drilling rights, and then everybody and their dog got into it."

"Well this *Argos Fire* was fetching oil in the Black Sea, and that was the same ship involved in that engagement with the Russian Black Sea Fleet a couple days ago."

"Look," said Maeve. "We need to consider the possibility that the Russians may have discovered some way to move in time. I know that incident with *Kirov* looked like an accident, but the Golem stream is producing evidence of numerous time shifts by that ship. It was involved with that big shooting incident with the US 7th Fleet in the Pacific, and then presumed sunk again."

"But it wasn't sunk," said Paul. "It shifted again, and I think I may know why. We had another massive explosive event when that volcano went off, and that was very near the last reported position of that ship. Suppose the Russians were on to something Maeve. Suppose they were trying to test some means of moving in time, at sea, on a warship like *Kirov*. Then they had an accident just as it was reported on that submarine—a nuclear detonation, and that jives with all the research Robert was digging up on the Russian nuclear testing program. Suppose they have some kind of technology that is catalyzed or energized by these massive explosive events.

"And the British?" said Maeve. "How to they pull off the same hat trick? It's clear that no submarine sunk this *Argos Fire* off the coast of Greece as it was reported. We know very well where that ship went. The only question now is how it got there. You say Fairchild claimed it had something to do with this key?"

"She said exactly that."

"And we strongly suspect the keys were engineered in the future," Robert put in.

"Correct," said Paul, "but we still haven't figured out what they have to do with these time fissures Fairchild mentioned. Here's an idea. Suppose something happened, a massive explosive event. Lord knows there have been hundreds of them on earth through the history—asteroid strikes, super volcanoes, even earthquakes releasing massive amounts of energy. And in recent years we've had a spate of these occurrences. We had the big 9.1 off the coast of Sumatra in late 2004, then the 9.0 off the coast of Japan, and that had a nuclear spin to it as well."

"Fukushima?"

"Exactly. Then we've had all these big volcanic eruptions, the Bardarbunga rift event on Iceland that eventually went ballistic, then the Demon Volcano in the Kuriles. That was worse than Pinatubo—even worse than Krakatoa. And we all know Cumbre Vieja is very unstable. We've tamped down that nightmare twice, but it could go on its own, even with no help from the Assassin Cult."

"So what are you getting at?" Maeve was tapping her finger on the desk as she listened, her eye taking note of a small imperfection in the grain of the wood.

"These fissures had to begin somewhere," said Paul. "They had to be caused by a natural event. Assuming the Russians were on to something, and large explosive events can rupture spacetime, then what could have been the cause of these time fissures?"

"We have no knowledge of them," said Nordhausen, so how can we determine their cause?"

"Fairchild knew about them," said Paul. "This came right from her."

"How did she learn about them?" asked Maeve. "In fact, how did she come by that key herself? Who gave it to her?"

"That's just one reason I have to go back," said Paul. "Assuming these keys were engineered in the future, then that is where they had to come from. Someone either brought them to the past, or sent them here. She also said she believed the keys were used to secure these fissures in time—or to grant access to them! She used those exact words."

"Alright," said Maeve. "If these fissures or time rifts exist, even though we know nothing of them now, they would likely be discovered in the future. Of course they would be an obvious threat to the integrity of the continuum, festering like an open wound. Anyone who wandered into one could shift in time and cause profound changes. So if they discovered these rifts, it makes sense they would have made every effort to secure them."

"You mean put them under lock and key?" Nordhausen smiled. "So what was this Fairchild lady up to? How did she get back in 1941 to look for the key in the Selene Horse?"

"She said she had instructions," said Paul. "Suppose the location of one of the time rifts was revealed to her. Hell, suppose its somewhere off the coast of Greece, and she was given the exact coordinates."

"By who?"

"That's the mystery, but my bet, particularly given our experience, is that it is some operative from a future time."

"Well if she wanted that key, she sure went about it in a sloppy manner," said Maeve. "The Selene Horse was in the British Museum."

"No, it was moved to the London subway system with some of the other Marbles during the Blitz," said Nordhausen. "That, and the invasion buzz, prompted the British to transport some of them to the United States."

"Yes, said Paul, "but did they even know what they had? I discovered that key by chance when that packing crate shifted and the sculpture was chipped."

"Interesting," said Nordhausen, rubbing the back of his balding head. "Then that damn key could have been embedded in the Selene Horse for ages. Hell, perhaps Phidias put it there!"

"Phidias?" Paul gave him a questioning look.

"He's the famous Greek sculptor that work was attributed to. He also carved the image of Zeus at Olympia, regarded as one of the seven wonders of the ancient world, and his sculpture appears all throughout that era, particularly in the Parthenon. His work surpassed all the rest. Hell, suppose the old boy wasn't who he seemed. Suppose he was from the future?"

"An interesting thought," said Paul. "Look, we've already discovered that someone has been meddling with time. We thought we were the first, but it now appears that is not the case. I've suspected that someone has already altered our own history, and it may be that these keys have something to do with that as well. If that key turned up in this ancient Greek sculpture, then somebody put it there deliberately."

"That would have been quite a trick," said Nordhausen. "The Selene Horse was a solid piece of marble. It was placed high up on the east pediment of the Parthenon. I think it had to be placed there while it was being carved, either by Phidias, or one of his assistants."

"It does sound suspicious," said Paul. "If the keys are associated with these time fissures, does this mean one extends all the way back to ancient Greece?"

"That would be a logical assumption," Maeve reasoned.

"How could we not know about it?"

"Well, suppose these rifts formed very recently. In that case, no one prior to our time would have known about them—yet someone from the future would. We know they extend to the past, and if they were discovered, they may have been navigated by future time travelers, and then well hidden and secured. Why they did this is really no mystery—the rifts are very dangerous. They could allow anyone to slip through and alter the continuum. So assuming they were natural, and not manmade fissures, they would have to first locate the source or cause of each rift in order to secure them. Who knows how far back they extend into time? The fact that this key was seeded in an artifact carved in the past is a fairly strong clue. They may have followed the rift back to its end point, and put some security in place there."

"Sounds logical. We already know that the Assassins established secret archives and bases in the past, and had agents in place posted all along key meridians in the history they were targeting. Can we be certain this isn't the work of the Assassins?"

"I'd think it was more like the Order to fashion these keys," said Paul, but we don't know that. Neither side could be involved. It could be a player we have yet to uncover. So I have to get back there and talk with this Fairchild woman again. We need to know more about the key she possesses."

"You think she knows the answer to all of this?"

"She clearly knows something about it. She said she had instructions. I need to find out who gave them to her. There's more to this, and she's involved. So I arranged a meeting on the Azores. Kelly is programming the numbers now. Fairchild wants this key, so let's see if we can find it."

"You said it went down with *Rodney*," said Maeve. "How will you manage that?"

"Oh, if I do go back to August of 1941, we won't find it there. But we can look for it somewhere else."

Those words held far more than Maeve was prepared to entertain at that moment, for clearly Paul had another time shift in mind.

"Somewhere else?" she said, an edge of suspicion creeping into her voice.

Chapter 15

"**Where?**" Maeve folded her arms, a determined look on her face. She could sense that there was another time mission in the offing here, and not just a friendly jaunt to the Azores to chat with this Fairchild lady.

"Anywhere," said Paul. "You said yourself the key was just sitting there in the Selene Horse, in the British Museum. If we target a time before the Blitz it should still be there."

"So you think you can just waltz into the British Museum with a rock hammer, chip a piece off the Selene Horse and say thank you very much?"

"Something like that."

"Oh, be realistic, Paul. There will be security there. Alarms, guards. The risk of apprehension would be very great."

"Well then how about we target the time they were being moved into the subway system?"

"I can help on that," said Nordhausen. "I've been looking into the Elgin Marbles while you were gone, Paul, and I found out where they were stored during the war—at the Aldwych branch of the Tube. The entrance was on the Strand. In fact, it was once called Strand Station before they renamed it, and it's Charing Cross today. Stephan Walter mapped it all out, including all sorts of historical oddities found beneath London. Did you know they found old Viking weapons, and a helmet dated to the battle of Waterloo, in that vicinity? It was also known as the suicide hotspot of the Thames."

"And they stored the marbles near there?"

"Right beneath New Oxford Street, just up Kingsway from the Strand. The British Museum station was very close. Well, they suspended passenger service for that line on September 21st, 1940, and then made them available as wartime shelters. It's a lucky thing they were moved there, because the Duveen Gallery where they had been displayed was badly damaged by German bombing. So they had it all planned out, and even called the whole thing "Operation Elgin." Most of the Marbles remained there in the Tube until the 25th of November, 1948. Only a few were eventually moved in that shipment on *Rodney*. I've got the whole thing wired."

"How did they move them?" asked Paul.

"They were all crated up, about 100 tons, and then transported using what was called a low-loader lorry. They went to the London Transport Depot at Lillie Bridge, Kensington, and then they were moved over the rail line to the Aldwych Station. A bit of a roundabout way to get them there, but I suppose they knew what they were doing back then. When the Blitz started, and the Germans used 1000 pound bombs, they started to think the Tube was not safe enough. That's probably when they got the idea to ship them over to Boston, though I know of no planned shipment other than the one on *Rodney*."

"Interesting that the Selene Horse was moved," said Paul. "Could they have known about the key?"

"I hardly think so," said Nordhausen. "It wasn't chipped at the base and exposed until you were there aboard *Rodney*."

"Well, that whole chain of custody there gives us ample means for intervention. I could pose as a truck driver, lorryman, loader."

"You?" Maeve protested. "I hardly think you look the part."

"I would do much better," said Nordhausen. "I can manage a fairly good British accent, and pose as an official from the museum wanting to fret over the shipment somewhere en-route. It will have likely happened anyway, and to the workers involved I would just seem another bothersome official wanting to stick my nose in it. Just tell me how to find the key, Paul. I'll fetch it double quick!"

"Still risky," said Maeve. "And your assignment to the mission is a large part of that."

"What? Me? Look here, I've made a firm resolution not to muck about in the history. Lord knows we've seen the damage it can cause."

"Yet they'll be crated," said Paul. "A hundred tons of them. You would have to go through the crates to find the one housing the

Selene Horse."

"Well, they also used part of that Tube as a air raid shelter. That's another angle to get us close during an air raid."

"A lot of people crowded into one place," said Maeve, "and most likely well segregated from the artwork storage areas. No. What we need is to find a way to get at them without all these human obstacles, drivers, laborers, museum officials, guards, and crowds of frightened people. It's not the sort of environment you can go crate hunting in, let alone breaking into the crate and willfully damaging a priceless piece of artwork."

"There is one other idea that came to mind," said Paul. "We could try getting to the Marbles before they got shipped into London."

"When was that?"

"Early eighteen hundreds," said Nordhausen. "The 7th Earl of Elgin actually wanted them for a home he was planning to build, and he was using one of his own ships after he finagled a way to get at them in the Parthenon. It was called the *Mentor*, and it suffered a little mishap on the route home."

"That's what I was thinking of," said Paul. "The ship went down in a storm."

"Correct," said Nordhausen. "Sea transport of heavy items is always chancy. I'm amazed the British tried it in World War Two. Just two days out of port, the *Mentor* encountered rising winds and seas, and the Captain, a man named Hegland, found the ship was taking on water. He advised they run for the nearest port, which was Avlemonas on San Nikolo Bay, on the Island of Kythira. As they approached the port both of their anchors failed to secure to the seabed, and the ship was in very heavy waters. They tried to maneuver, but ran afoul of some rocks, and the whole thing went down, marbles and all. They eventually hired seven divers and mounted a salvage operation, but it took a full two years to get everything up."

"I like that," said Paul. "If we could get to them first, then we could get the key before it ever reached London."

Maeve shook her head. "You propose doing a little scuba diving yourself? Didn't you hear? It took them two years to recover everything."

"I won't do the diving, but I know someone who can—that ship, the *Argos Fire*. They'll have well trained divers, even a submersible."

Maeve rolled her eyes. "And just how do you propose to commandeer their ship, then move it in time to the desired point for this little salvage operation?"

"Alright, forget the submersible. Perhaps we could just borrow their divers."

"And how do you get them there? When did this happen, Robert?"

"17th September, 1802. I did a good bit of research on this since Paul told us how he found that key. But she has a good point there, Paul. We can move you about easily enough, but divers?"

"Never mind that for now," said Paul. "First I have to keep my appointment in the Azores. I'll meet with them, propose these operations, and see what they say. That ship moved in time, and we still don't really know how for sure. If they had some other means of pulling that off, I'd like to know about it, wouldn't you, Maeve? After all, here we are trying to salvage this operation, and we've got these ships shifting into WWII! We need to get to the bottom of this, and if need be, to find a way to get to the bottom of San Nikolo Bay on a quiet night in 1802. It's perfect! No one will see us, because it will all happen underwater. We find the Marbles using hand held radar gizmos, or night optics. Then we locate the Selene Horse and get that damn key. If it does secure another time rift, then I think I can tell you where it is. I copied those numbers I found on the shaft of the key, and I've done some checking. They're map coordinates!" He smiled, a mischievous light in his eye.

* * *

The longer they looked at the readings the more precarious the situation became. The Golem Module had clearly identified the initial Point of Divergence as emanating from the accident on July 28th, 2021, and involving both the Russian submarine *Orel* and the battlecruiser *Kirov*. While *Orel* was destroyed, *Kirov* was displaced in time by almost exactly 80 years. Yet the data stream now showed the ship's position in time did not remain stable, and the damage it was causing to the integrity of the continuum was considerable every time it moved.

"I don't understand how the ship is moving in each case," said Paul. "A few of the displacements seem to be the obvious result of these massive explosive events, but there are others where that is not the case. Their second shift was also catalyzed by the use of nuclear weapons, and they end up moving slightly forward in time, into 1942. That's when they wreak havoc with the British Operation Pedestal."

"Some real oddities crop up there," said Nordhausen, his eyes running over the Golem reports. "This one didn't end with a bang, but a whisper. You'll want to read these reports I've managed to pull out of the data stream. It seems they cut a deal with the British and were ready to accept internment at St. Helena, but they vanished."

"That had to be another time shift," said Paul. 'This is what I mean. What catalyzed that shift? There was no reported explosion, not natural or manmade. Yet they turn up in the Timor Sea a day later, and there is no way they could have sailed from St. Helena to the Australian coast in that time."

"Alright," said Nordhausen, "they raise hell with the Japanese, yet the data shows a marked difference from the history when they arrive."

"Yes, Yamamoto forsake the Midway operation in favor of a plan aimed at isolating Australia. The Japanese operation in the data was to strike at Darwin, and push further south from the Solomons. But the actions of this ship end up causing so much disruption to the Japanese plan that they fail to coordinate. The Americans produce another miracle victory north of the Solomons, and the Japanese carriers are busted up almost as badly as they would have been at Midway."

"At least they did something right," said Maeve, cringing at all these deviations in the history.

'Well it seemed to set the war back on a normal course in the Pacific," said Paul. "Then the ship moved forward again, and without any explosive event. Correct Robert?"

"Correct. I find nothing indicating they used nukes on the Japanese, and no natural event of any consequence near the action."

"Goddammit," Paul swore. "How are they moving?"

"The Russians clearly have something up their sleeve Paul," said Maeve, "Robert did some digging and it looks like they were playing with time effects in the nuclear testing program."

Paul stroked his chin, thinking. "It must have something to do with their reactors. That's a nuclear propulsion system on *Kirov*— dual naval reactors. The energy driving these unassisted shifts has to be coming from that propulsion system. Robert, are you sure you haven't missed anything?"

"I was very thorough," said Nordhausen. "If the Russians did come up with a technology they could use in tandem with their nuclear propulsion system, then they've kept the secret well."

"Alright…" Paul spread out a chart he had been drawing, with lines indicating the known movements in time they had postulated for the Russian ship. "The war starts revving up in the Pacific, and *Kirov* puts to sea," he said. "It is involved in that big incident with the US 7th Fleet, and then vanishes again. This time we have an assist— the Demon Volcano. Where did they go?"

"1945," said Nordhausen. "I've got variation data in the Kuriles very near the ship's last reported position in 2021. They supported Russian operations there, then moved south and ran into the American Pacific Fleet. Then all hell breaks loose. First off, there is evidence that the ship did not move alone this time. I have data on at least two other vessels."

"Most likely part of the battlegroup *Kirov* was operating with in

2021," said Paul.

"My God," said Maeve, clearly bothered. "Three ships now? What did they do?"

"Oh nothing much, they sunk an American aircraft carrier, and a battleship, and with a nuke. It pissed off Halsey and the Americans so bad that they bombed Vladivostok."

Maeve looked at the ceiling, agonizing over the damage to the history. "That's in the data stream?"

"I'm afraid so," said Nordhausen.

"Then why don't I know about it? That would be one of the most significant events in modern history."

"Because they weren't finished," said Paul grimly. "Maybe you did know about it at one time, but then they continued to operate, and things changed again. Unless we were safe in a Nexus Point, we would have changed right along with that history."

"You're saying that as long as they remain a free radical in time, that the history cannot solidify?"

"Correct. Their actions in 1945 may have generated a Heisenberg Wave to migrate changes forward to our time, but it could have been swamped by a larger wave generated later. That nuke they used in 1945 moved them in time again."

"All three ships?"

"No," said Robert. "Two were reported sunk. Only *Kirov* moved."

"Where?"

"To 1908."

Maeve's initial silence underscored the gravity of that development. "They went further back in time?"

"Apparently so," said Robert. "And this is where we really get red lines all through the history module. The whole course of events begins to spin off in wild directions. There's a big battle in the Tushima Strait near Oki Island that was reported as an engagement with a rogue Russian armored cruiser, but it re-starts the Russo-Japanese war, and this time the Japanese don't settle so easily. They occupy all of the Kuriles, Sakhalin Island, and even invade and occupy Vladivostok. It's a major variation in the history of the Pacific."

"Of which I know nothing whatsoever," said Maeve again.

"Because the Heisenberg Wave hasn't reached us and finalized those events," said Paul.

It was something right out of his Time Theory, but a principle they had seen in very real terms after their missions. Changes made in a past meridian would begin to migrate forward in time, but they could not finalize until the Nexus Point occupied by the initiator of those changes was terminated, eliminating any further possibility of revision. "This whole thing is still in play," he explained. "The ship is still in the past, and has not returned to our time, as far as we know. So things are still riding the whirlwind they've created."

"Then there's a chance that none of this crap will ever happen?" said Nordhausen. "The Golem stream is picking this stuff up as if it were history."

"Because that is what the meridian will look like if the Heisenberg Wave *does* complete its work," said Paul. "Remember, what happened during the *Bismarck* operation? We got all sorts of conflicting possible outcomes in the data stream. One version showed the British sinking *Bismarck*, another showed the ship making a safe return to Saint Nazaire in France. One showed *Bismarck* docked at Brest, and a fourth showed it turning out into the Atlantic to link up with a German oiler and raising hell for two months. The Golems were just indicating the most probable outcomes as a weight of opinion, yet they could reach no conclusion, because our operation was still underway, and we were in a safe Nexus Point here, still capable of changing things. That Russian ship is still out there somewhere, operating in time, and so these events cannot yet solidify to a certain outcome. "

"Then the Heisenberg wave isn't moving?"

"It is, but slowly. It moved forward to the 1940s, because the ship did as well. Now it's stuck there, just like that ship, and only moving with the arrow of time, day by day. It could even dissipate when it strikes Paradox Time on July 28, 1941. This whole series of events could be re-written by the backwash."

"Thank god for that," said Nordhausen, because the outcomes being reported are frightening deviations. Russia's civil war never ends. The nation fragments into several warring states. Sergei Kirov finally consolidates power in Moscow and leads the Soviet State, and his chief rival jumped from the Reds to the White movement, assassinated Denikin, and founded a state being called the Orenburg Federation."

"Who?" asked Maeve. "Was it Stalin?"

"Nope. That was one thing that bothered me. I could find no mention of the man of steel. Come to find out, he was killed in 1909—assassinated while in prison."

"That's a *huge* variation," said Maeve.

"No argument there. Then the Orenburg Federation goes on to side with Nazi Germany in 1940, and Russia faces a war on two fronts."

"Who led that federation?" Maeve looked almost pallid with shock.

"A man named Ivan Volkov—a real mystery figure in the history. He was active as early as 1909, and battled Kirov for control of the Bolshevik party until he was finally ousted. But the data on this man is very nebulous. I could find nothing on his parents or ancestors. And another name keeps popping up—from the Free Siberian State. I have data indicating he joins Sergei Kirov and leads the Siberians in the fight against Volkov."

"Who?" Maeve sounded like she had caught someone in her library messing up the careful order of her books.

"A man named Karpov—Vladimir Karpov, but the Golem readings on him are somewhat obscure too. I'm focusing my research on the Siberian, but I can't find any roots on this man either."

"Show me," said Maeve, the light of battle in her eyes.

Part VI

The Mirror

"I saw, not with the eyes of the body, but with those of the mind, my own figure coming toward me ... As soon as I shook myself out of this dream, the figure had entirely disappeared."

— Johann Wolfgang von Goethe

Chapter 16

Karpov could sense that something was wrong, even as Tasarov and Dobrynin had heard the impending edge of Paradox in that deep, unaccountable sound, though he knew nothing about that. It was not a sound for him, but something deeper. It was not even a vibration, but more a sense that he was being watched, his every move noted and marked, and the eyes were jealous and vengeful.

He could not shake this uncomfortable feeling. Something was taking account of him, measuring, considering, musing on his fate. Was it Kymchek? He was saved from the meaty fists of Grilikov, and now adorned in his new General's uniform, but Karpov knew he was still a dangerous and scheming man. Is that what tickled his mind with this odd sensation of alarm? No. Kymchek could be managed, controlled, leashed and ridden. And no single man like that could account for this strange mood that had fallen over him, a feeling that his every move was being watched—not just now, but every step he had ever taken in the past, and every choice he might make in the future as well. It was most disconcerting, and it did nothing to calm his volatile temperament.

Was it his own face in the mirror, the face that seemed to be haunting him every time he looked into that glass? Was it that old, guilt ridden mouse of a man he had once been, his weaker self, returning to plague him in this trying time? It was most unnerving, so much so that he had abandoned his personal headquarters there at Ilanskiy, and moved back aboard the fleet flagship. It was a very fateful decision.

The massive shape of *Tunguska* hovered in the sky, high above the tiny hamlet of Ilanskiy, tethered to a temporary mooring pole augmented by ground anchors. Beyond this, both *Irkutsk* and *Novosibirsk*, a pair of sturdy battleships, rode at elevation, and *Abakan* circled on a wide perimeter patrol, along with *Talmenka*. Karpov was taking no chances that he would be surprised by Volkov's fleet, though he did not think the man would be so foolish as to sortie here again.

Yet our losses were heavy in that last engagement, he thought, damn near half our fleet. *Angara* will be repaired within the week, and that gives me six airships to work with. Kolchak is already making inquiries, and he'll soon want his two battleships back. The need to cluster the fleet here means I have nothing on the Ob River line watching Volkov's troops. It will be another month before my second T-Class airship can join *Tunguska*, but when that ship is ready, we will be in a better position. What to call it?

Kolchak has suggested *Baikal*, but that would lead him easily to claim the ship for the eastern task force. There is some merit to that. The Japanese are breathing right down his neck, and soon it will be December. In fact, they could enter the war at any time, and we must be prepared. Yes… the Japanese. They carved themselves out a nice little empire in Manchuria and by invading all of Primorsky Province, and then some. They hold all of Sakhalin Island, a good chunk of Khabarovsk, and even have troops in Amur, Chita and Mongolia. The threat they pose is significant. They have an estimated 25 divisions in their Kwantung army, and we have yet to determine what their war plans may be now.

They have the far east. The bastards took it from us! I could have prevented all that, rolled them out of Sakhalin Island, and occupied all of Korea… if not for the betrayal of my own comrades. Volsky and Fedorov have no idea what damage they have done to the nation. Look at Russia now! Yet Volkov is the greater threat for the next several months. Tyrenkov has detected no buildup on the part of the Japanese. No. I think they will make the same foolish mistake they did in our history, and strike south into the Pacific. To do that, they know they must take and hold the Philippines, and that means war with the United States.

All things in time, he thought. I will decide what to do about the Japanese later. For now, I have more urgent matters to consider, the least of which is my own personal fate.

Yes, he could feel it again, rising like a thrum of anxiety in his chest, a pulse of adrenaline that was most uncomfortable. Yet that was good, or so he believed. I cannot afford to be comfortable and sedate, nor can I simply wait on Volkov and the Japanese. I must act, but before I can realize any plans, there is the matter of late July to consider. What will happen?

He had given the matter some thought earlier, and even discussed it with Tyrenkov. July 28th was just around the corner now, a few days away. The ship had first arrived here on that day, but would it come again? How would that be possible if it was already in this world? How could I be sitting there on the bridge of *Kirov* and yet be here?

It was only a very brief interlude, he thought. *Kirov* was only here for twelve days, and then we vanished after I pounded the American fleet to teach them who they were dealing with. How was I to know it would blow us into the future again? We knew nothing of Rod-25 at that point, and nothing of Tunguska.

His eyes strayed out the viewport, seeing the imposing shadow of his fleet flagship on the small hamlet below. Yes, he thought, *Tunguska*. Here rides the ship with magic in its bones. I was able to ride those storms through time itself, and perhaps I can do so again. It should be easy enough. I'll just go up and find another good thunderstorm, and go... elsewhere. But where? Would I appear in the past again? The future?

He thought deeply now. Somehow I knew that I would return here when I left 1908 in *Tunguska*. I could feel it, sense it. In fact I demanded it! Destiny needed me here, to re-write that stupid little book Tyrenkov found. But where does destiny need me now? Yes, I am fated. I know this. I can feel it. Yet my fate seems to be haunted by a shadow now, something I can sense and dimly perceive, but not really see. Does it have something to do with the coming of the ship, our first arrival here?

On the one hand, how could *Kirov* manifest here given the deeply fractured history of this world? The building of that ship rests on the whole convoluted structure and future development of the Soviet Union. First the cold war must settle in, and then we must design and build the four ships in the early *Kirov* Class. Our ship was built from their bones, rising from the decrepit ruin of the Russian Navy to sail again for the Rodina. Will all of that happen? Will Volsky and Fedorov and all the others join the navy and find themselves on that ship again? Will I do that, fighting my way up through the ranks to win that seat in the Captain's chair? So many dominoes must fall for that to happen, but suppose it does pan out that way. It would still take that stupid accident aboard the *Orel* to trigger the incident that sent the ship back through time. How could all that repeat itself with the Russian civil war still raging even as Germany now invades the Soviet Union?

His logic was much the same as Fedorov's in this, though he could not know that. Yet behind it, he had the same feeling he might have upon discovering a young ambitious man in the ranks below him, a rival aiming to climb higher, just as he had. Only this time that man was his own self! If Kirov did return, it would be that other Karpov that would now threaten his hard won position here.

I am here, am I not? I am sitting right here in this chair, staring at myself in the mirror. Look at me now... Look at that scar on my cheek... look at my eyes... Power has a way of draining a man at times, even as it feeds him. I have been feeling very odd of late, thin and attenuated, as though I was not really all here.

That thought gave him pause, because he knew he did not belong in this world. Yet his very presence here, the image he was staring at in that mirror, all depended on that first coming of *Kirov* in 1941. It argued that event simply *must* occur, or how could he even be sitting there considering all of this?

The world we first entered was not like this one, he thought. Russia was not fractured, and Fedorov's history was so intact that he could count the hairs on Admiral Tovey's head with his library of books. But this world... My god, it is a nightmare of variation, ripped apart by our own blind intervention, and I am much to blame for that. Yet now the ship is already here. It slipped in through the back door this time. Tyrenkov tells me he believes it first appeared here in June of 1940! They were probably just trying to get home but, for some odd reason, any time the ship moved forward it got stuck here in this damn war again.

Why is that? Are the powers of Rod-25 limited? They obviously had that damn control rod aboard *Kazan*, otherwise how did that sub get back to 1908 when they came after me? And Fedorov was there earlier, unless that radio call I received from him was another lie. Yet when they shifted forward from 1908, they got stuck here again, and they have been here ever since. Perhaps the shadow this war casts on time is simply too deep to be easily penetrated. Yet I was able to go forward from this time by using that stairway at the inn. I arrived there too late. The war in 2021 had already started, and there was nothing I could do at that point but retrace my footfalls back down those steps.

So perhaps we were all sent here again for some reason, just as I appeared here at a most opportune time when I rode that storm aboard *Tunguska*. It is as if destiny calls us here, keeps us here...

Now he had that feeling again that this time was becoming a prison cell for him, and that he was sitting there, staring at himself in the mirror, while waiting for his own execution.

What will happen to me if I take no action, and simply remain here? Does that ship really arrive again from the future, and is another version of myself sitting there in the Captain's chair on the bridge? Is that even possible? How could there be two versions of the same person?

Now, as he stared into the mirror, he had the strange sensation that the face there looking back at him was that other self, a dark ghostly self, waiting to manifest here and claim his life when it did so. He was sitting there, looking at his own doppelganger, and it gave him a chill just to see his own face.

Perhaps I could find out what happens, if we could get that damn stairway finished in another few days. We'll have to test it, of course. Someone will have to go up those stairs—definitely up, because it will be too dangerous to do the inverse. Going down to the past could change everything in this reality again, and that could be even more dangerous than these things I now contemplate about the ship's imminent arrival. So someone must go up those stairs.

Tyrenkov? He's an able man. He had the presence of mind to fetch that book the last time, and that was most useful intelligence. Perhaps he could determine what happens by simply going to the future and reading the history. Then he could come back and tell me whether the ship vanishes again, and if it does he could find out where it goes. Tyrenkov is very reliable.

Yet it is not his fate at stake here, but mine. I am the one with my ass in the chair aboard *Kirov*, even as I sit here now. Something tells me that arrangement will be very uncomfortable for Mother Time. She'll have to do something… yes, but what?

For safety's sake, I must plan to take some operation before the 28th of July. I must either complete that stairway, and hope it still works, and that failing, I must pray for bad weather and take to the skies again in *Tunguska*. If take the latter course, nothing can be left to chance. July can be very warm, yet perhaps I can use my computer jacket to fetch up historical weather data. Yes, I must do this.

He looked out the window again, having the strangest thought that as he did so, the image in the mirror continued to stare at him. He could not stop himself from glancing at the mirror again, and of course, he would meet his own gaze there and find his suspicion had been correct.

He was being foolish, he knew, but that was the essence of how he felt just now. He was being watched… Something was considering him, just as he ruminated on all these strategies and options, all these unseen dangers and fears. The ticking of the clock on his desk suddenly seem a loud and annoying thing, so much so that he stood up and batted it aside, sending it clattering to the floor, the glass face of the timepiece shattered, just like the history he was living out now. He looked at the calendar, edgy, harried. Then he reached for the telephone on his desk and rang up his chief of staff.

"Solokov—find me the weather master. I want to know his outlook for the coming weeks. And get me the chief of engineers. I want a full report on that construction project and expected completion time, within the hour. Then have dinner sent here to my offices, and invite Kymchek. I want to speak with him tonight."

"As you wish, sir," came Solokov's dull voice—right out of his sullen, dull head, thought Karpov.

If I do mount an operation, and leave this time by one means or another, will I ever get back? Thinking I can impose my will on time is one thing, but in *Tunguska*, I really have no way of controlling the displacement that occurs. At least that stairway seemed to be more predictable. But what if it does work again? Then let me assume that *Kirov* does appear here on July 28th. What then? Will that other Karpov do everything I did before? That is not possible. The British are thick as thieves with Volsky and Fedorov now, so the damn Royal Navy would not be hounding us at all. That world we came to no longer exists. If the ship does return, then it will be to some other world, and not this one.

One question tumbled after another in his mind now, and behind them all was that thrum of fear. What if they *do* arrive here? What if there is only this one world, and no others? I'm supposed to be right there on that ship, and yet here I am at Ilanskiy. And what if that ship stays put this time, and never leaves? If I go up those stairs, I might escape this little Paradox, but then I might be trapped in any future time I reach, and prevented from returning to this place because I am already here! If I use *Tunguska* and try to find another storm, who knows where I will end up this time? I might find myself back in the past again, with all of this to live over. This is madness!

Pacing sometimes helped, a way to burn off the fight or flight reflex, and make the looming potential energy in his mind kinetic. Yet the notion that he was being tried and judged still harried him, and he knew it was more than the old pangs of guilt that once shadowed his every thought.

I did what was necessary, he thought stubbornly. The Americans had every round I fired coming, every missile, every warhead—yes, even the special warheads I was forced to use when they persisted.

They were behind the misery that had befallen the Russian Republic he grew up in, slowly engineering the fall of the Soviet Union with careful subterfuge, clandestine intelligence operations, deception, economic bullying, and sometimes even military threats. They lined up their armored cavalry and heavy tank divisions in Europe for decades, until the real center of gravity in the world centered on the whirlwind of the Middle East.

Both Russia and the United States courted client states there, arming them, and then watching them quarrel with one another, until the desert sands became a proving ground for the weapon systems each side so willingly supplied to tyrants and sheiks of the wayward, oil drenched sands.

When they wanted something, the Americans just took it, thought Karpov. Saddam took Kuwait, then the United States took it back, and all of Iraq for good measure, until they found out what a hornet's nest the whole place was. After ten years of fighting in Afghanistan and Iraq, they eventually pulled out, and then ISIS swept in like a bad squall at the edge of the so called "Arab Spring," and undid nine years, and nine hundred billion dollars worth of nation building in Iraq, in only 90 days.

The Democrats wanted nothing more to do with the wars the Republicans left them. Instead they pursued their agenda by other means, smiling diplomacy and economic incentives offered to Ukraine, until the Prime Minister they put in place there balked and got too cozy with Putin. They worked to quickly remove the man, and shepherd Ukraine into the NATO camp, but Putin would have none of that. He took back the Crimea, armed and supported Russian Separatists, and within months there was all out war in the Donbass, one of the Soviet Union's old industrial heartlands, as essential to Russia's sphere of influence as the old industrial middle states of America had once been—before they came to be called the "Rust

Belt." Karpov admired Putin in many ways. He was a man who also did what was necessary, and when he saw what was rightfully his, he simply took it.

Once I struggled to be a man of that ilk, he thought. Once I had to wring my hands and agonize over whether I should try to take a single ship, but no longer. What I need to do now is unmistakably clear, and it must begin by eliminating Ivan Volkov from the pages of this badly re-written history. Ivan Volkov—the prophet—Ivan the Terrible. Yet now you meet your match, and then some—Vladimir Karpov, Vlad the Impaler, Vlad the Destroyer—and you will be my first order of business.

But soon there is this little matter of Paradox I have been contemplating. I have two means of avoiding it, yet I don't like the idea of turning tail and running now. What if I do nothing, and simply stand my ground here? After all, I fought for it. I earned the power I now hold, and I am a real force in this world, much unlike the witless Captain I was when kibitzing on the ship with Volsky and Fedorov.

It was all I could do back then to muster the courage to try and take the ship, and I needed Orlov for that. I could not do it on my own. No! I'm not going anywhere. I'm going to stay exactly where I am, and stare time right in the eye come July 28th. I am Vladimir Karpov! We will see who blinks first, and who she chooses to cede the hours and days that follow in this world. Time is no fool. That other Karpov, the man I once was, did not have an ounce of the iron that now runs in my veins. If any man could rightfully call himself Stalin, the man of steel, it would be me.

So time must choose. My actions here have made my case well enough. Without my opposition, it is very likely that Ivan Volkov could help Germany to an early victory in this war. Time must certainly know that. What can that other Karpov do but quibble with Volsky?

He felt a quiet tremor in his hand, unwilling to interpret it as jangled nerves or anxious fear. Instead he clenched his fist to chase it away, a determination forming in him now. Yes, time would soon have to make a very important choice…. Very important indeed. And yet, like so much of Fedorov's muse on all of these issues, he was wrong.

Karpov's own sense of self-importance had gone to his head like too much vodka. He was not indispensible, for time had used and discarded so many others before him, men who call themselves great and believed they would live forever. They had their moment, and died, like all things must, and they were now all in their graves. The deserts were littered with the ruins of their achievements, and graven images sat weathered by wind and sun, now mocking testimony to their hubris and arrogance.

So as Mother Time sat listening to him, watching him, waiting for her hour of vengeance, the thought that Karpov was too essential, too important to all that was now transpiring never entered her head. Yet, not even Time was all powerful, and something had happened, born of Karpov's inner weakness, not his strength, that would now change everything. Harried and fearful, he had moved from his headquarters at Ilanskiy to the Admiral's stateroom aboard *Tunguska*, and that small decision was going to count more in the equation of his fate than all his devious planning would ever know.

Chapter 17

In spite of his inner bravado, that bothersome feeling of anxiety would just not leave Karpov. It was more than the inevitable security threat now that he had joined in open war with Orenburg. Even though he had captured Volkov's number one security man, he was under no illusions about Kymchek at this stage, and he knew the man had labored for years to build a network of spies and agents that was still a serious threat.

He was pleased to hear the knock on his stateroom door at precisely the correct time for the day's intelligence briefing. Tyrenkov was very punctual, and a moment later he stood before Karpov's desk, handing him a plain manila envelope.

"How is our new recruit? Are you watching Kymchek closely? You and I know quite well that he would never have turned so easily. Yet we must be discreet here, and give this dog the leash to see where he might end up sticking his nose. Perhaps he will dig up a bone or two."

"Of course," said Tyrenkov. "Yet that uniform you have given him will open quite a few doors."

"You will arrange a nice little honor guard for our newest general. Yes? Just make certain there is one door he never opens, and you know of what I speak."

Tyrenkov certainly knew of that door, though he had only seen it in another time. Even as they spoke, he could hear the carpenters and engineers framing out the new door and surrounding the nearby hearth with paneling to restore the dining room. In time that door would be right there again, as would the stairway it would lead to, though all fresh and new. Would it work as it did before?

"It will not be long now, Tyrenkov," said Karpov, changing the subject. "Kirov has moved five more rifle divisions to join us on the upper Volga, and he has also promised tanks and engineers for the crossing operation."

"Will it be enough sir? Volkov has all of his first and second armies watching that sector."

"Which means those two armies cannot be further south. What we must do now is put in a credible attack, and see if we can pull in his reserves there. Then we will see how long he can hold his position on the Ob River line."

"The information Kymchek has given us this far checks out well enough," said Tyrenkov.

"Of course it does. Do you think he would be stupid enough to feed us misinformation at this stage? He knows your organization would expose his lies easily enough. No. He will be much more subtle. He is a very clever man."

"Indeed," said Tyrenkov.

Karpov opened the envelope Tyrenkov had delivered for the morning intelligence briefing, taking out a stack of photographs.

"Where did you get these?" said Karpov.

"Our Cairo operation. We've been monitoring British reinforcements arriving through the Suez Canal. They just received a big shipment of tanks, yet as far as I know, none of these vehicles were in that convoy. These photos were taken some weeks earlier, when the British moved troops from Egypt to Lebanon to support their Operation Scimitar. They were so heavy that they had to move by rail."

Karpov took up his magnifying glass, leaning in to have a closer look, his eyes narrowing. "Astounding," he breathed. "This is not possible. These could not have been built by the British. Look at their size! See that man there for scale? Why, it must be at least 30 feet long!"

"Yes sir. That is twice the size of their main heavy Matilda tanks, and is even ten feet longer than the Soviet KV tanks. They have taken great pains to camouflage it, but if you look closely, you will see the main gun is pointing backwards for easier transport. If rotated forward this tank would be 45 feet from the tip of that gun to the rear."

"So this is what has been causing all the trouble for the Germans in the Middle East," said Karpov. "It is very much like modern tank designs from my day."

"Our engineers estimate that it must weigh at least 60 tons."

"Where was it developed?" asked Karpov quickly.

"We don't know."

"You don't know? What is wrong with your operational teams in the United Kingdom? It had to be shipped out of a British port."

"That's the problem, sir. We have not been able to identify any production facility in the United Kingdom, so now we are looking overseas—possibly in India."

"That is preposterous."

"Yet that is the only place outside England where they might have been built. Our thinking is that they were then transported in through Sudan. There aren't many eyes there, and it would be a clever way to sneak them into Egypt."

Karpov nodded his head. "So now we see how the British were able to stop a full German Panzer Division in Northern Lebanon. I didn't believe the reports at first. When news came of the Turkish capitulation, I thought the Germans would kick the British out of Egypt within months. How in the world did they pull this rabbit out of their hat? This is an important development, Tyrenkov. Get me all the information you can on this new British tank."

Being a navy man, Karpov did not immediately recognize the British tank as a Challenger II. The photograph was taken in low light, very grainy, and hastily shot, as the agent was obviously at great risk.

"That is what will eventually win this ground war," said Karpov. "Tanks! It is the one area in which we lag well behind the other powers. There is too little industry here in Siberia, and we will have to rely on cooperation and handouts from Sergei Kirov. My god, we strained to simply build these airships, and there is no way we will ever have any tank production here of any consequence unless Kirov builds them. Do you know we built entire new cities in the Siberian Urals? There was a massive armaments plant called Uralmash at

Yekaterinburg, but it has not been built in this world. We must consider rooting better production facilities there."

"Perhaps you should bring this up with Sergei Kirov at your upcoming meeting," Tyrenkov suggested.

"Don't worry. Kirov will soon be packing up his factory equipment and shipping it all east. Over 1500 factories were evacuated in Soviet Russia and moved here. For the moment, we will just have to make do with the manpower resources we have. But rifle divisions will only take us so far. Volkov is building tanks in Orenburg, and he still controls Chelyabinsk, Magnitogorsk, and Omsk, which were all places where the Soviet factories were relocated. We control Yekaterinburg, and so we must keep it well defended. I predict that place will again become a major armaments production center, as in the history I know, and in exchange for welcoming Sergei Kirov's factory workers and equipment there, we will get our fair share of tanks. Yet that is a year or more off, and much will happen in that time. What is the situation on the German front?"

"They have crossed the border in force. The Soviet air force was smashed at the outset, and the Germans are making rapid progress. Yet much of that is because Kirov has ordered his troops to fall back—especially his armored and mechanized divisions."

"He is no fool, Tyrenkov. Remember, that man knew about the stairway at Ilanskiy. Who knows how many times he went up those stairs? If he did so, and it took him to these years, then he would have seen much of what was happening in the war. So it will be no surprise to me if the Soviets try to avoid the major encirclements and massive losses they suffered in the summer and fall of 1941. If Kirov is crafty, he will trade space for time, husband his armor, and build strong defenses on the Dnieper. That will be the major obstacle to stop the Germans this year."

"At the moment, the Soviets appear to be falling back on Minsk."

"Yes, but they will not save that city, and if they attempt to do so they will lose 600,000 men in the Minsk pocket. Did you send that message packet I prepared to Kirov?"

"Yes sir. The information was delivered securely, and with no problems."

"Good. Then Kirov will know what happens at Minsk. He will be much better off screening Moscow and holding at Smolensk, or forward of that position if he can. And he must hold Kiev as long as possible, and all the line of the lower Dnieper. As for us, we must do all we can to deal with the significant threat posed by Volkov. That man will have just enough force to tie down hundreds of thousands of Soviet troops on the Volga. How is the planning going for Autumn Wind?"

"We have most of the Tartar and Cossack Cavalry Divisions moving through Perm now," said Tyrenkov. "The first six rifle divisions will deploy through there soon, and ten more will follow. Soviet buildup on the upper Volga has been slow, so we cannot yet assign a firm jump off date for the offensive."

"And Volkov?"

"As you predicted, sir, the Ob River offensive has been cancelled. In fact, Volkov has pulled his mechanized divisions out, and he is moving them west to the Volga front."

"Of course," said Karpov. "He will leave five or ten rifle divisions on the line, and a strong reserve at Omsk, but I have every intention of taking that city back as soon as possible."

"Yet we have only eight divisions on that front," said Tyrenkov.

"That will change," said Karpov. "We will raise ten divisions every month and, by autumn, we will be ready to launch a major offensive on the Ob simultaneous with the Autumn Wind operation on the Volga. 1941 will all be about buildup and re-rooting the Soviet industrial capacity. The Germans will soon overrun two thirds of the existing Soviet coal mines. Luckily we have resources in abundance here, and soon Sergei Kirov will be sending us the engineers, skilled labor, and all the machinery we need to make good use of those resources. On that note, tell Bogrov to get the ship ready for a long haul operation."

"Sir? We are leaving Ilanskiy now?"

"Don't worry, Tyrenkov. I think Volkov learned his lesson with that last little disaster he planned here. I have told Kolchak that I will need both *Irkutsk* and *Novosibirsk* to stand by here in my absence. He can have them back after *Baikal* is delivered to the fleet next month. In the meantime, I am taking *Tunguska* to Moscow to meet with Sergei Kirov and discuss these matters. We need to get our piece of the pie. I will show Kirov that he simply has no hope of winning this war without us, and extract considerable concessions."

"What about the Japanese, sir?" said Tyrenkov. "Kolchak is always droning on about the Japanese."

"They will not pose a serious threat until later this year. I wonder if they will attack Hawaii as planned?"

"Hawaii?" Tyrenkov seemed surprised. "We know they are rehearsing some big naval operation, but the target has not yet been determined. Several of my operatives believe it may be Singapore or Manila."

"Oh, it will be both," said Karpov with a smile, "and more. In my history, the Japanese attacked the big American naval base at Pearl Harbor on December 7th, of this year. That kicked off their major campaign into southeast Asia. They already have significant holdings in China and Primorskiy, so I see no reason for them to try and push further into our territory. No. I think the Strike South camp will now win by default in Japan. They will push all the way to the Solomons, and possibly farther, and come very close to destroying the American Pacific Fleet in doing so. Don't forget, Tyrenkov. I know every plan, every battle, and every mistake they will make. Kolchak has nothing to worry about for the time being."

"Yet he can be very persistent, sir. He is already complaining that the buildup here serves no purpose. Soon he'll be demanding more than those two airships. He'll want divisions to pad his defenses along Lake Baikal."

"Then get rid of the fool."

That statement fell like hot coals in water, and Tyrenkov inclined his head, wanting to be certain Karpov was serious. "Are you instructing me to plan his removal?"

"He's a nuisance, Tyrenkov, just as you say. He will question every operation I plan, haggle for troops and material, pull on my resources. If I'm to get anything done here, I'll need a free hand. I have accepted this role as his Lieutenant for appearances only. It is clear who is really running things in Siberia, and so I see no reason why we should not make that a permanent truth. Get rid of him. Do it carefully, and make it look like Kymchek planned the whole thing. In fact, we'll arrange to have him confess whatever we decide to do. For now, I'm off to Moscow to negotiate with Sergei Kirov. By the time I get back, the restoration of the inn at Ilanskiy will be complete. Then you and I have some very interesting options to consider. Volkov may soon have more to worry about than the buildup on the upper Volga or his pathetic defensive line on the Ob. Remember what we can do with *Tunguska!* Yet for the moment, I must cement our position with the Soviets and get a good deal for Siberia."

Tyrenkov nodded, seeing that distant look in Karpov's eye again, as if he were seeing things yet to come, and realizing that he may be doing exactly that. It was an eerie feeling to know this man was from the future, to realize that he had even seen a tiny glimpse of that future when he went up those stairs. What was he planning, he wondered?

"One more thing," said Karpov. "Have we found all of Kymchek's sleeper cells here in Ilanskiy?"

"We've identified several suspicious men, but the investigation continues."

"Get them all, Tyrenkov, every last one. I've had the most uncomfortable feeling that someone was watching me of late. Round up these agents and deal with them."

"Won't that make Kymchek suspicious?"

"Of course it will. We wouldn't want him to get too comfortable in that new uniform of his, would we?"

"I understand, sir." Tyrenkov saluted, and withdrew, thinking things over.

So, you want Kolchak out of the picture, he mused. Very well, Admiral, I can arrange that. And yes, I will keep my place as your trusted Lieutenant for a time as well. But there may come another time when I have to deal with matters myself, and let us hope that you do not present any obstacles to me. After all, I control the entire intelligence network, don't I. You will know only what I tell you, and in time you will do only what I tell you as well. But first things first— Kolchak.

Chapter 18

Tunguska rose into the darkening sky, with lightning licking the flanks of rising clouds, and the wind up at 30 knots. Air Commandant Bogrov eyed the barometer and wind speed indicators warily, knowing full well how unpredictable the weather could be in Siberia. Even in July, these sudden storms could rise over the marshy taiga, and produce occasional drenching rain.

His imperial majesty wants another storm, he thought. Why else would we be taking to the skies in these conditions? He noted *Irkutsk* and *Novosibirsk* riding at storm anchor on the new mooring towers that had been built, one at Kansk, the other at Ilanskiy. *Abakan* had pulled duty that morning for overwatch deployment, and was up high at 3000 meters to ride out the coming front.

We'd best steer northwest, right into the wind, thought Bogrov. That will slow us down considerably, but we'll soon pick up the lower Yeseni River north of Krasnoyarsk, and I can follow that due north for a time so we can stay clear of nosy airship patrols that Volkov might have up out of Omsk. Then I'll turn west, and fly well north of Omsk and head for Perm. Karpov wants to see how things are with his second army supporting the Soviets on the upper Volga. Rig for long haul operations, he says. That's nearly 2500 kilometers to Perm, then another 1000 kilometers to Moscow. It appears his lord high minister of Western Siberia has a hankering to chat with Sergei Kirov again. Well enough. Our fate is tied to the Soviets now, so we had better get on the same page in this opera.

I'll give Karpov one thing, he mused. The man knows a traitor when he sees one, and he won't hesitate to do what is necessary here. Ivan Volkov is a demon from hell, and may he burn there for all eternity when this is all over. Word is the Germans are raising hell itself out west. They've taken Minsk, and now they're hammering at the Fortifications outside Kiev. And up north they've already pushed within 150 kilometers of Smolensk. The whole center of the Soviet line has taken one blow after another from the news I've heard, and I hear quite a lot in my position.

So what's on Karpov's mind this time? Why the urgency to leave now, with the weather loading up and winds like this? Last time we steered for thunderheads things got very strange. That was after that first meeting in Moscow, and the audacious little run over Berlin.

Bogrov smiled, for that was the one moment in his tenure with Karpov where he actually thought he liked the man. The bastard had the audacity to bomb Berlin! It was nothing more than a pin prick, mere symbolism, but that took nerve. Herr Hitler isn't likely to forget it, and so whatever Karpov is cooking up in the stew with Sergei Kirov, it had better be nice and hot. If things keep on out west as they are now, the Nazis will be closing in on Moscow by mid to late autumn. Then what? Can they take the place, or will General Winter show up and save the day for us as he did when another little tyrant thought he could beat us—Napoleon.

Yes, I almost thought I could like this man when he stuck it to Berlin. But that last maneuver he pulled in the fight with Volkov galled me, and a good many other men in the fleet. When he burned Big Red like that…. Well I wanted to choke the man. And that slap on the face he gave me, right here in front of the entire bridge crew… I'll have my revenge for that one day, by god. For now it's off to Moscow we go, and another little secret meeting with Kirov.

Assuming we get there… He eyed the storm front again, gauging the height of the clouds ahead. That thunderhead there looks to be 25 kilometers wide, and we can get cells that rise up over 18,000 meters here, with strong convention even above that. So it's no good thinking to ride over top of that little monster. I'll give it a wide berth.

* * *

Karpov sat in his stateroom aboard the ship, looking out the port side windows. He could see the storm building, and it only seemed to feed the inner sense that something was terribly wrong. He had been feeling very harried of late, and very wary. It was as if someone was watching him, which made him take to the airship and forsake his ground quarters at Ilanskiy.

The back stairway is nearly ready, he thought. The engineers are putting the last of the structure in place today, just as I ordered. I told Tyrenkov to put the inn under a double guard, 24 hours per day, and to keep a good eye on Kymchek. In fact, I sent our new General to Kansk, just to be certain he poses no problems.

Time is running thin now, he thought. It's just a matter of days before I have to decide what to do. Should I postpone this meeting in Moscow? Should I head for this storm and see where it might take me? This could be my last chance. Then again, the stairway at Ilanskiy is largely complete. Should I just get down there and try my luck? What if it no longer works as before? What if it comes down to a matter of a centimeter or two and the carpenters made an error? Or should I just do what I decided earlier—nothing—stare time down and dare it to try and lay a hand on me. We'll see who prevails. I don't go down that easily, though perhaps it might be a good idea to design one of those nice little escape pods into *Tunguska*, just like Volkov had on the *Orenburg*.

His eyes strayed furtively to the mirror on the wall, and there he thought he suddenly saw a shadow behind him, some dark formless shape that sent a chill up his spine. He turned quickly, his eyes wide with alarm and fright, but there was nothing there. Looking back at the mirror it seemed as though he had a dizzy spell. His vision blurred momentarily, and he thought he saw himself twice there, another Karpov resolving from the darkness that had been behind his image, a blurry double that told him he must be experiencing the effects of the sudden altitude change.

He shook his head, trying to clear his vision, and reached for the emergency oxygen flask, covering his mouth and nose with the cup and turning the knob with a shaky hand. A moment later he was breathing clean oxygen, and his mind cleared after a few breaths. Yes, he thought. It's just the altitude, the pressure gradient of the storm we're approaching.

Yet it was more than he knew or could even realize at that moment. For far away, in that strange oppressive fog on the seas of oblivion, *Kirov* had plunged that control rod into the glowing heart of its reactor core and rolled the dice on time's roulette wheel for the last time, in a desperate attempt to escape the choking uncertainty that had fallen upon them.

Karpov never heard the last P.A. announcement that Admiral Volsky had made to the crew, nor did he share in that final, quiet moment on the bridge, listening to the men cheer below, and the sound of their joyful song echoing through the ship. He had slipped away from his former comrades like a fallen angel, descending into the hell of his own making, and deciding it was better to rule there than to serve anywhere else.

His every effort after that fall had been to rebuild himself by outwardly restoring his power and authority, his sense of control, and the notion that he was somehow consigned to this fate for a grand purpose. He did not really know whether it was his actions in the past, in 1908, that had caused Russia to fragment as it did, but discovering that Ivan Volkov had also found a way into the past at Ilanskiy was a great shock, another fallen angel that was soon rising to challenge him.

When he realized Volkov could not ever be trusted, he decided he had to be destroyed. Yes, there were many demons in hell, but only one Lucifer—only one could rule, and Karpov was determined to be that man. After learning he could find and destroy Volkov in the future, before he ever set foot down those stairs, he had the heady feeling that he was again the master of all fate and time, and the deciding factor in all these events.

I spared Volkov's life when I could have easily sent Tyrenkov up those stairs with a sub-machinegun squad to finish him, because that was too uncertain an outcome. I could not be sure what his death in the future would do to this time, this world so blighted by his shadow. And another thing—I wanted to do the killing myself. I wanted to show Volkov that I could beat him, man to man, in spite of the fact that his fleet was three times the size of my own.

Now he knows that, and soon he will know even more. I'm going to raise divisions from the Urals to Lake Baikal. Soon all of Siberia will be sending me its sons, men so hardened to the winter that is now befalling the world that they will surely prevail when we join this fight. Yes, soon all of Siberia goes to war, and our first order of business will be Ivan Volkov and his little Orenburg Federation.

We'll muster at Perm, then come down to the upper Volga to join Kirov's troops there. I can move on Ufa, and once I get a good bridgehead there, it will cut off all the troops Volkov has on the upper Volga bend. He'll have to fall back, and he'll be lucky to keep his industrial city at Almetyevsk when he does so. Interesting that he placed a refinery there, just as in our day. That city was not even built until the 1950s. No matter, he won't be able to hold it, and the line will settle between Ufa, that city, and Volkov's big Volga stronghold of Samara. That will be the real prize. Once Kirov takes that, then he can move east towards Uralsk to make a strong attack aimed right at Orenburg, Volkov's precious capital. For my part, I'll command the northern pincer, and drive on that city after I take Ufa on the river.

He could see it all now, the movement of troops and the tanks Sergei Kirov would give him in the bargain he set out to negotiate. I'll offer Kirov fifty divisions, and all the resources of Siberia if he needs them. In return, he'll give me tanks, artillery, aircraft from his factories, and I'll use them all to destroy Ivan Volkov.

He could see it all now, feel that it was coming, that it was all inevitable. He would re-write the entire history of WWII with his campaigns in the east, striking down the Kazakh traitors and re-conquering all that territory for Mother Russia. He would do this as Kirov's ally, and yet, behind this, he knew he had the power to remove that man as well, and eventually seize control of the entire Soviet State.

Yes, he thought, Kirov already knows I have that power. He obviously went up and down those stairs as well. That is always my Ace in the hole, for he can't get anywhere near Ilanskiy unless I allow it, and of course I never will. No. He'll simply have to take my bargain, arms and equipment for my manpower and the strategic ground I now control. Then, once he has armed my forces, there will be little he can do by force to change my control over Ilanskiy. As long as I have that, and this airship, of which he knows nothing at all, I'll still be the master of time.

All these thoughts should have bolstered him, but why did he still have the uncomfortable feeling that he was dangling by the barest thread here?

Then it happened.

Lightning rippled through the sky, and he heard a strange sound, deep, hungry, searching, like a pack of wolves on the taiga hunting for prey—hunting for *him*, hungry for his very being. Something wanted him, reached for him, sought his life.

"Not yet…" the words slipped from his mouth, quavering on the still air. "No, not yet, it isn't time!"

Then a stabbing pain took him in the chest, and he stooped forward, eyes clenched, a cold sweat breaking out on his forehead. Was he having a heart attack? Had his time finally come? I'm not even forty, his mind argued, and yet the stress I've been under….

The pain subsided as quickly as it came, and he noticed no other symptoms, no shortness of breath, and his heart and pulse did not seem elevated or distressed. But a strange feeling came over him, a sensation of terrible dread, accompanied by a chilling cold. The ship was rising, rising, yet the ambient air temperature should not produce such a chill. There was a darkness in that cold, deep and penetrating, and he reached for the oxygen again, thinking all of his distress was the giddy height of the ship.

A thousand thoughts came to him in that moment, like the faces of a thousand demons. Memories flooded his mind, the sound of his voice, high and shrill as he railed at Sergeant Troyak in that first failed attempt to take the ship… Volsky's fist pounding the table when he finally came to him afterwards… then came the sound of missiles firing, explosions, hot white contrails scoring the sky. He could see ships at sea burning, the orange fire glowing in the night, and then the massive upwelling of a nuclear explosion on the horizon, the anger he had set loose upon the world so wantonly, time and time again. Then he felt as though some skeletal hand was reaching for him, clawing at him, and wanting to drag him away.

"No!" he shouted again, his voice strident as the ship itself shuddered and lightning rippled again in the sky. *Tunguska* was struck by the bolt, its airframe coursing with the energy, and glowing strangely again, just as before.

A sharp sound pulled his attention to the mirror again, where he feared he would see that darkness behind him, something terrible coming for him from places unknown. The mirror was suddenly broken with a web of cracks, his image strangely distorted, doubled and redoubled as he stared at himself.

He forced himself to stand, his hand on the pistol in his holster, eyes wide and fearful, as though the door to his cabin might burst open at any moment and the demons would rush in to devour him.

But they never came.

Lightning crackled in the sky and the storm roared, but if there were demons out that night, they were well harbored in his own dark soul. Then he felt a strange sensation of lightness, a giddy feeling that sent him reeling, and he collapsed to the floor.

Part VII

War Plans

"Let your plans be dark and impenetrable as night, and when you move, fall like a thunderbolt."

- **Sun Tsu**, *The Art of War*

Chapter 19

They formed up in the wide brick square before the tall gold dome of the Imperial Palace of Orenburg. Each company of 150 men was deployed in a dense square, their black uniforms making a checkerboard pattern on the lighter stone. Each man wore a black Ushanka gilded with a silver badge, two crossed swords over the letter V, and light gleamed from the long bayonets on their rifles. The deep throated shouts of their officers saw them snap to in well drilled movements, presenting arms, their rifles held stiffly at the leather belts crossing their chest. They stood, in long dark field overcoats and polished boots, tall and trim. Then a trumpet sounded, and every head inclined upwards to the high balcony where a single man appeared, his grey hair catching the pale diffused light in the slate sky above. The man raised two arms in a wide V, and a the men called his name, fifty thousand strong—*Volkov!*

The Guard Commander turned, like a carved statue, his arm stiff and mechanical as he slowly raised his sword to his forehead. Then, in one swift motion, he pointed the sword west, down the long broad road leading from the square. Every man turned in unison, the voices of Lieutenants and Sergeants calling out the drill. One by one the companies moved, dark serried ranks marching down the road. The sound of their boots slapped sharply on the cold stone square. The Orenburg Guard was going to war.

There were nine divisions in all, but only seven had been mobilized for movement west. They would march in long ranks through the city, out from the main square and through the central business district, where tall brick buildings hunched in dense city blocks. Out past the outer collectives and workers settlements they would go, the steady rhythmic beat of the march timed out on the division drums. Soon they would reach the tall outer battlements and fortified walls of the city perimeter, where dark grey towers rose at intervals along the wall, overshadowed by the tall zeppelin towers where three great airships rode at anchor. There the trains would be waiting for them, already loaded with the heavy equipment of the divisions—mortars, machineguns, AT rifles and cannon, crate after crate of ammunition, trucks, armored cars and light tanks.

It was Ivan Volkov's Praetorian Guard, his elite Orenburg Guard Legion, each man wearing a red shoulder patch identifying them as one of the chosen. As infantry went, they might match any other in the world, save perhaps the elite Brandenburgers and the tough grenadiers and fusiliers of the German Grossdeutschland Division. Most had fought for years on the Volga front, rotating in and out of regular divisions, until they were selected out in a special draft and sent to the capitol for extended training as guardsmen. Only these seven divisions would leave the city, for Volkov always kept at least two divisions close by, his personal security force at the heart of the warren of stone buildings and military bunkers in the Grey Zone. Trucks, trains, and airships came and went, bearing officers, men and the machinery of war as Ivan Volkov feverishly rushed to complete his general mobilization.

His armies stretched from the Ob river to the east, back through Chelyabinsk and then across the lower Urals to the upper Volga. There he posted his largest army, the 1st, all of twenty divisions standing watch on the long broad flow of the river as it wound down as far as the industrial city of Samara. Four other armies remained in the main force, the 2nd Army posted south of Samara to Saratov, then 3rd Army extending down to Volgograd. From there the line dog-legged southwest to the Manych River, the 4th Army sector, and then 5th Army took over at Salsk, where there had been heavy fighting for the last several months all the way along the line as far as Kropotkin on the Kuban River. Each of these armies were smaller, with ten infantry divisions, and a few supporting mechanized elements. The reserve 6th Army was on the Ob facing down the Siberians. Together they numbered 70 infantry divisions, with another five armored, five mech and several armored cavalry brigades. It was a force three times the size of every man Great Britain would put in the field during the war, and it would soon be further swelled by even more troops arriving from the vast hinterland provinces of Kazakhstan, and Turkmenistan.

Beyond Kropotkin, a patchwork force raised from local militias had been battle hardened into the Army of the Kuban, where they fought to slow the Russian advance towards the rich oil fields of Maykop. Here the divisions bore regional names instead of sequential numbers. There were Rifle Divisions from the Taman Peninsula, Krasnodar, Armavir, and the Talmyk and Kuban cavalry. On the shores of the great inland sea, Volkov's Black Sea Marines stubbornly anchored the line at Tuapse. They had been pushed out of the major sea port of Novorossiysk a month earlier, and now they were digging in for another expected enemy assault, but none came.

The long line was faced by an equal number of divisions on the Soviet side, but in recent weeks, offensive operations by the Red Army had tapered off in the east, and trains had been moving men and materiel west to the German front, where two-thirds of the Soviet army was engaged. Yet the need to keep at least sixty divisions and twenty other brigades on the eastern front meant that those troops would not be available to face the heavily mechanized juggernaut of the Wehrmacht. And considering the fact that every man now standing to arms under the black and red banners of Orenburg was one more man that should have been filling out the ranks of divisions raised to fight Germany, Volkov's forces weighed heavily in the equation.

And so it begins, thought Volkov. *The men assemble in their perfect uniforms and overcoats, and the drill is well rehearsed. Then off they go to the hell this war will soon become. How many of these men will survive?*

Even with its forces stretched over two long fronts, the manpower resources of Russia were vast, and the number of rifle divisions that would be raised in this war boggled the minds of German planners at OKW. Hitler was hugely overconfident. In the beginning he had boasted that, where Russia was concerned, 'it was only necessary to kick in the door, and the whole rotting structure would collapse.' And now the hard boots of the German troops kicked off their long planned campaign, the bloodiest and most costly military engagement in human history.

It started early, in late May of 1941, a month before the German Operation Barbarossa actually began in our history. Hitler has planned for a sharp, brutal, fast paced war that he hopes might last only six months, thought Volkov, yet even in these altered states, the bloody hand of war might still be at the throats of his generals for a good deal longer than that, and then comes 'General Winter.' If things progress as in the history I know, by April of 1942, a million German soldiers will lie dead in Russia—*a million...* That was more deaths than all the wars the United States had ever fought throughout its entire history, including the 600,000 dead on both sides in the American Civil war. Yet that first million dead in feldgrau will just be the opening round of this Great Patriotic War. Three more years of bitter fighting might follow—*if* Russia survives this first year. I must see that Kirov is defeated quickly, and that never happens. Then, once I'm in charge, I'll consider what to do about the Germans.

Volkov stood in the window, watching his dark clad Guard march off, and thinking about all that was coming. He knew every battle as well, and every mistake and wrong turn on the road. Yet this campaign might end up very different.

Yes, there will soon be misery at Stalingrad, Volgograd as Kirov calls it today. But I will be the wolf at the door this time, and not the German Army. And this time I must attack from the east. It will be no good trying to cross the river directly into the city. The fortifications there are simply too formidable. We've sat on opposite sides of that river for years now, trading artillery rounds each day. No. The only way I will take that city is by double envelopment. I'll launch my attack with the fourth Army in the south, and pull their reserves to that line. Meanwhile, my Guardsmen will move by train to the selected crossing points north of the city. All our intelligence indicates that line is very lightly manned. Kirov does not think we can cross there, but my Guardsmen will prove him very wrong.

Volkov rubbed his hands together, thinking. Once they get me a bridgehead, then I'll move the armor from both 3rd and 4th Armies across, and we'll push for Serafimovich on the Don. This time I'll put my 22nd air mobile units to good use instead of throwing them away at Ilanskiy. The Southern Air Corps can get several battalions in, and they can cut the rail lines Kirov will need to rush reinforcements to that sector. With any luck we can get over the Don before he can react strongly, and that will put us in a good position to cut Volgograd off, if I can scrape up enough reinforcements to support the attack. This time the Russians will be trapped there instead of the German 6th Army.

He smiled at that, yet he was under no illusions that it would be as easy as he hoped. His troops were already blooded in battle against the Soviets. The Bolshevik zeal was equal to his own, and the standing army Kirov now fielded was even greater than the one that faced the Germans in the history he knew.

And there has been no purge, he thought. That officer Corps is intact, the bumbling fools are still there along with some very good men. Many were simply promoted out of privilege and favor, but some are real army men, and they know how to fight. I know the men who will rise like cream and win this war for Russia: Zhukov, Konev, Malinovski, Rokossovsky, Vasilevsky, Chuikov, Yeremenko, Vatutin. A pity I can't get to them and eliminate them all now. Some are already in high level positions. Other are simply division or corps commanders. I should have foreseen this earlier, and ordered Kymchek to round them up. Yet, it is likely that other men would rise in their place, just as I so easily supplanted Denikin here. That said, I must see about some attempt at assassination where these men are concerned.

I have raised a fine army here, though there are limits to the manpower at my disposal. My front line troops are as good as anything Kirov can put in the field, though his tank production will become a major problem soon. Yet I must rely on the tribesmen of Turkmenistan and Kazakhstan to flesh out my reserve armies, and who knows how well they will stand up in a war like this. Even the Germans are about to get a nasty little surprise when they realize that they cannot easily stop the newest Soviet tanks.

In that regard, I must shift all my production to advanced weaponry as soon as possible. I have tried to help the Germans, pointing them in the right direction in their early missile trials, and removing obstacles. Yes, I could hand them the plans for a high performance missile tomorrow, but they could never build it. That technology relies on microelectronics, metallurgy, composite materials, and even propulsion fuels and explosives that could not be duplicated today. Yet I can help them take the right steps at the right time, and get them down the garden path six months to a year early.

Yes, if the Nazis can get missiles and jet engines developed soon, then things might be different. They might be able to stop the Allied bomber offensive, and save their heartland from aerial destruction. As for the tanks, the Germans will do well enough on that score. Yet this development of a new British tank is most troublesome. Damn, I wish Kymchek were still here. He would have photographs and hard information on this tank by now. I must find out where they are building it, and how it was designed. For my part, I will stick to the tried and true. We have all the plans for the T-34, and I can move directly to the 85mm gun. Yet my industrial capacity can only take me so far. It is likely that I will not have the strength to produce these tanks in the numbers that will be required.

So then I roll the dice, just as Hitler does, and gamble that this war will not last through those long murderous years of 1942 and 1943. We must make a quick end of things, and link up with the Germans in the south as soon as possible. Kirov was very clever, and he saw the danger easily enough. That is why he launched his Caucasus campaign well before the planned date of the German attack—to gain some breathing space and push that southern frontier away from the Germans, as much as to get his hands on the oil at Maykop.

Yes, that is the one trump card I hold, the oil. The Soviets have stockpiles for six months, a year at best, but if they do not find new sources, then it won't matter how many tanks Sergei Kirov builds. He won't have the fuel to run them!

So on that front, I must send the Khazak Armies from reserve as soon as they are fully mobilized. We'll launch a strong counterattack aimed at Rostov from the south, because the Germans will be pushing for the lower Dnieper in due course.

Volkov smiled, watching the precise movement of the men in the square below. Off you go, he thought. How many will live out the remainder of this year? These are the best troops I have, and I must use these divisions as a strong shock force and cause some serious trouble here. The Guard will lead the way, and then I will mass all the armored formations I can come up with, and plan one good offensive to stick a nice iron rod up Sergei Kirov's ass. After that?

He did not wish to think further, on what might happen if these tall strong men were not enough to get the job done. The horror of the Great Patriotic war was too much to contemplate, yet how could they fail? How could the Red Army possibly weather the hammering it is now about to receive?

We shall see…

Chapter 20

The footsteps in the hallway sounded hollow, a mocking echo against the stark walls and high ceiling. Up ahead two guards stood in stony silence, suddenly animating as Rommel approached, and then stiffening to a frozen posture of attention. He proffered a perfunctory salute, and the door was opened from within by a young adjutant, who turned to announce him as he entered.

"Ah, Rommel," said Keitel. "I hope you have had time to get the sand out of your boots."

Rommel ignored the remark, his attention transfixed on only one man at the table, leaning over a map, head down, and an air of ominous silence about him—Adolf Hitler. He waited, until the Führer slowly raised his head, his dark eyes enveloping him with unwavering attention. There was, in that moment, a sense of emptiness deeper and more profound than any Rommel had ever known in his life. There he stood, twice defeated in the deserts of North Africa, and this by a nation that would field little more than 30 divisions throughout the entire war. The shame in Hitler's dark regard was a palpable thing, and Rommel felt its crushing power, an agony that weighed ever more with each passing second. Several other men stood in the shadows behind the Führer, the harsh overhead light only falling on their gilded uniforms. Rommel knew one man immediately—Eric von Manstein. The others were in civilian clothing, and unknown to him. Then Hitler took his hands off the table, straightening himself, a movement of shadow and coal black ire.

"So you have taken back all of Cyrenaica… Again…" said Hitler. "Yet what good are your hard-earned gains if you immediately lose them?"

Rommel said nothing, knowing he would have to endure this, and most likely find himself removed from his position before this meeting concluded. Is that why Manstein was here, he wondered? Were they sending him in my place? So be it. The medals on my chest eclipse anything that man has ever done, but face it, Herr Rommel, he chided himself. That is all past glory.

Hitler spoke again, just one word. "Explain."

Rommel swallowed, his pride long gone, his throat still dry with the desert heat he had recently left behind. Then he mustered his inner strength and spoke.

"My Führer, the enemy is now fielding a heavy tank that is completely impervious to any weapon our ground troops possess. As a breakthrough weapon on the attack, it is unstoppable, and it fields a gun that can destroy my best tanks with a single shot. In fact, there were instances where the enemy fire not only penetrated the frontal armor of my Panzer IIIs, but also blew completely through the tank and out the other side. Against such a weapon, offensive operations involving my Panzer divisions are impossible. Almost all the gains delivered in my last offensive against Tobruk were achieved by the infantry."

"You were inside the perimeter of the Tobruk defenses?"

"We were."

"And you ordered a retreat?" Hitler's voice raised in volume, his eyes beginning to smolder.

"I did, and if I had not done so, those troops would still be sitting there—but surrounded by British and Australian troops and simply waiting for the next ship to come in before they were sent off to the prison camps. The enemy heavy armored brigade had already broken through our lines to the south—through the entire front of my 15th Panzer Division. I could not afford to leave my hard fighting ground troops to be cut off in Tobruk. They were already down to their last rounds. Without those men, all that remained in the north were the Italians."

"My Führer," said Manstein. "I concur with Herr Rommel on this matter. To leave those troops in a cauldron would have been most unwise. Given the circumstances, his actions were correct, and I would have done the very same thing."

"Oh? Well I suppose it matters very little now," said Hitler. "It is obvious we will get nowhere in that filthy desert against the British. Very well, Herr General, we have read your reports concerning these new British tanks. When this matter was first reported to me during your initial offensive, I did not take sufficient notice. Now you have my complete attention, and I will not be as hard on you here as I might. Steiner reported the very same thing in the Middle East—tanks! Huge tanks that could not be stopped. Have we no artillery? Do we not lay minefields and dig hard defensive positions?"

There was a slight quaver in Hitler's voice now, and Rommel could see, by the tremor in his hand, that he was struggling to contain the inner rage he must be feeling. "We stopped them in the first war when they came, by simply standing our ground! And that was with artillery falling on us the like of which you have never seen, and the men choking with the gas. Yet we held the line! We stayed in our trenches and fought to the last man, and you must learn to do the same!" He composed himself, taking a deep breath and running a hand through the hair falling on his pale forehead.

"My Führer," said Rommel. "I placed the best troops at my disposal on the southern flank—the Grossdeutschland Regiment you were gracious enough to send me. They were dug in with good positions on difficult ground, and yes, they held that ground. The enemy 7th Armored Division attempted a flanking maneuver in that sector, but they could not get through."

"You see! All it takes is the same iron in the will that we put in the tanks."

"Agreed," said Rommel. "Yet at the moment I would be happy for just a little more armor in the tanks."

It was a bold remark, but Rommel had spent many hours with the Führer in the past, and knew the limits of what he might say here. He had not yet explained that the enemy's new heavy brigade had not attacked Grossdeutschland, but further north. Instead he returned to the matter that he believed was his real undoing in the desert, the lack of adequate fighting power in his all important panzer forces.

"I will put it very simply," he said, gaining resolve and

determined not to be made a scapegoat here. "Grossdeutschland was tough that day, but the tanks they faced were not the heavy brigade. If those monsters had fallen upon Hörnlein and his boys, there would have been nothing they could have done to stop them. Yes, they would have stood their ground as ordered, and yes they would have died to the last man. The iron in the will is there, My Führer, unquestionably. But they would have died in place, because we could not put that same iron into the tanks and guns they were fighting with. I will tell you once more—this new enemy tank cannot be stopped! Oh, we did get one that threw a track and was left behind. The *Stukas* managed to put a couple 500 pound bombs on it. If Goering would be so kind as to lend me a few hundred planes, then perhaps I might be making a better report here today. That said, of the thirty *Stukas* we had at our disposal, half were shot out of the sky by these damnable enemy rockets."

"Rockets? The British ground forces have them as well?"

"They do, my Führer, and they were concentrated to protect this new heavy armored brigade—and thank god that is all it is for the moment—a single brigade."

"You are certain of this?"

"The Americans have a little fellow in Cairo," said Rommel, "an American liaison officer who has been making regular reports to Roosevelt using their so called Black Code. Fortunately for us, an Italian spy managed to filch the key to that code from the American embassy in Italy, so we can read it. This man sends his reports by radio, and my signals intelligence is very good. We have been intercepting every report this man has made to Roosevelt."

The man Rommel was referring to was none other than Colonel Bonner Fellers, who came to be called "the good source" by the Germans, who now knew everything Roosevelt did concerning operations in that theatre.

"A single brigade…" Hitler seemed even more frustrated now. "I gave you five divisions, and you could not crush a single brigade?"

"Unfortunately, my Führer, that brigade was not fighting alone.

I was also facing three or four commonwealth divisions, including two armored divisions. The British have been recently reinforced with new tanks arriving at Alexandria."

"More of these heavy tanks?"

"Strangely, no. From what we were able to ascertain, they received more of their Matildas, and a new light cruiser tank. We faced them in this last battle, and did well against them. Yet that hardly matters, the heavy brigade could not be stopped. Oh, I suppose if I could put ten divisions in the field, I could simply smother this brigade, and the rest of the British Army with it. But General Manstein knows, as I do now, that we simply cannot support a force of that size in the desert. We are barely able to sustain the divisions I already have."

"Well do not fret over that, Rommel," said Hitler, a biting edge to his voice now. "I am recalling the Grossdeutschland Regiment for Operation Barbarossa. It will form the nucleus of a new division. Don't look so sad. I am also pulling Steiner's SS division out of the Middle East. I was a fool to be distracted by these sideshows, and for the very same reason you just pointed out—logistics. Yes, we intimidated the Turks into allowing us right of passage through Turkey, but on what? The railways are a shambles. There is no rolling stock available. It took Steiner weeks to get his single division down into Lebanon, and now it will take him just as long to send it back. Face it. The British are of no concern to me at the moment. I will win this war by crushing Sergei Kirov. So unfortunately for you, I must recall these troops at once, and put them to better use."

"Yet the matter of these tanks is still of some concern," said Manstein. "Operations are already underway in Russia, and the campaign is off to a very good start. Yet we have also found that the Russians have new tanks as well. They are not the monsters you report in Egypt, Herr Rommel, but they are better than anything we presently have."

"Which brings us to the real reason for this meeting," said Hitler. "I did not summon you here to get your bad news and deliver my own. No. It is this matter of the heavy tanks we must now set our minds on."

Hitler turned to the men waiting quietly at the edge of the table. "General Rommel, these gentlemen have been ordered to get us back in the game. They will put the iron in the tanks to match the will of our soldiers. Here we have Mister Porsche from Stuttgart, and Mister Henschel from Kassel. And you will be pleased to learn that they have been feverishly working on new and better tank designs ever since you first reported this new heavy British tank last February. In fact, they have been working on this even longer than that, but I had not given it my full attention. That has all changed. We already have new designs, 45 to 60 tons, and with twice the armor on your best Panzer IIIs. We are calling this one the Tiger, and there are already two models under development. I have put every resource we have at their disposal, and we are now converting all our tank production to make ready for these new designs—the big cats."

"I am very glad to hear this," said Rommel.

"This is not all," Hitler continued. "There will be others, a new medium tank called the Panther, and another model we are calling the Lion, which looks to be very promising. And I am considering even bigger tanks, as powerful as a battlecruiser at sea, and with guns right from the naval shipyards I will take from Admiral Raeder. If the British want to place heavy artillery on their new heavy tanks, so be it. I will show them what heavy artillery is. Beyond that, we are committing ourselves to a crash development program for this new rocket technology. Unfortunately, the early results have produced exactly that—one crash after another, but we will be diligent, and I have been promised a working weapon before my next birthday. In this regard, Ivan Volkov has been most helpful."

"Ivan Volkov?" Rommel knew who the man was, but could not see how he figured in the matter.

"It is clear that the Russians have been working on new tanks as well," said Hitler. "This new T-34 has been quite a shock to us. And our existing 50mm anti-tank guns cannot defeat the enemy heavy KV tank either. These are not as advanced as this tank you describe in the desert, but they are better than anything we have at the moment, which is an outrage. Volkov has sent me intelligence on these new Russian designs, and we may take a leaf from their book as we build our own tanks in answer. Now then, I would like you to meet with these gentlemen and tell them everything you have learned about this new British tank. Give them a soldier's eye view of what our new tanks should be able to do, and how they must fight. General Guderian would be a good man to include in this meeting, but he is otherwise occupied for Operation Barbarossa. I can see now that everything you have warned about, and all you have said about the inadequacy of our own tanks, is painfully true. I should have listened to you earlier, Rommel. I should have known you could not fail on your own merits."

"If I had those tanks I would already be in Cairo," said Rommel.

"I do not doubt it," said Hitler. "You have done the best you could with what we gave you. Now we must do better. I am done with building battleships, much to Admiral Raeder's chagrin. He has sent the entire navy gallivanting out into the Atlantic, and the British simply chased it back into French ports! Doenitz told me we would never have a surface fleet to match the Royal Navy, and he is another man I should have listened to. Yes, the British have these deadly new rockets. They have stolen a march on us with that, but we will catch up very soon. In the meantime, I do not think they can use this new naval rocket against our U-boats. I have already cancelled the H-Class battleship program, and the steel will be put to good use building more U-boats and these new heavy tanks. And what you have said about those *Stukas* has also been heard. I have underestimated the effectiveness of the Luftwaffe, and we will correct that matter. Rest assured, you will get all the air support you ask for in the desert."

"Thank you, my Fuhrer," said Rommel. "Yet it could take years before we get these new weapons into production. In the meantime, what am I supposed to fight with?"

"Not years, Rommel, *months*. The whole weight of the Reich is being committed to this, every engineer, every factory, all our resources. Yes, we will keep up a modest production on existing models to replace combat losses in Russia, but I have approved the new designs, and the bulk of our production is already gearing up for these new tanks and aircraft. If, by some miracle, the Soviets survive this winter, then by next spring, summer at the latest, things will be quite different. A year from today I expect to have at least three new tanks at the heart of all our panzer divisions, and soon after that, we will have these rockets that have been so troublesome. The British will see that two can play at this game. I hope to deliver the first prototypes to the Lehr units in a matter of months. Soon the big cats will be prowling the steppes of Mother Russia, and I assure you, they will have very sharp teeth and claws."

Chapter 21

The Situation on the Russian front had been very difficult in the early weeks of July. The Soviets had suffered severe losses in May and June, but had managed to make a stubborn retreat, though not without great cost. Many rifle divisions had been ill equipped in transport, and fuel was rationed to a point where most units were relegated to moving by foot. The rail system had collapsed under heavy German air attack in the early weeks of the campaign, but it had slowly recovered, and was now the life saver of the Soviet Army. Running on coal, it was not hobbled by fuel shortages, as the Soviets had sufficient stockpiles of rail coal for at least a year. So rail was the primary means of strategic transport, and the Soviet Generals had used it most efficiently to rush the endless supply of troops forming into new divisions to the front.

The Germans would overrun and destroy a rifle division, only to find two more detraining and marching sullenly up to the front to reinforce the line. Yet Minsk had fallen, Kiev was besieged, and the Red Army had been pushed back behind the wide marshy flows of the Dnieper. Now Sergei Kirov was meeting in the Red Archives again with his intelligence chief, Berzin, and receiving a full report on the deteriorating situation after this intensive German offensive activity.

"They are making every effort to break out before we get too deeply entrenched behind the river," said Berzin.

"Give me the whole report, Grishin," said Kirov, using the old code name Berzin had adopted when he operated undercover in the Spanish Civil War. Kirov always called him that, particularly in any personal matter. And now these affairs of state had become very personal, for it was not only the fate of the nation at stake, but their own hides as well. "What is happening in the north?"

"No further developments. Army Group North has pushed as far as the Dvina River, and stopped. Our line there is anchored on the Baltic coast at Riga, and while the Germans have a single bridgehead further east, it is well contained. There is only one panzer division assigned to this group, and it appears the Germans are not planning any offensive aimed at Leningrad."

"That is a relief," said Kirov. "We may avoid the misery of that thousand day siege that was so grimly depicted in the material." He was referring to a cache of very secret documents he had collected during his numerous trips up the stairway at Ilanskiy during the revolution. With a history of WWII in hand, he had foreknowledge of how the Soviet Union would both suffer and yet prevail in the war against Germany, but this battle that had finally come was playing out much differently than in the material he had obtained.

"Yes," said Berzin. "No thousand day siege, but that will also mean the resources the Germans threw at Leningrad will now be deployed elsewhere. There is a much heavier emphasis in the south, as we predicted."

"And the center?"

"After Minsk fell, they have concentrated their panzer armies in a drive towards Smolensk. Unfortunately, Mogilev fell last night, and resources are becoming very strained. That counter offensive you ordered against Volkov has cost us. We've sent another fifty divisions to the Volga front, and for every one we send, he has managed to match us with reinforcements arriving from his outlying provinces."

"Yet his forces there will be limited," said Kirov.

"True, sir, but those were fifty divisions we could have used to save Minsk, and now it appears we may soon lose Kiev as well."

"Can we stop the drive on Smolensk?"

"That remains to be seen. There is a big penetration south of Gomel now, and the entire center between Gomel and Mogilev is under pressure."

"What about our secondary defensive line?"

"We still have troops digging in at Bryansk, but now we have more to worry about in the south."

"The South? I thought we had contained the bridgehead over the Dnieper north of Zaporozhe?"

"We have, but the Germans forced another crossing west of

Dnepropetrovsk. It's that damnable SS Corps, their very best troops. They have spearheaded their entire effort in the south, once they get moving, they are very hard to contain. They broke out yesterday and pushed a strong attack north between Poltava and Krasnograd. A single brigade pushed all the way north to the outskirts of Karkhov, and today they have reinforced that penetration."

"Kharkov? We cannot lose that industrial center—not at this stage. It must be held."

"We've sent everything we could find there in the last two days. Zhukov managed to scrape up ten to twelve rifle divisions, pulling them from Orel, Voronezh, and as far north as the Leningrad sector. We've formed them into the 10th Field Army that was building at Penza. And we have also pulled the reserves slated to launch that offensive on the upper Volga."

"It can't be helped," said Kirov. "That offensive will simply have to be delayed until we stabilize the main front against the Germans. But will it be enough to stop them?"

"Zhukov thinks we can, but now we must decide what to do with the troops along the Dnieper line. There are about 15 divisions holding from the breakthrough zone to Kiev, and another six to ten units at Kiev itself. Even if we do hold Kharkov, that German SS Corps could wheel west. Then the Panzer Army south of Gomel could act as the other pincer, and that entire force would soon be in a pocket. We cannot afford to lose another thirty or forty divisions in a cauldron battle. It would mean we would have to rebuild the entire front there between Kharkov and Bryansk, and we simply haven't the troops and resources to do so at this time—they're all on the Volga."

"What about the new tank corps we've been forming."

"It has been slow going," said Berzin. "Two corps came out of the new factory sites in the Urals sector, and got pulled right into the buildup on the upper Volga for that offensive against Volkov's 1st Army. Zhukov believes we are trying to do too much, too soon."

"Yes," said Kirov, "but Volkov has crossed the river north of Volgograd, and I will not allow him to push any farther into Soviet territory."

"He is also pushing hard south of Rostov, though we've stopped him there—another seven rifle divisions that should be elsewhere, but at least our line has held."

"And our counteroffensive?"

"We've certainly got his attention. That wedge he pushed towards the lower Don has been contained. We stopped him short of Serafimovich, but he crossed at Sirotinskaya further east. Yet as soon as we launched the pincer operation at the base of his penetration, he pulled all those troops north of the Don again. Now he is on the defensive, and our northern pincer is breaking through near Kamyshin. That said, he brought up five more Divisions from his 3rd Khazak Army. The situation is still undecided."

"Don't worry about Volkov," said Kirov. "How many of his guard divisions have we identified in that sector?"

"Seven."

"Then this is his main offensive. The drive in the Kuban is merely wishful thinking. I can raise another five rifle divisions in Rostov if need be, and that will be the end of it. And this offensive he's launched to try and outflank Volgograd and cross the Don is mere theater as well."

"That's a deep penetration sir," Berzin cautioned.

"And it will take him nowhere. It's well contained. The attacks we've mounted at the base near the Volga have done just what I hoped, and he's shifted reserves there. So now tell me how many Orenburg Guard divisions have been put on the line against our forces on the upper Volga?"

"None sir. He's sent them all to the battle for that Don crossing."

"See what I mean? Mark my words, the man will soon be pulling those seven guards divisions out of that operation and sending them up north, because his 1st Army hasn't the manpower to hold us off for very long there."

"That's his biggest army sir, all of twenty divisions."

"True, but it won't be enough. They can hold the line of the

Volga now simply because it can only be crossed in a few places, but that will change. The first real cold fronts will begin soon, and by September we might even get an early frost. Once that river freezes up, then the divisions he has doled out here and there to watch likely crossing points simply won't be enough. He'll have to break them down and disperse the regiments to cover more river frontage, and then we can hit them anywhere we wish. Face it, my friend. Volkov is having his fun now, and putting on a nice show for Berlin. Come winter things will be very different."

"The Siberians have come down from Perm sir," said Berzin.

"As expected and promised."

"They aren't well armed, but they fight very well. Hard men."

"And we'll put them to good use," said Kirov. "On that note, when is Karpov due in for this meeting?"

"Three days from now."

"He'll want to talk about getting better weapons for his troops, and see about new armaments factories."

"Most likely sir."

"Well, we'll need him. He controls all the locations in the southern Urals where we'll have to relocate our mining and production centers, so we'll have to throw him some red meat."

"I expect so, but are we really going to give him what he will ask for? He'll want tanks, aircraft, artillery."

Kirov nodded. "Yes… and in exchange we get the Siberian Army. Yet I'll need more than what he's sent me thus far. Let's see what he has under his hat. I'll want to put on a nice show—better than the last time. Get the Moscow band up and ready, and roll out some good thick red carpet. Treat this like a state visit, because believe it or not, Grishin, that man may be the difference between victory and defeat for us in this damn war. If he had sided with Volkov…."

Berzin nodded, but said nothing more.

"Very well," said Kirov. "And what of the British?"

"They stopped the Germans in Syria, and have consolidated in

Lebanon. It appears their vaunted plans as expressed in Hitler's latest Führer Directive are futile."

"Another Directive? How many so far?"

"Thirty-Two, sir. This one referred to an 'Operation Orient' involving plans for the Middle East. We picked up some information on this earlier, and the German Brandenburg Commandos in Iraq have moved north to the oil regions near Kirkuk."

"He needs the oil," said Kirov, nodding his head.

"Unquestionably, as we do. Now that the Germans have taken Odessa on the Black Sea, their *Stukas* prohibit any movement of oil by sea to Constanta. They still get shipments over the Turkish rail system, but not enough to really matter. The Germans are still relying on Ploesti for most of their imports. To that end, we believe they will complete the occupation of the Eastern Mediterranean islands by attacking Crete soon. To leave that in British hands would mean they might soon have bombers there that could reach Ploesti."

"Yes," said Kirov, "but don't hold your breath. The British only made a few small raids on Ploesti in 1941, with no more than five or ten planes each. The Americans aren't in it yet, and their first major air raid there doesn't come until August 1st of 1943, at least according to the material. Even that was considered a strategic failure. They started off calling it Operation Tidal Wave, until their bombers were shot to pieces. In the end the pilots referred to it as Black Sunday. So as to this German Operation Orient—what do we know?"

"Not much has developed, sir. They have even pulled 5th SS division out of Syria and moved it to join the SS Corps in the Dnieper Bend. The other crack units that were sent to Rommel have also been recalled. Both the Hermann Goering Brigade and the Grossdeutschland Brigade have been returned to France. They are being built up to full scale divisions for deployment against us."

"Churchill must be happy now," said Kirov with a half hearted smile. "The British complained they were alone in this war since 1939. Now they've simply handed it over to us. All but five of

Germany's divisions in active fronts are facing us. Face it, Grishin. This is our war now."

"Yet the material indicates the Japanese will soon attack Pearl harbor."

"Yes, and that will start the war in the Pacific if it happens. It might do Karpov some good, because I don't suppose the Japanese will be looking to push any further into Siberia. They'll want oil too, and all the developed sources in Asia are in the south."

"Then you believe the material will hold true? The Japanese will strike into Southeast Asia?"

"Most likely," said Kirov. "Then the British lose Hong Kong and Singapore, and the Americans lose the Philippines. And we must not expect much help from them now either. They cannot ship anything to us through Vladivostok, because the Japanese have been sitting there for decades. They can't send us anything through the Middle East now, not with Turkey in the grey zone and German troops minding the rail system there. Nothing gets in through Iran because of Volkov, and so that leaves only one route—the Murmansk convoys. They become crucial for us now. We can build the tanks, but we never seem to have enough time to build the trucks!"

"The first Murmansk convoy is staging to test the route now, sir. The British are calling it Operation Dervish."

Kirov smiled. "Just as they did in the material. See Grishin? This world may be fractured in a hundred pieces, but some things still hold true. Let us hope that convoy gets through without incident."

"I think it has good prospects," said Berzin. "The really big German raiders have all sought refuge in French Ports now after that big sea battle. They lost their only big aircraft carrier as well."

"Yes…" Kirov had a knowing look on his face now. "Those naval rockets were reported in use there, correct? I think our friends at sea may have had a good deal to do with that situation. What news of them, Grishin? What of the ship they had the good sense to name the *Sergei Kirov?*"

Part VIII

Doppelganger

"*After a great blow, or crisis, after the first shock and then after the nerves have stopped screaming and twitching, you settle down to the new condition of things and feel that all possibility of change has been used up. You adjust yourself, and are sure that the new equilibrium is for eternity. . . But if anything is certain it is that no story is ever over, for the story which we think is over is only a chapter in a story which will not be over...*"

- **Robert Penn Warren** – *All the King's Men*

Chapter 22

Fedorov sat in the sick bay, eyes closed, feeling very strange. He tried to sleep, but his mind was too active with unanswered questions. In time he decided he simply must return to the bridge, and convinced Doctor Zolkin he was steady on his feet. The Doctor gave him one last cursory observation, noting his eyes and sense of balance, and then certified him as fit for duty.

He slipped on his cap, and was out the door into the corridor, walking in a fog of his own thinking. A few men saluted as he passed, yet he was too preoccupied to notice. All he wanted to do was to get up to the bridge and see what was happening. The ship seemed fine now, the men going about their routine evolutions, and he was glad that he was not approached and pressed with questions. Yet as he navigated the passageways and ladders up, he thought he perceived a difference in the men that he could not quite identify. There was a lightness of heart in them as he passed. They were joking with one another, laughing easily in a way he had not heard for some time. Perhaps it was simply relief that they had come through the shift with no further damage or odd effects.

Finally he was up the last ladder to the main bridge hatch, where a solitary Marine stood watch. The man saluted, opened the hatch for him as he came, and Fedorov stepped through, glad to hear the reassuring hum of the equipment as he did so. He glanced over at Petrov manning the navigation station, and then looked to find the Admiral. To his great surprise he stopped, frozen, his hand instinctively seeking a hand rail on the bulkhead by the hatch to steady himself, but it was not the nausea again this time, not his sea legs... It was Orlov! The Chief was standing there leaning over the sonar operator's station, clearly alive and well.

In that moment his mind reached for any possible explanation, and all he could think of was that the Chief had finally phased correctly with the rest of the ship.

"Ah, there you are, Mister Fedorov," said Volsky. "I trust you have recovered?"

"I am well, sir. And I see the Chief is back after that last shift. Thank God for that!"

Orlov gave him a look, then a nod of his head, acknowledging the remark with a restrained grin, his attention still fixed on the sonar station. "See Tasarov," he said glibly. "Fedorov loves me. Do you love me too?"

A few of the men laughed at that, but it only increased Fedorov's surprise. "Tasarov? He's back too? My God! Then they weren't missing after all. That last shift brought them all back!" He looked to Nikolin now, seeing the young Lieutenant glancing at Tasarov with a bemused expression on his face.

"Yes, we are all back on our regular shift," said Orlov. "And now with you here, the bridge crew is complete. Take your station Fedorov. Petrov—you can take your leave now, but don't eat all the biscuits in the mess hall before we get there!"

Again a ripple of laughter from the junior officers, but Orlov's remark struck Fedorov oddly. He walked up to the Admiral, thinking to get an update on the remainder of the crew. "This is a great relief, Admiral. Was there any news of Kamenski? Has the crew roster been double checked to see if anyone else has gone missing?"

"Missing? Nobody was reported overboard, Fedorov. And who is this Kamenski? I pride myself in getting to know my crews, but that name escapes me? He is certainly not in the regular bridge crew."

Fedorov now had a sinking feeling that the Admiral was again experiencing the effects of memory loss, and this was very worrisome. "Director Kamenski, our guest. I know you forgot about him earlier sir, and Tasarov as well. We all did. I couldn't remember him until Nikolin came to me in the dining hall. Then you remembered… the gopher holes. Do you recall it now sir?"

The Admiral gave Fedorov a searching look, his eyes narrowing. "Are you certain Doctor Zolkin certified you as fit for duty, Mister Fedorov? What is all this about? Gopher holes?"

"Damn," said Fedorov, his frustration getting the better of him.

It was happening again. The shift had done far more than he believed. It wasn't just the dizziness and nausea many had reported to Zolkin, including his own condition. Time had given them something in the unexpected, yet welcome return of both Orlov and Tasarov, but it had apparently extracted a price. The Admiral had forgotten Kamenski again!

"You told me to ask him about the gophers, sir—in the Devil's Garden. That was stuck in your head for some time. Do you recall it? And what about Chief Dobrynin?" Fedorov said quickly, trying to take stock of the situation before anything else slipped away. Orlov had been listening out of the corner of his ear, but now he stood up, arms folded, a serious frown on his face.

"What about him?" said Volsky.

"Then you remember him? He's back again as well?"

"Sookin sym," said Orlov with a shake of his head. "What's gotten into you, Fedorov? Enough with this nonsense, and get to your station. Do I have to drag you off to see Zolkin again? What kind of medicine is he giving out these days?"

"What's the problem?" came a voice, and it froze Fedorov's blood. He stiffened, slowly turning his head towards the briefing room, his face white with shock, and a chill running through him as though he had seen a ghost.

It was Karpov!

There he stood beneath his sheep's wool hat, a clipboard in one hand, which he slowly handed to Orlov with a nod. "Fedorov," he said. "Did Zolkin get the wax out of your ears?"

Fedorov said nothing, his eyes wide, his face clearly registering distress, and now Volsky had a troubled expression. "I am not certain that Mister Fedorov is fully recovered from that fall," he said quietly, deciding something. "How are those sea legs, Fedorov? Can you get yourself back down to sickbay?"

Fedorov heard the words, but his mind was a turmoil of shock and fear. Now the full weight of everything that had been happening on the ship these last days seemed to fall heavily on him again, impossibly heavy, collapsing into his soul like an avalanche of doom. He felt his knees begin to buckle, a cold sweat breaking out on his forehead, and it was all he could do to keep on his feet. The Admiral saw him sway, and reached to steady him, nodding quickly to Karpov, a message in his eyes.

The Captain shook his head, reaching for the overhead intercom. "Captain to sick bay. Please send a medic to the bridge with a stretcher team. Mister Fedorov is still not well." He cradled the microphone and looked at the Operations Chief. "Orlov, where is Petrov?"

"I just dismissed him," said the Chief.

"Then get someone else." Karpov walked slowly towards the Admiral, and as he did so Fedorov instinctively backed off, his eyes riveted on the man, as if he were some spectral nightmare come to haunt him in this desperate hour.

Karpov... Vladimir Karpov, standing there in his Captain's uniform with an expression on his face that was half annoyed, and half curious.

"He's clearly still disoriented," said Volsky. "Stand easy, Lieutenant Fedorov. We will get you back to sick bay in a moment, and I want you to take the entire day off tomorrow. Eat well, rest in your cabin, and if Zolkin can mind his business correctly this time, and he certifies you as fit, then report your availability to Chief Orlov. You men—help Mister Fedorov to his chair until the medical team arrives."

Now the Admiral turned to Karpov. "It seems we have more to worry about than missing ships and submarines. Have there been any other situations with the crew?"

"We've been preoccupied here, but I can send Orlov to walk the ship and see to the section Chiefs," said Karpov.

Volsky considered that, but decided Orlov was not the man he wanted to press the flesh with the crew just now. He was hard on the men, even rough at times, and the Admiral instinctively knew this was not what was needed now. He looked at Fedorov again, standing there with a look on his face that betrayed real anxiety, and he wondered how the rest had fared. If any man had the pulse of the crew now, it would be Doctor Zolkin.

He sighed heavily, his eyes looking out the forward viewports where the grey fog was again close about the ship, isolating it, smothering it, choking off air and life. It came and went, one moment thick, and the next with the promise of clearing. When would it lift? The Admiral struggled to clear his own mind and come to grips with the situation, and soon the claustrophobic feeling he had, drifting slowly forward through the quiet mist, his ship almost blind and deaf, prompted him to act.

"If you gentlemen can keep your heads about you," he said to his two senior officers, "I think I will accompany Mister Fedorov to sick bay and see the Doctor. My head is killing me!" He slid off the command chair, and shuffled past Orlov, tapping his pocket. "I'll take that," he said quietly, and the chief handed him something. "Let the matter go, Chief," said Volsky. "The men are a little bewildered at the moment, as you can clearly see." He looked down at the device, an iPod Nikolin still used to store his music and decided he would make it a point to return it to the Lieutenant later.

"Very well, sir," said Orlov gruffly.

"I'll make sure the accommodations are in order this time in sick bay," he said to Fedorov, and the medical team came tramping up the stairs beyond the main hatch even as he said that.

"Medical team reporting sir." A young *mishman* saluted when he saw Volsky near the hatch.

"Please see Lieutenant Fedorov gets an easy ride to the sick bay," said Volsky. "Captain, you have the bridge. Keep me posted if there are any further developments." The Admiral was through the hatch and on his way below.

Fedorov could not take his eyes off Karpov, who was now drifting over towards Orlov at the sonar station. He was watching every move the man made, so familiar, and yet so shocking at the same time. He could not be here like this. He simply could not be here…

"Gone to see the wizard," said Karpov with a wry grin when Volsky left. Then he was all business. "This fog can't persist for very long. When it clears we should get the KA-40s up and have a better look around."

"Agreed," said Orlov, glancing over at Fedorov as the medics helped him onto the stretcher again. "Twice in one morning, Fedorov," he said gruffly, with a disapproving tone. "Now I have to get a third stringer up here to fill your boots, and Petrov gets the entire shift tomorrow. Get the lead out of your head! And don't think I won't remember to get you a nice double shift next week so you can pay back the Admiral's kindness."

"Forget Fedorov," said Karpov, casting an equally disapproving look as the men carried the Lieutenant through the hatch. "We have more to worry about than a dizzy navigator. I have a very bad feeling about this situation. It's plain as day, in spite of this fog. Unless all the equipment has completely malfunctioned, we should have *Slava* and the targeting barges clearly on radar by now. Failing that, the KA-226 should have seen them, but they're gone, just like *Orel*. This was an attack, Orlov, and most likely carried out by a goddamned submarine. If I'm correct, then we're at war."

* * *

When the Admiral arrived at the sick bay, two crew members were just leaving the Doctor's office, their heads lightly bandaged where they had apparently sustained minor injuries from the blast wave that had recently shaken the ship. They stiffened to attention, saluting Volsky as he went through the door, then rushed back to their posts, casting a wary glance over their shoulders and wondering what was happening.

"Leonid," said the Doctor with a smile, his eyes alight, drying his hands on a towel near his first aid station as the Admiral came through the door. "Don't worry about the crew," he said. "Just a few bumps and bruises here and there; nothing to be concerned about. But what is wrong with Fedorov? The same as before?" His eyes were bright behind his dark rimmed spectacles.

"He seems very disoriented, and unsteady on his feet. Are you certain there was no serious injury? He took a fairly good fall up there when this business started."

"I'll give him the five star treatment this time," said Zolkin. "But what is going on, Admiral? The ship took quite a jolt there, right along with Fedorov. Did we hit a mine?"

"I wish it was something that simple, Dmitri." It was plain the Admiral was quite distressed. "It is the strangest situation I have ever encountered. We've lost contact with *Orel*, and *Slava* as well. All the ship's equipment seems to be working, but it is as if it was as foggy headed as Fedorov. He'll be here shortly. The medics were arriving just as I left the bridge. I'll want him here under observation all night, if you have the room."

"Of course."

"If he can be discharged tomorrow, I've given him the entire day off to eat and rest."

"That will probably do more for him than I can. I saw no obvious signs, but he might have a mild concussion from that fall. But yes, he did seem somewhat disoriented earlier."

"He seemed very surprised to see Orlov on the bridge," said Volsky. "Almost as if he did not expect him there."

"Come to think of it, he did say something about Orlov. Yes... He was talking about Dobrynin too, and Lenkov from the galley."

"And again on the bridge just now," said Volsky. "He also mentioned another man... What was the name? Ah, a man named Kamenski. You know the crew better than most, Dmitri. Who is this Kamenski?"

"Yes, Fedorov mentioned that man when he was here, but I don't know him either."

"What do you make of it, Dmitri?"

"I'll give him a thorough examination this time. He might also be having a reaction to the anti-nausea medication. There was nothing in his medical file indicating that would be a problem, but I'll see to it."

"And what do you think of the rest of this crazy situation we find ourselves in?"

"This accident you speak of? Let us both hope it is exactly that. What you suggest about *Orel* suffering the same fate as *Kursk* makes a lot of sense to me, but this business about *Slava* is somewhat puzzling. Neither ship responds to communications hails? Then you will have to conduct a thorough search. Better *Slava* than *Orel*. Easier to find a surface ship than a submarine, and also easier to spot any sign of flotsam."

"We've sent the KA-226 out," said Volsky, "but they have seen nothing conclusive yet."

"I see," said Zolkin. "And the explosion?"

"I am thinking we have lost *Orel*," Volsky said heavily.

"An attack?"

"Karpov believes this. I am not so sure."

"Any deliberate attack would not happen in isolation, Leonid. A surprise attack upon a Russian naval task force would be a major international incident, yes? It would have to have some context to make any sense."

"Things were getting very difficult in recent weeks, my friend," the Admiral explained. "Why do you think we are out here for live fire exercises? This business in Georgia has the Americans all up in arms again. They want the place to keep the back door firmly closed on Iran, yet the presence of three of our motor rifle divisions just over the border is most unsettling for them. They rattle their sword, so we rattle ours."

"A little more talking and a little less rattling would be so much better," said the Doctor. "Have you tried listening on shortwave to see if the world has gone crazy again?"

That very simple idea had never occurred to Volsky. If there had indeed been a surprise nuclear strike upon his homeland, then something as simple as a short wave radio might provide information he needed. Why not simply tune in civilian radio stations and monitor that traffic for a while? Nikolin had been on secured military channels all this time.

"Good idea, Dmitri. Now… can you give me something for this headache?"

"Certainly, but I don't think it's the headache that's really bothering you." The Doctor gave him a cursory examination, looking at him with a warm expression on his face, puttering amongst his medication trays to fetch a couple of aspirin.

"That's a lot of crew to be worried about now out there on *Slava* and *Orel*. It's a heavy burden to carry them on your back, but if this was an accident, Leonid, you can do little more than what you have suggested. Investigate the matter thoroughly, satisfy yourself as to the whereabouts of these two ships, and then report home to Severomorsk."

"Karpov is edgy again," said the Admiral. "He is convinced this was a deliberate attack."

"Perhaps so, but why? The political situation was deteriorating. Why else would we be here shooting missiles in the middle of nowhere like this, just as you say? But it was not all *that* bad. I do not think the world is crazy enough to start World War III. We are still really not over the scars left by the first two."

The Admiral nodded, forcing a smile. "Well, I'd best make room for Fedorov. He'll be here directly. Let me know how he is when we meet for dinner this evening."

"I'm sure he'll be fine," said Zolkin, "And don't let Karpov get under your skin. He's your canary in the mineshaft. Listen to him, but use your best judgment. He'll fret and fume for a while, but things will settle down soon enough, you'll see."

"I had best get back to the bridge," said Volsky. "This idea about the shortwave might allow us to get our bearings again. Have you looked outside? Did you see the ocean?"

"Every crewman who has come in here in the last half hour was talking about the sea conditions. We should feel fortunate that Rodenko's weather report was wrong today, that's all. This is better than that storm front he was tracking."

"That's another thing that bothers me," said Volsky. "I've seen the weather change suddenly at sea many times, but that looked to be a major storm brewing yesterday, which is why I was rushing to complete these live fire exercises as soon as possible. Now the sea seems eerily calm…. Unnatural."

"Perhaps it is merely an algae bloom," said Zolkin. "Such things are not that uncommon. The ocean is as temperamental as Karpov. It's just a mood. It will pass."

Volsky nodded, heading for the bridge, but the Doctor's suggestion would soon raise many more questions than it answered.

Chapter 23

Fedorov could not believe what his eyes had seen on the bridge, yet he heard the man speak, he could feel his steely presence. He had been so shocked by what he experienced that he was speechless, nearly collapsing again when his legs felt so rubbery. For a brief moment he thought it was his own problem, that he was hallucinating, another bad after effect from their recent time displacement. Yet something within him knew the reality of what he had seen. It was Karpov, dark, brooding, wound up like a coiled spring. Yet how was this madness possible?

The medical team rounded the last turn and was hastening down the corridor to sick bay, edging aside when the looming presence of Admiral Volsky appeared. Fedorov finally found his voice, dry and thin as he looked at Volsky.

"Admiral…. I must speak with you!"

"Not now, Mister Fedorov. Let these men get you to the Doctor. I will check on you later. For now I have too much to consider on the bridge."

Fedorov was going to speak again, more urgently, until a pulse of warning made him hesitate. He leaned back, resting his head on the stretcher pillow, and breathed deeply.

The shift, he thought. Something went crazy during the shift, but what in god's name has happened? I was heartened to first think Orlov and Tasarov had finally re-materialized. Their disappearance might have simply been a phasing issue. They might have been out of sync when we first disappeared. Yet Karpov? How could he be here now? This makes absolutely no sense!

Now the little things returned to mind, after the numbing shock of seeing Karpov there on the bridge. He recalled his earlier conversation with Doctor Zolkin as they carried him into sick bay, and the odd little incongruities that had cropped up. Zolkin knew nothing of Kamenski, yet he seemed to think Orlov, Tasarov, Dobrynin and Lenkov were all alive and well. *I was worried his* memory might be affected, but my god, this is something entirely unexpected. Karpov? He was right there, standing three feet from me, just as I remembered him. How could this occur?

His mind raced through everything he had discussed with Director Kamenski, and all his speculations over what might happen to the ship when it finally faced the question of Paradox. Was this some strange effect from that moment? *Think,* Fedorov, he chided himself. What could have happened here?

"Back again, Mister Fedorov?" Zolkin gave him a warm smile. "I see I was a little too hasty in discharging you. Perhaps that medication I gave you did not settle with your system well. Get him up here, gentlemen." He slapped the examination table, and the men shifted Fedorov over from the stretcher station.

"Good enough," said Zolkin. "You two can return to your posts, and, as I have no line outside waiting for my attention, I can give Fedorov here a proper examination."

The men saluted and left, shutting the infirmary hatch as they went. Zolkin folded his arms, just giving Fedorov a quiet look at first, making a general assessment of the man. He could perceive much in that, the obvious anxiety on Fedorov's face, the sweat on his brow. Then he proceeded to take more note of his vital signs, fetching a stethoscope to check his heart rate and pulse, and ready to check blood pressure.

"Stressful business, all of this," he said to Fedorov. "It was no surprise to find a line of men half a kilometer long outside my door after that accident. Tell me, Fedorov, did you see what happened?"

"Accident? No. All I remember was the sudden jolt, and then …" He hesitated remembering the strange tingling and other sensations he had felt during the shift, but something told him not to talk about all that with Zolkin now. He needed to get his bearings, find his position in the scheme of things here, like the navigator he was, looking for latitude and longitude to make sense of all this.

"And then what? Zolkin raised his heavy brows.

"Then I was here."

"Yes, and I let you go without taking proper note of your condition. I'd like to run a few tests this time around, just to make sure. Then the Admiral tells me you are given the entire day off tomorrow. That is good for you, and I would have most likely ordered it in any case. Now then… Do you feel any numbness or pain?"

"No Doctor."

"Alright. Then Let's check your blood pressure, and as I do so just answer a few simple questions for me. To start with, how are things back home?"

"Home? Well enough I suppose."

"And where is that, exactly. I don't think we've ever talked about your family."

"Saint Petersburg. My mother and father still live there." Fedorov answered perfunctorily, yet he was still inwardly wrestling with a hundred questions. He knew what Zolkin was doing here, sizing up his mental state by asking these simple things.

"And your wife?"

"I've never married."

"Yes, of course. I remember reading that in your file earlier."

"Look Doctor, I know you want to see to my wellbeing here, but I can assure you that I am of sound mind." He knew Zolkin was assessing his sense of personal identity, his awareness of location, date, time, and the present situation. Disorientation was a definite altered mental state, and he knew it could signal a serious medical condition.

Yes, he thought. I know who I am, but does anyone else? I am Anton Fedorov, Captain of the battlecruiser *Kirov*, yet apparently that has changed. Orlov ordered me about on the bridge and was thinking to send me right over to the navigation station. He even dismissed Petrov when I arrived. And my god, it's clear that the ship has one too many Captains now. I know where I am, clearly aboard *Kirov*. The bulkheads and deck plates are hard and firm, and this is certainly no dream. Yet from what I have gathered, I took a fall on the bridge during the shift, and everything started after that. Was I seeing things? Was Karpov just a hallucination? He decided to test this possibility with Zolkin.

"Doctor... How long has Karpov been in his present position?"

"Weren't you at the ceremony when the command change occurred?" Zolkin gave him an assessing glance.

"Of course, sir. I know that Karpov came aboard last May, but I was asking about his time in the service." He was really just mentioning Karpov to see if Zolkin would know who he was talking about, and hoping the whole time that the Doctor would protest, knowing Karpov was long gone. Yet he was not going to find an easy solution to this dilemma that way. It was clear that there was nothing wrong with Zolkin's memory concerning Karpov.

"Too long, I'm afraid," said Zolkin. "No offense to the Captain, but there are many who would say the same thing, and wish that Karpov would take early retirement. Yet here he is, finally Captain of the fleet flagship, and I suppose we are all stuck with him for the time being."

And on the examination went, as Fedorov settled into the grim realization that something profoundly disturbing had happened. He was Anton Fedorov, but clearly not the man he was before they attempted that last shift. He looked down at his uniform jacket cuff, and there were the insignia of a Lieutenant. Zolkin had fetched a new coat for him, and now he remembered how he had referred to him wearing someone else's coat earlier.

So now even my uniform was different, he thought with some renewed sense of shock, noticing it for the first time. And now he began to make the same inner assessment that Zolkin was undoubtedly working through in his quiet examination. Who was he, where was he? What was the date and time? What was his present situation?

He was Anton Fedorov, aboard the battlecruiser *Kirov*, yet possibly not the same ship he had been Captain of only hours ago. As to the where and when of his situation, everyone else on the ship seemed to be wrestling with that same problem. And yet… He could clearly remember everything he had lived through and experienced, all of it, as far as he knew. He recalled all those battles they had fought in the Atlantic as clearly as the action the ship had only recently fought against the German carrier *Graf Zeppelin*.

Yet the world he had been sailing in was an altered state of affairs. The ship they had just attacked had never put to sea. Was this the same ship he had led through the Mediterranean, and against the Japanese? He knew how he could find out, with a few questions of his own.

"Doctor, is there any damage to the ship?"

"Nothing I am aware of," said Zolkin. "That was a fairly good jolt we took, and it rattled my teacups, but nothing broke."

"Then all is well—even the reserve command citadel?" He gave Zolkin a close look, for he wanted to see if he knew about the damage there, as he clearly should."

"Reserve citadel? Yazov was in there today for system checks. It was all he could talk about while he was in here earlier. He had a bout of nausea as well."

"He was working on the equipment in the reserve citadel?" said Fedorov slowly.

"Isn't that where he spends his time when he's not on the bridge relieving Rodenko? You know the officer rotations better than I do, Fedorov."

"Of course," said Fedorov. "Yazov is a good man."

"Tell me," said Zolkin. "Who is this Kamenski you asked me about earlier?"

Fedorov felt that reflexive caution again, and thought he had better not say anything more about the Director.

"Oh, just a *matoc* from the dock service crews in Severomorsk."

"Ah, than that explains why I did not know the man. He stayed there, yes? At Severomorsk?"

"Apparently," said Fedorov, suddenly hearing the sound of a helicopter revving up for takeoff. Zolkin took the opportunity to ask him about it, still casually questioning him to gauge his situational awareness.

"Now what are they doing?"

"A KA-40," said Fedorov, as the sound of the engine was unmistakable.

"Ah yes," said Zolkin. "The Big Blue Pig. I flew in on that one before we left Severomorsk. Frankly, I like it better than the other one they just sent up, what is it called?"

"The KA-226? You say they just operated with that helo?"

"I believe you were indisposed at the time, but yes, that is the one. I don't care for it. Yes, it's much newer, sleek and fast, but I rather like the Big Blue Pig myself. Maybe I'm just getting old." Zolkin smiled.

Fedorov took a deep breath when he heard that, knowing his blood pressure was not being helped by the realization that was now solidifying all around him, moment by moment. *This was not the same ship!* This was not the same *Kirov* he had been Captain of, promoted up by Admiral Volsky after Karpov's failed mutiny. We lost the KA-226 long ago, and even Zolkin would know that by now. And the reserve command citadel was made a smoking wreck by a Japanese pilot. The only thing Yazov could have done there was stack up supplies, as that's all we could use the space for. *This was not the same ship!* How was this possible?

I'm the same man I was, he thought, in spite of the uniform. There is simply no way I could have dreamed up everything I experienced. It's all clear in my mind, as if it happened yesterday. We were steaming with HMS *Invincible*, set to engage the German battlefleet. Then everything seemed to come apart, the ship itself experiencing odd warping, men missing, and Lenkov, poor Lenkov. Even the men left behind intact after our sudden disappearance were beset with a debilitating memory loss, but that is not the case for me now. I can remember everything, every missile fired, the anguish and torment of every decision we had to make.

He remembered it all, the hunt for Orlov, that strange event on the back stairway of Ilanskiy, Sergei Kirov, and the massive contamination he had introduced into the world with his own errant whisper in that man's ear. It was real, by god. No. It was not something he could have dreamed up in a thousand years. It all *happened*, but even as he asserted that, he had the sinking feeling that no one else on this ship would know any of this.

Then one more memory emerged from the montage he was playing in his mind—Turing's watch! It had been found in that file box, though Tovey reported that Turing claimed it went missing some time before that. He knew there was no way that he could have placed the watch into that file box—at least not in the world where he was standing, not in those horribly altered states they were just sailing through. It came from another world, another meridian of time, a remnant from that first sortie they had made to the Med. And here he was, plucked out of that altered history he had been sailing in, and set down here aboard the ship that first started this journey.

My god… where were they? Were they in the Norwegian Sea, or still in the Atlantic where they had last disappeared? I'm the navigator here, he thought. I'm supposed to know. It's a good thing I was shocked speechless when I saw Karpov on the bridge, because if I had blurted out any of this, than Zolkin would probably be certifying me as insane by now.

Something has happened. Time has played some cruel trick on us. We must have fallen out of the shift and into some confounding loop in the tormented fabric of time. This whole thing was twisted so badly that it has bent back upon itself, and here I am. This is the ship that just left Severomorsk!

Now he suddenly recalled Zolkin mentioning an accident, that jolt the ship had taken, rattling his teacups. I thought he was referring to the shift we initiated, but now I realize it could be the accident aboard *Orel*. Yes, that was the first cause. That's what lit up Rod-25 like a sparkler and sent us reeling through time. But if that is the case…

His mind was doing the reeling now, and with one throbbing

question. Did any of what I remember even happen? Are we sitting there in the Norwegian Sea, just moments after that first time shift sent us back to 1941—July 28, 1941—*Paradox Hour*. If that is so, what happened to the other ship? What happened to Volsky, and Rodenko, and Nikolin and all the rest? Time caught up two slippery fish in the same net, and she only had room in her boat for one. Did she simply throw the other one back? Was that ship and crew simply tossed away into oblivion, or is it still out there, sailing in that oppressive Atlantic fog? Would that mean that Doctor Zolkin has a double out there somewhere, a doppelganger sailing on that other ship? And if the man I saw on the bridge was Vladimir Karpov, what about the other man in Siberia? Were there two Karpov's now—two of every crewman on this ship that still survived in the ordeal we went through?

He remembered the logic he had settled on before—both ships could never occupy the same space, but two objects could easily occupy the same time—just not the same *spacetime*. Is that what had just happened here? Did this ship come through to 1941 from the future, just as I feared, even as the ship I was on came to this same moment from the past? If this was happening, then was I simply moved here, like Alan Turing's watch? And what about the other Fedorov, the man I was just hours ago, speaking with Admiral Volsky on the bridge as we decided to make that last shift with the reserve control rod? Did the other Fedorov vanish, just like Kamenski had vanished, or do I have a doppelganger out there as well?

No he thought. I am that man. I know I am. I'm the man who watched the sea red with fire when *Yamato* burned. That memory is etched in my mind forever. *I'm that man!*

Chapter 24

Fedorov had a very long time to consider his situation as he rested in his quarters, though his mind was so beset with questions that sleep did not come easily. He passed moments of deep sadness, realizing that the men he had known were gone now, the Admiral, the bridge crew, every man on the ship. Oh, they were still here, all around him, yet they were not the same. There was an innocence about them, and unknowing. At this very moment, they did not even know what had happened to them. They were here and gone all at once, and his mind and heart were shaken as he remembered that last speech the Admiral had given to the crew, and the sound of their voices cheering, singing, celebrating that last moment just before they shifted into oblivion.

And so it ended there, he thought with grim finality, even as it begins again here. A story never really ends, as a river never ends. It just flows on and on, turns round another wide bend, curls back on itself. Some leave it to find a longed for shore or the promise of the sea, others come to it beginning a journey they can never really see the end of. That was life. We were here, and hearty travelers all, and then gone. Yet here he was again, strangely changed, yet in the eyes of those all around him, he was still just Fedorov. Here he was, still aboard this old familiar ship, and everything in his quarters looked the same.

After he was finally released from sick bay, he made a point of taking a walk about the ship before he retired, almost as if he thought he might suddenly find it back the way it was, bruised, yet unbowed by every circumstance and trial they had faced.

The first thing he did was to go to the reserve command citadel. That was the place that had been demolished in the Pacific when a Japanese plane came careening down on the ship there. Only the heavy 200mm armored roof, and then the equally well armored floor, prevented the plane from penetrating deeper into the ship. Yet the battle bridge, as they called it, had been completely demolished, and everything there had been destroyed.

Before they returned to Vladivostok, they cleaned the space up, painted over the fire and smoke damage, and then covered the whole thing with a tarp. Once in port, the roof was sealed off with some new armor plating, but restoring the equipment there was impossible during their short stay in the Golden Horn Harbor.

Fedorov wanted to see the place again with his own eyes, and when he arrived there, finding it all in perfect working condition, completely undamaged, he knew his premise was now proven. The impossible had happened again. This was the ship they had started this whole journey on, and not the one he had commanded only hours before that last attempted shift.

Some sort of strange time loop was in effect here. Either time had made a choice as to which ship she would allow in this meridian, or *both* ships were here. The implications of that last possibility had already shaken him, for it would mean that everyone here might have a duplicate self out there somewhere, on that battered and weathered ship he had recently commanded. Yet he knew in his bones, with no doubt whatsoever, that he was the man from the ship that had fought *Yamato*, the ship that had been boldly engaging a German battlefleet just before they vanished into the grey fog of Paradox. He had taken the good counsel of Admiral Tovey, and given the same, and he had stood with restrained awe beside Churchill in the desert oasis of Siwa.

So now I wear this old Lieutenant's uniform, and not the Captain's hat I earned through all those harrowing hours at sea. But I am not that younger officer, naive and unknowing. I remember everything we did, every experience. So how did I get here? Was I moved here during the shift, just as Alan Turing's watch was moved to that file box? If that is so, what happened to the other Fedorov, the man I replaced here? Is he gone forever so that I might remain. Have I stolen away his innocence, his astonishment, the delight in his eyes when he first saw that Fairy Fulmar overfly the ship?

If the old ship is still out there somewhere, then they are probably realizing I am gone. From their perspective, I was just another crewman who failed to shift properly, just like Orlov and Tasarov. I wonder... Did time move them here as well? Is that where the missing men all went—to this new ship? No. Orlov gave no indication he knew anything at all. He was his old grumpy self, ordering me about like a schoolboy on the bridge. I knew that felt odd when it happened, but I was so relieved to see him there that I overlooked it. Then the real shock came—Karpov.

How could this have happened?

He thought deeply about it, unable to sort through the Paradox, and then a possible solution suddenly occurred to him as he lay awake, staring at the ceiling. It was born of his own tortuous logic when he had been trying to determine what might happen to the ship. He reasoned that the very existence of the ship, its design and building, rested on a long series of events that had been stored away in the icebox of the Cold War between Russia and the West.

I just could not see how everything would turn out the same, he thought, particularly with all the damage we were seeing in the history. With Russia fragmented into three warring states, how would events lead to the building of this ship, and to that very same mission to the Norwegian Sea to conduct live fire exercises? How could that same accident aboard *Orel* trigger everything as it did—the first cause. It seems so improbable that it simply could not happen. And yet... that same logic also told him that for him to be there in the past worrying about all of this, *Kirov* had to begin this journey somehow. That was an imperative. It *had* to happen, yet he could see no way it could repeat itself now.

The evidence of his own eyes told him differently. Here he was, Lieutenant Anton Fedorov, posted as Chief Navigator on the ship. It had happened again, and now he thought he knew why. The changes to the history were going to affect the future, that much was certain. Yet he had no idea how long it took for the damage to migrate forward.

I was assuming that when we change something in the past, the effects it might have on the future occur immediately. Maybe that was true of some things. Admiral Volsky had no trouble getting that letter I put in the storage locker at the Naval Logistics Building—except when Volkov intercepted it. Yet I wrote it in the past, and because that locker remained undisturbed for all those years, it turned up in 2021, almost immediately. Perhaps there were no other events in that chain of causality that could have interfered with it.

He shook his head. What about the Japanese? They occupied all of Vladivostok. Wouldn't that have interfered with the survival of that letter? No. At that point, Karpov had not yet even gone to 1908, so the letter got through. The locker proved to be a safe means of transmitting the information from the past to the future. I found that journal Orlov wrote that put me on his trail, and Kamenski had produced photos of *Kirov* in the past, and of *Orlan* in 1945. He turned up evidence of these events with no problem, but does that always happen? Do the changes migrate forward immediately?

What if that is not so? What if some events in the past are so profound, or so complex, that their consequences cannot be immediately reflected to the future. What if it takes... time?

Yes! Admiral Volsky and Kamenski were talking about something like this earlier. The Admiral wanted to know why we could not simply go to a history book and see what would happen during my rescue operation to fetch Orlov, or what Karpov would do in 1908. Kamenski said the events were still underway, and we were all involved, and with the power to change things. He used that term right out of the American Physicist's technical papers—nexus point. It was like the eye of a hurricane, or the center of a whirlpool in the river of time. Everything was caught up in the chaos of change around it, yet from within that point, a willful agent could move in many directions, enter the stream of events, effect further changes that would all bear on the outcome.

So what if *Kirov* was in such a place? What if it caused a nexus to form, and these events cannot completely migrate forward to the future until its actions in the past conclude? In this case, that future might still be intact. We noticed some effects at Vladivostok when we got back there. One man claimed his house was gone, and hung himself! But yet, the world seemed largely intact, right down to the restaurant where the Admiral and I had that dinner with Karpov. That was when I was first hatching my plan to go back and rescue Orlov. Yes… I was determined to do that, and convinced that Orlov was going to cause further damage to the history. He had his damn service jacket with him.

And look what I did to the world. I found Orlov, but I took a wrecking ball to everything else. And yet… We went forward again to get to *Kazan*, and that world was still remarkably intact. I had already whispered that warning to Mironov, but the world we entered seemed to take no notice of the fact that he would kill Josef Stalin! *So the change I introduced with that warning had not yet migrated forward.* The world we entered to board *Kazan* with Gromyko was not yet altered by my meddling! Yes, there were some changes, but they were very minor. The really big things were still in play. I was again determined to go back and stop Karpov in 1908, and that was going to have everything to do with the outcome on history.

Then his logic took one last leap. What if that world we returned to *was* the same as the one we left, with only these slight alterations? We stopped Karpov, and then tried to come forward again, but we could only reach 1940. There the changes Karpov caused in 1908— the changes I had caused with my warning to Mironov, had time to take effect. The world was clearly altered, drastically different. But those changes may not yet migrate to 2021, because *Kirov* was still in the past, still operating to effect the outcome. Our story had to resolve itself before the consequences of our actions could be fully determined. If that is so… My god! Then the ship that arrived here from the future—*this ship*—must have come from the original time meridian—the world that was as yet unaltered by our actions! So my complaint that events would never stack up to permit that was faulty logic. I was assuming the future was already changed, but that may not be the case.

Of course! That is the only way this ship could be here now—the only way Karpov could be up there on the bridge. Did he replace the other Karpov in Siberia? Did that man vanish when this ship arrived here some hours ago? That thought gave him some hope, because at this point, Karpov had not yet fallen into the darkness that consumed him. He was all potential, dangerous potential, yet the possibility of redemption still remained in him.

There were still so many questions in his mind. He needed to start getting some answers. First off, where were they? Was the ship in the Norwegian Sea? That seemed likely, because that was where *Kirov* was operating when the accident happened, the first cause.

Then will events play out the same way as before? Will we soon make contact with Wake-Walker's task force headed for Petsamo? How could that happen given what I saw? The history of the 1940s had clearly been overtaken by the wave of changes migrating from 1908. In fact, that was the theory posited by the American Physicist Paul Dorland. He called it a Heisenberg Wave, and claimed it acted to re-materialize the world to account for the changes made in the past. It migrated out from a major variation like ripples in a pool of still water. Here in the 1940s, we've already been overtaken by the wave that was initiated in 1908. But it has not yet reached the future in 2021! Not entirely. Some changes were seen, like the fact that the US entered the war earlier, but otherwise, things were still intact, and they should have been drastically altered.

My god... I think *Kirov* just came from that original time line, only it entered the meridian already changed by events in 1908! I've got to find out if this is so. I've got to find out what is happening on the bridge, but I must be very cautious here. As I recall events when we first shifted to 1941, we would have made contact with Wake-Walker's task force by now. Yet the ship is quiet. I heard the KA-40's return some time ago, and we are no longer at action stations. That would certainly support my theory that this ship entered the altered timeline. If I could just get to Nikolin, he would probably know what is happening. In fact, he's most likely off duty by now.

That thought prompted him to get up and steal down the

corridor to Nikolin's quarters. It was very late, well after midnight, and he knocked lightly on the door, waiting impatiently. Thankfully, Nikolin was a night owl, and he had been listening to his own short wave radio, still monitoring stations as he had been on the bridge. He opened the door, surprised to see Fedorov there.

"Fedorov, how are you feeling?"

"Well enough… May I come in? I need to speak with you."

A moment later the two men were sitting by Nikolin's desk, where he had been playing solitaire with a deck of cards while listening to the old style music being played on the radio. Nikolin explained that it was all he seemed to find—that and old news documentaries.

Fedorov's eye fell on the dark King of Spades, wielding a sword of doom, and arising from the very image of its own self, one king above, the other below. The image brought a strange feeling, a doppelganger, he thought grimly, just like Karpov.

"Listen," said Fedorov in a half whisper. "I need to ask you some things. I've been off duty a long time. Do you know our position and heading?"

"We're circling," said Nikolin. "Right where *Slava* was supposed to be waiting with those targeting barges. The Admiral wants to put a submersible over the side in the morning to have a look at the sea floor."

"Then we are in the Norwegian Sea?"

"Of course, where else?"

"Alright… Have you heard anything from Severomorsk?"

"Nothing. I can't get through to any of our normal military bands, but my equipment was very weak until just a few hours ago, Then I started picking up this stuff." He gestured to the small shortwave on the desk, illuminated by the cone of light from a metal hooded desk lamp.

Fedorov inclined his head, listening. "What have you found out?"

"It's very strange, Fedorov. There's nothing but these old news stories. That made the Admiral think there was no war, because every station would be alive with that news if something really big happened. They were just talking about the last war, bombing France, and things about the Russian front. Just old news from WWII."

"Did you get any details?"

"Something about German ships in France. It didn't make any sense to me. What would they be doing in France?"

Fedorov looked excited, nodding his head. "Did you hear any names? *Hindenburg? Bismarck?*"

"That's the one—*Hindenburg*. The BBC said the RAF was bombing French ports, and they claimed to hit that ship."

"No other news? Didn't the BBC carry live news feeds?"

"That's what's so scary. They only broadcast these old documentaries from WWII. There's been nothing else on the band for the last five hours. I've heard the same thing out of Reykjavik on the AM band. And I've heard shortwave from the U.S. and England. I'm still listening here, because Karpov and the Admiral will want my report first thing in the morning."

"Were these broadcasts dated?"

"Just the old dates from the documentaries."

"What did they say?"

"Well, that's what is so odd. It's as if they were doing some commemorative replay of the old news reels, because they're just reporting the news from this very day. Seems odd, especially since this is preempting all other local and international news. It's as if nothing else is happening but this damn documentary."

"The date, Nikolin. Can you remember it?"

"Sure—this broadcast here was BBC, and they time stamped it 28 July, 1941. That was two hours ago—the 11:00 newscast out of London. It's past midnight now."

That was the date Fedorov expected, yet hearing it sent another chill down his spine. It was Paradox Hour, and now it was behind him. He had finally come through to the other side of midnight, and yet he was still alive, his memories all intact, but strangely here on this phantom ship. It had arrived from the same world he left so long ago, and he was the only soul here that knew anything of all that had happened to them. He suddenly felt very lonely, but he put that emotion aside and asked Nikolin his next question.

"Have you tried using our coded ship-to-ship transmitting band?"

"Just once, right after this thing started. I tried to raise *Slava*, but nothing came back. And all my satellite links are dead too. The Captain thinks this was an attack, Fedorov, but it's gone eerily quiet since that fog lifted."

"Good. I Think I'll go out on deck and have a look at the stars. If I have to plot manually tomorrow I'll get a good fix on things tonight. What else is happening on the bridge? Any idea what the Admiral is planning?"

"Karpov wanted the KA-40s up all night, but they could find nothing so they pulled them back in. Tasarov heard nothing on sonar, and you know how good he is. I was with him for evening mess and he said he's never heard the sea this quiet before. It's very strange, Fedorov. But what happened to you?"

"It was nothing. I think I had a reaction to some medicine the Doctor gave me for that dizziness. I'm fine now." Fedorov hesitated briefly, then decided to risk one more question. "Look Nikolin," he began cautiously. "Do you remember anything else that seems odd to you. Anything about that old war?"

"You mean the documentaries? I was never good at history, Fedorov. That's your hobby. Me? I like riddles and good music. I have some Beatles on my iPod if you want some tunes. The Admiral gave it back to me after Orlov took the damn thing today."

Fedorov smiled. "Then you don't remember anything about battles at sea, airplanes attacking?"

"What do you mean?"

"Oh, nothing I suppose. You're right. I'm the history buff here. When do you go back on duty?"

"Morning shift as usual. You coming on duty? Karpov has been bullying your replacement. When he couldn't get GPS coordinates and had to manually plot, he was taking too much time. He called Petrov back for the last shift, but that's three shifts he pulled yesterday."

"I'll be back in the morning."

"Well be careful. Karpov isn't too happy. He stayed up on the bridge real late, and then ate by himself like he always does. That man is spooky."

Fedorov nodded. "I'll be careful. Say Nikolin, tomorrow morning do me a favor. Try our ship-to-ship one more time. Maybe Severomorsk has sent out a salvage task force."

"We haven't heard anything. I've received no messages from home at all."

"Well just send out an 'all ships respond' signal—but use our coded ship-to-ship, use 272, and put it on long range transmission. Can you do that?"

"I suppose so. The Admiral has had me monitoring Fleet command link channels, but I haven't used the coded ship-to-ship, except that one time."

"Good. Do it first thing when we come on duty. Maybe we'll get through to another ship close by, and that will be a nice feather in your cap."

I can't tell him what I'm really looking for here, that the only ship he might get through to on that channel would be *Kirov*—our ship, the one I was Captain of just a few days ago. That was our designated channel. This is going to be very scary if he does get through. What will they think? What will he think when he hears his own voice talking back to him? How will I handle that on the bridge?

"Make sure you wait until I come on duty before you try," said Fedorov. "I don't want to miss anything."

No thought Fedorov, I wouldn't miss it for the world.

Part IX

Backwash

"I believe that life is chaotic, a jumble of accidents, ambitions, misconceptions, bold intentions, lazy happenstances, and unintended consequences, yet I also believe that there are connections that illuminate our world, revealing its endless mystery and wonder."

- David Moranis

Chapter 25

"**Astounding.** That single Russian ship caused all this?" Maeve shook her head, unable to admit the consequences that were now threatening to destroy the entire course of modern history.

"That's the odd thing," said Nordhausen. "I can see no direct link as to how the ship could have caused all these events, particularly the demise of Stalin and the rise of these other figures in Russia. It's as if something else is operating here. Are we certain that future generations are not still meddling? Are we certain they still don't have agents in place, or working Arch complexes? They must have seen these variations, even as we have. Wouldn't they operate to try and take advantage of this situation?"

"All we have is their word not to do so," said Paul. "And the considerable threats Maeve made should we discover any further tampering."

"Well no offense, my dear lady," said Robert. "But it appears your steely regard was not sufficient. Someone is clearly operating to effect these changes. It can't simply be this single Russian ship. Something else is going on here, and I just can't nail it down. "

"That's where these damn keys come in," said Paul. "Look, whatever does happen here, our friends and enemies in the future will have a better perspective on it, assuming they have survived. I think these keys were part of their solution. It's clear they were engineered in the future, and now we also have a firm connection to these natural time fissures the Fairchild woman was talking about."

"I still think it odd that we would not have known about that," said Maeve.

"The world holds many secrets," said Paul. "Our knowledge is limited at this point on the continuum. It could also be that these fissures have been well secured since they were discovered, and only now come into play."

"Yet we got no alert warnings," said Maeve. "Wouldn't the existence of these time rifts have caused some effects that were significant enough for us to detect a variation?"

"Possibly."

"Fairchild knew about these rifts?"

"I think she was told about them. She said she received instructions on how to utilize one, and that is apparently how they managed to get that corporate ship to also move in time. If there are other keys, then there are other rifts. That could be the reason for some of these other variations we've detected."

"You suspect someone else is using a natural time rift to effect these changes?"

"How else can we explain this altered Russian history?"

"Alright," said Maeve. "Let's assume that is the case. Wouldn't we see other variation flags?"

"Well, we've got red flags all the way back to 1908," said Nordhausen."

"Nothing earlier?"

"Not much of anything. There was a yellow flag in 1815, but it didn't have any corroboration, and no consequences I could determine."

"What was it?"

"Just a Golem report indicating there had been an assassination attempt on the life of Marshall Ney."

"Marshall Ney?" said Paul, his eyes widening. "Le brave des braves?"

"That's the man."

"Who tried to kill him? Did the data reveal that?"

"No. It was just an incident during the Waterloo Campaign, where the Marshall was fired on by a sniper. But the attack wasn't successful. He wasn't even hit. His horse had reared up at that very moment, and the assassin missed. There was nothing else about it, just a few lines in a report written by an adjutant in the campaign."

"Interesting," said Paul. "Ney was certainly a Prime in that campaign. It looks like time did its best to prevent that attack."

"And it also sounds suspiciously like something the Assassin cult would do," Maeve warned.

"Kill Marshall Ney? Whatever for?" Then Paul considered the matter, thinking. "Wait a second... let's consider this a moment. Ney's errors were a big reason Napoleon lost that last battle. He failed to promptly secure the vital junction at Quatre Bras, and then was late counter-marching to the engagement Napoleon was fighting with Blucher at Ligny. He recalled D'Elon's Corps at a vital moment, and it was never committed to battle, and then, in the main battle at Waterloo, he committed the whole of the French Cavalry in a fruitless charge, mistaking Wellington's "backward step" as a retreat. That had a lot to do with the outcome of that battle. Yet why would the Assassins want to eliminate him? Suppose they did so, and Bonaparte wins the battle of Waterloo? That helps France, for a while. Were there any other outcomes in the resonance?"

"Nothing," said Nordhausen, "just this one little blip in 1815, and nothing more. The attack failed, and that seems to be the end of the matter. It could have just been a little aberration."

"Little things have a way of becoming big things," said Maeve. "This could be evidence that someone else is still operating in the continuum. That affair in 1908 can be attributed to the Russian ship, but we have no evidence it ever went any farther back in time."

"Nothing that I could see," said Nordhausen.

"Then who tried to kill Marshall Ney?" asked Maeve.

"Well we can't immediately assume it was a time traveler," said Paul.

"Then why was it flagged by the Golems?" Like an ill placed crumb on her table, Maeve was immediately suspicious. "They don't just report history—they report *variations* on the history. This incident was not in our touchstone database, it's something new."

"Yet it seems to indicate no unusual consequences," said Paul. "Look, we've enough on our hands now with this damn Russian battlecruiser. Let's leave Marshall Ney alone for the time being."

Maeve took a deep breath. "Agreed," she said. These other variations with people and ships popping into World War Two are the immediate concern."

"That's an understatement," said Nordhausen. "Everyone starts crashing the party. I've got major variation data on the North African campaign now, and reports indicating a Russian submarine was also operating in the past. Just ten minutes ago I got a further variation flag that showed other modern British vessels discovered in the past. I even got a photograph—a ship called *Ulysses*. It was from a file buried deep in the Royal Navy archives, but the Golems managed to dig it up. The Brits use it as a troop carrier in our day."

"The same ship sunk yesterday in that ballistic missile strike?"

"Not sunk, my friend. It's turning up in the data stream now for 1941, along with all the other ships in that convoy that went missing. Christ! Things happen in this damn war, they hit CNN, and ten minutes later we get them in the Golem history variation data."

"It's all still in play," said Paul. "We have a nexus open here now, and that Russian ship is creating one as well. The longer *Argos Fire* remains in the past, the greater the likelihood that a nexus will form around that ship as well. In fact, that has probably already happened."

"I still don't see how this single Russian warship can wreak such havoc," said Maeve. "How in the world will we operate to cure this? It's catastrophic damage to the continuum. And now we learn of these physical rifts in time, yet we have no idea what caused them."

"Fairchild knew more than she was telling me," said Paul. "Once Kelly runs his numbers, I'll get back there and find out all I can. They clearly have information that we've been unable to turn up."

"Alright," said Maeve. "The keys are at the heart of this. You seem to think that ship was there to look for the very same key you were after. This Fairchild woman knew about it, and she also had yet another key in her possession. That makes her a very suspicious character in my book. I'd go so far as to suspect she might even be an operative from the future."

"She said nothing of that," said Paul. "But I'll take the matter up with her when I get to the meeting in the Azores. Yet one thing struck me. She used terminology right out of my own lexicon on time travel—Grand Finality."

"She used that exact terminology?" asked Maeve.

"Yes! I even told her I was the one who first coined the phrase. Now look—no one in the past would know of that, and only *we* know of that in our time. Correct? So if this woman used that term, then she had to hear it from someone— "

"In the future," said Maeve with equal finality. "Alright. You've convinced me we have work to do here, particularly after what you said about these natural time fissures. What would happen if they continue to develop?"

"Who can say," said Paul, "but it will not be pleasant. Think of it like cracks spreading slowly through glass, or a mirror, and here we are peering into that looking glass, seeing a reflection of the history in all this data we collect. In the beginning the glass holds, the mirror still reflects properly with only mild distortion. But, as they progress, things get worse. The glass weakens, and at any moment it could completely fail. The mirror becomes so riddled with fissures that everything it reflects is now badly distorted. See what I mean? Grand Finality. We've seen that time has the ability to smooth over some minor alterations—like that variation Robert turned up concerning Marshall Ney. There were no consequences—no cracks forming from that event. Yet time can only take so much punishment. Operations in the past create circumstances that may be very stressful. Perhaps even the annihilating power of Paradox cannot account for these things, or prevent permanent damage to the continuum. Once that happens, it can spread, progress, become fatal. Then, all at once, like the sudden triggering of an earthquake, the glass shatters, the mirror breaks, and then when we look, we see nothing at all. That's a Grand Finality. Time simply ceases to function as we have known it."

"The ambassadors from the future reported odd things happening," said Maeve. "They wouldn't say much, but it was clear to me that it was causing them great distress, and they did not know how to handle it. If something as powerful as Paradox cannot cure this, then what chance do we have?" She gave him a frustrated look, the anguish obvious on her face.

"I know how you feel, Maeve," he said, "But we have to try. We might be able to do some good here. Perhaps these keys were an attempt by future generations to try and stem the damage, and halt the progression of these natural time rifts. We have no idea how long it might take them to spread to a fatal failure state. In fact, we have no idea how far off their future is."

Maeve nodded, realizing there was nothing more they could do but try. They had a functioning Arch complex, and fuel to operate. A nexus point was open here and they were all standing in the center of that maelstrom. So her steely logic pressed forward, girded for battle.

"You said these keys had information machined on the shaft? Geographical coordinates?"

"I didn't realize that at first, but given what I learned from Fairchild, I looked at the numbers I copied from the shaft of that key when I had it. Entering the number as a geographic coordinate produced a location. Not any number will do that—this one did. Have a look."

He reached in his pocket, and produced a folded paper, opening it to show a long number: 36126225-05345633. "Two sets of numbers, separated by a dash" he said pointing at the note. "Eight characters each, or a total of sixteen numbers. That got me thinking it had something to do with computers, as everything is a permutation of eight bits to the byte. I went round and round with that, and could not make any sense of the numbers. It could have been anything. In fact, it might have just been a code of some kind. Then, when Fairchild said these keys were associated with a rift, I took another look at my number. I fooled around, and just for yucks I looked into the possibility that they were geographic coordinates. Look here... If I put a decimal point after the first two digits of each eight number set, I get a valid coordinate. Make that dash a minus sign, and place a comma at the end of the first set of eight digits, and look what comes up!"

He went over to a computer, called up Google, and simply

entered the number for a search: 36.126225, -05.345633. Maeve leaned in, seeing the results clearly returned a map at the very top of the page, and an arrow indicating the geographic location.

"Well I'll be... A map!" she breathed.

"Interesting, isn't it," said Paul. "Those folks mentioned that the shipment on *Rodney* had something to do with the Kings business, and look where the number on that key takes us. We have a major variation associated with this location, correct?"

"You mean to say that there may be a physical rift in time there?"

"Or the entrance to one," said Paul. "That place has been a British haunt for ages, and I also find it very curious that the key was sitting right there in the British Museum for decades, before it took that ill-fated journey on *Rodney*. Now... throw in a CEO from a British corporation on what was once a Type-45 destroyer. There she was, with yet another key that looked identical to the one I found. I thought it was actually the same one until she said otherwise. Think about it... Physical rifts in time that no one ever knew about, each one secured by a key engineered in the future. And the British had at least two of these keys."

"Where is that location," said Nordhausen, leaning in and squinting at the map on the screen. "Zoom out, Paul. Let me see where it is."

Chapter 26

He planned to shift back again in his old guise, Lieutenant Commander Wellings, USN. Maeve and Robert conspired to draft authentic looking new orders for him, in the event he would have to jump any security hurtles. Kelly Ramer had come in with his numbers on a laptop, fresh from the Arion supercomputer at U.C. Berkeley. He had already run the data in internal systems, but wanted a solid second opinion from the most powerful computer he could get to.

Targeting the Azores spatially was no challenge, but they needed to get the temporal coordinates perfect for August 1st, 1941. Paul knew he was taking a great risk by shifting again so soon, particularly to a meridian that had already been profoundly affected by a Heisenberg Wave.

"This is going to be dangerous," he told Maeve privately, not wanting to bother the others.

"You worried about phasing incorrectly again? You got back OK this last time."

"True, but this is different. I huddled with Nordhausen and Kelly for an hour and we had a good long look at the chronology line to assess variations. We're seeing evidence that a Heisenberg Wave is already in play, and it originated in 1908."

"Something the ship did?"

"That's what is so confounding. We just can't make any connection. Nordhausen's premise is that the data we found concerning that rogue Russian cruiser engaging Admiral Togo's fleet must be the lever. He suggests that it prompted the Japanese to renege on the treaty with Russia and reinitiate hostilities. He's dug up variation data indicating they occupied all of Sakhalin Island, and then invaded Vladivostok in reprisal. They eventually pushed into Primorskiy province, and he thinks the loss of that port, and Russia's entire position as a Pacific power, must have led to the early collapse of the Czar."

"He's got data on that?"

"No. It's just speculation, but what we do have is one major Prime going down—Josef Stalin. His assassination seems to be the key lever on events in my mind, but neither Nordhausen, nor I, can link that to anything the Russian battlecruiser did. It could have been happenstance."

"The death of a Prime Mover like Stalin would not come off that easily," said Maeve. "Time is stubborn, and she protects Primes like her own children. Remember those assassination attempts against Napoleon from our mission to Egypt to look at the Rosetta Stone? Someone took a pot shot at him, several men in fact, and each and every one had their muskets misfire."

"Yes," said Paul, "historians attributed that to the muggy climate right near Suez affecting the powder, but it did seem rather strange."

"Just like this little blip Nordhausen found about Marshall Ney—another assassination attempt that went bad," said Maeve.

"Well, Stalin didn't fare so well, and the result was that Sergei Kirov eventually took over the Bolshevik movement. That struggle, particularly with this new figure, Ivan Volkov, led to the complete fracturing of the Russian state. Yet I just can't connect the dots. We have to be missing something, so as dangerous as this is, I've got to go back. Perhaps this Fairchild woman can shed some light on all of this."

"It should be an easy shift," said Maeve. "The Azores isn't under threat for this date."

"It's not that," said Paul. "It's the Heisenberg Wave. It's clear it is already swept forward from the assassination of Stalin to affect all the history between 1909 and 1941. In fact, there may still be a lot of residual energy there. Kelly says he's detected something odd for this time period centered on late July. I think I know what it is."

"Paradox," said Maeve darkly.

"Correct. July 28 1941 was the point of initial divergence according to the Golem flags. Somehow, with all these time displacements, the damn ship ended up in 1940, a year before it first arrived, which means it's approaching its own point of entry into the time continuum, but from the past."

"Not very tidy," said Maeve.

Paul took a deep breath. "Well it's going to cause a problem. That event is sitting there like a rock in the stream. The Heisenberg Wave is hitting it right now, yet Paradox Time is completely immune to Heisenberg variations. Ever see a big wave break on a shoreline rock? All that quantum energy is going to be like a storm front at high tide meeting an impregnable rock. Sea spray everywhere— quantum foam, and a hell of a lot of variation risk, because the wave is going to be split as soon as it reaches that Paradox."

"What will happen?"

"You've seen wave dispersal patterns. A single tsunami set that encounters an island at sea could split and form two dispersal wave sets. The Heisenberg Wave might do the same thing, and then we get into a real witching hour—very odd effects, and very unpredictable."

"How so?"

"Two Heisenberg Wave patterns will form, and they'll also overlap and influence one another. A kind of temporal moiré will form on the other side of the Paradox time, a zone of chaos where we could see very strange events, and that is dangerous."

"I'm not following you, though I'll grant you the physics has some reason for this."

"Too many cooks spoil the broth," said Paul. "The Heisenberg Wave is trying to re-order the continuum to account for the variations introduced in 1908. That's what it generated from. Now it encounters Paradox, splits into a dual wave set, and then all hell breaks loose. Anything could happen as both wave sets attempt to migrate forward from the Paradox Hour. Each one could act independently. They will no longer be in sync, and the altered states they give rise to could conflict with one another. It could manifest in any number of ways, something small, or something very big."

"Example?" Maeve crossed her arms, waiting.

"If this Paradox is really solid, it generates a new Heisenberg

Wave as well, which then influences and alters the waves migrating forward from 1908. It could also reflect a good deal of that initial Heisenberg Wave backwards at the point of contact. Then we get backwash, a wave flowing in reverse order, and against the arrow of time. That causes more variation, only it migrates to the past."

"How does it manifest?" said Maeve. "Put it on a personal level so I can grasp it."

"Well… You'd get things like Déjà vu, Jamais vu, Presque vu."

"Already seen, never seen, and almost seen," said Maeve, translating the French.

"Yes, people could be beset with Déjà vu, thinking they have already lived experiences due to the ripple effect of the backwash migrating through their past. Then again, they might lose memory functionality, and suffer Jamais vu, thinking familiar or routine events were all new and completely unique. The third is when you've got something on the tip of your tongue, but just can't get it out—a sensation that something you know is impending, right on the cusp of happening or being expressed, but inhibited in some way."

"But Jamais vu is fairly rare syndrome, isn't it?"

"Yes, but it can sometimes lead to the Caprgas Delusion."

"Enlighten me," said Maeve, not being familiar with that condition.

"Psychologists think it's a delusion where a person comes to believe an associate, friend, or even a close family member or spouse, has been replaced by an identical imposter, a double."

"Invasion of the Body Snatchers?"

"Not quite, but you have the general idea. It's called the 'delusional misidentification syndrome,' and patients with extreme cases have even claimed they believed time was warped, or that they were trapped in some kind of recurring time loop."

"Now you've got my attention," said Maeve. "You think this isn't really a delusion at all."

"I have my suspicions, because things like this can happen in a Chaos Zone. These patients might have been experiencing something very real. Beyond that, you get memory loss, because lived events are suddenly being reordered, and time has to account for the memory of those events in living persons. You see, our brain is like Kelly's RAM bank—our Touchstone Database. We keep it running here at all times, and protected by a low order nexus point. A human brain is like that, only it won't be protected—unless it's also in a nexus bubble. That's why we remember the history and don't suffer the memory loss. You see how disturbing this is? Events change and things you once knew simply vanish, like that key that was hanging around my neck."

"Scary," said Maeve. "You mean I might suddenly lose a Shakespeare play and never know it was gone?"

"Worse than that—you might suddenly lose a *person* and not even remember they ever existed. And there are other effects that could arise from the dual Heisenberg Waves after the Paradox is encountered. This can cause *real* time loops, replays, echoes, phasing events, things falling out of sync with their own time, even the shifting of physical matter. The duality of the Heisenberg Wave also introduces another dangerous possibility. A doppelganger could arise—a double walker… perhaps more than one."

"Your Capgras Delusion made real?"

"Exactly. That may not matter if the duplicate is just another nobody, but if it happens with a Prime…"

"I see where this is going," said Maeve. "I had never considered this possibility."

"Yes," said Paul. "The problem is, if we do get one, it *will* most likely be a Prime, because they tend to inhabit Nexus Bubbles, which can protect them from Paradox effects. You were worried about Stalin, well suppose he were still alive in that milieu when this Heisenberg Wave splits, and the world ends up with two men of steel. Can you imagine the consequences—two Stalins? And that is just the little stuff."

"My god," said Maeve. "What else?"

"It's easy to see that all these effects can cause real chaos. In fact, now I'm beginning to really see the danger that Fairchild spoke of when she use my terminology—Grand Finality. Things could come flying apart to such an extent that time is unable to restore a viable continuum. In effect, the meridian suffers a fatal break—it shatters."

"But wouldn't that just mean things spin off onto another meridian?"

Paul gave her a long look. "You don't understand," he said slowly. "Forget the many worlds theory, that's all bunk. A meridian is just a possible reordering of events. You can have an infinite number of them, but only one universe. Everything settles onto one meridian in the end. All the others are 'also rans.' They are just possible outcomes arising from a variation introduced in the continuum by a time traveler. That variation generates a Heisenberg Wave, and as that wave moves forward, it slowly weaves all the various strands from these possible meridians back into one—but only one remains in the end. All the others never happen. Once the Heisenberg Wave completes its migration, the entire universe settles back into one meridian—the *prime* meridian. We all think it's the one we were born to, and we are correct, because you never leave the prime meridian of time, Maeve, but it changes… it changes… The one we are standing in now stretches all the way back through time. But in 1908, it started to fray, and that loosened thread is migrating forward like a run in good hosiery."

"And when it gets here?" Maeve's eyes held as much fear as anything else as she waited.

"Then God help anyone who is not in a protected Nexus Point."

There was a long silence between them after that. Maeve's eyes reflected the seriousness of what Paul was telling her now. It could all come unraveled. It might be so badly frayed that time cannot hold the rope of causality together, and that rope was now grinding and stretching against the sharpened rock of a major Paradox event.

"How long before the wave reaches us?"

"I don't know," said Paul frankly, "but we'll certainly see it coming. The Golem modules will see the variations, and we'll be able to monitor the progression of the damage on the chronology line. Right now we have solid green before 1908, except for that one little yellow blip in 1815 that seemed to have no consequence. Yet in June of 1908, things go from yellow, to amber, to red, and the damage to the meridian as it passes through WWII is quite profound. Now we see black on the chronology line for the first time, right at 28 July, 1941—Paradox."

"The ship," she said in a low voice.

Paul nodded.

"That damn Russian ship... What was the code name Nordhausen said the British once use for it?"

Paul looked down, thinking, then remembered the word.

"Geronimo," he said, and the silence returned.

Maeve finally met his eyes again, understanding. "So this is why the voices from the future went silent.... Yet you've said the Heisenberg Wave is still in the 1940s. Only minor variations have been detected here."

"Yes, the Golems are having difficulty finding variation data from beyond July of 1941. Paradox has a very strong penumbra, a shadow that can be quite impenetrable. So we aren't sure if the main Heisenberg Wave has passed through that point in time yet."

"Then what causes the minor variations we have detected here?"

"The P waves," said Paul. "Predictive waves, precursors. When an earthquake happens, the seismic waves migrate through the earth's crust. There are those that migrate through the deeper crust called body waves or P waves, and these are very fast, often reaching seismic monitors before the real damaging waves that follow. The P waves often produce low frequency acoustic energy as well."

"You mean you can hear them?"

"Not unless you have very good ears. They manifest as ultrasound, very low amplitude sound, and other ambient vibrations. Then the main surface shock waves come, which create the real shear and roll in the crust that causes most of the damage in an earthquake. My theory posits that a Heisenberg Wave acts the same way. First it sends out rapid waves that are precursors to what is going to happen. So I call them P waves, as they can be predictive of what is to come— yet they don't cause the real damage. Ever get a sensation of imminent doom? That's a P wave passing through, you sense it, feel it on some level, though you can't really hear it. They just begin introducing minor variations and other odd effects. Think of them as outliers, harbingers, little foreshocks of the damage yet to come. As to the future, they are at the greatest angle of divergence, so they get the worst of these P wave effects."

"Angle of divergence?"

Paul thrust out both arms in front of him in a V. "Two roads diverged in a yellow wood," he said. "As they do so, they are very close to one another in the beginning, yet the farther they go, the farther apart they become. Think of those roads as two possible time meridians. There are actually hundreds, thousands, perhaps even an infinite number of possible meridians, but let's just stay with these two for this example. When they are close together, they are very similar, with only minor variations. Yet as they diverge, that gulf between them sees them become very different. The farther they go, the wider the divergence, and the greater the variation. So... these precursor waves, these foreshocks, well they can cause minor alterations to both meridians, which are retained when these two roads must eventually become one road again. That's what the Heisenberg Wave is doing, pulling the two possible meridians together again into one new altered prime meridian. Think of it like a zipper, to mix metaphors here. So, way out in the future, these precursor shocks are much more severe than they are here. It's like a whip cracking. The energy flows in a wave along the whip, from the point of initial variation at the handle, to the snapping crack of real change in the future at the far end."

"You mean they are going to suffer more damage than we will at this point. The changes become progressively worse the farther on in time you go." Maeve was grasping it now.

"Correct. They could have all these effects I've described

underway there, only much worse than we'll get them here. The Ambassadors even hinted at that. Remember? Soon the main Heisenberg Wave will migrate forward, the S wave that can shear and roll events into an altered state, and it eventually settles down, joining all the possible meridians back into one new prime. We're just starting to see some of the effects here—that phase shift I went through was a perfect example. In the future, it will be much worse, possibly bad enough to stifle those voices."

Maeve nodded, with only one more question in her mind now, and it was soon on her lips. "Can we stop this? Is there anything we can do?"

"I'm not really sure, but we can damn well try."

Chapter 27

Kirov was at the heart of it now, they could all see that. Even if all the connections to the major variations had not yet been mapped out, it was clear that the ship was going to cause severe trauma to the continuum because of its presence at a point in time prior to its first displacement to the past. Paul thought deeply about the impending Paradox event, and knew what he believed might happen.

"One thing is certain," he told the team members. "That ship has already displaced from this present meridian. The event has already occurred. *Kirov* was reported missing in that Norwegian Sea accident. Then it mysteriously returns in the Pacific, evading detection by a very capable US Navy, not to mention the spy satellite networks, so that means it was arriving from some point in the past. Then after the eruption of that Demon Volcano, the ship is reported as being sunk in that recent engagement with the 7th Fleet, but I don't think that's what happened. I think the damn ship displaced again, and the Golem variation data we've got here is ample evidence of that."

"Agreed," said Robert. "So then what happens to the ship that was approaching Paradox Hour from the past?"

Paul smiled. "There aren't two ships, Robert, only one. The ship that vanished again in the Pacific recently is the same one approaching Paradox Hour in 1941. We may speak of them as if they were separate entities, but in reality, they are one and the same."

"Then how is there Paradox here?"

"Because in 1941, the ship is now about to enter time reserved for their initial arrival—Paradox Time. That is not possible."

"But you just said there was only one ship, so it's not like there's any real collision here. We have only one entity. Why wouldn't they just sail on into Paradox Hour and simply become the ship arriving from the future?"

"There you go again. There isn't a separate ship arriving from the future. *They are that ship*, and in order for them to be there at all, the first arrival event *must* occur. It's an imperative. So time will not permit what you suggest."

"Christ, how did they end up displacing to a time before their first arrival?"

"I haven't mapped out all the time they may have made, but it's clear that they somehow managed to get to 1908, and then attempted to move forward again."

"They were most likely trying to get home," said Maeve. "Yet we still haven't accounted for how the ship moves each time. We have several very energetic events that explain some of its shifts, including the nukes they were flinging around, but at other times we have evidence of a displacement that seems to have no direct cause."

"Yes," said Paul. "I'll see if Fairchild knows anything about that, but my guess is that it has something to do with the ships nuclear reactors."

"A lot of ships use nuclear propulsion, but they don't just start shifting in time," said Nordhausen.

"True, but this one does. That's a given. We have to work from known facts."

"I still don't get what you said about there being only one ship," said Kelly, finally joining the other team members after setting up his shift program for the planned mission to the Azores.

"Of course there's only one ship," Paul said flatly. "The last attempt they made to move forward created a real anomaly. They fell out of their displacement event prior to first arrival. Who knows why, but that caused a real nightmare, because the ship in the past cannot enter the same timeframe they occupied during first arrival, as I've just explained."

"They were in 1941 for twelve days," said Nordhausen. "Then they shifted out somewhere."

"Right," said Paul. Well those 12 days stand like a great stone wall, and the arrow of time is pushing the ship towards that wall from the past, yet it cannot enter that time—it's Paradox Time, and therefore completely impregnable."

"Do you think they know this?"

"We can't say. Who knows, someone aboard may be trying to sort this out, but if they did, they are sure playing chicken here."

"What do you mean?" asked Maeve.

"If they see the Paradox ahead, they should get the hell out of there before they reach that time."

"Golems haven't found any evidence of that attempt yet," said Nordhausen. "But they're still working, particularly Golem 7. It's taking a real long time to process data sets now."

"We need more computer power here," said Kelly, "but for now we have to work with what we have."

"So what if they don't move, or can't move again to avoid the Paradox?" asked Maeve.

"I think that would be impossible," said Paul. "That's the nature of Paradox. It draws a line and says it will not be possible for the ship to cross it, and it has considerable power to enforce that line—the power of annihilation."

"You mean if the ship persists and does not displace prior to reaching the Paradox time, it could simply be destroyed? Annihilated?"

"That is very possible," said Paul, "yet then we get a time loop. The ship arrives from the future as first cause dictates, and the whole mess repeats itself—with only one catch—the ship displacing from the future will reach a meridian in the past that has already been altered by the Heisenberg Wave that generated in 1908."

"I see," said Maeve. "Then the next loop is going to play out quite differently. The altered meridian the ship enters may not give rise to the same circumstances they dealt with the first time."

"Correct," said Paul, but the ship remains there in the past, and it has a momentum that is going to start this whole chain of events again."

"You mean it must all play over again, their sortie to the Med, those battles with the Japanese?"

"We don't know what may happen yet," said Paul, "because the Golem modules can't seem to reach a weight of opinion. I think the shadow from the Paradox is inhibiting their performance. Also, the Heisenberg Wave is at work here now, so all of that history may be rewritten, and may never occur. The initial events after first arrival may seem strangely similar to what happened the first time, but the longer this goes on, the more variation we will likely see. At this point, there is still no outcome that can be expressed with any real certainty. Yet I do know that ship cannot enter Paradox Time while approaching it from the past, any instance of Paradox Time, and now there are a good many locations on the continuum where those barriers had formed. I believe the next one will be in late 1942."

"Right," said Nordhausen, looking at his notes. "I have them in the Mediterranean in August of 1942. They got involved with the British Operation Pedestal."

"But isn't that on a different meridian?" asked Maeve.

"It's being revised into a new prime meridian by the Heisenberg Wave," said Paul. "That work will surely be complete for every day they live out between their initial point of entry and that next Paradox Time in August of 1942. But you say they only remained in 1941 for twelve days after the first shift."

"Yes, then they turned up in the Med a year later, and twelve days later they vanished again and re-appeared in the Pacific off Australia, yet only a day later."

"They won't be able to pull that trick off again this time, because that's Paradox Time as well. See what I mean? Their ability to move in time now is more restricted. They can't displace to any timeframe they visited before."

"Which means they can't get back to 1908 and do whatever they did there to generate the Heisenberg Wave."

"Correct, but there's still too much haze around those events. We don't know what they really did there, where the Pushpoint is that really caused the wave to form."

"Interesting," said Nordhausen. "This is going to be very interesting." As I read it, the first series of time displacements saw the Russians mixing it up with the Royal Navy, but later they seemed to mend fences and sailed as allies."

"Yes," said Paul, "I suppose the initial hours and days after the ship arrives are going to be very... interesting, just as you say."

"Is this a predetermined loop?" asked Nordhausen. "Are they fated to make the same choices and experience the same events as before?"

"Not likely," said Paul. "It's not even remotely probable. The historical milieu they are entering now is completely altered by the Heisenberg Wave. Some circumstances they encounter may be similar, but otherwise, things will be very different. And remember, nothing is ever certain when you get willful agents making choices. The ship is mechanical, but the officers and crew determine what they do with it. So we may not see them make the same time displacements as before."

"Let's hope they're good little choir boys this time around," said Nordhausen. "Maybe we should plan a mission to that ship, and we can tell them to behave themselves."

Maeve rolled her eyes. "Not bloody likely," she said.

"Yet the British in that milieu will soon detect the arrival of this ship, assuming Paul is correct," Robert pressed on. "Won't they assume everything is still chummy? Perhaps if things start off on a better footing at the outset, we can avoid some of the damage that was done in that first loop."

"That's the only ray of hope I see here," said Paul. "Actions they take now could serve to revise and alter the history the Golems have been digging up. In fact, we're already starting to see that in the Golem data. Those events from 1942 in the Mediterranean are starting to lose their certainty factors. They are falling below 40% probability now, and some may never occur."

"You mean they already started re-writing their own history?" Maeve raised an eyebrow at that.

"Apparently," said Paul. They got to 1940 somehow, and their actions there will bear on things they already did earlier when they visited 1942. Yet there will be some events that are like load bearing beams in a house. They form a chain of causality that got them there to 1940 in the first place. So while some things change, others may be much more stubborn."

"Sounds encouraging," said Nordhausen. "At least we know all of this damage hasn't solidified yet."

"That's what I'm hoping," said Paul. "The backwash from the Heisenberg Wave striking Paradox Time will stir things up. In that environment, things may take longer to solidify into a new Prime Meridian. That's probably why the wave is still stuck in the 1940s. Yet, as hopeful as that sounds, this whole situation is still very grave. There are other considerations in play here."

He gave Maeve a furtive glance and she realized he was referring to their earlier private conversation. Other considerations... dual Heisenberg Waves, backwash, fragmentation and phasing issues, time loops, and then the possibility they may end up with a doppelganger somewhere in the mix, not to mention the grim prospect of a Grand Finality forming at the end.

"Backwash," said Kelly. "I thought the Heisenberg Wave only moved forward, with the arrow of time."

"This is an aberration," said Paul. "But backward migration is a very real phenomenon in quantum physics. We have laboratory proof that quantum particles can alter their state and position in order to create a certain outcome from their past. It's referred to as backward causality, and it's one of the conditions prevalent when we get a backwash event like this. The whole situation is very dangerous. I gave Maeve an earful on that a while ago, but I won't go into it again now."

"Well, here we go again," said Maeve. "This ship has every potential to help us now, but it could still continue to ravage all this history. We can't assume their next intervention will be benign. Like it or not, the Russians are Free Radicals, and the senior officers, the real decision makers, may even be regarded as Prime Movers now. This is going to be a very chancy thing."

"And there are still several loose threads we haven't uncovered yet," said Paul. "I want to nail down how this *Argos Fire* displaced in time, and what these keys are all about. And if I can get some answers as to how *Kirov* is making these unassisted shifts, it would help us plan some kind of countermeasure as well."

"Yes," said Maeve. "We still aren't seeing the whole picture. We have no clear chain of causality between *Kirov* the ship, and the man it was named for. In fact, we still don't know why Stalin was assassinated, or who really did it."

"I'm hoping to find that out on this mission," said Paul. "And I've got a little coinage to trade for the information they might give me, like my idea about retrieving that key that went down with the battleship *Rodney*. Fairchild may be very interested in that. The British may also be very interested to learn the location of the door that particular key opens. Remember, I've deciphered the coordinates."

"First things first," said Maeve. "Let's get you there and back again in one piece, and then we'll see where we stand."

"Yes," said Paul. "Let me get this mission to the Azores under my belt. When I get back, we'll be in a much better position here. Come on Kelly. You have good numbers?"

"Solid," said Kelly adjusting the fit of his Giants baseball cap."

"Then let's get started."

* * *

They wasted no time getting to the lab monitors. Kelly manned the shift module, as always. Nordhausen and Maeve took up work at the Golem module. Between the two of them, they would closely monitor the Golem fetch data stream during Paul's mission to see if they could detect new variations. Paul was back in uniform and down through the long access corridor and elevator to the Arch. There he stood calmly in the pre-scan position, while Kelly took a double reading to generate and store his pattern signature. It was a bit like a quantum fingerprint, or DNA, describing who and what he should be when manifesting in the stream of infinite particles that defined the world.

The technology they had developed could only hold Paul safely in another time for a limited interval. Then he would have to be pulled back, though, basically, to get him to another time, the Arch was going to do something with the particles that formed his being. And to bring him back again, they simply had to cease that activity in as controlled a manner as possible. It was as Kamenski had described it to Fedorov, there were no 'places' in time, only activities and expressions of reality. To go anywhere in time, one had merely to learn how to dance with infinity. The Arch complex achieved that, though only Paul could really say how it worked, and he seldom ever tried. But it did work, and that was all that mattered.

After the tingling energy of the pattern signature capture, Paul heard Kelly's voice in the intercom wishing him well. The power revved up, with the Arch suddenly coming alive with the scintillating energy that accompanied time displacement. He stared at the broad yellow line on the cold concrete floor. Stay on this side, and you remain a movement in the here and now. Take one step across that line, and you become a movement somewhere else.

The great anaconda of causality lay coiled at your feet, and through the Arch, you could walk along that serpent's back, traversing the scales of ages past, and move to another time. The moment he took that first step, however, the only thing in the here and now that remembered him were the memories of the other team members, and that pattern signature stored safely in the massive data banks of the Arch facility computers.

As always, Paul closed his eyes to lessen the shock and disorientation of the shift, and he whispered a silent prayer that Kelly had all his numbers in order. They had experienced any number of mishaps in their many missions, and things were already critical enough without any further problems arising from their own equipment failures, or operator errors.

He reached up, straightened his naval officer's cap, and then took a deep breath. Maeve had it so right, he thought. Here we go again. Then he took that one forward step, closing his eyes, and felt the cold chill of infinity closing in around him.

It was happening…

Part X

Loose Ends

"If you lack the humility to go back and tie up the loose ends in your past, then be prepared to forever be haunted by ghosts, all of whom will come into your present and your future— staining everything and everyone with their leftover emotional and mental garbage."

- C. JoyBell C.

Chapter 28

Hornsrandir was a wild place that night. Situated on the northernmost cape of Iceland on the Denmark Strait in the Westfjord region, it was cold and cheerless, even in the summer when the light seldom faded. The winds were fierce on the exposed cape, moaning with sounds that seemed unearthly at times, like demons lamenting their fate in some unseen hell. Few people lived in the region, where only a scattering of old farm houses and hunting cottages dotted the landscape. It was a green desolate preserve, pristine in its simplicity, with emerald swards that swept up at near 45 degree angles to the edge of a jagged coastline that suddenly dropped off in sheer cliffs to the rocky shore and cold sea below.

There two men stood a bleak and lonesome watch, where even the stubborn sun, high in the sky, could not chase away the eerie green fire of the auroras that night. Fedorov had come up with the idea that they could set up a generator and *Oko* panel radar team in a small cottage, the Ice Watch, as they called it, to keep an eye on the Denmark Strait. A pair of radar technicians from the ship, and one local guide named Oleg held forth in the cottage, and Oleg was coming up to the place on the thin stony trail after a long day's hike from the nearest settlement. He carried a small backpack with gifts for the men in the cottage, tea, fresh cheese and bread, and some good hard sausage, with two bottles of wine.

Bad out tonight, he said to himself, one hand tight on the strap to the rifle slung over his right shoulder. It wasn't for protection from the Germans, and certainly no other Icelander would ever pose a threat to him, but these wild lands were said to be haunted by… other things. There was always a chance that he might find a hungry polar bear that had come up from the coast, or an occasional Arctic wolf on the prowl. Yet those were things he could deal with well enough. He would see a bear very easily in the open terrain, and so he felt reasonably secure… Until the ice fog came.

It rolled in from the coast like frosty smoke, the breath of Odin, hoary white. Soon his visibility dropped to just a very few yards, and he stopped, suddenly feeling a deep, bone chilling cold. High above, the impenetrable fog seemed to glow with milky green trails, and he knew it must be the auroras still dancing in the late summer skies. Some said the Huldufolk would creep out from their hidden rocks and glens to dance beneath the lights. The ancient reclusive elves, according to legend, might be celebrating a marriage, or the birth of a new child. Oleg was not a superstitious man, but he believed the tales, for he had seen too many strange and unaccountable footprints in these wild lands, and things he could never explain. Even in modern times, a survey of the population found that over half the people on the island believed in the Huldufolk, and he was one of them.

Oleg stopped, his eyes tight as he watched the green light color the hoarfrost all around him. He tightened his coat and pulled up his collar against the cold, and then the sound came, the dolorous moaning that was part wind, part wolf, and everything that spoke of death and foreboding. Fear struck him, and he slipped to one knee, huddling down near the ground as if to hide from some unseen demon in the mist. The sound became a roaring rumble, and he felt the earth quiver beneath his feet. Then all was still and silent, and the pale green lights slowly dissipated.

Soon a cold wind began to stir the ice fog around him, and curling eddies of frosty air swirled about the jagged edges of nearby rocks, which loomed like the dark stony shoulders of trolls as the landscape slowly cleared. Then the wind subsided, the deep cold abating, and there came only the mournful call of some wild thing on the distant bleak shore.

Shaken by the experience, now he wanted more than ever to reach the safety and warmth of the cottage, and the company of the two men there, manning their lonesome watch. He hastened along, skirting around the large boulder that lay on the broken ground beneath the stony rise that led up to the cottage. The sight of the thatched roof, and the thin stream of wood smoke from the chimney, gave him heart, and he hurried on. Soon he came tramping up to the outer porch, taking a deep breath, much relieved as he knocked firmly on the door.

He called out a greeting in Russian, one the men had taught him in their long hours at the post, but no one answered. Casting a wan look over his shoulder, he looked for any sign of recent activity out of doors. Then he tried the handle, finding the door unlocked, and nudged it open. The hinges creaked as he eased inside, thinking he might find the men dozing by the fire, or lost beneath those strange headsets they used when minding their equipment, yet, to his great surprise, there was no one there.

Why would they be out with the weather so unpredictable like this? Perhaps that sudden fog had fouled their radar set, and they went up to the cape to check on it. So this is what Oleg decided to do, yet his discomfiture only increased as he went back out and looked up the sloping rise to the high point where they had set up their devices. Nothing was there... He looked this way and that, thinking the men may have moved the equipment somewhere else. Could they have been recalled to their ship, he wondered? Did that strange whirlybird come just now, devouring them and taking them up into those fluorescent green skies? Was that what he had heard moaning through the ice fog, the deep growl of the engines on that flying contraption?

He took a long look around, shaking his head, and then going back down the rise to the cottage. Once inside he shifted off his pack, and set his rifle down by a chair. Then he saw something on the bare wooden table that seemed odd, a pot of freshly brewed tea, the steam still curling from the spout of the iron kettle. One cup was half full on the table, the second broken and spilled on the wooden floor.

He could picture the men in his mind... at least he thought he could. Suddenly it seemed very difficult to summon up the memory of their faces, though he had spent many hours with them there in the past. Frowning, he scratched his head, looking about, and finding absolutely no sign of the men, not their equipment or books, no boots and coats, nor any possession—only those two cups of tea, one half empty, the other broken. He walked up to the wooden table, pulling off his gloves and feeling something was very wrong here. One hand touched the side of the iron kettle, finding it still very warm, as though taken from the fire just minutes ago.

And yet, with each minute that now passed, his mind seemed to be enfolded with the same deep ice fog that he had encountered earlier on the trail. Why had he found it so necessary to walk all day and come up here to the hunter's lodge? He knew damn well that pickings were very lean in the summer. He might find an occasional fox or minx, enough for a good pelt or two, but little more. And who had taken the liberty just now to make themselves at home in his cottage?

They must have seen me on the trail, he thought, and when that fog bank rolled through on the wind, they took the opportunity to slip away. Then again, it might have been the reclusive Huldufolk, curious about his isolated haunt, and creeping about in the fog to see what they might find. That he had come there that day, bearing gifts for two strange Russian men, never entered his mind. It fled like the thin, insubstantial tendrils of a dream, the images fading, recollection losing its grip, memories lost. Never again would he think about them, sitting there before those strange humming boxes and winking lights in the night, their eyes watching the odd sweep of a phosphorescent clock face as the green hand swept in endless circles. He knew nothing of the two Russians, nor anything more of the fact they had ever been there.

He was simply Oleg, out that morning to visit his hunting lodge, and curious as to who might have been in his private little domain, helping themselves to his tea.

* * *

First Able Seaman Thomas Winn was back at his station, staring oddly at the new equipment in the radio room he would monitor from time to time. It had been brought in by the Russians, quietly installed and fed power from the ship's electrical system, and he had been taught how to use it, bemused at first by the many new dials and switches. Yet Winn was an old radio man, with many years of experience, and he soon learned that this one worked much like the other equipment he was so familiar with, once he got used to the dials and switches.

There had been very little traffic on the device of late. The fleet had moved south to the Azores, where a gathering of several new and unfamiliar looking ships had been secreted away in a broad bay. Crewmen pointed and whispered about them, wondering what they were, but in time, the men got on with their business and let them be.

From time to time, *Invincible* had sortied out with a pack of destroyers, watching the waters east towards the bay of Biscay for any sign of enemy activity. HMS *Glorious* was on station there to look for the Germans, but they never came.

Old *Hindenburg* and the rest took a little spanking and went running off to France, he thought. Yet we lost a good ship in *Rodney*, and word is we damn near lost *Glorious* as well. But we made them pay, or so it's been said. Jerry had a carrier out here too, and it never made it to France. The Russians put the fire to that one, and sent it down, or so I've been told.

Funny thing that they slipped off like that, right in the thick of things, and haven't been seen or heard from since. The Admiral has been down here nigh on every other day, and always with the same bloody questions—any news of the Russians? Any messages on the secure comm link channel? He seemed good and worried about that ship, and so maybe we lost more than *Rodney* that day. Maybe the Russian ship went down as well, ran afoul of a U-boat and took a torpedo that ripped open her sides and sent her down so fast that no one could even get off an S.O.S...

Yes, I've seen it before when I was with the convoys out of Halifax. Damn U-boats would come prowling like sharks, nipping at the flanks of the convoy, and then a ship might just light up with fire and smoke, all on a moment, and be gone the next.

Yet we had no sign of that with the Russians. Watchman Jimmy Corkle has a few tall tales to tell about how it went missing—just like that, one minute there, and the next minute gone. But Jimmy Corkle has told more than his fair share of tall tales from the mainmast, and could not always be taken seriously. Still, the silence on that radio set was deepening with time.

Then it happened.

He was sitting there that day, minding his signals traffic on the British set, where plans were being made for some visit by that other odd ship, the *Argos Fire*. It had been riding at anchor out in that secluded bay with the rest of those new ships, the funny fleet as the men called them now. A message came in on the Russian radio set, and he quickly typed it up for the Admiral, glad he would have something to hand him when he came down today with his questions. Then it happened, that strange glitch, the green fire, the tingling in the air all about the room.

He saw what looked like static fireflies around him, and particularly near that new equipment set he had learned to monitor. Thinking the damn thing might be shorting out, he reached for it to turn off the power, and then felt a sharp pain, as if his hand had been bitten by something, or burned on a hot teapot. He yanked it back, cupping it in his other hand, his eyes still wide with surprise and shock as the light danced around the radio set, green fire enveloping it, but held at bay by a shimmering sheen of scintillating blue.

Then there came a sudden chill, and a moaning sound, like the braying of the Hound of the Baskervilles. He felt a sensation of dread, a clammy fear settling over him, as if something was coming for him, to this very place, with an anguished hunger that wanted everything here dead and gone.

"God save me," he breathed, leaning back away from the infernal Russian machine. Amazingly, he saw the device shudder, alight with that strange green and blue fire, and then the moaning trailed off, long and distended. The cold abated, and things settled down.

The quiet that followed was eerie and still, the quiet of fog, the stillness of death, the chill of things done and forgotten. But unlike Oleg in his cold, lonesome cottage, Tommy Winn remembered everything just as it was. There sat that radio set, the lights gleaming red and green, as always. The momentarily fit had passed, and now the silence abated, and the room was suddenly humming with all the other equipment, as though nothing had happened.

Yet he could still feel the sting in his hand, and when he looked there, he saw his fingertips looked red and inflamed, as though singed by fire. He had the distinct feeling that he had survived something very dangerous just now. It was as if something had reached for that damn Russian radio, clawing at it, wanting it, a ravenous hunger. Yet when the green fire came, that icy blue shield around the device had staved off that hunger, and stilled its deep growl.

He felt like a man on a fishing boat, merrily going about his business and baiting his line when a great white shark reared up, jaws gaping, serried white teeth wet with seawater as its endless maw opened to devour him. But the jaws snapped shut, finding nothing to clamp down on! The demon was gone as quickly as it had come, leaving him shaken, wet with fear, his pulse racing, but otherwise alive and well.

He crossed himself, whispering saints be praised, and he was grateful he was still alive, though he could not think what he should be afraid of. He was sitting on the most powerful ship in the Royal Navy, behind nearly a foot of solid steel armor plating in the conning tower, and yet, at that moment, it was as if he was sitting at the edge of perdition itself, his hand burned by the fire when he reached for that machine.

Lucky me, he thought. Once burned, twice shy, and I've been burned more than a few times in the past. That damn thing must have suffered a fit, and I might have shocked myself senseless if I had laid my hand on it. Pulled back just in time, and all seems well and in order now. I'll have to report the problem to the maintenance chief, and see if they can have a look at the power feeds. The Russians said they had to put something they called an adapter on the plugs, but maybe things have fallen out of order. Bonkers in here just now, wasn't it? How did it get so bloody cold? And look at me here now, sweating like a school boy before the master and thinking I've a swat from a sturdy cane waiting for me.

Tommy Winn would never know just how close to perdition he really was that moment. Now that it had passed, all seemed well as before, but something had indeed reached for the Russian radio set, the green fire and endless hunger of Paradox. Yet it had been frustrated, held at bay, kept safe in the strange nexus point that had formed around a very special Admiral, on a ship that now skirted the swirling edge of the whirlpools of time, HMS *Invincible*. She had lived up to her name in that hour, steadfast, stalwart, invincible, and Tommy Winn was living proof.

And so was the Russian radio set, still sitting there unharmed in the silence of its electronic dreams, even as another similar set, its first cousin, sat in similar bliss safely aboard the *Argos Fire*. Something had reached for it that day as well, but it had survived intact the same way Tommy Winn's set had prevailed, the hunger of Paradox frustrated by some arcane twist in the logic of Time.

Chapter 29

It was that radio set which would suddenly come to play a very important role in what would now happen aboard the battlecruiser *Kirov*. Fedorov passed a sleepless night, slipping in and out of dreams, waking up and thinking all he had just experienced was just a bad nightmare, until he heard the voice of Chief Orlov on the ship's intercom, summoning the crew to the morning shift. A feeling of fear and alarm jangled his nerves when he again realized where he was, an old soul on a new ship, a changeling spirit, spared from the wrath of Paradox, and given this new life.

Will this happen again and again, he wondered? He thought of all that might lay before him, and the daunting challenges he now faced. First off, how could he convince the Admiral and Captain Karpov that the ship moved in time? That should be much easier now, he thought.

I did it before, and even when I wasn't entirely sure of what was happening myself. So now, with all I know, it should be easier to prove my case. I must find a way to speak with the Admiral. Karpov will be very difficult at first, but I know how I convinced him before, and maybe those same old tricks will work again.

Can I just come out with it? Of course not. They'll think I was absolutely insane, particularly after that fall I took and all the time I spent in sick bay. No. I must be very cautious at the outset, and very clever. I must wait as evidence begins to present itself, and then interpret that evidence as I did before. Yet the situation is very perilous now. Beginnings are always chancy affairs. Last time, we encountered that British task force, though that isn't likely now. Nothing in my *Chronology of the War at Sea* is likely to be reliable, though that remains to be seen.

From what I gathered with Nikolin, the German fleet made it to France—at least *Hindenburg* did. That will mean Admiral Tovey and Home Fleet will most likely be standing a watch against any further breakout attempt. Those ports are right on Britain's life line to the

Middle East. It will probably mean the British bases in the Azores will become the center of gravity for Home Fleet now, and not Scapa Flow. So I must look for news from there, and perhaps I can find a way to contact Admiral Tovey. The important thing at the outset is to prevent this ship from reflexively engaging the British as we did the last time. Tovey is the key to that.

As he made his way to the bridge, his feet felt leaden, his body and soul weighted with the burden of being the only man on the ship that knew what was really happening. Up the last stairway and through the hatch he went, easily adopting his old role as navigator, for in truth his Captain's hat had never fit him all that well.

"Fedorov," said Orlov, seeing him come on the bridge. "Sleep well with Zolkin last night?" He chuckled with that, winking at Samsonov.

Fedorov gave him a peremptory salute. And made for his post, warily looking about to see who was on duty. He eyed Nikolin, who had also just taken his station, and gave him a silent nod of his head. The junior Lieutenant began checking his equipment, doing all the routine things he would normally accomplish as he started his shift. But as he put on his headset, he gave Fedorov another look, and the two men passed a knowing glance. There was a question in his eyes, and Fedorov gave him a quiet nod in the affirmative. Karpov wasn't on the bridge yet, nor the Admiral, and Fedorov hoped Nikolin might get that message out on the coded ship-to-ship channel and learn something.

He heard Nikolin speaking quietly on his headset microphone, sending out a standard 'all ships' hail, and awaiting a reply. Orlov inclined his head, and thought he would see what Nikolin was doing, drifting over from the CIC where he often hovered with Samsonov.

"Ready with your report, Nikolin?"

"Sir? You mean on the radio transmission intercepts? Yes sir."

"Good, because the Admiral will want to know everything as soon as he arrives. And you Fedorov? Is Petrov's manual plot correct?"

"It is, sir. I have us still circling at 10 knots over *Slava's* last reported position."

"Today we get the submersible down for a good look at the sea floor. Alright, be sharp. Karpov will be here soon as well."

"Aye sir."

Orlov drifted away, off to find coffee in the briefing room, and Fedorov realized that was the last anyone saw of him on the old ship. He passed a moment, wondering if this Orlov might have come from the old *Kirov* again, but he could see no sign that Orlov was in any way distressed, and did not think the Chief would handle these events so calmly if he had shifted here. No. This was the old Orlov, the man he was before Karpov tried to take the ship, and he was busted down to a lowly Lieutenant and sent off to Troyak and his Marines. Yet here they were, sailing in a world that other man had done much to shape. It was Orlov's discontent that led him to jump ship on the KA-226, and that ended up starting that long journey to find him again, a journey that led to Ilanskiy…

Fedorov looked at Nikolin again, waiting and wondering whether he had any response. The other man just gave him a silent shake of his head. Nothing, and something more died in Fedorov as he realized the other ship might be gone. Surely they would have heard that coded message, though he still held out a little hope in thinking the old ship might very well be in that same eerie fog as before, out there somewhere, elsewhere, and perhaps destined to appear again one day. Yet there was no certainty there, and he could not invest too much hope in that. He had to deal with things here and now.

Kirov was gone, at least for now, yet still right beneath his feet. The King is dead… Long live the King. This ship now ascended to the throne of fate, and he was its real Captain, that he knew, even though he no longer wore the rank. It was his responsibility to steer the ship safely now, and prevent this situation from spinning off on a course that would cause even more harm.

So now he set his mind on how to proceed. The Admiral was the key factor here. He held the real authority, but Fedorov wondered if he would again suffer that debilitating collapse, an effect from that first shift, that led to Karpov taking command at a most inopportune time. If that happened again…

"Admiral on the bridge!"

Orlov had been leaning over Samsonov's station again, and he stood up straight, saluting as Volsky appeared through the hatch, breathing a bit heavily as he always did.

"One day we will get elevators installed on these ships," he said with a smile. He noticed Fedorov at once, and took a moment with him.

"Mister Fedorov, welcome back. I trust you are well?"

"I am sir. The dizziness has passed and I feel fine now."

"Good, good. Mister Orlov, is the submersible staged for launch?"

"Ten minutes, sir. Byko is checking the seals on the hatch."

"Very good, then I will take Mister Nikolin's report, unless we have any further contacts. Rodenko? Tasarov?"

"All clear sir," said Rodenko.

"No undersea contacts, Admiral. All quiet," Tasarov gave his report, seeing Fedorov watching him closely, a strange look on his face, like he had found a long lost cousin.

"Then Mister Nikolin can tell me what he was listening to on the radio last night. Any news?"

"Just the same, sir. Old WWII documentaries. They just keep playing the same old news, something about Barbarossa, and Smolensk was the latest."

"Barbarossa? That was the German attack on Russia in 1941, am I correct, Mister Fedorov?"

"Yes sir," said Fedorov, eager for any interaction he could get with the Admiral. "The First Battle of Smolensk was fought between mid June and September, 1941. It was the first instance where the Red Army recovered enough to put up stubborn resistance, and delayed the German advance on Moscow for two full months."

"That's our resident historian," said Volsky. "So that battle would be at its height now. Yes? Perhaps they are commemorating the 80 year anniversary of these war events. Yet no other news, Nikolin?"

"Just this old war news, Admiral."

"Still no GPS feed," said Fedorov, wanting to stay engaged. "And I have no Loran-C data from Jan Mayen—nothing from the Met."

"The Met?"

"That's the weather station at Metten on Jan Mayen. There's a four man team there year round, and then the main installations at Olonkin City and Helenesanden. Most activity has moved there, but we still call the station the Met." This had been important evidence the first time around, and Fedorov wanted to get it on the table as soon as he possibly could.

"I see... Can we signal them, Mister Nikolin?"

"I can try, sir."

"Good. Get the weather report while you are at it, and see what they know. Do it now."

The intercom sounded a single tone and they heard the voice of Chief Byko reporting that the submersible operation was ready for launch.

"Order them to proceed, Mister Orlov."

"Aye sir."

Fedorov knew that Nikolin's call on any normal channel to Jan Mayen would go unanswered. That would only deepen the mystery, and he knew it was his first real chance to get control of events here. It had been his suggestion that they take a helicopter to that Island that was key in providing real evidence that something profound had happened to the ship. None of those installations he had just talked about were there in 1941, not even the landing strip that was used by Norwegian *Hercules* cargo planes to supply the island. There was only a small Norwegian weather team, always wary of imminent German attack.

It did not take long for Nikolin to report no contacts, and

Fedorov was watching the Admiral very closely to gauge his reaction. He nodded, settling into the Captain's chair, just as Karpov was announced.

"Captain on the bridge!"

"As you were, as you were." Karpov huffed in, all business, stepping to the Admiral, and giving Fedorov a sideward's glance as he passed.

"Any news?" he asked brusquely.

"Nothing. Nikolin reports the same old war stories, and we can't even raise the Norwegian weather station on Jan Mayen." Volsky gave him a searching look.

"This is most irregular, Admiral. Nothing on the BBC? Nothing from Severomorsk? Nothing from Iceland or Norway?"

"Only the same stories we heard last night. They are still commemorating the war years."

"Nonsense," said Karpov, looking around, scanning the sea through the viewports. "And still no sign of *Slava*? Well, when we get that submersible to the bottom of the sea, we may finally get to the bottom of this little mystery as well. I fully expect to find wreckage there, and if this is so, then our situation here takes on a rather dark tint. Are we at battle stations? I heard nothing on the intercom."

"We have no contacts within Fregat range, and Tasarov certifies no undersea threat. So I see no need to put the ship on a wartime footing until we know more."

Karpov seemed unhappy with that. "We lose both *Orel* and *Slava*, and can no longer raise Severomorsk, or anyone else for that matter, and you see no need to take precautions? We should be more careful, Admiral."

"Let us test your supposition, Mister Karpov. The submersible is in the water now, and on the way down. They will use both radar and sonar down there to give the seabed a good looking over. If there is wreckage, they should find it with no difficulty, as it would still be very warm on infrared. If we do find wreckage, then we have another scenario on our hands, but until I can determine what happened here, we will not yet assume it is World War Three."

There it was, thought Fedorov. Karpov's instinct for battle was not really misplaced, yet the Admiral's caution and calm served to keep a lid on things. Fire and ice. He saw the Captain fold his arms, shoulders hunched, his eyes tight.

"Consider the situation carefully, Admiral," he said. "there was clearly a detonation of some kind before we lost contact with *Orel*. The fact that now, more than 24 hours later, we still have no GPS or satellite links, is very telling." He looked Fedorov's way now. "Correct Lieutenant? I see you are finally back at your post."

"Correct sir. No GPS or satellite data. No Loran-C out of Jan Mayen, though that signal has not been much used since 2006."

"So you are plotting manually?"

"Yes sir, Petrov had correct coordinates."

"Good...." Now Karpov lowered his voice slightly, speaking to the Admiral as Fedorov strained to hear their conversation.

"No satellites. Why is that, Admiral? We have gone over our equipment here from top to bottom. It is not a system failure. If those satellites are up there, then we should be able to bounce a signal off of them and get a response. But we get nothing! What does that tell you?"

"I agree, it is most alarming," said Volsky. "Yet here we sit, the flagship of the Red Banner Northern Fleet, and surely a prime target of any war aim if a conflict were underway. Yet we have been cruising in circles over *Slava's* last reported position for eighteen hours, and no one has bothered us. We've seen nothing, not a ship, nor any plane on our screens."

"And let me suggest why that may be so," said Karpov, lowering his voice to a whisper now. "If they hit us, then we surely hit them back. And they most assuredly hit us, Admiral, or we would not be looking for wreckage on the sea floor now."

"That may be so," said Volsky, "but yet we may have something else here, a simple accident. As I have said, until I know World War Three is actually underway, I have no intention of starting it myself.

Now calm yourself, Captain. Set an example for the men. We will get our report from the submersible soon enough, and then the senior officers will discuss this, and we will decide what to do."

Yet soon enough was not soon enough.

Tasarov looked over, the light of alarm in his eyes, and spoke.

"Con, Sonar. I have screw noise. Analyzing possible range now, but I'm estimating it is at least 80 kilometers out. Bearing 180 degrees… two distinct contacts, yet they are traveling together."

"The Fregat system won't pick them up for some time sir, said Rodenko. My Over the Horizon signal's processor isn't returning anything yet. It might still be suffering the effects from that incident with *Orel*. I can say one thing. I have no long wave IFF data. No recognizable signals emissions at all. They must be running silent."

"There," said Karpov. "Don't tell me that is *Slava* towing those targeting barges. Two ships creeping up on us like a pair of thieves. They are most likely British destroyers, and if we had a helicopter up we would have seen them long ago. Recommend action stations and rig for missile defense at once!"

Chapter 30

The warning sent Fedorov's pulse running faster, for he knew this contact would appear to be just what Karpov suggested, ships running up, emissions silent, hoping to appear by stealth. Yet his mind raced to find a way to head off what could soon become a fatal collision. He looked at Admiral Volsky as he considered the situation.

"Mister Nikolin," said the Admiral. "Hail those ships. Use English please, and request positive identification."

True to form, Volsky's instinct was to talk first and shoot later, just the opposite of what Karpov might have done. The Captain looked at him, waiting, and Volsky obliged him by ordering the ship to action stations.

"We will come to level three alert as a precaution, Mister Karpov. Let us see what develops here."

"Very well. Make it so, Orlov. But think, Admiral. Two ships, with no IFF data and no signals emissions? It is obvious what they are doing, sir."

"Yes," said Volsky, "but yet it makes no sense. Our operations here should be no mystery to them. We were overflown by British reconnaissance planes three days ago, so they know we are out here. And they most certainly know our capabilities. Are you suggesting they are planning to attack us?"

"That may have already happened," said Karpov sharply.

"Yet here we sit, without a scratch. How do they hit *Slava* and *Orel* with such precision while missing the main event? If these ships were the culprits they could have launched a missile attack long ago. Why move into visual range, and direct line of sight for our Fregat system? Would you attack in this manner?"

Karpov folded his arms, his face hard, but Volsky's arguments did make some sense to him. No, he would not attack in so foolish a manner as this. His missiles would have been in the air long ago if this were a wartime scenario. Yet his impatience was obvious.

"Nikolin?" He looked at the communications station, waiting

tensely for more information.

"Nothing sir. I get no response to my hails."

"Not very friendly, Admiral," said Karpov tersely.

Volsky frowned. "Keep trying, Mister Nikolin."

"Admiral, sir." Fedorov was unable to remain silent at the edge of this critical moment. "I suggest we send up helo at once and get eyes and cameras on this contact. I believe I can identify it easily if the helo gets me a profile."

Karpov gave him a hard look. "If it isn't shot down first," he said with a scowl. "Mind your navigation plots, Mister Fedorov."

Volsky considered, still waiting on Nikolin, but the young Lieutenant just shook his head. "I get no response, Admiral. They are running silent."

"And yet they obviously know we have detected them… Tasarov, can you give us a fix on their course or speed?"

"Yes sir, they appear to be steady at about 20 knots. I've sent the data to Fedorov."

"Sir," said Fedorov again, eyeing Karpov warily. "I have plotted the exact heading and course from that data. They are not on an intercept course. If they continue without turning they will miss us by at well over twenty kilometers. I don't think they are even aware of us yet."

"Close enough," said Karpov. "We are already well within range of their missile systems now. Why don't they answer our hails? We are now within our rights to fire a warning shot. Perhaps that will loosen their tongues."

"Mister Karpov," said Volsky, somewhat irritated. "I have passed a hundred ships at sea, and many have not taken the time to chat with me on the radio. I might have ignored this contact myself in peacetime, but given the present circumstances, I requested identification. And I have seldom found it necessary to shoot at these passing ships, whether they bothered to fraternize or not. You are making many assumptions here that have not been proven. Are these warships? Civilian traffic?"

"Up here?" Karpov shook his head. "Where would civilian traffic be going? NATO was well aware, as you say, that we were here to conduct live fire exercises."

"Yes? And they also may have determined that something has gone wrong. These ships could simply be investigating that possibility, as we might if the shoe were on the other foot. They might even be thinking to render assistance."

"Then why don't they contact us?"

"That remains a bit of a mystery." Volsky thought for a moment, then turned to the Operations Chief. "Mister Orlov. Order the helo bay to send up the KA-226. They are to approach the contact, stating their identification and origin, and obtain a live video feed so that we can positively identify these ships. It appears our Navigator has plotted the most prudent course at the moment."

"Aye sir." Orlov was immediately on the intercom. "Helo bay— execute emergency launch. KA-226. Approach and identify seaborne contacts to the south. State ID and origin en-route on all channels. This is Chief Orlov."

"I don't like this sir," said Karpov. "What is wrong with their radio sets? They are acting as though this were a wartime scenario, emissions tight and radio silent. I recommend we rig for missile defense and obtain targeting information now."

"Our sonar system already tells us where they are," said Volsky. "Mister Tasarov, pass active contact information to the C.I.C. Mister Samsonov, activate both Klinok and Kashtan close defense systems, but do not go live with targeting radars until I order this. Understood?"

"Defensive systems only?" said Karpov. "This is dangerous. At this range we would have just a few seconds to react if they launch a missile salvo."

"I am well aware of that," Volsky said quickly as they heard the sound of the helicopter engines turning over for liftoff, yet Karpov persisted.

"Our holds are crammed with surplus missiles for the live fire exercises. One hit sir… That is all it will take, and it need not even be in a critical location. If we get a fire…"

Volsky held up his hand, stilling the Captain's warning. "Yes, Mister Karpov, everything we do at sea is dangerous, particularly in a situation like this. We are like two men here, with a bucket of gasoline between us. They know that as well as I do, and I do not suppose either one of us thinks lighting a cigarette is a very good idea now. Let us wait. They will see our helicopter launch as standard operating procedure. It will not be unexpected, particularly given their silence."

"That is what concerns me," said Karpov. "They clearly hear our hails, yet they remain silent. They can see what we are doing with the helicopter. Why don't they respond?"

"I am considering all possibilities now," said Volsky. "First off, they may be just as confused by the lack of outside radio transmissions as we are. We cannot raise Severomorsk, and they might not be able to reach their home bases either. You saw the effects in the sea and sky. Perhaps something bigger happened here, a solar event of some kind. It took us hours before we got our equipment sorted out. Perhaps theirs has not yet recovered."

"Yet they also have helicopters, at least if this is a modern British Type 45 out there. The lack of radar signatures could also be a deliberate attempt at deception."

"Or an abundance of caution," Volsky said quickly. "I would not be so foolish as to maintain radio silence in this situation, but I have known many Captains who sometimes do foolish things at sea, particularly under stress—or under orders."

"Agreed," said Karpov, "but that suggests they have moved to a wartime footing, as we should by default given what has already happened. Where is *Orel*, Admiral? Where is *Slava?* We are the aggrieved party here, and we have every reason to assume the worst."

"I do not disagree with you, but I choose to proceed as planned with the helicopter. If this is the Royal Navy, or perhaps Norwegian ships, then we will know in a matter of a few minutes. Which reminds me. Mister Nikolin, what did you learn from the weather station on Jan Mayen?"

"Nothing sir. They did not respond either."

Now Volsky folded his arms, the situation becoming more serious with each passing moment. Why no radio response, from these ships or the facility on Jan Mayen? There was clearly a detonation of some kind, he thought. If Karpov was correct, then that was a submarine attack, possibly intending to take us out as well. Yet Tasarov is very, very good. He might have failed to detect a stealthy British sub, particularly if it was just lying in wait for us here, but he would have certainly heard torpedoes in the water, and without question. So I do not think *Orel* was targeted deliberately, yet the disappearance of *Slava* is most disturbing.

"Any word from the submersible?"

"They report all clear below, but they are still searching."

Volsky nodded. Yes, where was *Slava*? That is the difficult piece of this puzzle. If there was an accident aboard *Orel*, we were much more vulnerable, within 5000 meters of that boat when it happened. Yet *Slava* was over 30 kilometers to the south, and well out of harm's way. For it to simply disappear like this is a strong argument for Karpov's view of things. One accident I might believe, but two, and both at the same time? That is preposterous... unless...

Sabotage...

That thought arose in his mind now like a dark shadow. The political situation has been very grim of late. There are many back home who are set on taking a hard line, just as Karpov might here. It is not outside the realm of possibility that someone would take such a rash action. Two old ships suddenly suffer catastrophic loss, but not *Kirov*, no, not the fleet flagship. *Slava* was ready for the bone yard, as was *Orel*, but this ship would be needed if it ever came to war. We are the heart of the entire Red Banner Northern Fleet.

"Nikolin," he said. "Have you sent out an all ship's respond on command level channels?"

"I have sir, on 272, but I get no response from any fleet unit." He glanced furtively at Fedorov as he finished.

"Quite the little mystery here," said the Admiral.

"Yet one that paints a very dark picture, Admiral." Karpov still had that warning in his eyes.

"No response from any ship or submarine? You know as well as I do that a 272 coded message designates it as coming from this ship, the fleet flagship, and therefore from me," said Volsky, "the current commander of that fleet. It demands a response, and yet we hear nothing, as if—"

"As if they were not there," Karpov finished, "just like *Slava* and *Orel*."

"You are suggesting that our enemies have destroyed every ship in the Red Banner Northern Fleet? Every submarine? Yet they overlooked us?"

"Those two ships out there may be here to finish the job," said Karpov. "You and I both know what happens if they fire first. Our defenses are very good, but something might get through."

"KA-226 is on approach," said Nikolin. "I can hear their salutation, but there is still no response."

"Mister Rodenko," said Volsky. "I wish to know the moment you detect any targeting radars painting that helo."

"I've been watching, Admiral, but nothing."

"Rodenko," said Fedorov quickly. "have a look down at 39.9MHz, then try 85MHz and finally 600Mhz. Look for 3.5 meter wavelengths."

Rodenko gave Fedorov an odd look. "They shouldn't be using that. British Sampson radar is in the S band, in the microwave spectrum, but I suppose there's no harm in looking elsewhere."

"Full of suggestions today," said Karpov looking at his Navigator. "I did not know you were trained for radar, Fedorov. Kindly leave that job to Rodenko."

Some tense moments passed, but soon Nikolin spoke up with an update. "I'm getting live video feed from the KA-226," he said.

"Put it on the overhead," said Volsky, and all eyes were now focused on that screen, a wide HD panel that could link with the ship's Tin Man optical systems, and receive feeds from all the helicopters. The KA-226 was particularly suited to scouting and reconnaissance, with an array of very powerful cameras. Volsky squinted at the screen, seeing two ships there in the sea haze. It was difficult to make them out, particularly as they were steaming bow first, but the helo soon began to angle away at about 10,000 meters, swinging around to get a silhouette view.

The moment was coming, thought Fedorov, for he knew what they were most likely to see now. Yet how to convince the Admiral and Karpov that these were old WWII class vessels? He reached quickly for his silhouette book from the small library he kept at his station, waiting tensely. There they were, three stacks amidships, slightly inclined, and the center stack thicker than the others. The ships looked to be approaching 10,000 tons, and he knew exactly what he was looking at.

"Very odd," said Volsky. "That certainly does not appear to be a Type-45 destroyer, and they look much too big to be Norwegian or Danish frigates. They are certainly not Type-23 Class British frigates either. Am I correct, Mister Fedorov? You said you could identify these ships. Any thoughts?"

It had to begin somewhere, thought Fedorov. Yes, the insanity had to begin. It was already started, and well underway, except he was the only one who knew that now. So his course was clear, his mission obvious. This ship and crew would eventually determine that what he was now about to say was the truth, as impossible as it might sound. So there was nothing else to do here but to speak that truth, as convincingly as possible.

"Sir," he said, clearing his voice as Karpov frowned at him again. "This will not make any sense, but I believe those are a pair of *County* Class heavy cruisers, Royal Navy ships. See the three stacks amidships? That is very distinctive of this class. There were several variations, and that would be in the *Kent* subclass. This other ship would be in the *London* subclass, but it's very similar. I have the silhouettes right here, Admiral." He held up his book, all the world's fighting ships, and he was reaching for his pad device where he also had several applications stored with digital imagery of many WWII vessels.

"*County* Class?" Volsky adjusted his hat. "I am not familiar with that class. Is it something new? These ships do not look like anything else in active service with the Royal Navy."

"Not in our day, sir." He let slip that first subtle hint, but did not lean on it too heavily.

"Let me see that," said Karpov, huffing over, an irritated expression on his face. He squinted at Fedorov's book, hovering over his station like a shadow, his finger running down the ship silhouettes as he shook his head. "This is useless," he said. "This is old data, Fedorov."

"Here, sir," Fedorov pointed. "Now have a look at that video feed."

"Karpov glanced up at the screen, then back at Fedorov's book, still shaking his head. "Yes, there is a clear resemblance, but you are seeing a bear in the kitchen, Fedorov. What is this, one of your old WWII books? Don't be foolish."

"But sir, look at those gun turrets on the video!"

Karpov looked again, a sudden silence settling over the bridge. The guns… yes, those nice big twin 8-inch gun turrets up front, in a shape and configuration that had not been used in naval ship design for decades. They were sure to get attention, a commanding presence even in this video feed. The image zoomed as the KA-226 switched to high powered optics, and the image focused to a sharper resolution. There was no hull number, but an obvious wartime camo scheme was painted on the hulls.

"Those are 203mm gun turrets, two forward and another two aft. This is a County Class vessel. I am certain of this. There was no other ship built to this configuration."

"But certainly very old, yes Fedorov?" Said Volsky. "When might these have been built?" the Admiral swiveled in his chair, listening to what Fedorov was saying now.

"They were laid down in the mid 1920s, sir. May I ask Nikolin to do something here? I think it can solve this mystery once and for all."

"More bright ideas, Lieutenant?" said Karpov, his tone obviously irritated. "You want to be Captain, Mister Fedorov? Then complete your training back in Severomorsk. Otherwise, leave these matters to the senior officers."

"Just a moment," said the Admiral. He had heard that Fedorov was a very astute young officer, and his file looked very promising. In his time aboard the ship, he had always found him competent and level headed, and his studious nature and penchant for naval history made him very likable in his eyes. "Let the Lieutenant speak," he said. "Fedorov, what do you suggest?"

Karpov looked furious, but Fedorov knew he could not allow himself to be cowed by that man's anger now, nor that of Orlov, who was also looking at him with a very unfriendly expression on his face.

"Sir... Have Nikolin send this—in English please. *Geronimo, Geronimo, Geronimo.* Home Flag respond as per fleet signals protocol one. That's a command level channel for Royal Navy operations," he explained to Volsky.

"What is going on here, Fedorov?" Karpov began to raise his voice. "Fleet signals protocol one? You are working for the Royal Navy now? Sit down and mind your damn station! Admiral, I recommend we increase to alert level one and prepare for combat. I don't care who or what they are. Either they respond to our hails or we must take stronger measures."

Nikolin looked from Karpov to Volsky, and then back to Fedorov. The tension on the bridge was thickening, and he did not know what he should do. Thankfully, the Admiral spoke next, and his authority was final.

"Mister Nikolin, I will indulge our young Lieutenant, for no better reason than the unpleasant alternative the Captain now insists upon. Send that message. I do not know what this is all about, Mister Fedorov, but the ship will also come to alert level one, and Mister

Samsonov, you will now activate the forward 100mm bow gun."

"All hands," said Orlov on the intercom. "The ship will come to alert level one and man all battle stations!"

The loose end of Time's tangled thread had come full circle, but the knot that would now be tied would have everything to do with the fate of all days to come.

Part XI

Chaos Zone

"*There are only patterns, patterns on top of patterns, patterns that affect other patterns. Patterns hidden by patterns. Patterns within patterns. If you watch close, history does nothing but repeat itself. What we call chaos is just patterns we haven't recognized. What we call random is just patterns we can't decipher.*"

- **Chuck Palahniuk** - *Survivor*

Chapter 31

Azores, August 1, 1941

They sat in the Admiral's stateroom aboard HMS *Invincible*, anchored in the channel between the small islands of Pico and Faial. Less than four miles wide at its narrowest point, the channel served as a makeshift harbor there between the small fishing ports of Horta and Madalena. Seven other merchant ships were clustered to one side of the channel, "the funnies," as the navy rats called them now. There also, was the sleek white hull of the *Argos Fire*, its tall mainmast and prominent Sampson radar dome marking its lineage as a former *Daring* Class destroyer.

The long stately lines of HMS *Hood* also graced the anchorage, where both Admiral Holland, and the ship where he still set his flag, were enjoying the sweetness of a life they both might have lost months ago in another telling of these events. They had come late to the engagement with the Germans fought some weeks ago, but now formed an important part of the standing watch the British Home Fleet had established here, along with the *Repulse,* and the fleet's newest addition, the battleship *Duke of York.* Her twin sister ships, *King George V* and *Prince of Wales* were both in the Celtic Sea with the carriers *Ark Royal* and *Illustrious,* enough power to face down the German fleet should it attempt to sortie again, at least until Tovey could hasten northwest from the Azores with reinforcements.

Two other light AA cruisers rode at anchor in the channel, and beyond them there were numerous destroyers keeping a watchful eye, though the presence of HMS *Glorious* in the Azores was a powerful deterrent to German U-boat activity in the vicinity. Her aircraft patrolled ceaselessly, keeping watch for U-boats on the surface, and the destroyers prowled the waters off the islands to listen for any boat bold enough to try and creep up submerged.

Captain MacRae had assured Admiral Tovey that he had sonar that was more than capable of detecting any undersea threats long before they could pose a danger, but the Admiral chose to maintain his regular ASW patrols nonetheless.

"Well now, Miss Fairchild, gentlemen, welcome aboard." Fairchild was there with MacRae and Mack Morgan, and a third man dressed out in a white naval coat and trousers of the American Navy, a Lieutenant Commander by rank.

"I have not had the pleasure of meeting you sir," said Tovey, extending a handshake. "Didn't know you fellows were out here. I'm to understand that you are serving as a fleet liaison officer?"

"Forgive me, Admiral," said the man. "I was introduced to you as Lieutenant Commander Wellings, USN, but I must confess that identity, and this uniform along with it, was put on simply for purposes of security. I am Professor Paul Dorland of the Lawrence Berkeley Labs in the United States, and I have recently met with Miss Fairchild and company concerning events that played out in the recent fleet action with the Germans."

Tovey gave him a puzzled look. He had been told by Fairchild to expect a most unusual visitor for a very important discussion, though he did not yet know the details.

"I'm told you were with Captain Dalrymple-Hamilton aboard the *Rodney*, God rest her soul."

"I was, sir."

"He speaks well of you—says you did everything possible to persuade him to take a course that might have avoided that unlucky engagement he fought. A pity I couldn't get there in time with *Invincible* to help out. Speed can make all the difference at sea, and I'm afraid that was not a strong suit for *Rodney*, or things might have turned out differently. But tell me, Professor, just what is it you do in this laboratory of yours, and why do I find you here, insisting on this meeting with these good people." He gestured to the Fairchild camp, where they sat at the opposite end of the conference table.

"It concerns several matters you will be familiar with," said Dorland. "The first is *Rodney* and the cargo it was secretly carrying in its hold, now unfortunately lost, at least for the moment. The second is the fate and whereabouts of another ship, the battlecruiser *Kirov*. As for my business in that laboratory, it would take some time to explain it. Suffice it to say that the facility could not be found if you were to travel to America at this moment—for it simply does not exist in 1941. Like your Russian allies, and Miss Fairchild and company, I have come here from the year 2021."

"I see…" Tovey did not quite know what to make of that, though his experience with the Russians, and the Fairchild group had taken the sting and shock out of such a statement, and made the impossible real to him in more ways than one. There was *Argos Fire*, and seven other ships from 2021, their decks crewed by interlopers from that same future time. And in the deserts of North Africa, a brigade of extraordinary fighting men and machines still stood to arms for Britain, their very presence neutralizing the whole of General Rommel's formidable Afrika Korps, and assuring the safety of the vital British bastions in Egypt.

"Quite a party you people are throwing here," he said. "Will there be any more unexpected guests? And how you manage to come and go as you please I may never understand, but we'll leave that off for the moment. What is it you have come to discuss?"

"*Kirov*," said Dorland, "the ship that once went by the code name *Geronimo* when you first encountered it, though that moment is about to be re-written by events now underway. From my perspective in 2021, I have the advantage of history to let me look over my shoulder to these days and learn things that occurred. Unfortunately, circumstances are no longer the same here, and that history is now badly frayed. Whether it will ever be saved is in grave doubt."

Tovey nodded. "Yet given what you have just said, you must certainly know the outcome of all these events."

"That was once quite true," said Dorland, "at least for the broad strokes of history. Most events in human experience go unrecorded, and only the big things stand the test of time and survive as recorded history. But now, not even that can be relied upon. The interventions made by this Russian ship have changed everything. From our vantage point in the future, we could see many of those changes manifesting as variations against the history we already knew. But when these things happen, it takes time for the changes to migrate forward to the future—to our time and beyond."

"Yet the Russians were clearly aware of events about to unfold in this war—at least to some extent."

"It is that certainty that is fading now," said Dorland. "Nothing can be relied on in the history at this moment, particularly now, for we have entered what I call a kind of zone of chaos after the 28th of July. You are aware of the significance of this date?"

"I was told it was the date the Russians first arrived here. That was on Wake Walker's beat, but I know this only because of a few very odd file boxes where I seem to have written up reports on the entire affair. They were found at Bletchley Park by our Mister Turing. I hoped he could be here for this meeting, but the plane is running late. Might you have any explanation?"

"Let me try," said Paul. "Whenever something moves in time, it opens a temporary hole in the continuum, or to put it another way, it creates a little whirlpool in the stream and slips through. Sometimes other things can be dragged along with it, particularly things related to events it may have altered during its time in the past. As we have seen, those events can cause serious harm to the continuum of future events. So these little things can be very dangerous, like contaminates or waste byproducts from the intervention. The easiest way to think of it would be to imagine Mother Time trying to sweep up bits of broken China on her kitchen floor. Sometimes she can be very meticulous. Other times things can happen in a haphazard or random way, particularly in a Chaos Zone. That refers to intervals of instability that accompany objects and persons moving through time.

And when we get an entire battlecruiser, with a crew of over 700 men doing that movement, the disturbance can be quite significant."

Tovey was able to follow the logic of that easily enough. "According to the reports from my own hand, I didn't personally encounter the Russian ship until August 4th, cruising south of Iceland. Are you saying that one of these chaos zones has formed around that date—the 28th of July? The young Russian Captain was particularly concerned about that day. He kept referring to it as a Paradox."

"And rightly so," said Dorland. "Well... It has just occurred, and because the Russian movements in time also took their ship as far back as 1908, changes that took place at that time have been migrating forward, and they have obviously reached the 1940s. This world seems quite different, a completely different history in many ways, though still very familiar to the history we knew in other aspects."

"Yes," said Tovey. "Now that you mention that, I believe my last statement was in error. I think I first set eyes on that Russian ship as a very young man, a Lieutenant serving aboard the armored cruiser *King Alfred* out of the China Station. We were involved in that big battle—the Second Battle of the Tushima Straits, and I'm certain it was the Russian ship we faced there—until it vanished, just as it did a few months ago while steaming some 500 meters off the very bow of this ship!"

"In fact," said Dorland, "that was an alteration of your own personal timeline, or meridian as I use the term. You were never supposed to have seen that ship, and there was no such battle ever recorded in the history I know. These things all happened as a consequence of *Kirov's* intervention in time. We only just perceived these variation flags in our research systems, and we have seen the changes occurring that far back, to 1908. Now changes from that day are reaching this time, though they have not yet reached my time in 2021. Think of these changes as moving in waves, like a tsunami, and they have finally reached this shore of 1941. Yet that date—July

28th—did indeed present a Paradox. The Russian ship was here, approaching it from the past, yet it was the date of its first appearance, so that would create quite a problem. Too many cooks spoil the broth. You say *Kirov* vanished in May, and there has been no further sign of it since that time?"

"Not a whisper on the radio sets they left with me."

"I beg your pardon… Radio sets?"

"Yes, they brought over some of their equipment to facilitate secure communications. I believe Miss Fairchild received it as well."

"Confirmed," said Elena. "We've a Russian set aboard the *Argos Fire*, for secure encrypted comm-links with *Invincible* and *Kirov*. The Russian Submarine has the same, but we've no contact with it."

"Submarine?" Now Paul remembered that Nordhausen had mentioned he had data on that, along with a photo of these new ships at anchor, the funnies. "Yes, we just learned of that. Frankly, you can tell me much more about it than our researchers are likely to find."

Elena took a moment to explain, as far as she had learned it from Fedorov, how the use of Rod-25 in conjunction with a nuclear reactor had enabled *Kirov*, and then *Kazan*, to move in time.

"Amazing," said Paul, surprised to hear all of this. "Then that control rod was still aboard the Russian submarine?"

"As far as we know, though it may have been transferred back to *Kirov*. In any case, both vessels are gone now, and that all occurred during that little naval spat we recently concluded in May. I'm sorry to say there was a nuclear detonation involved as well."

Now Fairchild told the professor about the presence of the *Astute* Class submarine, obviously escorting the small transport flotilla they had inherited.

"Yet another interloper," said Tovey.

"Yes," said Elena, "only this one probably did not realize what had happened. It appeared here, perhaps because of an event that occurred in 2021, and then probably detected the Russian sub.

"The two got into quite a scrap," said MacRae, "and one side or the other must have made a donnybrook of it when they used a nuclear tipped torpedo."

"So we get another rip in the continuum at that time," said Paul, shaking his head, "along with all the others connected with these keys. I'm beginning to think that all this is related now—these natural rifts in time we spoke of earlier, Miss Fairchild. Yet let me ask you something directly if I may. What meridian are you native to?"

"I'm not sure I understand."

"When were you born?"

"Professor Dorland, one never asks a lady to state her true age, at least not one over thirty. If you mean to ask if 2021 is my own native time, then you are correct."

"You have not moved here from any future time?"

"Certainly not."

"Very well. I had to ask that, and I will of course take your word on the matter. I raise this issue because we've had… dealings with other operatives from the future, so I can empathize with you, Admiral Tovey, in having to put up with all of us tramping through your garden."

"Well," said Tovey, "as you chaps seem to be doing a good deal of weeding while you're at it, I have no objection. But this business about Chaos Zones does seem a tad disturbing. Might you expound on that further?"

Now Professor Dorland explained how the Heisenberg Waves emanating from 1908 might split into two distinct wave sets when they encounter the Paradox he had spoken of earlier. He took up pencil and paper and drew a diagram to help them visualize it.

"See how the dual wave sets now overlap one another on the other side of Paradox Time? That's where we are now, in the Chaos Zone. Things can get very strange there, though there is a hidden order at the heart of chaos itself. This business with the radio sets you mentioned—neither set should have survived here in this milieu after July 28th. The Russian ship and sub were conveniently gone when the final bell tolled on July 28th, but those radios are the kind of loose ends often cleaned up by Paradox. They should have been annihilated, but the fact that they remain here is very curious, and also somewhat alarming."

"Like those file boxes we discussed?" Tovey put in.

"Perhaps," said Paul. "But the radio sets may have been protected by a Nexus Point. That's rare, but it can happen. All of you have been so enmeshed in these events that you may have become what I call Prime Movers, important willful agents that can affect the course of time and events. Primes, and things around them, can be very resilient in chaos, and even when facing Paradox. And so here we all are. Here I am, thinking I might possibly find some way to set things right again, though the history looks completely broken as I see it now."

"And all the king's horses and all the king's men couldn't put Humpty together again," said Tovey.

"Quite so," said Paul. "Beyond that, we have another problem with the discovery of these natural fissures in time. I assume that is how your ship got here, Miss Fairchild? Am I correct? Was the location of a natural fissure inscribed on the shaft of that key in your possession?"

"Not at all," said Elena. "I received my orders to go to a specific point, the Oracle of Delphi. I was to excavate the shrine, and was very surprised to find a well engineered passage way. It was certainly nothing that could have been built in antiquity, not even in this time. There were precision milled doors and hatches, all opened by my key, so I assume the Watch received this information by other means."

Now she shared the strange message she had found in the box, presumably sent by Admiral Tovey himself. She produced the note, handing it to Paul, who read it with studied intensity.

'Should you read this your mission will have concluded as planned. Keep this device within a secure room aboard Argos Fire at all times and it will serve to hold you in a safe nexus. As of this moment, you are now Watchstander G1. Godspeed.'

Paul looked up at Elena, a question in his eye. "Miss Fairchild," he said quietly, "why do I get the distinct impression that you know a good deal more about all of this than you have yet spoken?"

"Because I do," Elena said with equal calm.

Chapter 32

"**Have** you told him about the box?" said MacRae, not knowing whether or not he was revealing some great secret.

Elena looked at him, then simply shrugged. "You may as well know everything," she said. "We were ordered to the Delphi Shrine by the Watch, the Group supposedly established by our good friend Admiral Tovey here, though he has yet to live those days out, and now may never do so if this Heisenberg Wave you speak of takes down that little sandcastle and washes the shoreline clean."

"Yet it did occur once," said Paul, "and you remember it because you are now clearly a Prime Mover, and this ship, and your own, are in a Nexus Point, a kind of safety zone in the chaos of time when things begin to change. We all share it, otherwise the Heisenberg Wave would be affecting us all here at this very moment."

"That's how she explained it all to me once," said MacRae.

"Yes," said Elena, "and I used that very same phrase, not because I had any innate knowledge of it. It was simply information I received from the Watch, and they purportedly got it from the future... Until the voices and information from there went silent."

Now she told Paul her full story, and how the Watch had received those strange transmissions from the future, information from another time!

"Yes," said Paul. "I'm afraid I pioneered the technique when we were trying to clean up a little mess involving the *Bismarck*, though that was before these radical changes migrating from 1908."

"Then do you also know about Tunguska?"

Paul gave her a searching look now. "What about it?"

"The Tunguska Event," said Elena. "That occurred in late June of 1908, and we have learned that it may have caused some very significant damage to the continuum of time, as you refer to it."

Yes, thought Paul, Tunguska! It was a major explosive event, and we've already learned what can happen when they occur. Why didn't I think of this earlier? There it was, right in 1908. Did Nordhausen mention anything about it? Then the revelation Miss Fairchild made next struck him with equal surprise.

"I believe the box we found at Delphi may contain a fragment from the Tunguska Event—a massive explosion that disturbed both space and time here when it occurred, and ever since then, other explosive events have continued to fracture time. This is how we learned of these natural fissures."

"This was information from the future?" Paul asked quickly.

"I believe so," said Elena. "I can't say I was really told everything, even though that note there seems to elevate me to the top of the list where membership in the Watch is concerned. This talk of Paradox and Chaos Zones has me worried. We learned that time may have been badly fragmented by that event, like pottery or glass that's been cracked."

"And it's getting worse," said Paul. "So this is why you knew of that other term, Grand Finality."

"I was told that as well," said Elena, though I can't say I fully understand it."

"I don't suppose anyone really can," said Paul.

"Well whatever happened, time has a crack in it," said Elena, "more than one, and now any big explosive event seems to cause additional damage. Remnants of a strange element found near Tunguska also seem to have this same effect, opening time, creating one of those whirlpools you spoke of. I don't know what metaphor best describes it now. It's very confusing. British intelligence first thought this was something the Russians were experimenting with. We even managed to obtain a few samples of a material we thought was from Tunguska, and now we've learned that it can be catalyzed by nuclear detonations as well. Then we learned the Russians were using it in the control rods of the nuclear reactors aboard that battlecruiser—*Kirov*. It took a good long time for us to discover that, but we eventually learned about it. And that box we found at Delphi contains a Tunguska fragment. It was activated when I used my key."

"I see," said Paul. "Are there other boxes associated with keys like the one you possess?"

"Not that I know of. In fact, I didn't even know how this one would work, though I was aware that other keys existed, other passages securing rifts in time. The Watch learned of that, but it seems much of this has been embedded in British history for a good long while. Frankly, Mister Dorland, I have come to believe this history has been tampered with many times in the past. Yes, we've found evidence of keys associated with hidden passages, and always they were places under British control at some point. Delphi was a bit of an oddity, however. We never held Greece, though we've fought there. In any case, we've kept them very secret, known to very few living souls. So when I received my key, I had some inkling of where it might eventually take me. In fact, I thought our little foray to Delphi was going to be a farewell journey through one of those fissures in time, but all I found was that box."

"So that your *ship* could move here," said Paul, leaping ahead. "I see... the box must have amplified the effect, extending the shift radius, almost like that control rod did aboard *Kirov*, as you've explained it."

"So it seems," said Elena, "yet I could not fathom why, unless I was meant to join forces with Admiral Tovey here and fight the good fight with *Argos Fire*."

"And that you have," said Tovey.

"Thank you, Admiral, but the military assistance I can offer you has some hard limits."

"Aye," said MacRae, "We're down to just seven missiles remaining after that last little foray, at least for the ship killers. Our air defense systems are a wee bit stronger, but as Miss Fairchild has it, we'll eventually run out of those as well."

"Well not just yet," said Mack Morgan. "One of those ships in the flock we're shepherding now is a fleet replenishment vessel. I've kibitzed with her Master, and they have a nice little snake pit over there, several cases of Aster-15s and a few more Aster-30s. No GB-7s, as that was a private special order for this ship, but they do have Harpoons, and we might easily adapt our firing systems to utilize that missile."

"You've just won yourself a new feather for that cap. The job is yours Mack. See to it."

"Aye, Mum, I'll take care of everything with the ship's engineers."

"Well that's encouraging," said Tovey. "The Russians had a good deal to do with our holding off the *Hindenburg* and other bad company. Now that they're gone, I'm realizing how crucial their contribution was to our effort here."

"All this is very interesting," said Paul, taking these revelations in now. "As to those keys… You said there was nothing machined on the shaft of yours?"

"No, I said the was no clue as to location there, at least a spatial location. My key was apparently designed to work anywhere in tandem with that box I retrieved from Delphi. Yet there was a series of numbers on the note we found in that box. They were temporal coordinates, a date, which is why I knew we might end up in 1941. I thought it was just a means of saving a chosen few, the Keyholders, and I was grateful my ship and crew could come along. When I first went to Delphi I thought it might only allow me to take a small contingent through that passage. Then I found there was no rift or passage there at all."

Paul nodded. "So the box, and the hidden Tunguska fragment you suspect it contains, must have been tuned in some way to open the continuum to 1941." Paul was analyzing all this new information, slowly piecing the puzzle together.

"Your guess is as good as mine," said Elena, "but here we are. Yet I wondered why. Then I remembered another part of the story of these keys. The Watch knew there was once one hidden in the Elgin Marbles, only we didn't discover that until it had already vanished, when the damage to the Selene Horse revealed it had once been there. You see, my key might fit into that impression left in the statue like a glove, which is why we knew it might be a very special key indeed. Then here you come in that uniform claiming you were the man who first discovered the key, and the very reason it disappeared."

"Yours truly," said Paul. "Guilty as charged. So when all this shenanigans started up again, and my key simply vanished, I came back to try and see if I could find it the very same way I encountered it the first time, in the one location where I knew it must exist—the hold of battleship *Rodney*. Well you may be interested to know that particular key is also associated with a hidden passage. Because I can tell you where it is. The shaft of the key had numbers engraved on it, and I deciphered their meaning."

Elena was silent for a moment, then simply stared at him. "Do go on," she said quietly.

Dorland reached into his jacket pocket and produced a paper with the number clearly printed out: 36.126225, -05.345633. "Unlike the number on the note you found in that box," he said, "those are spatial coordinates. Why, in our time you could punch them into Google and get a map of the exact location."

Tovey frowned, "Google?"

"It would take too long to explain just now, Admiral, but please indulge me. Let me make it a little easier for you, since I don't think we have a nice handy internet connection to 2021. The key from the Selene Horse was targeted to another long time British possession— Gibraltar—a specific place on the Rock, to be precise, deep beneath Saint Michael's Cave."

Tovey was lost when the man spoke of an 'internet,' but mention of the Rock, and Saint Michael's Cave brought him right back into the thick of things here.

"Yes," he said grimly, "a former British possession indeed. That was where the garrison made its last stand. The Germans have it now."

"Most unfortunate," said Paul, "because that was one of those nasty little changes to the history. They never took it before the Russian ship went back to 1908 and generated a Heisenberg Wave. In fact, Admiral, this ship was never even built. All this is an altered meridian, and we, my friends, are now riding the edge of that very same Heisenberg Wave, and right into the Chaos Zone behind that Paradox. Who knows how far the zone of instability exists, how many days? Things will settle down again soon, or I can only hope as much."

"Well this key can hardly matter now," said Tovey. "It's lost. We can't use it, and neither can the bloody Germans. Do you suppose they've discovered what it might open? Might they have found that passage beneath Saint Michael's Cave?"

"I would hope not," said Elena, "Even if they did, it would take some doing to get through the door. The works I saw at Delphi were heavy titanium alloy, and very well made."

"Yet the Germans can be very industrious," said Paul, "and very determined. If they ever did stumble upon that passage, then it would certainly make them very curious. And as we have no way of knowing where it might lead..." The implications of what he was saying now were obvious to them all.

"Well," Mack Morgan spoke up again, "all the more reason to make sure the Germans lose their lease on the Rock as soon as possible."

"Here, here," said Tovey. "Sir Winston has been in anguish over the loss of Gibraltar for months now. We all have. It was the most strategic base outside of England I could name, save perhaps Alexandria and Suez. Yet the loss of the Rock has closed the entire Eastern Med to convoy shipping. Yes *Invincible* made it through, with the able assistance of the Russians and *Argos Fire*, but none of our merchantmen would fare so well. I can say that Churchill would be in favor of anything we could tee up to get Gibraltar back, but I wouldn't expect any major operation would be possible for some time. We just haven't the capacity to make any sizable amphibious attack, and the only way to come at the place by land would mean we would have to control Spain, and that isn't bloody likely in the short run. Get the Americans in it, and we'll have another look at things, but it's all we can do to hold onto Egypt and half of the Middle East right now, and that only by the grace of Brigadier Kinlan's unexpected arrival."

"What about a smaller operation?" said Dorland. "Might a commando team land secretly to gain access to that passage?"

"Possibly," said Tovey. "We've some good men in the service of those misdeeds."

"As do I," said Elena. "My Argonauts have specialized equipment, night vision, and other technology that can make them very good in such an operation."

"And we certainly know the ground well enough," said Tovey. "We built the place, and have every nook and cranny very well mapped. But this is all academic, because that key is quite lost now, and with no blame to heap on Mister Wellings this time around—or is it Professor Dorland."

"In the flesh," said Paul. "At least for a while. But suppose I told you that exploring such an operation would not be a fruitless mental exercise, Miss Fairchild. Suppose I told you exactly how we might find that key again. You see, it remains lost here now, on this clear day in August of 1941. But at any *other* time, it might be found very easily." He smiled, a mischievous look in his eye.

"Something tells me this visit was for more than idle chatter," said Elena. "You have a plan?"

"Most assuredly," said Paul. "Yes, I certainly do. But there is one further matter we must discuss before we get to that. You may have wondered why I spoke so harshly about the presumed fate of those Russian radio sets."

"I assumed you meant they might have been pulled away to wherever the ship itself has gone," said Tovey.

"In a manner of speaking," said Paul, "but it's a little more devious than that. I thought they would be annihilated, because they simply should not be able to exist in this time now."

"And why not," said Tovey. "Ours was a bit giddy the other day according to my radio man, on the 28th now that I think of it. But it seems to have settled down again, and functions normally. I was able to discuss arrangements for this meeting with Miss Fairchild and had no difficulty."

"Yes?" said Paul. "Well all that equipment should be gone, because it should not be able to co-locate with itself when the Russian ship arrived here again."

There was a momentary silence, and then Tovey leaned forward, looking at Dorland intently. "Arrived here... again? You mean just as it did before?"

"Precisely," said Paul. "That was the imperative driving the Paradox. The ship simply *had* to arrive for *Kirov* to be here in the past. And that day has come and gone..."

"Then you believe the ship is out there? This very moment?"

Before Paul could answer there was a knock on the stateroom door, one of those moments of synchronicity that sometimes happen as though they were cleverly written fiction.

"Excuse me, sir," said the orderly. "But you asked to be informed immediately of any message received on the Russian radio set. It was acting up, but we got it sorted out. One's come through, sir, right on channel 272... the one you insisted we monitor."

"Well man?" said Tovey impatiently. "What was the message?"

The man simply walked over and handed a paper to the Admiral, who scanned it with a mix of surprise and delight in his eyes. He looked up at the others and spoke slowly. "*Geronimo, Geronimo, Geronimo. Home Flag, please respond, as per fleet signals protocol one.*"

Chapter 33

The Zone of Chaos following Paradox Hour was widening in all their minds now, for the implications inherent in that message were not lost on anyone present.

"It seems they're back again," said Tovey, "Volsky, Fedorov and the whole bloody ship. Good to have them."

There was a note of caution in Dorland's eye now. "Yet not in the way you might expect if this has actually happened," said Paul.

"Explain," said Elena in the way she often made her questions orders.

"If this happened as I believe, then it is a recurrence of first arrival. The officers and crew will be experiencing events as if they were happening for the first time, and therefore, they may have no recollection of anything that occurred earlier."

"I don't understand," said Tovey. "Is this not the same ship that vanished some weeks ago? Why would they forget anything."

"Yes, it is the same ship, in one respect, the same officers and crew should be there as before, but they are the crew that arrived for the very first time. The ship is the one that actually arrived here on July 28th, 1941, and this is, for all real purposes, that first arrival."

"But this world is entirely different," said Tovey, "at least I've been told as much. To me it is the world as it has always seemed, completely in order, except for this bloody war."

"Yes, it would seem that way to you, but remember, the wave of change the ship initiated in 1908 may have reached this time, but not the year they are now arriving from—not 2021 in our day. Precursor waves may have reached there, but not the real damaging waves with the power to radically change things. I believe they will just have to start over, and sort through their situation from square one, the square they presently occupy in this crazy game."

"Good lord," said Tovey. "Then what has happened to the ship that was with me in May? What has happened to Admiral Volsky. That man had a good head on his shoulders, and a heart to go with it.

I learned his caution and desire for accommodation saved some very difficult situations in our first encounters. You're telling me the man there now remembers nothing of the interaction we have had since they appeared here?"

"Not only that," said Paul, "but most everyone outside a safe Nexus Point will have no recollection of those events either. The Heisenberg Waves presently sweeping through these years can have the effect of wiping such memories clean, though there are exceptions. Persons safely harbored in a Nexus Point will retain their memories. Think of them as safe zones, protected bubbles in the stream. They have limited range, however, and leaving them can lead to some rather strange disorientation. I believe a nexus has formed around this ship, Admiral—more specifically, around you, a Prime Mover at the heart of all these events. The same should hold true for your ship, Miss Fairchild. Your crew should have no memory loss if I am correct."

"Yet when we take the launch back over to *Argos Fire*—what then?"

"I think you are also a Prime, or possibly a Free Radical, if you'll pardon the expression. Your presence here was not an accident, it was willful. That tends to put you right inside a nexus, and where you go, it goes with you. As for the ship you knew, Admiral, when it vanished last May, that may have been the result of the impending Paradox. I do not presume to know exactly what may have happened to it, or to those good men you came to know. They may have entered some undefined region, where minutes and hours there could manifest as months and years here."

"Could they reappear? They did this vanishing act many times before, in the North Atlantic, then off the island of Saint Helena, and again in the Pacific. The reports I supposedly wrote on those encounters clearly spoke of that."

"Of this I can be certain of only one thing," said Paul. "They could never reappear here at any time occupied by the ship that has just arrived. From what we were able to determine, they were here only twelve days initially."

"Yes," said Tovey. "Their Captain Fedorov explained that to me. It had something to do with a maintenance cycle on the ship's propulsion system, and it occurred every twelve days. He said it took them some time before they discovered this. According to my reports, I did not encounter them until eight days after their arrival, on August 4th. But just a moment... With all due respect to your theories, Professor Dorland, there is something quite irregular about this message we just received. It uses a code word I personally assigned to that ship—*Geronimo.*"

"Yes, I was wondering if you might notice that."

"Well, see here—my reports indicate we didn't assign that name to the ship until after it vanished, on August 8th. I spent hours and hours reading all that material after our Mister Turing discovered it. I'm quite certain of this."

"Interesting," said Paul. "We picked up the reference between the ship and *Geronimo*, but there has been very little time for deep research. In fact, we haven't been able to account for all the moves the ship made through time just yet, but I'm sure my people are working on that back home. Yes... This is very interesting."

"Furthermore," said Tovey, "the message has requested a response using a coded protocol that was arranged in Alexandria for private ship-to-ship communications with our newfound Allies. It was for command level access only. Whoever sent that message was obviously aware of this, which means they had to be in the know when we were at Alexandria in late January. The message is meant for this ship, the flagship of the Home Fleet, and requests signals protocol one. It was meant for me personally, and it is a request to use the equipment we spoke of earlier, the radio set the Russians provided for this very purpose."

"So no one on that ship now should know that," said Elena.

"Yet someone clearly does. Are you certain of your theory, Professor Dorland?"

"Nothing in all of this is ever certain, Admiral. Yet if what you say is true, then something very strange has happened here. It could be that one or more members of that crew were so significant to the outcome of these events, that they were also protected in a safe nexus. Their memory of past events might be still intact, or it could be that they might begin to recollect those earlier lived events by slow degrees. This is the only explanation I can offer."

"Yes… I've experienced this very same thing—memories, arising from some deep place within me—things I know I never consciously lived through, as they purportedly happened next year! Yet I seem to recall these unlived events as if they had already happened. It's a very odd feeling akin to *déjà vu*. As for more recent events since *Kirov* appeared here in June of 1940, I certainly haven't forgotten one bit. I can clearly recall old Admiral Volsky, and that enterprising young Captain of his, Mister Fedorov. I've spent hours and hours discussing all this with them, and planning fleet operations between us. You told me why you think this is, why I haven't lost these memories, and by Jove, I think the same must have happened on the Russian ship! Who knows, they might all be well and good there, and simply a bit bewildered after they've reappeared. You said yourself that months here might only be minutes to them. They vanish here last May and then suddenly turn up somewhere else. Huff Duff encoding at the bottom of this signal intercept indicates a point of origin… Very strange. They've moved well up into the Norwegian Sea. That's just where they first encountered Wake Walker in the reports I wrote."

"Yet that isn't likely to repeat," said Paul. "Is it?" He could see a wry grin on Tovey's face.

"They say history never repeats itself," said Tovey. "But in this case I believe it rhymes. Your Mister Twain was thought to have said that once, well, I'll say it now. Admiral Wake-Walker was recently put in charge of preparations for the planned convoy operations to Murmansk. Operation Dervish is the code name we've given to the first, and it's teeing up even as we speak. Wake-Walker is up there in the Norwegian Sea. We thought we might raid the German airfields at Petsamo and Kirkenes, until Mister Fedorov advised me against it. A bit like ringing the bell before all the guests have arrived. He said it might only alert the Germans to a heightened state of vigilance, and prompt them to reinforce those airfields. For that matter, he also disclosed that this particular raid was actually attempted in the history he knew, and it was a bloody disaster. So I persuaded the Admiralty to cancel the raid, and instead we assigned Wake-Walker to the Dervish convoy. It's out a bit earlier than we initially planned, but to answer your question, yes, it is very likely that the Russians might encounter our Force P up there. Two Carriers, *Furious* and *Victorious*, a pair of good heavy cruisers, and a destroyer flotilla."

"I think we had better get to that Russian radio set as soon as possible," said Paul. "If all this is so, then someone on the Russian ship is trying to communicate. Let's get to the bottom of this, shall we?"

* * *

"**How** long do we wait?" said Karpov. "They've come right up on our horizon by now. Rodenko, what is the range to those ships?"

"34,000 meters, yet Fedorov was correct. That range is holding fairly well, over the horizon. I don't think they know we're here."

"Just an assumption," said Karpov. "The British radar is every bit as good as ours, and they had to have seen our helicopter. They are just playing very coy here."

"But we have no signal intercepts on normal microwave bands for any British set I know," said Rodenko. "I do have signals down where Fedorov advised me to look just now—but they are very weak."

"Interesting," said Admiral Volsky. "What were those signals bands, Mister Fedorov?"

Fedorov swallowed, giving Karpov a quick glance, but he was not the same young man he was when he first arrived here. The experience of all those many time shifts, and the battles he fought, had hardened him, and steeled his will. He had been made Captain of the ship by Volsky long before the hat fit him, but in time he developed considerable skill in that post, and the mindset of command to go with it. So he cleared his throat and spoke.

"Those ships we have on video feed are *County* Class cruisers, Royal Navy, and of a very old vintage. So I chose radar bands that might have been used in early British equipment."

"How early?" asked Volsky. "Didn't they first develop radar sets in WWII?"

"Correct sir."

"This is a waste of time, Admiral," said Karpov. "Old ships, new ships, you can see the guns on those forward decks as clear as I can."

"Yet they should not be there," said Fedorov quickly. "Those guns are obsolete, as are these ships. They should not be at sea."

"Don't be stupid, Lieutenant! They *are* at sea, no matter what you wish to call them. Can't you see the video feed?"

"Correct," said Fedorov, ignoring the insult and remaining calm. "And I also know what I'm looking at, Captain—two *County* Class cruisers. They are clearly there, yet they *cannot* be there, not in the year 2021, and if they are, then something very strange has happened here." There it was, his first assertion that something more than an accident had happened to the ship.

"Are you telling me these ships were dragged out of the bone yards and put back in service? We may have to resort to such measures, but our fat capitalists here do not."

"That could not be the case here, sir."

"Why do you say this?" Volsky cut in, holding up a hand when he saw Karpov's growing anger. He knew his Captain did not want to hear from junior officers like this in a command situation, so he quickly intervened before Karpov exploded.

"Because the last *County* Class cruiser, the *Cumberland*, was decommissioned, sold, and broken up for scrap in the year 1959. Believe me, Admiral. I know these ships very well. I have studied this all my adult life, as many here know."

"You say they went to the scrap yards? All of them?"

"Every last one, sir. I know what I am seeing in the video feed, and it is an exact match for my silhouette book on this class. Yet every ship in that class is long gone. Two were sunk by the Japanese, in the last war, one was scuttled, and all the rest were scrapped between 1948 and 1959."

"Then it's a goddamn replica," said Karpov. "Maybe it has to do with those old war documentaries Nikolin reported on the radio. Either that or you are quite mistaken, Fedorov. That knock on that head of yours must have shaken something loose. Now sit down, mind your business, and keep those stupid history books to your off hours, or I'll have Orlov collect every last one and throw them overboard."

"Easy… Easy…" said Admiral Volsky, slipping off the Captain's chair and walking slowly over to the navigation station. "Let me see that book, Fedorov. The Captain may be right, but let me satisfy myself and have a look."

Fedorov was relieved when Volsky came over, for he knew he simply had to get the Admiral to see his viewpoint, or they could start something here that would complicate everything.

"Why do you pander to his stupidity, Admiral? Fedorov, I think you need a few more days in sick bay. Have Zolkin examine your head again, because he clearly did not get it right the first two times."

In spite of Karpov's lashing tongue, Fedorov maintained his composure, handing the silhouette book to Admiral Volsky, and pointing out the reference. The Admiral looked up at the helo video feed, then down at the book."

"It is certainly a good match," he said.

"Then we are looking at a ghost fleet?" Karpov protested. "This is preposterous! I have heard a lot of guff in my day, Fedorov, but this tops it all. It's nonsense, I tell you."

"Yet there they are," said Admiral Volsky gesturing at the video. "You were just beating Fedorov over the head with the video feed. Yes? Or are you suggesting the British are feeding us this video footage with some new electronic warfare device?"

Karpov raised his eyebrows, thinking a moment. "That may be possible, sir." His eyes widened as he spoke, quick to latch on to anything that would allow him to fit what he was seeing into some understandable point of reference, and dispel the illusion that Fedorov was spinning out. Fedorov knew what was coming out of his mouth next, an eerie echo of the same reaction he had the first time they were here.

"This could all be part of some elaborate ruse, designed to confuse us," said Karpov. "Some kind of electronic warfare, perhaps a NATO PSYOP. That strange explosion we experienced hours ago may have been the opening salvo." It was clear to him that such a deception would be much more plausible than anything Fedorov was saying now.

The strange replay of these events gave Fedorov the shivers, yet he knew he had to take a stronger line here, and the Admiral was the key to winning this argument before the missiles began to fly, and things got out of hand.

"Orlov?"

The Admiral wanted to know what his Chief of Operations thought, but Orlov looked as confused as anyone. He had idled with Fedorov at times, the two of them also sharing stories of the second war where both their grandfathers had served, but this was difficult to believe.

"I don't know what to think, Admiral. But, as it is clearly impossible that the British could resurrect ships decommissioned and demolished decades ago, then we must give further thought to what the Captain suggests. As for Fedorov, he did take a good knock on the head the other day. Perhaps he needs another one?" He gave the navigator an unfriendly look, a warning in his eyes.

"Impossible, you say, yet this very ship has risen from the dead, has it not?" Volsky's voice was a strange echo of the past, heightening the sense of déjà vu for Fedorov.

Karpov took a deep breath, stiffening, gratified that Orlov had again reinforced his position. "Enough of this game," he said. "If this is a PSYOP then the British have gone too far! These ships may be responsible for everything we have been dealing with here."

"A moment ago it was this submarine that was responsible for all of our problems," said Admiral Volsky. "Now you suggest the British are running some elaborate psychological operation aimed at confusing us?"

Karpov frowned, clearly unhappy with the Admiral's remark, yet he persisted. "If they do not identify themselves under international protocols, then it is permitted to give fair warning and fire a shot across their bow, sir. Everything we have endured here has been a clear provocation. It is time we let them know that the Russian Navy will not tolerate this nonsense." He folded his arms, his anger apparent, and the look he gave Fedorov was clearly meant to silence any further comment on his part.

The Admiral rubbed his forehead, the headache he complained about returning again with the stress of all that had happened. The next time he looked up to check the video feed, he seemed to sway on his feet, his eyes glazed over, and he began to fall.

"Admiral!" said Fedorov with alarm, quickly taking Volsky's arm to steady him. Yet those thick legs could not hold him, and he fell to the deck.

Orlov shouted, and two Yeomen ran quickly to render assistance. "Call the Doctor," he said. "Better yet, go and fetch a stretcher and we will take him to sick bay ourselves."

Volsky's eyes were open, yet he said nothing, clearly distressed by a severe attack of what seemed like vertigo. The lights above him, the milky green glow of the radar and combat stations, all blended with the faces of the men as they leaned over him, and he closed his eyes to fight off the nausea. As he did so, he had the distinct feeling that he had lived through something like this before, and a pulse of alarm that warned him of grave danger, not for himself, but for the ship.

No, dear god, not now, thought Fedorov. This wasn't supposed to happen yet! It was many days before the Admiral collapsed like this, and by that time, Karpov had already been convinced that they had shifted to the past. Yet now, in this critical moment, command of the most powerful ship in the world would suddenly fall to the Captain, and what might he do?

"Careful men," said Karpov. "Easy with him through that hatch." He looked at his navigator now, seeing a look on his face of shock and distress. "You wish to join him, Fedorov? Because this nonsense you've been spouting here is just this far from crazy."

Karpov held up a thumb and finger, an inch apart. He stood tall, moving towards the Captain's chair. "Ships that were scrapped over 70 years ago do not miraculously re-float themselves, so with your nose always in those history books, you are seeing too many goblins in the woods. As senior officer on the bridge, I will now exercise my own judgment on this matter and get some results. Mister Samsonov... prepare to fire a warning shot over the bow of those ships out there. Activate the 100mm bow gun."

"Captain," said Fedorov quickly. "Don't forget the helicopter. If you fire now they might take it down!" He said anything he could to buy time, though Karpov was not happy to hear his voice again.

"I told you once, Fedorov—sit down and see to the ship's navigation. Another word out of you and—"

"Signal on secure channel 272!" said Nikolin suddenly. "He had been watching the growing tension and conflict on the bridge, and with an odd inner feeling of fear, believing he had sat in this chair before and felt the same dark thing. There was something about Fedorov now... he seemed different. For him to stand up like this and engage the senior officers, particularly in the face of the Captain's obvious anger and displeasure, was most unusual. He remembered the conversation they had the previous night, and how he had warned Fedorov to be careful around Karpov, but the Navigator seemed intent on something here. That message he had suggested was very strange, but here was a response!

"What is it Nikolin, quickly please." Karpov had one eye on Fedorov, his head slightly inclined as he listened.

"It reads back just what Fedorov said, sir. 'Roger Geronimo. Ready on fleet protocol one, HMS *Invincible* standing by—over."

"HMS *Invincible*? That was one of their aircraft carriers. Yes? Now we're getting somewhere."

Karpov rubbed his hands together.

Part XII

The Second Coming

"History never repeats itself, but the Kaleidoscopic combinations of the pictured present often seem to be constructed out of the broken fragments of antique legends.... no occurrence is sole and solitary, but is merely a repetition of a thing which has happened before, and perhaps often."

— **Mark Twain**

Chapter 34

"That will not be an aircraft carrier," said Fedorov, realizing his position was very precarious on the bridge now after the demise of Admiral Volsky. Thankfully, Orlov had accompanied the medic carrying the Admiral to sick bay, but Karpov could be very volatile, and quite unpredictable. Nikolin's interruption had helped just a little with the report of that signal, but soon the inevitable conflict with Karpov would have to play out, and the last time he had challenged the Captain, Karpov had him relieved.

How to avoid that, he thought? How do I engage Karpov so that he will not merely dismiss me? How to convey what is happening now in a way that might persuade him?

"Not a carrier?" said Karpov.

"It was decommissioned in 2005, sir, and sold to a Turkish company to be scrapped in 2011."

"Then this is a new ship?"

"Not by that name sir. You and I both know there is no HMS *Invincible* currently in active service with the Royal Navy."

"So we are receiving messages from another ghost ship here?" Karpov smiled. "Or perhaps they are still playing out their little game."

Now Fedorov decided to take a very grave risk. He had to do something dramatic, something that would be so striking that it would arrest the inevitable escalation that Karpov would surely initiate here.

"Captain, if you take that radio call, you will be speaking with a man named Admiral John Tovey, commander of the British Home Fleet. He will likely ask to speak with Admiral Volsky, or to me."

"To you?" The notion that the British would even know of Fedorov was preposterous. Karpov shook his head, his anger becoming disdain. "So Orlov was correct, Fedorov, and the Doctor still has work to do with you. Now it's delusions of grandeur."

"Take the call sir. This is what you wanted, isn't it? They are standing by. You can finally get to the bottom of all of this.”

Karpov gave his Navigator a dismissive wave of his hand, his attention now pulled to Nikolin’s station. “Damn right,” he said, striding over to Nikolin’s side. “Get yourself back to sick bay, Fedorov. Nikolin, have them identify themselves again,” he said gruffly. “And I want it straight. Get the speaker’s name, rank, position and ship number. Send them the same information from us, and identify me as acting Captain.”

“Aye sir.” Nikolin toggled a switch and sent out a response. “Roger Geronimo, please say all again. Identity, name, rank, position, and state ship name and pennant number. This is the Russian Navy ship BCG *Sergei Kirov*, pennant number 072, presently in the Norwegian Sea south of Jan Mayen. Over.”

There was a brief pause, and a voice came back, speaking English, which Nikolin quickly translated. “This is Admiral John Tovey, Commander of Home Fleet, Royal Navy, aboard HMS *Invincible*, fleet pennant number 50.”

“Commander of the Home Fleet?” Karpov looked surprised as Nikolin listened, an odd look on his face.

“Sir… He’s requesting to speak with Admiral Volsky… or Mister Fedorov!” He looked at Fedorov strangely, obviously as surprised to hear this as Karpov was.

“Fedorov?” Karpov turned, eyeing his Navigator with a suspicious look. “How could you know what that man would say?” He pointed at the radio set, turning to Fedorov. “How could you know his name like that? And why in the world would he be asking to speak with you, a simple minded Lieutenant in the Russian Navy?”

A moment ago he had glibly suggested Fedorov was working for the Royal Navy, yet now a thrum of real suspicion pulsed up, and he looked at Fedorov with new eyes.

“Because I personally know the man, sir,” said Fedorov quickly. “In fact, I have met with him on that very ship, HMS *Invincible*. He is exactly who he claims to be, Admiral John Tovey, Commander of the British Home Fleet. This man can identify those other two ships we've been monitoring. He will know the deployments of all Royal Navy ships."

Karpov was looking at him, a hard, suspicious look now. "You know him personally? The Admiral of the British Home Fleet, is it? Leaving aside the fact that there *is* no British Home Fleet any longer, at least not that I am aware of. It's been simply called Fleet Command, since the 1970s. Yes, Fedorov, I went to the Naval College as well, but it seems you've forgotten a few lessons." He nodded his head Nikolin's way. "Look up that pennant number. Find out what ship this really is."

"Aye sir, keying the ship data bank now."

"You won't find it in our data," said Fedorov. "And if you will meet with me in the briefing room, sir, I will tell you why."

"Correct Captain," said Nikolin. "No ship by that pennant number or name is correctly active in the Royal Navy."

Now Karpov's suspicions redoubled.

* * *

"**Standby** *Kirov*," said Tovey, switching off his radio microphone and turning to the others. "Well this is one smelly kettle of fish," he said. "They're back alright. I recognize that young lieutenant on the line that Admiral Volsky always used as a translator—a Mister Nikolin. Yet I'm told the Admiral is presently indisposed, and the acting commander of the ship is being named as a Captain Karpov. This was the name of the officer that caused such a row aboard that ship earlier, but how could he be there now? Admiral Volsky made no mention of any planned meeting with the man."

"Are you certain?" said Dorland.

"That was the name I was just given. Captain Vladimir Karpov."

"Strange," said Paul. "We were having a look at that name, as it cropped up in our research—a prominent figure in the Siberian State."

"That's the man," said Tovey. "I was told he was a former officer on the Russian ship."

"Aboard *Kirov?*" In all the rush to plan this time shift to the Azores, they had never had time to fully investigate the key officers on the ship. Paul assumed his people were running all that down, but he had been too eager to shift again, and had not been briefed.

Mack Morgan cleared his throat and spoke up now, remembering some intelligence he had collected before this meeting. "Karpov? He was en route to a meeting with Sergei Kirov in Moscow, at least according to radio intercepts my boys collected. He left Siberia a few days ago. In fact, he should be in Moscow now."

"Well the Russians have just stated they are presently sailing in the Norwegian Sea near Jan Mayen," said Tovey. "Could he have traveled all that distance?"

"Not likely," said MacRae. "That would be some 3000 miles, and that's taking the direct route up over the pole, and with no stops and fair wind. They might make it in three days, but I wouldn't bet on it, and not with a stopover in Moscow for this meeting Mack has just mentioned."

"Just a moment," said Paul, turning to Admiral Tovey. "Are we talking about the same man here? You're saying this Siberian leader was a former officer from the Russian ship?"

"That's what I'm told," said Tovey. "They believe he was lost in an incident that occurred earlier. The very same incident I talked about before—in 1908. Then Admiral Volsky and that Captain Fedorov were quite distressed when they learned the man was still alive, and had apparently moved forward in time with the ship. I don't know all the details, but they seemed convinced that the Siberian was the same man that served aboard *Kirov*. I've never met the man, but I'm told he's a bit unsavory."

"Good lord," said Paul, thinking. "Could this be so?"

Tovey gave him a penetrating look. "What are you thinking, Professor Dorland.

Paul took a deep breath and tried to explain as best he could. "Admiral, as I explained earlier, the ship we're presently in contact with is not the same one you last saw steaming off your bow last May. In one respect it is the same, but this is the ship that first arrived in 1941. That happened in the Norwegian Sea, just where you say this ship now claims to be sailing. So this officer, this man Karpov, he's right there aboard *Kirov* at this very moment."

"And how could he be there and still making headlines as he meets with Sergei Kirov?" said Mack Morgan.

Paul looked at him, a very serious expression on his face. "When this event occurred—the Paradox Hour we spoke of—one of several things could have happened. The first possibility is that the Heisenberg precursor waves could have found a way to alter the history of 2021 to try and prevent *Kirov* from shifting back, but that wasn't very likely. It would have denied that first cause, and in our day, the ship did indeed vanish on July 28th."

"Aye, said Morgan. "It was in the news, and we all heard it."

"So *Kirov* was coming, and there was no way to prevent that, which means the second possibility, that the ship you last sailed with, Admiral, might simply replace it when it arrived here again—well, that isn't very likely either. The two ships were not in the same location."

"And the third possibility?" Tovey prodded.

"That *both* ships manage to survive the Paradox—again, very unlikely. Co-location is very rare. The theory doesn't entirely forbid it, but it is usually factored out of any possible shift equation, and precisely because it gives rise to Paradox. Yet what we have here is a very peculiar situation, the Chaos Zone I spoke of earlier. The wave of change emanating from 1908 encountered Paradox, then split and formed two wave patterns. These are the conditions that can give rise to real anomalies. Is this is the first contact you have had with the Russians since it last vanished."

"Correct," said Tovey.

"Interesting... And there's someone aboard that ship who clearly knew of your special communications arrangement—fleet protocol one.... Gentlemen, Miss Fairchild, I believe we have a situation here, something that has arisen from that Chaos Zone after the Paradox. We're still in it now, and the waves of chaos abound all around us. Someone on the Russian ship is experiencing intense déjà vu at this moment, so much so that memories of past lived events were retained when he shifted here. And if this Vladimir Karpov is presently there aboard that ship, and also in Moscow as your Mister Morgan seems to believe, then we've got a real problem here. We've got a Doppelganger…"

Tovey raised his eyebrows. "A duplicate? The same man alive twice in the same world? I thought you said this couldn't happen. You clearly didn't think we would end up with two ships here."

"Yes, that's a great deal of mass to duplicate, even for a Dual Heisenberg Wave. I'm not saying it isn't possible, but just not likely. It would mean Time would have hundreds of personal time meridians unresolved, one for each crew member on the two ships. That's a lot of work, very untidy, so time resists that with Paradox, and the power of annihilation that can accompany such an event. You see, I believe that ship you were last sailing with has vanished for good, Admiral, as much as that may pain you to hear it. I believe it was completely removed from the meridians of possibility, as long as the first arrival occurred, and it seems it has. The presence of this man Karpov aboard argues strongly to that. Yet this other Karpov, the Siberian, well he should have also been annihilated. Paradox should have removed him from the continuum here. If Mister Morgan's report is correct, and he is at that meeting in Moscow with Sergei Kirov, then something happened to prevent that, and it is a very rare and unusual event."

"What could have done that?" asked Elena.

"I can't say at this moment, assuming this is all true. There were, however, several factors that could have contributed to this outcome. The man was obviously a significant player in this history—at both ends of this twisted time loop. He becomes a Free Radical soon after arriving in the past, and in time, he becomes a Prime Mover on key events, as we all are here. That gives him some clout, in a manner of speaking, and some measure of protection from Paradox, though a Prime is not entirely immune. Most of that protection might derive from the fact that Primes tend to move in a Nexus Bubble, and Primes that travel in time have an even greater layer of protection that way. Yet if there was something else, perhaps some physical anomaly involved, then that nexus field around a Prime might have been strongly reinforced."

"You mean he might survive, just like this bloody radio set?"

"There you have it, Admiral. Something protected this radio set from annihilation, possibly the same energy in the Nexus Point that surrounds and protects you. It could have been something as simple as your personal proximity to the equipment at the time of the event. We've learned these things have a given range relating to the intensity of the nexus. Who knows, perhaps this man's personal nexus was so strong that he was spared the ravages of Paradox, but I tend to think there must have been something else involved, though I can't say what that might be at the moment."

"Yet how could there be two instances of the same man?" asked Elena, not understanding how this could be possible.

"Time has that same question on her lips," said Dorland. "She undoubtedly worked very hard to prevent such a thing from ever happening, but like the marvel of DNA, she makes mistakes, and that makes all the difference. There's been an error here, a blip in time, a mistake, yet those same errors when made by DNA give rise to all life. So something has been born from this little blunder, and it is very dangerous—a Doppelganger. I never thought I would see that possibility proved true in my theory, but we may be looking at exactly that."

"Yet how? Are you saying the man mutated and split in two, like a cell dividing?"

"Not at all," said Paul. "This is difficult to explain, but nothing really moves in time, only information moves. Once it is sent here, that information reassembles the moving person or thing from particles present in the local environment. At least this is how the device I use to travel in time works. We take a pattern signature, right down to the quantum level, and have just enough computing power to store that information. Then we open the continuum with a spinning singularity and send it on through. Once it gets here, it does what nature does effortlessly enough when it spins out trees and birds and all the rest. Everything around you is just information, just particles assembled in a unique order for a given interval, always changing, always a dance—order from chaos, if you will. You vanish into Elsewhere, and then reassemble at another point on the continuum. It's just a transfer of information from one time to another. When there is a dual Heisenberg Wave like this, that information can be… copied."

"Copied?"

"Yes, think about saving a file on your computer. You have two options. The first is save with replace—that's what Paradox does, or what it should have done here. This Karpov in Siberia should not have survived Paradox Hour. He should have been removed from the continuum, erased, annihilated to allow for first arrival to occur, which was an imperative. If he did survive, as your intelligence chief here believes, then it was like a save as a separate file. It's like two versions of the same novel residing on your hard drive, even though one may have revisions and material added that the other lacks. They're both the same story, but slightly different, and they both exist. I believe all the legends concerning the existence of Doppelgangers may have arisen from this, and it appears we've got a case like this on our hands now, and a very dangerous one."

"Astounding," said Tovey. "A Doppelganger. Lord knows that man Karpov was more than enough trouble here the first time through the tube. Now he's riding the train again! Why, he would have no knowledge of the delicate alliance we made with the Russians. In fact, the first time around he went to war with the Royal Navy. Could that happen again?"

"That's quite possible. This situation is very perilous. It must be handled very carefully."

"Good Lord," said Tovey. "I've got ships up there teeing up the Dervish Convoy operation to Murmansk. It's very likely that Russian ship will soon spot them with their advanced radars. I should get word out to all fleet units about this."

"Well," said Elena. "This Captain Karpov is standing by this very moment. Shall we have a chat with him?"

As if in an eerie response to Elena's suggestion, the radio speaker crackled and the voice of Nikolin was heard again. *"BCG Kirov standing by. Do you still copy HMS Invincible. Read Back for Check. Over."*

"Be very cautious," said Dorland, looking at the Admiral. "It's likely that this man does not yet know what has happened to his ship. Things are riding on the razor's edge just now, and they could easily tip one way or another."

Chapter 35

Far away, in the tumult of the storm as *Tunguska* approached Moscow, Professor Dorland's theory had been put to a most exacting test, for another Prime Mover in all these events, Vladimir Karpov, lay on the floor of his stateroom aboard the airship *Tunguska*. There came a bump and a shudder, the glowing energy striking the ship and sending that luminescent glow through its bones, as if an X-Ray had been taken. Yet, within that metal skeleton, the exotic particles mined from the river valley the ship was named for stood as that one missing factor in Dorland's equation.

Yes, Karpov was a Prime Mover, a Free Radical, and a key initiator of so many of these deep variations that had so violated the continuum. Time did not look kindly on the man, and the stabbing pain he had felt in his chest was the cold, steely grasp of her jealous and spiteful hand, clawing at his soul and wanting it crushed to oblivion. But like the radio sets that had been spared from annihilation when the hour of Paradox finally transpired, Karpov was there aboard *Tunguska* as it skipped out of the here and now, into the ethereal realm of Elsewhere, if only for the barest moment. Then the ship shuddered with the roll of deep thunder, lightning rippling through the dark clouds, and returned, just as it was, impervious, immune, unbowed by time and the tumultuous tides of wind and sky.

It was the very same effect that had also served to preserve the unique life and mind of one Anton Fedorov, for at that moment, when the Admiral and crew of *Kirov* finally faced the advent of Paradox, Fedorov held a strange artifact in his pocket, the key that had been deliberately left on that nightstand for him to find by Director Kamenski. It had served to keep the Director safe through many similar riptides of fate, preserving his memories over the years, though the world had changed around him many, many times.

And old man at the end of a long and very full life, Kamenski had finally grown tired of his days as a Keyholder, and he had found in Fedorov the perfect young protégé, a man with a keen and curious mind, and a penchant for sorting through the confounding mystery of time. He left no note, and said no farewell, but after that long conversation they had shared together, Kamenski had quietly finished his last pipe, and then reached into his pocket for the key, hefting it in his hand for a moment with a smile.

"Let us see what you can unlock with it, Mister Fedorov," he had said aloud to himself, and he set it quietly on the nightstand as he slipped into his bunk, turning out the light there for the last time. He would never be seen again.

There was something in that key that opened hidden doors, not only in the physical world but in time itself, and the presence of the key in Fedorov's pocket when *Kirov* made that last shift had everything to do with his survival. In like manner, there was something in the bones of *Tunguska* that had a similar effect, and the metal skeleton that now surrounded Karpov's stateroom at the heart of the ship acted like a shield. Paradox had reached for him, wanting him gone, wanting him dead and vanished, but it could not take hold.

And so he survived.

He awoke, bleary eyed, as though emerging from a deep unsettling sleep, where nightmare dreams haunted him, the images of the faces of men he had doomed, the ships and planes he had destroyed. Struggling up onto his hands and knees, he felt an enervating sense of fatigue, a weariness, as though the very particles of his being had fallen into an apathetic stupor. The lethargy lay heavily upon him, his arms and legs leaden, and only slowly recovering.

He managed to pull himself up onto the chair by his desk, reaching for the oxygen mask again. He slipped it on, breathing deeply, and feeling his mind and thoughts clearing as he did so. As he slowly came to his senses, he realized where he was again, saw the uniform, his Admiral's cap there on the desk, and heard the thrumming of *Tunguska's* engines.

Karpov... Vladimir Karpov, Admiral of the Air Fleet, and Viceroy of the Western Oblasts of the Free Siberian State. He stared in the mirror again, remembering the shadow he had seen behind his own reflection, and the deeply unsettling feelings it had spawned in him. That feeling he had, that he was being watched, stalked, hunted by some unseen evil, had finally passed, yet in its place there was a strange sensation of absence.

He found himself involuntarily searching his pockets, as if something had been taken from him, stolen from him while he lay in a daze on the carpeted stateroom floor. I must have passed out from the altitude, he thought. Better men than me have done the same, and I've been under a great deal of stress lately.

Yes, there was something wrong still, something missing, something stolen from him, but he could not see what it was. Then he realized that this damnable storm could have sent *Tunguska* careening through time again, and he looked to find the telephone on his desk, cranking the handle and ringing up the bridge. Bogrov's voice was the first reassurance that there was life beyond the four walls of this stateroom, and he passed a moment of relief, though he did not know why he should feel that way.

"Bogrov? Is the ship alright?"

"Aye sir, just a little rough weather, but I've made a turn and we're steering to avoid the next thunderhead. Things should settle down soon. We'll be mooring over Moscow within the hour."

"Good," said Karpov, again with a sense of relief. Though he realized he must have been unconscious on the floor for a very long time. The ship was already at Moscow... but in what year? We could be anywhere, he thought. We might have shifted somewhere else.

"Bogrov... send Tyrenkov to my stateroom, and ring the galley. I'm famished."

"Right away, sir. Will that be all?"

"Yes, I just need food and information. Tell Tyrenkov I need him immediately."

"Aye sir, Bogrov out."

Karpov had never been a drinking man, but now he sought out the good bottle of Vodka that is never very far from a true Russian, opening the drawer to his desk and taking out two glasses. He started to pour the first glass, his hand quivering, and then stopped, staring at the glasses, a strange feeling overtaking him. Slowly he set the bottle down, his eyes staring at the scene, one glass empty, the other half full, and he did not know why he was so transfixed by that.

There sat one glass, empty, waiting, yearning, all potential, nothing realized. There sat the other, the heady liquor glistening in the light of the desk lamp like the fruits of long experience, the laurels of battles fought and victories won, and yet still not full, wanting more, a fulfillment that was as yet just beyond its reach. Strange, he thought. Just drink the damn vodka, you fool, and stop gawking at it. But instead he decided to wait for Tyrenkov, heartened to hear the knock on his stateroom door.

"Come," he said, the sound of his own voice seeming hoarse and hollow.

"You needed me sir?" said Tyrenkov coming in with a salute.

"Sit," said Karpov. "Drink with me..."

Tyrenkov removed his hat, striding to the desk, his uniform immaculate, and took the seat offered. The Admiral had been locked away in his stateroom for two days as *Tunguska* navigated to the meeting with Sergei Kirov at Moscow. The summer heat had given rise to a ripening storm, and he first thought that the ship might end up someplace quite unexpected, but they had arrived at Moscow safe and sound, and apparently with no strange occurrences, except that one moment when the lightning came, rippling through the ship's skeleton when it struck the forward lightning rod.

"What day is it?" said Karpov.

"August 1st."

"And the year?"

"The year sir? 1941. All is as expected. The meeting with Kirov is all arranged. Bogrov is maneuvering to the mooring tower near the Kremlin as we speak. Didn't you see the city below as we approached?"

"I was... occupied."

Tyrenkov looked at the Admiral, studying him very closely, noting the pallor of his face and cheeks, his disheveled hair, the lean, hungry look of the man.

"Are you alright, sir? You did not answer any calls these last two days, but, as you gave orders that you were not to be disturbed..."

"Correct," said Karpov, not saying anything of what had happened, of how he had sat in terror at the edge of oblivion, staring into that mirror. He saw the shadow behind him grow and grow, and could feel its icy chill on his shoulders, but he was resolute. It would be his life or that of the other Karpov, or so he believed, and he was determined to prevail.

Now, as he realized he was still alive, exhausted as he was, a awareness of that finally dawned on him. He *had* prevailed. He had done exactly what he decided he would do, and stared Time and Fate right in the eyes as he looked at his own haunting image in that mirror. And Time had blinked; Fate had shirked away, and what remained was Vladimir Karpov.

"You do not look well, sir," said Tyrenkov.

"Too much work, that is all. It's nothing that a good meal and a stiff drink will not cure. In that instance, pour yourself a drink, Tyrenkov. I want to discuss something with you before the meeting."

"Very well, sir. Thank you." Tyrenkov naturally filled the empty glass, and then was about to lift it to a toast when he realized his glass held more liquor than Karpov's. So he tipped the bottle to fill the Admiral's glass, and was careful to see it held just a little more than his own.

"To our meeting, sir. To your health. To victory!" he said, clinking his glass against Karpov's. "Nostrovia!"

"As to the meeting," said Karpov, "I have little doubt that I will get all we need, and all we have planned now that the Germans have crossed the border. What is happening on the front?"

"The enemy has made remarkable progress, sir. They have not crossed the Divina, but are making a thrust towards Smolensk. Both Minsk and Kiev have fallen, and Kirov has had to abandon the whole line of the Dnieper and has fallen back to the Donets River. The Germans are outside Kharkov, and there has been a mad rush to get reinforcements there. Unfortunately, many of those divisions were pulled from the reserves set aside for our Volga offensive against Orenburg, which may have to be postponed. Our guards divisions obtained the bridgeheads as you ordered, but the Soviets are not prepared to launch a general offensive there now."

"I will discuss this with Sergei Kirov shortly," said Karpov.

"There is more, sir. The Germans have taken the Perekop Isthmus, and it looks like they are planning a general offensive against the Crimea. At the same time, they are pushing east from the Dnieper, and a big offensive is being aimed at Rostov."

"As we expected," said Karpov. "Does it look like the Soviets can stop them?"

"That remains to be seen, sir. They have already withdrawn numerous armored brigades that were sent into the Kuban for the drive on Maykop. Two rifle divisions were also pulled off the line there, but Volkov is up to his old tricks again. He moved his 1st Kazakh Army to the south Volga Front, relieving his 5th Regular Army so it could build up and concentrate for an offensive."

"Of course," said Karpov. "It's the least he can do, to keep pressure on from the south."

"The Soviets are being very stubborn. They fight for every village and hamlet now."

"As they should," said Karpov.

"Yet nearly a third of the nation has been overrun!" said Tyrenkov. "Hitler has made a declaration annexing all of Ukraine west of the Dnieper as a permanent German province."

"That may look like a fact on the ground to you now, Tyrenkov, but believe me, it is just talk. Things will change come winter. You will see. Believe it or not, the Soviets are doing quite well. In the history I know, the Germans did not even begin their offensive until June 22nd, and the first battle of Smolensk began around July 10th! Their initial offensive was a spectacular success, but here, Sergei

Kirov has avoided many of the terrible cauldron battles where the Soviets lost hundreds of thousands of men, and instead he has conducted a deliberate, and very skillful withdrawal. Yes, the German war machine is at the height of its power now, and it will be difficult to stop, but I am telling you that their offensive is already well behind schedule."

"The Soviets have had to transfer most of the armies in their strategic reserve to hold the line," said Tyrenkov.

"Don't worry, they will raise more. Now then… There is another matter I wish to discuss, and it concerns that Russian ship operating in the Atlantic. Is it still mising?"

"The missile cruiser? Yes sir. It transited the Straits of Gibraltar in May, and there was that big engagement I reported on."

"The Germans are still in their French ports?"

"Yes sir, and the British fleet has consolidated in the Azores, with a strong patrol also in the Celtic Sea."

"Then nothing more was seen or heard of the Russian ship?"

"Not as yet, sir. The speculation is that it may have been sunk."

At this, Karpov laughed. "No, Tyrenkov. It was not sunk, of this I can assure you." He gave his intelligence chief a searching look, thinking. "I want you to focus your signals intercept teams on the Norwegian Sea."

"Sir? There isn't much happening there. We believe the British are preparing to mount a convoy operation to Murmansk. The code word *Dervish* has been picked up, and we think it pertains to this operation."

"Correct," said Karpov. "That was the first convoy to Murmansk, and not the last. But look for that Russian battlecruiser, Tyrenkov. Look for it in the Norwegian Sea, and I want to hear about it the instant you have any further information, even if I am cheek to cheek with Sergei Kirov when the news comes in. Understand?"

"Very good, sir. I assume you have plans concerning this ship?"

"My ship, Tyrenkov. Yes, I have plans concerning *my* ship. I am its rightful Captain. Don't forget that. But I want to know if you find it there, in the Norwegian Sea, and I want to know immediately. Focus your attention on Jan Mayen. Can't we get a fishing trawler out there with signals intercept equipment?"

"I have some good men in Norway, sir."

"Well get them busy. Focus on the region near that island, the Denmark Strait as well. Oh… one more thing… Have you any information on a possible meeting between Churchill and Roosevelt?"

Tyrenkov looked surprised. "Nothing has come up concerning that," he said.

"Be wary. Keep your ear to the ground. What are the Americans doing now?"

"Not much, sir. They are rattling their sword in the Pacific, by way of a warning to Japan. In the Atlantic they have relieved the British on Iceland, and sparred with a few German U-boats. They made certain declarations there concerning a 100 mile wide naval exclusion zone."

Karpov smiled. "Yes," he said, "I sailed right down the middle of it, and raised hell the whole way."

"Sir?"

"Never mind, Tyrenkov. Don't forget about that meeting with Churchill and Roosevelt. See if you can get some men over to Nova Scotia and Newfoundland… Have a look at Argentia… Placentia Bay. Snoop around. The Americans will be setting up bases there soon. And see if you can ascertain the whereabouts of one of the British battleships, the Prince. Yes, the *Prince of Wales*. I want to know of its movements, but first and foremost, I want you to find me that Russian battlecruiser. Put everything you have on that."

"You can rely on me, sir."

Chapter 36

Tovey stared at the radio, realizing the situation was very grave. He had never met the man he would be speaking to, the Russian officer that had been involved in a mutiny, and the man who was most likely responsible for those reports he read in the file boxes Turing had found.

It was this man, he thought. He was the reason this ship put fear into our souls, for with men like Volsky and Fedorov at the helm, *Kirov* became a bulwark for the defense of the realm. Then it really wasn't the ship I supposedly set a watch on, establishing that secret group within the Royal Navy, it was this man. He put the darkness in the shadow this ship became for us, and the fear. Karpov… And here he is again, like some rough beast, his hour come round at last. Yeats was in his mind as he thought this, a poem called *The Second Coming*.

Here he is, unknowing, still thinking he is sailing in his own time, unaware of what has happened to him and his ship. The danger here is measureless. This man could undo all the careful planning and cooperation I've worked to achieve with the Russians. He could become the deadly foil that ship was when we first encountered it, events I stand at the edge of this very moment, yet things I can literally read my own hand on, as I documented the whole affair once before!

What to do here? The key thing now is to diffuse any potential conflict in the immediate local area of this ship. I must get a message off to Wake-Walker, and tell him to hold the *Dervish* convoy at Iceland. He'll need to pull in his cruiser screens, and I'll also have to get hold of Vian and rein him in as well. He's up there with Force K off the Norwegian coast. Yet how to speak with this man, here and now. He's standing by, and every moment of delay attenuates the thin rope we may now be dangling from.

Think Tovey, he chided himself. What would they be doing now on that ship? I'm told there was some sort of accident. That was what sent them here in the first instance. So they will be somewhat disoriented, perhaps investigating what may have happened, and each and every bit of evidence they uncover will seem an impossibility. It's likely that this is what created the tension and conflict on that ship, and led to this attempted mutiny. So I must do everything possible to tamp things down here…

Tovey narrowed his eyes, and then made his call.

"HMS *Invincible* to BCG *Kirov*, this is Admiral Tovey. Come back."

"*BCG Kirov reading you loud and clear. We Copy, HMS Invincible. Over.*"

"*Invincible* here. This message is for the Captain. It appears we have a situation on our hands here, and I am presently giving orders that all Royal Navy ships in your vicinity should immediately withdraw. Should you require any assistance, we will, of course, be happy to lend a hand. Otherwise, in the interest of peace, orders will be transmitted immediately to any British ship in the Norwegian Sea to withdraw to friendly ports. We wish no hostilities. Over."

There was a good long wait before a message came back. "*We copy your message, HMS Invincible. All Royal Navy ships will withdraw to friendly ports. No assistance required, and no interference with the investigation we are presently conducting will be tolerated. Do you copy? Over.*"

"Message received. No interference contemplated. We will stand by on this channel should you wish any further communication. HMS *Invincible*, over and out."

The Admiral turned to the others, a concerned look on his face. "Well, he said. It appears we've just struck our first bargain with the devil. He may be exactly that, this Captain Karpov, or he may be something more, a guardian angel, as this ship was for us in our hour of greatest need. I suppose only time will tell which it will be. If they keep to their maintenance schedule, then the ship may only be here ten more days. Yet, in that time, it managed to sink and damage many ships, kill thousands of men, and loosed a terrible weapon on the world that ended up doing only one good thing—it brought the

Americans into this mess, once and for all. That was in my reports as well, though I realize we have no way of knowing if that will ever occur. I suppose it all rests with what is happening on that ship. This time it isn't armies and fleets that will decide things, but the delicate tension strung out between the senior officers on that ship."

"What I wouldn't give to be a fly on that wall," said Professor Dorland. "Someone on that ship has survived this shift with their memory intact. Either that, or they are experiencing intense déjà vu, but the result is the same. They knew your secret communications channel, and that means they retained memories of their experiences, at least insofar as that meeting in Alexandria you mentioned. Admiral Tovey, do you have any idea who that person could be?"

"The list is very short," said Tovey. "Only three men attended that meeting. The ship's commanding officer, Admiral Volsky, then Captain Fedorov, and the young Lieutenant they were using as a translator. Oh yes… there was one other man, a civilian. I believe his name was Kamenski. Yes, Director Kamenski. He told us quite a tale when we were easing Admiral Cunningham over the line in all this business."

"Admiral Cunningham?" said Paul.

"Well, he had to be informed," said Tovey. "He was commander of the Mediterranean Fleet, and that Russian battlecruiser sailed right up through the Suez Canal and onto his watch, so there had to be some explanation."

Paul looked a bit distressed. "Then he knows that *Kirov* was from… the future?"

"As amazing as that still sounds, yes. But he's a most capable and reliable man. In fact, as I'm apparently fated to establish this group called the Watch, I'll make him one of my first recruits."

"Who else has been told what was really happening?"

"A few more good men. Wavell is in the know, as is General O'Connor. This Mister Fedorov from the Russian ship found it necessary to bring both men over the line when Brigadier Kinlan's troops suddenly appeared in the desert."

Paul rubbed his forehead, remembering Maeve's anguish that the situation was so badly fractured now that it might never be put back together in any way that might resemble the history they knew. An entire modern armored brigade, complete with all that technology and weaponry… It was unimaginable. The implications were staggering.

"I can see by the look on your face that all this is somewhat disturbing," said Tovey. "Believe me, Professor Dorland, you stand there worried over how all of this affects your future, while I stand here worried how it will all play out in the here and now. Thankfully, these interventions have proved benign, as far as the British Empire is concerned, though things went quite a bit differently in those reports I supposedly wrote, and now that this ship has arrived here again, they could easily spin out of our careful control."

"Does anyone else know what has happened here?" asked Paul.

"One man who was perhaps fated to know all this, our Winston Churchill. There was a meeting at Siwa, with Wavell, The senior Russian officers, and Churchill. It was necessary to get the Prime Minister on our side of the fence. Otherwise he has a tendency to insist on things, in a manner of speaking."

"I understand," said Paul, "but you realize the implications of this. If you could point to one single man as perhaps the most significant Prime Mover in the history of this era, it would be Winston Churchill. Now I'm standing here wondering just how far this knowledge will spread, who will know, and what effect it may have."

"Impossible to say," said Tovey. "I don't mean to offend in saying this, but none of you belong here at all. You are all uninvited guests here, and every man woman and child alive today will have to live with the things that happen because of your presence. Some of those things may be good. I'm the first to admit that the support of the Russians, and their ship of miracles, has been a saving grace for us. Yet I'm told by Mister Fedorov that many things have already happened here that were never meant to be, this ship we're standing on being one of them. I can't imagine the Royal Navy without good old HMS *Invincible*, but he tells me it was never supposed to have been built. That said, and understanding your obvious concerns, the genie is out of the bottle, Professor. I for one cannot see any way to correct that situation, and so we had better learn to live with what is happening here, as I don't think it will be easy to change things."

Paul pinched the bridge of his nose, realizing the terrible truth in everything Tovey was saying. The Dragon had awakened. It was inevitable that they would encounter a situation like this once time travel was proved to be possible. Here it was... The Dragon had roused from its long slumber, and the thought that he, and Maeve, with Robert and Kelly, could put all this back as it was, now seemed a farcical impossibility. What could they do? Could they slay this beast now that it was loose on the world? Perhaps not, but they could learn how to ride its back.

He looked at Tovey, a man caught up in the whirlwind of World War Two. There he was, commanding his ships, seeing to one small matter after another, until the guns roared with their anger, and the killing began. He felt a sudden kinship with the man, for he could not know the enormity of all that now lay ahead in this war, through the long years of 1942 and 1943, then on into 1944, and beyond.

They would fight to clear the Vichy French from North Africa, and then to defeat Rommel in the desert and drive the Afrika Korps back to the continent. Then would come the invasion of Sicily and Italy, and the long planning for Operation Overlord, the D-Day invasion. After that there would be the grueling battle in France, the headlong breakout and the miraculous German recovery in Belgium and Holland. Operation Market Garden would attempt to break through, but it would lead the British Army into the meat grinder of the battles for the Rhineland, and the Germans would again strike with their Ardennes offensive. And this was just the Western theatre. Would any of that ever happen now? How would this history play out given the variations they had already seen here in 1941?

He's standing there just like I am, thought Paul, wondering how in the world he can salvage this situation, preserve his nation and way of life, and possibly prevail against the might of the German war machine now. So I'm no different, just another general fighting the war here, and we'll just have to take it one battle at a time.

"I'm under no illusions," he said. "I know what lies ahead for us is extremely dangerous, perhaps fatally so. And yet, if you can believe it, I once faced the prospect of reversing an intervention that would have altered the entire course of Western history, to the point where all of Christendom might have been eliminated in Medieval Europe, and the United States itself might not have been discovered as it was, being colonized by another power. In that, my very own existence was at stake, as it may be here for all of us as we now proceed. That situation came down to a very few key points on the time meridian, where levers existed that allowed us to move events back on track. It took one good woman on a horse, a message in an apple, and the death of two men to reverse that catastrophe, so you see, little things that change at just the right time can have dramatic effects. I call them Push Points, and I must believe they also exist as levers we can use in this crisis."

"Can we find them here?" asked Elena. "Can your research team ferret out something we can work with?"

"Possibly," said Paul, "though the situation we're now facing is extremely grave. We have had a near catastrophic intervention in time by this Russian battlecruiser. Beyond that, our situation in 2021 is now very precarious. We were nearly put out of business when the Chinese lit off that EMP attack over the Western US. Thankfully, our facility has emergency power generators, as long as we can provide the petrol to keep them running, and our equipment was wel shielded. At this stage, I came here to discover who was involved in all of this, and what was really going on. It looked impossible, this history skewed as it is, and with so many Primes now having knowledge of what has happened—not to mention Kinlan's Brigade in North Africa, and now a small flotilla of merchant Marine ships out there as well."

"These concerns were raised at the conference in Siwa," said Tovey, "and at the meeting in Alexandria. Six men now know the truth, and I think that they shall form the first six recruits in that little group I'll call the Watch. We have resolved to limit general knowledge of these events to as few key players as possible. As for the rank and file on the ships, and the troops Kinlan now commands, we have some control, which is why that brigade has been kept where it was, in a very isolated place, and why we have these new ships segregated here in the Azores."

"Laudable, and quite important," said Paul. "Yes, you must do everything possible to limit knowledge of what has happened. For at this moment, time itself is on the verge of rupturing and tangling in a way that could be absolutely fatal. This ship has ravaged the continuum once already, and the man that drove that energy has now returned for a second loop—a Doppelganger, something that I thought might never occur. We now face the very real possibility that the original Karpov still exists in Russia, and it is likely that he may soon gain knowledge that his own duplicate exists as well. This could lead to a real calamity, events introducing so much variation into the continuum that it simply cannot recover. It is not something that *may* happen, ladies and gentlemen, I strongly believe that an event I call a Radical Transformation is already underway, and it will lead us to only one certain outcome if we do not find a solution—that Grand Finality you spoke of Miss Fairchild."

"What is it?" said Elena, the fear obvious on her face.

"A kind of Gordian knot in time," said Paul. "These variations and Paradox events get time so doubled back on itself, that an insoluble looping begins to occur. Time cannot find a way to resolve it, and so it gets stuck in an endless replay. If this happens the future simply ceases to exist, because time cannot progress beyond the point of the finality…"

"Ceases to exist?"

"As terrible as that sounds, that is what the theory predicts. Since the future cannot be created in the line of causality, it must be destroyed, and that shadow ripples backwards on the continuum like a backwash from Paradox. That may be the reason the voices from our own distant future have all gone mute, for there, the impact of all these changes will be most severe—annihilation—and that is a silence that will eventually roll back upon us all…"

A small measure of that silence fell on the room at that moment, stilling every voice there. Only the quiet hum of the radio set thrummed in the background, a cold and lifeless pulse on the airwaves of time, a mechanical Doppelganger, something there that should not exist, an insult to the very fiber of the universe itself. Then Admiral Tovey spoke, the words coming from that same poem by William Butler Yates he had running in his mind moments ago. It seemed, in that moment, to hold all the fear and uncertainty, and the intimation of utter doom that each of them felt.

> *"Turning and turning in the widening gyre*
> *The falcon cannot hear the falconer;*
> *Things fall apart; the centre cannot hold;*
> *Mere anarchy is loosed upon the world,*
> *The blood-dimmed tide is loosed, and everywhere*
> *The ceremony of innocence is drowned…"*

The Saga Continues…

Kirov Saga: Nemesis

The second volume in the third season of this long running tale carries the story into the turbulent waters of the north. With Admiral Volsky fallen ill, Fedorov struggles to prevent Karpov from repeating the awful events that ended in nuclear fire, and the explosion that again sent the ship reeling through time. With his memory intact, knowledge of Rod-25 and everything Karpov would do, he sets his mind on gaining control of the ship, yet must face the dangerous wrath of Karpov if he is to succeed.

Meanwhile, the Siberian, as the second Karpov is now called, has struck his bargain with Sergei Kirov, but one that could bring about another fatal collision in time. Learning that *Kirov* has reappeared, he sets his mind on trying to find that ship, and in so doing gain control over the most powerful weapons in the world. Unaware that his duplicate self even exists, he soon finds he has a shadowy accomplice.

The war continues on the Russian front as the Germans slowly begin to introduce new prototype tank designs, born of the shock and fire delivered by Kinlan's heavy brigade. The story takes us into this action on the Soviet front, as the Germans launch their final assault aimed at winning the war in 1941, Operation Typhoon. Meanwhile, the German Navy licks its wounds in French ports, but still remains a dangerous threat on Admiral Tovey's watch.

With the thorny problems of time travel finally resolved, the action takes us boldly into the war in 1942, even as Professor Dorland and the Meridian project team struggle to find the strange key that was lost on *Rodney*, and unravel the mystery of the Keyholders.

DORLAND's TIME GLOSSARY - Terminology

ABSOLUTE CERTIANTY - A condition brought about by willful determination that serves to limit variation in the continuum, creating a kind of tunnel in the time *Meridian* that restricts outcomes to an absolute resolution.

ALTERED STATE – A new prime meridian that has been recreated or radically altered to incorporate consequences and changes due to variations in the original meridian. See also: *Prime Meridian*

ATTENUATION - A property of an incomplete Time shift, where the traveler manifests across a range of several milliseconds, slightly out of synch or phase with his correct manifestation point.

BACKWASH – The reflection of *Heisenberg Waves* that propagate backward in time after encountering *Paradox*. *Backwash* can create *Backward Causality*, and literally alter past events.

BACKWARD CAUSALITY – A quantum event where entangled particles in the present or future serve to alter the quantum state of particles in the past, leading to the alteration of events in the past because of something that happens in the present and future, usually a *Paradox* event. See Also: *Quantum Entanglement*

CHAOS ZONE – A kind of time moiré when dual *Heisenberg Wave* sets overlap on the other side of *Paradox Time*. *Chaos Zones* can be very unstable and create unexpected or odd effects. See also: *Dual Heisenberg Wave*.

CLARITY – Clear or good understanding of a temporal locus, pattern, event, *Outcome* or *Consequence*.

CO-LOCATION - The presence of an object or person transported back through time to any point or Meridian on the continuum where that object existed. This is expressly forbidden by Time, and therefore generally thought to be impossible. In like manner, no person can ever shift in Time to a point where they co-locate with themselves, which will create a Paradox if attempted. *EXCEPTION: See Dual Heisenberg Wave and Doppelganger*

CONSEQUENCE – An undesired result achieved by a temporal *Transformation* – Usually referring to the negative. (i.e.) Sometimes certain *Consequences* must be accepted in order to achieve a desired *Outcome.*

CONVOLUTION – The relative difficulty or complexity of a given temporal event or condition.

DEEP NEXUS – Sometimes called a "Void" – A crucial, significant *Nexus Point* where radical alteration of the time line is possible. A Deep Nexus has a universal effect on all moments in Time until resolved, and can therefore be a portal into any potential Meridian passing through the Nexus.

DENSITY – A relative term describing factor counts in temporal events. The more density, the more difficult it is to discern possible outcomes on a meridian, and plan intervention.

DOPPELGANGER – *"Double Walker."* A duplicate of a person or object arising as a result of a *Dual Heisenberg Wave* during *Paradox Time*. *Doppelgangers* are rare and unique duplications of information in the time continuum. They can only arise when one information set, object, or person, is protected in a *Nexus Point*, or protected by some other force, during *Paradox Time,* particularly if the second duplicate information set, object or person is associated with an *Imperative* or *First Cause* event that must occur.

DUAL HEISENBERG WAVE – A *Heisenberg Wave* that has separated into two wave sets after encountering *Paradox Time* on the continuum. Such conditions give rise to a *Chaos Zone* in the hours and days immediately following *Paradox Time*, and can also lead to many strange effects, like Déjà vu, Jamais vu, Presque vu, alterations in physical matter, memory loss, and the creation of a *Doppelganger*.

ELASTICITY – The tendency of Time to resist alteration and reassume its original shape.

FACTOR – An element contributing to convolution in temporal events.

FINALITY – A catastrophic *Grand Imperative* (like the Cuthulu asteroid strike that led to the eradication of the dinosaurs and other life.) See Also: *Grand Finality and Imperative.*

FIRST CAUSE – A crucial event in a chain of causality that initiates all following events. A first cause is often associated with a *Time Loop*, and it becomes more and more imperative the longer the looping occurs without proper resolution.

FREE RADICAL – A dangerous, erratic variable in the course of temporal events – usually only existing within a *Deep Nexus*.

GOLEM - A special search program written by Kelly Ramer and distributed to hundreds of thousands of computer users via the Internet. Golems are able to search and report on information on the net, and can perceive data on every Meridian during a time of *Deep Nexus* through the phenomenon known as "Resonance." Golems are arranged in to modules, and one notable module responsible for fetching crucial variations was designated "Golem 7."

GORDIAN KNOT – A series of time loops that cannot be untangled, even by using the annihilating power associated with *Paradox*. Such a knot can occur when objects or persons are protected from the effects of *Paradox* by one means or another. The presence or existence of a *Doppelganger* is a warning that a *Gordian Knot* is starting to form from a *Time Loop* influenced by *Paradox*.

GRAND FINALITY – The inevitable end or result of a *Radical Transformation* to the time continuum. Such an occurrence can permanently rupture the meridians of time, creating infinite *Time Loops* that can never resolve. In effect, time becomes hopelessly tangled into a *Gordian Knot*, and this can lead to the annihilation of the future, as events cannot progress beyond the point of the knotted or looped time. Grand Finalities differ from natural finalities in that they are the result of willful action, and not acts of nature.

GREAT VOID – An interminable shadow or *Penumbra* cast by a *Grand Imperative*. It can also refer to the void in time created by a *Grand Finality*.

HAZE – Obscurity in the understanding of a temporal situation.

HEISENBERG WAVE – The transforming effect of an intervention in time, which propagates forward along the continuum to radically alter all subsequent events. All major variations in time, including *Paradox*, result in the creation of a Heisenberg Wave, like a stone thrown into a still pool. See also: *Time Tsunami*.

IMPERATIVE – An event in Time which <u>must</u> happen – Usually a natural event, but not always, as in the case of a *First Cause*. A *Grand Imperative* is a natural event of special significance. Some *Grand Imperatives* can become a *Finality*.

INEVITABILITY – A progression of events that is inexorable and unalterable.

INITIATOR – A person directly responsible for a new *Time Meridian* (Like Mohammed, or Christ). A *Prime Mover* of great significance.

LEVER – A secondary contributor to movement in a series of events.

MERIDIAN – An established line of temporal events on the continuum. A possible line of causality. See also: *Prime Meridian*

NEXUS POINT – A point of connection, intersection or branching of one or more possible *Meridians* in the Time continuum.

NODE – A specific point on a *Time Meridian.*

OUTCOME – A desired result achieved by a temporal *Transformation* – Usually referring to the positive.

P-WAVE – A "predictive" or "precursor" Heisenberg Wave that acts as a harbinger of changes to come, but does not introduce major changes to any meridian. *P-Waves* resonate across all possible meridians, and can therefore be detected as possible variations in the *Resonance* around a series of events. Minor effects may accompany P-Waves, which are often perceived as a sense of emotional dread.

PARADOX – Time's way of correcting errors in the Time continuum. *Paradox* arises when an insoluble conflict occurs in the continuum, and time attempts to avoid or correct that problem. It is therefore a real force, and quite dangerous. It kills or erases people and objects from the *Time Meridian* when unaccountable complications arise from their actions. A Paradox is NOT simply a thorny problem; it is a real effect and the force of annihilation—a kind of "Anti-Time." See also: *Heisenberg Wave,* and *Time Loop.*

PARADOX HOUR – The moment when an object or person in the past reaches the moment of their first arrival at a point on the continuum, their birth, or moment of first cause. The annihilating force of *Paradox* attempts to resolve potential conflicts by removing them from the continuum or any contact with *Paradox Hour.*

PARADOX TIME – The time prior to, and during, a *Paradox* event. Odd effects of *Paradox Time* can begin occurring, hours, days, weeks or even months before the actual *Paradox* event, as a result of the subtle generation of *P-Waves* in the Heisenberg field.

PENUMBRA – The shadow of influence on future events cast by an *Imperative*, often impenetrable or a great obstacle, to time travelers.

POINT OF DIVERGENCE – The point of initial vitiation in any previously established time meridian.

POINT OF ORIGIN – The temporal locus where a person or object becomes a *Prime Mover.*

PRIME MERIDIAN – The initial or first meridian of time, and the one that all other potential meridians must return to after a variation. Heisenberg Waves created by variations serve to rejoin potential altered meridians back into one new prime, which could then be a *Altered State.*

PRIME MOVER – A primary causative lever or agent for an event – usually a person but sometimes an object.

PUSH POINT – A moment of insignificance that gives rise to a key event on a *Time Meridian.* Often associated with a *Prime Mover.*

QUANTUM ENTANGLEMENT – A relationship between two quantum particles where the state or condition of one causes the other related particle to also alter its state, location, spin or other condition—instantaneously. *Quantum Entanglement* can lead to *Backward Causality* and other strange time effects, as the two entangled particles need not be in the same *spacetime*.

QUANTUM KARMA – The influence of causality on a *Time Meridian*. Each moment on the Meridian affects the next with a kind of momentum, and certain Prime Movers accumulate an aura of Quantum Karma around them that also has profound effects on the configuration of future moments in Time.

RADICAL TRANSFORMATION – A catastrophic alteration of the *Temporal Condition* that can lead to a *Grand Finality*.

RESONANCE - Information available in the intersection of a Nexus Point, where many alternate Meridians "resonate" data concerning the possible outcome of events. This data can be picked up by the Meridian Team *Golem* software, registering as potential variations in the history in conflict with data stored in the *Touchstone Database*.

TEMPORAL CONDITION – The matrix, pattern or state of affairs in a given time period.

TIME LOOP – A replay of events that occurs as a result of a *Paradox* event. Movement to any point on the continuum prior to one's first appearance in the past is dangerous, as the arrow of time slowly brings that person or object forward on the continuum to approach the point of its first entry. The prohibition against *Co-Location* creates a *Paradox*, and associated *Paradox Time* when the object or person arriving from the past encounters the moment of their first arrival, or moment of *First Cause*. Time loops can result in a *Gordian Knot* if not properly resolved, which can lead to *Grand Finality*.

TIME TSUNAMI – A series of *Heisenberg Waves* generated by a

Grand Paradox and initiating changes and transformations so profound that they create a *Finality*.

TOUCHSTONE DATABASE – The history of all known recorded events as established in a protected RAM bank by the Meridian Project Team at the outset of their project. This data is thought to define events native to the Prime Meridian, prior to the first opening of the continuum on the team's initial time mission. This data is often used as a reference to indicate a variation in time has occurred when the *Golem* search modules fetch resonance information that conflicts with that in the database.

TRANSFORMATION – Any change in a *Time Meridian* that alters a future *Temporal Condition*.

TRANSFORMER – A person who causes a *Transformation*.

VANISHING POINT - The exact moment in Time when an object is removed and transported elsewhere in the continuum.

VARIATION – A subtle change in a *Time Meridian* that does not significantly alter *Temporal Conditions*.

WEIGHT OF OPINION - The culmination and likely outcome of future events as a result of a potential *transformation*, as perceived and reported by the Golem search cloud.

WILLFUL EVENT - Events resulting from decisions or actions taken by human beings

ZOMBIE - The walking dead. A person, fated to die, but whose life has been spared due to a willful intervention in a Time Meridian. Paradox will allow the elimination of a Zombie by restoring the moment of his natural death to the continuum.

Discover other titles by John Schettler:

Award Winning Science Fiction:
Meridian - Meridian Series - Volume I
Nexus Point - Meridian Series - Volume II
Touchstone - Meridian Series - Volume III
Anvil of Fate - Meridian Series - Volume IV
Golem 7 - Meridian Series - Volume V

The Meridian series merges with the Kirov series beginning with Book 16, Paradox Hour

Classic Science Fiction:
Wild Zone - Dharman Series - Volume I
Mother Heart - Dharman Series - Volume II

Historical Fiction:
Taklamakan - Silk Road Series - Volume I
Khan Tengri - Silk Road Series - Volume II

Dream Reaper – Mythic Horror Mystery

Made in the USA
Lexington, KY
27 March 2015